SEALS
THE WARRIOR BREED
CASUALTIES OF WAR

H. JAY RIKER

AVON BOOKS
An Imprint of HarperCollins*Publishers*

This is a work of fiction. Names, characters, places, and incidents are products of the author's imagination or are used fictitiously and are not to be construed as real. Any resemblance to actual events, locales, organizations, or persons, living or dead, is entirely coincidental.

AVON BOOKS
An Imprint of HarperCollins*Publishers*
10 East 53rd Street
New York, New York 10022-5299

Copyright © 2003 by Bill Fawcett & Associates
ISBN: 0-380-79510-8
www.avonbooks.com

First Avon Books paperback printing: December 2003

Avon Trademark Reg. U.S. Pat. Off. and in Other Countries, Marca Registrada, Hecho en U.S.A.
HarperCollins® is a registered trademark of HarperCollins Publishers Inc.

Printed in the U.S.A.

10 9 8 7 6 5 4 3 2

To Nina—

**companion, comrade, survivor, fighter . . .
a Warrior Breed unto herself**

SEALS

THE WARRIOR BREED

CASUALTIES OF WAR

RIGHT PLACE, WRONG TIME

Casey used his rifle's nightscope to probe the darkness of the open hangar. He could easily make out the shape of the Learjet parked inside. He could also see the forms of several soldiers scrambling for cover, including a couple of men with rifles crouched behind some fifty-five-gallon drums close by the far wall.

An ambush.

"Throw down your weapons!" the PDF officer called.

"Shift right! Take cover!" Casey called over the tactical channel. They needed to get out of the line of fire, to get clear of this kill zone. There was a light aircraft on the runway to the right that might provide cover. Some of Golf One's SEALs were already there.

And then time ran out. One of the Panamanians opened fire. Suddenly, muzzle flashes flickered and winked from three sides—from the hangar and from each flank—a storm of full-auto gunfire.

The SEAL assault force had just walked into Hell.

Prologue

Halstead residence
Balboa Park, California
1812 hours

"I . . . um . . . have some news, honey," ETC Greg Halstead said as he came through the front door. "I got my new orders today."

Wendy Halstead came out of the kitchen, drying her hands on a blue and white dish towel. She looked wary, Greg thought, perhaps a bit cornered. He sighed. He was not looking forward to this.

"Where this time?" she asked, her voice flat, almost emotionless.

"Oh, right here in San Diego," he replied, keeping his voice bright. "Coronado, in fact."

"Oh, Greg . . ."

"Honey, they want me back. I'm back with the Teams."

"Damn it, Greg! You *promised* me! . . ."

"I promised no more secrets," he told her. He held out his arms, trying to welcome her. "This is different."

She pushed him away, snapping the dish towel at her side like a whip. "How different? Just tell me how!"

"Honey . . ."

1

"Damn it, Greg! A phone call in the middle of the night, and you're up and packed and gone and you can't even tell me where? I'm left here night after night watching the news and wondering which crisis in which damned little third-world hole in the ground is *it,* the place they've sent you, and, God damn it, if you *die* over there they won't even tell me where it was or what happened. . . ."

"Wendy, listen to me! I'm being stationed at the school! I'm going to be an instructor! I'll be down at Coronado turning tadpoles into SEALs!"

"And how long will that last? Greg, once they have you . . ."

"Wendy, they already have me. They always have. Once a SEAL—"

"Always a SEAL," she snapped, finishing the line. "And the only easy day was yesterday. Hoo-yah!" She flung the towel at him. "Why can't you get into an honest line of work for a change? I'm sure the Mafia has a place for someone with your skills!"

That stung. "That's not fair!"

"It's not fair to make me a widow while you're still breathing! It's not fair that you think more of your damned SEAL friends than of your wife! It's not fair that Mark is growing up without a father! . . ."

"And you knew I was in the Navy when you married me. You knew damned well what I was, and what it meant to be in the Teams!"

"*You're* in the Teams, damn it! Not me!"

"You're a Navy wife! And you know that when I get my orders—"

"I've *done* my tour of duty!" She was screaming now, her face red, her eyes wet. "I've goddamn fucking done my tour, and I want *out*! I want *out*! Do you hear me?"

She whirled away from him and ran down the hall. The

door to their bedroom slammed hard enough to rattle the framed photographs on the living room wall.

Greg stood unmoving, hands clenched at his sides. After a moment, he reached up to touch his dress blue uniform jacket, his fingers brushing the heavy gold Budweiser pinned above the ribbons on his left breast. Eagle and trident, flintlock pistol and anchor, the proud if gaudy emblem of the Teams.

Once a SEAL, always a SEAL. . . .

No more secrets. . . .

The hell of it was, he'd meant that promise two years ago, after his return from a highly classified op in Iran and the Persian Gulf. Promoted to chief four months later, he'd put in a request for a duty transfer and ended up conning a desk at the San Diego Naval Station for Navy Intelligence.

No more secrets? Well, working Intel with Top Secret clearance, there were still plenty of things he couldn't discuss with Wendy, but at least he'd been keeping regular hours, with his only weekend duty being a stretch of on-call every other week.

He felt a stab of guilt, though, for the one piece of information he'd deliberately not shared with Wendy—that over six months ago he'd requested a return to the Teams and had pulled every string he could to make that happen.

Damn it all . . .

He walked down the hallway to their bedroom door. He tried the knob. Locked.

"Wendy?" He tapped on the door. Then, louder, "Wendy!" He could hear her sobbing on the other side.

"Open the door, Wendy! Damn it, quit acting like a child!"

"Go away! Go play with your SEAL friends!"

"Wendy, we need to talk this through. What can I do?"

"You can give me a *divorce*!" Something heavy slammed on the other side of the door . . . a thrown book, possibly.

"Wendy, we can make this work. . . ."

"Just stay out of my life! I'm leaving!"

"You're not giving me a chance!"

"Fuck you! I've been giving you chances for twelve years! And you've blown them! Every one! I am *out* of here!"

Greg closed his eyes, wondering how he could fix this, what he could do. . . .

And outside the house, in the suburban backyard lined with palm and fruit trees, ten-year-old Mark Halstead closed burning eyes and wondered what he could do. He'd been playing war with Dave and some of the neighbor's kids—a longtime favorite game, with him and Dave as the SEAL commandos, pulling sneaky-Pete crawls through the shrubbery to ambush the others with plastic guns. His current op had brought him right underneath his mother's window, and he'd heard every shouted word.

Mom? Leaving? She'd been acting pretty stressed lately, but . . . leaving?

He tried to keep the tears from coming, and failed.

Chapter 1

16 December 1989

Outside Paitilla Airfield
Panama City, Republic of Panama
1415 hours

"They're crazy," Master Chief Halstead said, scanning the airfield slowly with his binoculars. "They are absolutely, guaranteed nucking futs."

Boatswain Chief Fred Jaco grunted assent. "I hear you, brother. But the Powers That Be have declared it to be so. Blessed be the Powers That Be, now and forever, amen."

"Fuck that. And the horse they rode in on. SEALs have no business assaulting an objective like this. This is an Army Ranger job."

"You know it, I know it. But someone farther up the chain of command doesn't want the Teams left out of the medal competitions."

An American helicopter, a UH-1, clattered overhead. The two SEALs were crouched behind a low, stone wall atop a seven-story Panama City apartment building perhaps a kilometer from Paitilla, a vantage point that gave them an excellent view of the entire airstrip. The Huey angled in toward the American section for a gentle touchdown; it was odd, given the extreme tension between the American military and the local Panamanian Defense Force, to see both sides using the same air facilities.

Both SEALs were wearing civilian clothing, Jaco a yellow sports shirt, Greg a gray T-shirt, the idea being to keep a low profile with the locals. Their heavy binoculars, however, weren't exactly tourist-issue. A stiff breeze from the sea whispered across the roof of the apartment, ruffling their short hair. Despite the breeze, though, the mid-December air was hot and oppressively humid. Greg's shirt was already drenched with sweat.

"Who drew this plum little assignment?" he asked.

"We did, Team Four. Lieutenant Commander Tuohy." Jaco grinned. "An up-from-the-ranks mustang."

"Tuohy? Yeah, I know him. I thought he was Six."

"He was, actually. Now he's with Four. We're glad to have him. His tour with Six gave him experience in commanding units of forty men or more."

Greg continued to study the airfield, an airstrip with the main runway terminating at the edge of a cliff above the roiling surf of the Pacific. Though this was a civilian facility, a lot of military was in evidence, both U.S. and Panamanian. American Air Force transports were using the field to bring in supplies and troops—supposedly for maneuvers—and the local Panamanian Defense Force had boosted its presence as well. Through the binoculars, Greg watched a band of tough-looking PDF troops marching in formation past the control tower, brandishing AK-47 assault rifles. To the right, on the far side of the runway, were several large, open hangars, and he could see PDF troops lounging inside in the shade or standing guard outside.

"Is that Pineapple's getaway plane?"

"With the guards? Yeah. That's the objective. A Learjet kept fueled and ready for *el presidente*'s personal use."

Greg lowered the binoculars and gave an exasperated sigh. "Shit. I could pop that plane's tire from here with a

Barrett fifty-cal. Or a rufus round in one of the engines, for chrissake. Why call for a large-scale assault?"

Jaco made a face. "ROEs," he said. "The goddamn Rules of fucking Engagement. The brass is afraid of missed rounds causing 'unacceptable collateral damage,' as they put it. Especially rufus rounds."

A rufus round was a .50-caliber rifle bullet hollowed out and filled with explosives, the perfect weapon for disabling a light aircraft's engine at long range. A Barrett M-8 .50 could reach out and touch someone with deadly accuracy at a range of over a mile.

"Bullshit," Greg said. "SEAL snipers don't miss."

"Maybe not. But the brass is damned worried about this one. When Blue Spoon goes down, a lot of innocent civilians could get hurt. Washington is already having a damned tough time selling this op to the rest of the world and to the American people. A high number of civilian casualties could turn this thing into a disaster, even if we win."

"Gee, a whole new approach to modern warfare," Greg said, his voice sarcastic. "Zero casualties and everybody feels good about it afterward."

"So what's USSOCOM going to do about it?" Jaco asked.

"Damfino. I'm down here as Team Three's intelligence liaison with USSOCOM. I'll report to Fort Bragg on my way back, of course, but I doubt that anything I say will have much of an impact. They have their own ideas about warfighting right now."

"Yeah, but are things any better now than they were at Grenada? That was a class-A cluster fuck."

"A cluster fuck and a half," Greg agreed. "I suppose we won't know the answer to that one until we see how things go down here."

USSOCOM—the U.S. Special Operations Command— had been created in the aftermath of the invasion of

Grenada, in October of 1983. Grenada had been a victory, officially. The communist coup that had toppled the government of Prime Minister Paul Scoon had been on the point of falling into anarchy, American medical students on the tiny, tropical island were at risk, and President Reagan had ordered the invasion, ostensibly to avoid another hostage situation like the one that had paralyzed America for 444 days in Iran.

In fact, Operation Urgent Fury had been launched to stop further communist expansion in the Caribbean. Cuban advisors were working with the Grenadan revolutionaries, and Cuban engineers were lengthening an airstrip to accommodate Soviet cargo planes. The invasion had restored Scoon to power and sent a clear message to the world that the United States was drawing a line against further communist expansion in the Western Hemisphere.

But if the invasion of Grenada had been a political success, it had been an operational nightmare. Army, Navy, Marine, and Air Force elements had worked poorly together, as often as not getting in one another's way. Every service arm had wanted a piece of the Grenadan pie, but the mission planners had overlooked key elements necessary for successful joint ops. Communications had been hopelessly snarled, with some units in the field unable to talk to others. Timing for the invasion had been a real screw-up; some planners had been using Zulu time—GMT—while others were using EST, five hours earlier. In fact, it was a miracle that the invasion had been carried off at all.

Old Man Murphy had vented his special wrath on the SEALs. In an attempt to plant radio beacons at the airstrip at Point Salines two days ahead of the invasion, members of Team Six had parachuted into the sea off Grenada—in full darkness instead of twilight, and in twenty-knot winds. Four heavily laden SEALs had drowned. After being recovered from the sea, the rest had made two attempts to get ashore and been thwarted both times by drowned-out engines. Rangers parachuted onto Point Salines Airfield and had taken it without help from SEAL radio beacons.

Other elements of Team Six had reached the Government House and rescued Prime Minister Scoon, his wife, and nine staff members safely hiding in the basement, but then they became trapped by superior enemy forces. They'd had to hold on for over twenty-four hours before a detachment of U.S. Marines finally reached them. Still other SEALs, sent to capture a radio transmitter at Beausejour, found themselves in a ferocious firefight with superior enemy forces, including several armored personnel carriers. They managed to fight their way free to the sea and were eventually picked up by an American destroyer. The transmitter, it later turned out, was more of a political target than a military one, and the mission would have been more properly assigned to better-armed and supported conventional forces.

So Grenada had indeed been a cluster fuck, to give it its technical name, especially where the Navy SEALs were concerned. As a result, Senate Armed Services Committee meetings had been held leading to the creation of a new command tasked with overseeing all U.S. special operations forces. USSOCOM had been the result, a military command embracing the entire special warfare community—the Army's Special Forces and Delta, the Air Force Special Operations Group, and the Navy SEALs.

So far as most SEALs were concerned, membership in the close-knit SPECWAR family was a decidedly mixed blessing. It seemed at times that the Teams were drowning in Army green, and the orders and regulations coming down from the top tended to favor the Army's way of doing things, not the Navy's.

Besides, the Teams historically were there to support the fleet. Would they still be able to do their traditional job for the Navy while toeing the line drawn by Fort Bragg?

"You wanna know how things are going to go in Panama?" Jaco said after a long silence. "I'll tell you, and it doesn't take a psychic to see it, either. The damned armchair strategists and REMFs are moving in lock, stock, and regs manual. They're already passing down so many damned ROEs you can't tell who's fighting who anymore."

"Vietnam all over again," Greg agreed, "only worse. You'd think Washington would learn its lesson."

"Vietnam, hell. This is *worse*. In Vietnam we weren't allowed to hit targets without authorization, couldn't cross certain lines on the map, half the time couldn't take a piss without filling out the proper forms. But, damn it, in Nam SEALs weren't being used as heavy infantry."

"Well, sometimes they tried," Greg said. "But platoon commanders have been known to stand up on their hind legs and refuse orders. It's not real good for the old career track, but it's been known to save lives."

"Yeah, well, every man in the Teams knows we're not trained and equipped to take out an objective like *that*." He nodded at the airfield for emphasis. "Not with a goddamn frontal assault."

"So who has the terminal case of testosterone poisoning?"

"Damfino. Every service wants a piece of Blue Spoon, and some of them were using any excuse, any justification to grab one. I don't know if this screw-up is from a SEAL farther up the chain of command, or from some Army bastard in SOCOM."

"What about Tuohy? He has a say in this thing, surely."

Jaco shook his head. "Not really. Not enough to be heard. Ever since this damned SOCOM takeover, they've had us on a real short leash." He grinned. "Hell, you'd think someone up the chain thought we were going to embarrass them or something. The Rules of Engagement are so tight we can't fucking spit without authorization in triplicate."

Greg made a rude noise, then took another long look at Paitilla Airfield through his binoculars. "I've got some contacts in Intelligence," he said at last. "One of 'em's at Fort Bragg, USSOCOM S-2. Maybe I can have a word with him."

"That's why I wanted you to see this shit, bro. A fucking disaster in the making."

The trouble was, there just wasn't going to be that much Greg could do. Since the creation of USSOCOM a few years earlier, the entire shape, scope, and feel of the Teams had changed. Training was still just as tough, for the most part. The Teams were still elite in every sense of the word. But they didn't have the same independence under the new regime that they'd had before. That translated as less flexibility, less opportunity to choose their own ground, less chance to operate independently, which was where SEALs and their expertise at small-unit tactics truly shone.

"So, speaking of a piece of the action," Jaco said, "I heard you got loaned out to Team Two."

"Yeah. They've had me training for the op against Pineapple's personal Navy."

"Yeah? How's that going?"

"Pretty smooth, so far. At least we're doing classic SEAL work."

"And the water's a lot warmer than at Machrihanish."

Greg's home Team was SEAL Team Three, based in California. Operations in the Caribbean and Latin America, however, were usually tasked to Team Four, operating out of Little Creek, Virginia. Lately, Team Two had also been brought into the picture for Blue Spoon, but Two, also out of Little Creek, spent most of its time training for ops in northern Europe, with their advance base at Machrihanish, in northern Scotland. As Jaco had suggested, Panamanian waters were balmy in comparison.

None of the West Coast Teams had a part in Operation

Blue Spoon, the liberation of Panama from *"el piñe"* Noriega and his thugs. Because of his years of work with Navy Intelligence, the SEAL West-Coast command had given Greg a temporary assignment with Team Two, ostensibly as intelligence liaison with SOCOM and the Panama operation.

In truth, Greg had the feeling he was being expected to spy on SOCOM's plans for the Teams. It was a hell of a note when the Enemy was the same people who were supposed to be on your side.

"So," Jaco asked after a time. "You married?"

"Yeah." He didn't volunteer more than that. He was still married to Wendy, but the marriage was shaky at best, had been ever since she'd first threatened to leave back in '82, when he'd told her he was going back into the Teams. He'd talked her out of divorce then, telling her that they needed to stay together for the sake of their son. Mark had been ten at the time, but they'd endured several separations since then. For the past four months, Greg had pretty much been on his own, living and training with Team Two in Little Creek, with occasional flights back to San Diego to see Mark and to try to patch things up with Wendy.

And two days earlier, sure enough—and just as Wendy had complained six years before—a phone call had come in the middle of the night, and six hours later he'd been on a military flight to Panama. If Wendy knew, she'd be going crazy right now.

Hell, maybe she did know. Navy wives tended to be downright psychic when it came to knowing what was really happening with their husbands' orders and deployments, and SEAL wives were better at that ancient game than most.

They needed to work things out. Mark wouldn't be available as an excuse any longer. He'd graduated from high school the previous June, then joined the Navy on his eighteenth birthday. He'd already graduated from Boot Camp and Boatswain's School and was on his way now to BUD/S. Mark was going to be a SEAL, like his daddy.

Greg was button-busting proud of his son, proud of what the boy had already become, proud of the fact that Mark wanted to follow in his father's footsteps—correction, his swim-fin steps—as a SEAL.

But Wendy had reached the point a long time ago when she just downright hated the Teams and everything about them. Greg wasn't entirely sure she'd still be there at the end of this deployment, when he finally returned home.

"Just tell me one thing, Halstead," Jaco said.

"What's that?"

"Tell me this whole thing isn't just being staged to get the canal back."

Greg chuckled. "Wish I could, but I can't. I don't know that's what's happening, but . . ."

"But it stinks to high heaven. I've got a family back in the World, too. Wife and two daughters. Who's going to explain to them that their dad got killed over some kind of silly-assed political brinkmanship down here?" He sighed. "What the hell was Carter thinking when he gave the canal away, anyway?"

Greg shrugged. "He probably thought it was the decent thing to do. And we *did* at least retain the right to intervene militarily if the canal is threatened."

"Which is what we're doing, isn't it?" Jaco asked. "Even though the official turnover isn't supposed to happen for another ten years. You ask me, I think they're setting Noriega up as a straw man, someone to take down when they need an excuse."

"Maybe," Greg agreed. "But the son of a bitch is still a monster. He needs taking down."

"Yeah, he is that. Why do *we* have to do it, though?"

"If not us," Greg said lightly, "who?"

"We're not the world's policemen," Jaco said. "Noriega ought to be Panama's problem."

"Maybe. Most Panamanians don't like him any more than we do. But Pineapple and his thugs have the guns. Maybe it's just up to us because we're here."

Most Panamanians liked the *norteamericanos*. The people of Panama—thanks to their historically close relationship with the U.S. over the Panama Canal and the American military bases guarding it—remained friendly, for the most part, friendlier, indeed, than the citizenry of most Latin American countries in this era of drug wars, covert campaigns against the communists, and the worsening image of *el americano feo*—the Ugly American.

The problem, so far as the U.S. government was concerned, was Noriega and his henchmen.

Manuel Antonio Noriega, known as "*el piñe*," the "Pineapple," because of his hideously pocked face, was, frankly, an unfortunate invention of the U.S. intelligence community and the DEA. A promising army officer and a graduate of the Canal Zone's Army School of the Americas, he'd become head of the Panamanian Defense Forces' intelligence branch in 1972, and during the next decade he'd forged extremely close connections with both the CIA and the DEA.

In 1981, his mentor and patron, the dictator Omar Torrijos, had been killed in a convenient plane crash—a crash that most in the intelligence community believed had been engineered by Noriega himself. Noriega became head of the entire Panamanian Defense Forces and the most powerful single man in the country.

During the turbulent '80s, he'd been invaluable to the U.S. intelligence community. He'd provided a safe haven for the deposed shah of Iran, provided intelligence on the drug-trafficking cartels of Colombia, and served as middleman between the U.S and the contras fighting the communist Sandinista regime in Nicaragua.

But Noriega was greedy and wanted more—more money, and more power. By 1989, the U.S. government believed he was running a widespread and profitable drug cartel of his own and even providing meeting places, money laundering, landing fields, and technical support for drug traffickers from Cuba, Colombia, and Peru. There was also proof that he'd been passing on American military secrets to anyone with hard cash, including Cuban Intelligence. When his bid for president of Panama had failed in the elections during May, he'd invalidated the results and seized full control of the country for himself. An attempted coup in October by disaffected PDF officers had been ruthlessly crushed.

By now, Noriega had his sticky paws in half of the dirty deals in the Western Hemisphere, and he'd done it by using his contacts with the CIA and especially the Drug Enforcement Administration, a genuine case of adding insult to injury. For months Washington had been applying pressure to Noriega, trying to control him, then to indict him, and even to capture him in a covert Delta Force op that had gone quietly wrong.

The pressure had been building steadily to the bursting point. Just the day before, on 15 December, Noriega had addressed the country's National Assembly, naming himself Maximum Leader and declaring that a state of war now existed between the United States and Panama.

"'The Maximum Leader,'" Jaco said, as if reading Greg's mind. "If a war is what that madman wants . . . he's got it."

"The poor SOB won't know what hit him," Greg agreed. "I've seen all I need to see here. You ready to go?"

"Yup. The thing is, I'm afraid it's gonna turn out like

Grenada. There is absolutely no question in anybody's mind that we're going to wipe the sidewalks with Noriega. Like you say, he has no idea what he's up against. But there are people on our own team who aren't shooting straight, and good people are going to get hurt or killed because of it. If we can avoid hitting ourselves in the foot, well, I'd like to help manage that."

"I'll do what I can. I just have to say again, I doubt that my views are going to get much of an airing, in Fort Bragg or in Washington."

"At least we tried, right? Hoo-yah!"

"The only easy day was yesterday," Greg said, repeating the old and well-worn training phrase from BUD/S. "Let's get back to Howard."

"There's cold beer waiting."

They walked down the apartment building's stairwell, emerging on the street minutes later. It was only mid-afternoon, but the traffic in the streets of Panama City was heavy. As they climbed into the nondescript Chevy they'd signed out of the Fort Howard motor pool, Greg nudged his companion. "Watch it. We've got a tail."

"Shit. PDF?"

"Not unless they're plainclothes. Digbats, most likely."

"That's not so bad, then. Those assholes can't find their heads with both hands."

The PDF was the regular Panamanian army. The Dignity Battalions, however, a name shortened by the Americans to "digbats," were more like gangs of thugs or vigilantes. Noriega had used them extensively during the May elections to crack the skulls of political rivals and break up his opponent's victory demonstrations. Greg had spotted five of them in a battered red pickup truck across the street, two in the cab, three on the flatbed in back. They were wearing civilian clothing, but he'd glimpsed the AK-47 one held as he tried to put it out of sight, and the dark expressions on their faces as they watched the Americans getting into their car told Greg all he needed to know.

"You think they're upping the ante?" Greg asked as Jaco put the car in gear and pulled into the street.

"Could be. This whole thing has been one long war of nerves, ever since before the election. If you ask me, we should have moved in two months ago, during the coup attempt."

"They were probably planning just that, but someone got cold feet. Shit. They're following us. You packing?"

"Smith & Wesson is my copilot. You?"

Greg nodded. He was wearing a belt holster clipped to his waistband, up high beneath the tail of his T. The little Walther PPK wasn't good for much but a holdout weapon, but it was better than nothing.

"We have some firepower under the rug in the floor in back," Jaco said.

Turning in his seat, Greg lifted the rug and retrieved two Uzi submachine guns and a black canvas satchel with loaded magazines. "Nice. Where do you do your shopping?"

"Shit. The Israelis are all over the country, man. They've been helping Pineapple organize and train the PDF. You just gotta know who to talk to."

Jaco turned left onto the Via Italia. Their vigilante shadow followed, caught in the traffic about three cars back.

"Not much of a car chase when you're stuck in a traffic jam," Greg said.

"Yeah, but it makes it easier to lose 'em."

"Good. The streets are a bit too crowded for gunplay."

"It won't come to that. The digbats and PDF have been harassing U.S. service personnel some, but nothing real serious. Couple of guys I know, they've planted coke on 'em and then arrested 'em. Mostly, though, they just try to keep tabs on us. Hold on to your lunch."

Jaco accelerated sharply, pulling around the left sides of two cars ahead and making a sudden and highly illegal turn against the light onto Avenida 6 Sur, heading east. Horns blared and drivers swore and gestured as he broke into the traffic stream, racing clear of the intersection.

"All-righty, then," Greg said in a sing-song voice. "Do we get arrested for dope possession or reckless driving?"

"Hey, this is Panama, man. Reckless driving is the fucking national pastime."

They swung onto a traffic circle. Jaco leaned on the horn to clear a way across two heavy lanes of traffic, exiting the circle onto Calle 53 Este and heading north. Greg peered out the back window but couldn't see their pursuit.

"Nice moves, Jac. I think you lost them."

"All in a day's work, man. All in a day's . . . shit."

"What?"

"Up ahead. Looks like a PDF roadblock."

A guardrail barrier had been erected across the street just in front of the bridge over the Río Matáznillo. Uniformed PDF soldiers watched from trucks on either side of the street and from behind sandbag barricades. The Panamanian flag fluttered in the breeze above a concrete-block structure that had the gray and institutional look of a government building. Cars had backed up in front of the barricade and were being allowed through one at a time, after a prolonged conversation with each driver.

"I don't like the looks of this," Greg said.

"Yeah. They're checking papers. We should be clean."

"What about the weapons?"

"As long as they don't search, we're okay. Just chill and play nice."

"I will," Greg said agreeably. "But what about *them*?"

He nodded at the rearview mirror. The digbat pickup was crowding its way up the line of traffic fifty meters back, the driver leaning on his horn and the men in back angrily waving their weapons to force cars to pull left or right out of their way. The racket had already attracted the attention of the PDF guards at the bridge.

"Well, well," Jaco said. "How do you want to play this, Halstead? We can let them arrest us, we can try walking, or we can John-Wayne it."

"There are too many civilians around for a firefight, Jac."

"I know, I know." The line of cars ahead began to move, and Jaco followed. They were completely hemmed in now between cars, buildings, and sidewalk.

A trio of armed PDF soldiers were coming down the line of cars, weapons at the ready, looking in at the occupants of each. *"Allá!"* one of them called, pointing.

"Shit. They made us," Greg said.

"You two!" the PDF soldier shouted. "Out of the car!"

"Buenas tardes. Hay un problemo?" Jaco asked the soldier, smiling.

"You are Americans, yes?" the soldier said. He was a beefy, heavyset man with a bushy mustache and captain's bars pinned to the collar of his green utilities. "We wish to question you."

"Now, just a moment," Greg said. "You can't—"

"Papers. Passports. ID. *Ahora!*"

"Capitán!" another soldier cried. *"Mira!"* He reached into the back of the car and pulled out the two Uzi SMGs.

Jaco folded his arms. "I think we'd better take this discussion inside, don't you, Captain?" he said. "My friend and I are Israeli. We're here training elements of *el presidente*'s personal guard. *Entiende?*"

The soldier blinked piggish eyes. "Israeli?"

"Sí! Es verdad! I don't think your superiors would approve of this."

"We will check. This way! Move!"

Soldiers closed in on the two SEALs and ushered them ahead, toward the gray building. Someone prodded Greg hard between the shoulder blades with the muzzle of a weapon.

"Well, man," Jac muttered. "The only easy day was yesterday."

"Hoo-yah." Greg glanced around. "The water is your friend," he said.

"I'm with you, partner."

"Do it." Greg dropped and spun, snapping his foot toward the nearest soldier's knee.

Chapter 2

16 December 1989

Mataznillo Bridge
Panama City, Republic of Panama
1535 hours

He caught the muzzle of the soldier's AK-47 with his elbow, smacking it aside an instant before his foot slammed into the man's right knee. The soldier screamed and crumpled, clutching his knee; Greg reached under his T-shirt and pulled his PPK free, chambering the first round with a sharp snick.

"Cuidado!" someone shouted, as Greg raised the small pistol, nearly engulfing it in both hands.

The PDF trooper who'd discovered the Uzis stood a few feet away, mouth agape, clutching both weapons uselessly by their barrels. He took one look at Greg's PPK and let go of the SMGs, raising both hands high.

"Fuego! Fuego!" someone yelled at Greg's back.

The flat, rattling crack of an AK echoed down the street. Greg dropped into a crouch, pivoting swiftly, bringing his PPK to bear on the gunman. He heard the hollow *chunk-chunk-chunk* of rounds punching through the side of a car, heard the snap and hiss of other rounds cleaving the air above his head. He triggered the PPK twice, and the gunman stumbled backward, arms pinwheeling, AK flying. A woman screamed nearby.

Jaco had taken down two of the soldiers closest to him hand-to-hand and now had his own S&W bulldog out. He fired once . . . twice . . . a third time, the bulldog's bark deeper-throated than the crack of Greg's PPK.

The PDF guards, those still on their feet, had decided discretion was definitely the better part of valor and taken to their heels. The digbat thugs, however, were out of their truck and rushing forward. Civilians were running everywhere, fleeing the sudden gunplay.

Greg stooped, scooping up the AK dropped by the crippled guard next to him, racking back the cocking lever to chamber a round. "Head for the water, Jac!" he shouted. "I'll cover!" He fired, aiming well above the close-packed cars on the street, spraying a short burst over the heads of the Dignity Battalion troopers.

That single burst was enough to convince them that they weren't in quite such a hurry as they'd believed. Two sprawled flat on the pavement; the other three fled. Civilians screamed and scrambled for cover; some were abandoning their autos, leaving others to helplessly lean on their horns in frustrated immobility.

Turning, then, Greg raced after Jaco, who was already vaulting the red-and-white-striped guardrail at the checkpoint. Greg leaped the rail right behind him, and the two SEALs raced out onto the south end of the bridge.

A gunshot followed them. Greg turned and loosed an AK burst in the direction of the concrete block building, where several PDF soldiers were just emerging. His shots sent them tumbling back inside. He slung his weapon then, took a running leap up onto the low barrier along the side of the bridge, and without breaking stride launched himself out into space.

Jaco hit the water ahead and to his left; Greg landed a

second later with a stinging, spread-arm splash designed to keep him from going too deep. The Mataznillo was a broad, sluggishly meandering river through the heart of the city, deep enough in the center for small craft and work boats, at least, but he wasn't sure what the depth was or how wide the central channel might be.

He surfaced, blowing and snorting. The water was oily and dark, thick with mud and bearing the unmistakable reek of raw sewage. *Just like home*, Greg thought, as he gulped down a double lungfull of air and ducked back underwater. There was a mud flat behind the beach at the BUD/S training ground at Coronado that smelled a lot like that; at least he didn't have a SEAL instructor over him, bellowing in his ear as he struggled through an evolution involving bench-pressing creosote-soaked telephone poles with half a dozen other slime-coated, shivering pollywogs. SEAL training was designed to toughen trainees, yes, and to weed out the unfit, but above all the lesson hammered into every BUD/S recruit was that the water was a SEAL's best friend. Any time a SEAL was cornered, his first thought was to reach the safe embrace of the water.

And it's a sure bet no one would follow us in this *stuff,* he thought, stroking hard. Underwater, visibility was effectively zilch, with only a faint haze of light filtering down from the surface. That didn't matter. He kept on his original course, swimming underwater at a diagonal that would take him away from the bridge and out toward the center of the river channel.

All too soon, his lungs burning, he came back to the surface. As soon as his head broke water, geysers of spray cracked and splashed around him, as gunfire crackled from the shore. Greg was not particularly worried; he had a low opinion of PDF training and especially of their marksmanship, but with enough lead slamming into his general part of the river it was possible that someone might hit him through sheer chance. He took another breath and submerged again, going deep enough so that the trace of light from above all but vanished, and the water acted as a shield against the odd lucky shot.

The water also cut off the sound of gunfire like a heavy blanket. He'd always particularly liked that about underwater work—the silence, the feeling of peace, even if that feeling happened to be illusory. The water also transmitted sound more efficiently than air; if it cut off the racket of gunfire from above, it magnified the sounds within the river itself. He could hear the dull clang and clank of something mechanical in the distance, could hear the deep, rumbling rush of the river itself, and in particular he could hear a far-off but growing throb—the turning screw of a fair-sized boat, it sounded like.

Time for another breath. He rolled over onto his back, unslung the AK hanging from his shoulder, and surfaced with the weapon trained in the direction from which he'd come, back toward the roadblock at the bridge. He was unpleasantly startled to see how close he still was; SEALs could manage long stretches underwater on one breath, but he was hampered now by the weight of the AK, by the street shoes on his feet, and by the sodden mass of wet clothing clinging to his body. The PDF gunmen were perhaps fifty meters away, firing down at him in wild, uncoordinated bursts.

He squeezed the trigger on the captured AK, not really aiming the weapon but trying to put down some suppressive fire, maybe make them think twice before showing themselves like that. The worst problem was that there were tall buildings in his line of fire beyond the bridge. He tried to keep his aim low, firing into the bridge itself.

Bullets slammed into the bridge and the abutment, sending up puffs of dust and concrete chips like tiny explosions. One PDF soldier standing on the bridge jerked and spun, toppling over the bridge railing and splashing into the river. The wonderful thing about the AK-47, Greg thought as he swept the bridge with a long, stuttering fusillade, was its sheer, dogged, hoo-yah reliability. Drop it in the mud or drag it through a river and it kept on firing.

The weapon ceased abruptly, the last bullet of its thirty-round banana magazine expended. The PDF soldiers had scattered again or were flat on their bellies. Greg released the AK, letting it sink to the bottom of the sluggish river, and began swimming toward the middle as hard as he was able.

On the surface, he could see the source of the heavy, underwater throbbing. A cargo lighter, a clumsy, twin-screwed vessel of perhaps 600 tons, was wallowing slowly down the center of the channel. It was flying a Panamanian flag but wasn't armed. He doubted that the crew had heard the altercation on the river just now.

He kept swimming, rising high every few strokes in an attempt to spot Jaco. He couldn't see the other SEAL, however, and had to assume he was spending most of his time underwater.

Which was still a good idea, Greg thought, as rounds continued to splash on the surface in his general area. Taking another deep breath, he dove, frog-kicking and breast-stroking toward the lumbering cargo lighter.

A heavy thud hammered Greg in the back and lungs and ears, rolling him over in the water and nearly driving the pent-up breath from his lungs. The bastards were tossing hand grenades now, hoping to bring him to the surface like a dynamited fish, belly-up. Sound wasn't the only thing transmitted by water. It also magnified the detonation of a half-pound or so of high explosives into an underwater shock wave that could easily render him concussed and helpless.

He kept swimming, biting back his breath. Another explosion rumbled through the water, but far enough off this time to convince him that the PDF troops didn't really know exactly where he was. *Let's hear it for opaque water*, he thought, pulling himself along stroke after stroke after chest-burning stroke. When he could stand it no longer, he forced an extra three strokes from his agonized body, then rolled onto his back, gulping down air without fully surfacing. He couldn't tell if the troops ashore had seen him. At least there were no more grenade explosions.

He'd made good progress this last stretch. The lighter was twenty meters ahead, idling downriver. He gauged the remaining distance carefully, took six more deep, deep breaths to boost the oxygen content of his blood, then dove and swam, aiming for the lighter's bow.

He could feel the boat approaching, feel the buffeting from its bow wave. As dark as the water was, it suddenly became much blacker still as Greg passed beneath the vessel's keel. He pulled harder than ever now; he was all too aware of the churning, pounding threat of the twin screws aft. If he tangled with those, he would be dead by the time what was left of him reached the surface.

The water grew lighter again, but he kept swimming, putting as much distance as he could between the lighter and himself. When he surfaced at last, he was perhaps ten meters on the far side of the craft; he could see several Panamanian crewmen on deck, all on the port railing, looking toward the shore from which he'd come. They were probably wondering what all the noise and confusion over there was about.

Good. Let them wonder. He turned and kept swimming for the river's north bank.

Where was Jaco? It took another ten minutes to complete the swim to the river's northern bank. When he felt the silty bottom dragging at his shoes, he treaded water for a moment, searching. Had he passed in front of the lighter, coming ashore close to the north end of the bridge? Or had he angled himself upstream, crossing aft of the vessel in order to lose himself in its wake and stay well clear of the bridge? The first choice would be the easiest one, since he wouldn't need to work as much against the current. Jaco was a SEAL, however, and could be counted on to do the unexpected. Greg started swimming slowly upstream, away from the bridge.

There. He saw something floating in the water thirty meters upstream, close by the shore. Heart quickening, Greg swam toward the object. If that was Jaco, he wasn't moving at all. . . .

It was Jaco—or, rather, it was Jaco clinging to a large, waterlogged wooden cargo pallet adrift in the river. When he saw Greg, he lifted his arm, but the movement was weak.

"Jac!" Greg called, raising his voice just enough to reach the other SEAL. "Jac! You okay?"

"No problems," Jaco said. He released his make-do raft and started dog-paddling toward Greg. Together, they made their way to the muddy bank of the river, clambering out and collapsing against a crude seawall of broken concrete chunks.

Jaco was bleeding. His trousers were torn and a bright red patch showed against muddy skin just above his left knee. "Shit!" Greg said. "You're hit."

"What, this?" Jaco snorted. "Cut myself worse shaving."

"Can the macho crap. God knows what's living in this water. We need to get you back to base."

"I'm with you." Together, they rolled over the concrete wall and onto the street beyond, studying the bridge, the nearby roads, the towering buildings around them. Traffic was heavy, and pedestrians looked at the two men curiously or with open distaste.

"So what do we do," Jaco asked. "Hail a cab?"

Greg frowned. One of Panama City's infamous *diablo rojo* public buses cruised past in a cloud of diesel fumes; some of the passengers stared down at the two mud-covered Americans in the street. They were in the heart of the city here, and he was feeling very much out of place. "I feel about as inconspicuous as a tarantula on a china dinner plate," he said. "We need to get inside, out of sight."

"I'm with you."

They could hear shouting from the south side of the bridge, mingled with honking horns. Judging from the confusion over there, the PDF troops were milling about in total confusion. Several had ventured halfway across the bridge and now were staring down at the water. The lighter had hove to, its crew members calling back and forth with the troops ashore, but if anything like a serious and organized search had been initiated, it was well hidden behind a façade of Keystone Kops chaos.

Still, they would be sorting themselves out soon enough and had probably already telephoned for backup. They would also be able to guess where the two SEALs had come ashore. Fortunately, traffic was still heavy enough that it was moving at a rush-hour's pace. It would take them a while to get to where they were.

Greg pointed at a windowless building across the street, dwarfed by the skyscrapers beyond it. Like much of Panama City, this neighborhood was an odd—to North American eyes—mixture of the ultramodern and the poverty-stricken, gleaming modern towers mingled with crumbling façades that would have made a gringo ghetto look good. The sign over the seedy-looking door read LA VIDA NOCHE CAFÉ.

"Think they'll let us in?" Jaco quipped. He looked down at himself. Both men were as mud-coated as any BUD/S pollywog fresh from the mud pit and at least as aromatic. "I know that place. Tony nightclub for the under-twenty-five set. Ten dollar cover charge, and forget even going through the door if you're an old fart like us."

"What, they've never heard of the 'grunge look' down here?" Greg raised one hand and stepped into the slow-moving stream of traffic. Brakes squealed, horns sounded, angry drivers vented torrents of Spanish invective, but Greg helped Jaco hobble across the street.

The nightclub looked closed, but when Greg pounded on the door, a young Latino with a suspicious expression opened it a crack. *"Cerrado!"* he snapped. Then his eyes widened as he took in the mud-covered Americans.

"Estamos norteamericanos, señor," Jaco replied. *"Necesitamos su ayuda, por favor."*

"I speak English," the man said. He glanced up and down the street. "Inside. *Rapido.*"

They slipped inside, stepping from the bright glare of the afternoon into air-conditioned coolness and dark. The nightclub was empty, with chairs upturned on tables. A mop and bucket stood in the middle of a large dance floor. A bandstand occupied the back wall, a large bar another. An attractive, olive-skinned woman in shorts and a red T-shirt eyed them suspiciously from the bar. *"Amado,"* she said. *"Quién es?"* The look of suspicion changed to one of disgust as she got a better look at their condition. Her nose wrinkled. *"Mangajos!"*

Amado replied with a burst of Spanish. Greg spoke a little, but this was beyond the abilities of his high-school comprehension. "What's *'mangajos?'*" he asked Jaco in a whisper.

"Local slang," Jaco replied. "Means really filthy people."

Greg looked down at himself. "The woman has a knack for understatement."

"Big crowd tonight," Jaco observed.

"We don't open until evening," the man explained. "I'm Amado."

"You're the owner?"

"The bartender. This is Maria, one of our hostesses. Who did this to you?"

Greg hesitated. Admitting that they were on the run from the *Guardia Nacional* could get them turned in for a possible reward.

On the other hand, Amado had let them in *after* he'd heard they were North Americans. Most Panamanians, he reminded himself, hated Noriega and his thugs.

"We, ah, had a bit of a problem at a roadblock over the river," he explained, watching Amado's eyes for a reaction. "We had to swim for it."

"The Dignity Battalions?" Amado asked, nodding. *"Sí. Ladillas!* They hassle everyone. Anyone who hates what *el piñe* is doing to our country. Come on. Let's get you two washed off. Is your friend hurt?"

"They were shooting at us in the river," Jaco said. "I just got grazed, is all."

"I have a laundry sink back here." He rattled off another incomprehensible burst of Spanish at Maria.

"First," Greg said, reaching for a telephone sitting on the end of the bar. "I need to make a call. *Con su permiso?"*

"Sí, sí. Go ahead."

Fifteen minutes later, both SEALs were sopping wet but considerably cleaner, having hosed each other down at the laundry sink. Greg had placed a call through to the U.S. Naval Station at Fort Rodman. Help was on the way, but it was anyone's guess how long it would take them to get there.

"I do not wish to appear inhospitable, gentlemen," Amado told them, "but—"

"But you're going to have soldiers all over the place any second now," Greg said. He was putting the finishing touches on a gauze wrapping over Jaco's leg. Maria had produced a first aid kit from behind the bar. The wound, clearly and fortunately, was only superficial; the bone hadn't been hit. Still, it was bleeding a lot and Jaco was hurting when he put any weight at all on it.

"Maria tells me there are soldiers across the street, checking the riverbank. They could come here at any moment."

"My friend isn't going to travel far without transport," Greg said. He reached over to the tabletop next to him and picked up Jaco's Smith & Wesson. Somehow, the SEAL had held on to his weapon during his swim, though it was somewhat the worse for wear now. They'd rinsed it off in an attempt to get the river mud out of it, but the snub-nosed handgun wasn't as robust in such conditions as an AK-47, and they had neither the time nor the tools to clean it properly, or ammo to replace the rounds in the cylinder. Greg didn't know if the thing was going to fire at all.

He held the weapon up. "You know, if the soldiers think you helped us, you could claim we took the two of you prisoner. Forced you to help us."

"Sí. Posiblemente. We hope it won't come to that, eh?"

As if in reply to Amado's hope, a heavy pounding sounded at the door. *"Este es la Guardia Nacional!"* someone bellowed outside. *"Abra la puerta! Ahora!"*

"Quickly! Maria! Hide them in the storeroom in back." He raised his voice as the pounding sounded again. *"Uno momento!"*

"This way!" Maria said. Greg lifted an eyebrow. He'd not known she could speak English.

The storeroom was a large and dirty cement-block chamber turned into a maze by metal canning shelves, stacked cardboard boxes, musical instruments, and cases of beer and soft drinks. Rats the size of small terriers scurried out of the way when Maria switched on the light. "Hide yourselves," she said. "And for God's sake, be quiet!"

"Miss?" Greg said as she turned to leave. "Thank you. *Mil gracias.*"

"Thank us if we get out of this alive, gringo." She closed the door behind her.

Greg stepped up to the door, listening carefully. He could hear muffled shouts coming from the front of the nightclub.

"If they give this place a careful search," Jaco said, "we've had it."

"Then let's make sure they're not careful," Greg replied. There were two naked, overhead light bulbs in the room, just within arm's reach. Working quickly, he partially unscrewed first one bulb, then the other, plunging the storeroom into complete darkness.

"Good plan," Jaco said, as Greg felt his way back to the side of the other SEAL. They took cover behind some high-stacked soft drink cartons to the right of the door. If someone did come into the darkened room to look around, they would be dazzled by the light coming through the open door on the way back and, Greg hoped, not be able to see them. He clutched the useless Smith & Wesson in the dark; if they were caught, he might at least be able to bluff an opportunity for escape.

They waited, long minutes passing in an agony of slow-ticking seconds. Somewhere in the darkness, a rat's claws scrabbled on concrete. Greg thought he heard more muffled noises from beyond the closed door . . . someone shouting, perhaps.

But the words were unintelligible. There was a long, long silence . . .

. . . and then the storeroom door was thrown open.

Light spilled into the room, a rectangular splash of illumination against the cement floor partially blocked by a human shadow. The shadow moved, and they heard the *click-click-click* of the light switch being thrown up and down several times.

"Hijo de puta," a voice growled. A soldier, half-lit by the

light in the hallway behind him, took the two steps down into the storeroom. The SEALs were barely breathing, not even looking at the soldier directly. An article of faith among most of the men in the Teams held that you could *know* through an eerie sixth sense when someone was staring at you. They held their bodies and their minds both still as the soldier took another couple of steps into the room. Greg found himself thinking over and over *no one here . . . no one here . . . no one here . . .* as if he could telepathically implant the thought in the PDF trooper's mind.

The soldier stumbled against a crate and cursed. A rat scampered for cover and the man jumped, swinging his AK-47 in the direction of the skittering noise.

"Hey, Enrique!" a voice called from the front. *"Ven aquí!"*

The soldier took a last look around. *"Nada aquí,"* he muttered. Then he pounded up the steps and through the doorway, leaving the storeroom door open. The two SEALs remained crouched in the darkness, listening.

The voices were much clearer now with the door open, but the words were coming too fast for Greg to follow them. "What are they saying?" he whispered.

"Shht." Jaco hissed. Then, a moment later, "Shit."

"What?"

"They know we were here. They found mud on the floor . . . and blood . . . and one of them's laughing about the gringo stink in the air. They're accusing Amado of being . . . uh . . . not sure. 'Traitorous pig,' I think. Amado's telling them we broke in, forced them to help, and that we're gone. Out the back way through the alley, he said. I'm not sure they're buying it."

"Damn. How many of them are there?"

"Dunno. Four or five, at least." Jaco stirred in the darkness. "Why? You're not going out there."

"Shit, Jac. We got these people in trouble."

"What are you going to do? Rush a squad of armed PDF soldiers with a popgun that probably won't work? Get real, man."

"I know, I know . . . but we've got to do *something*."

" 'Something' does not include getting them killed, and yourself killed with them. What's the matter with you? That little blue button gone to your head?"

Greg bristled at that. The "little blue button" was the Medal of Honor he'd won in the closing acts of the Vietnam War. He naturally received more than his fair share of ribbing about the decoration from other SEALs, and more than once had found bureaucratic obstacles thrown in his path by armchair types who didn't think it appropriate for an MOH winner to go in harm's way.

Hell, the award was a mistake in any case. He'd gone back for a wounded CO on an op gone wrong in the DMZ. The fact that his CO himself was an MOH recipient might have had something to do with the importance attached to the act, but so far as Greg was concerned, medals had nothing to do with it. A SEAL did *not* leave a fellow SEAL on the beach, period, end of conversation.

"Jac—"

"Shht. Quiet a second."

Greg fumed in the near darkness, listening to the rapid-fire voices. He wished his Spanish was better.

"Okay," Jaco said. "Noriega's boys are putting them both under arrest. One of 'em said 'take them to the special detention facility in El Cangrejo.' Hold it . . . I think they're leaving."

Greg heard a door slam. Rising from his hiding place, he started toward the door.

"Watch it!" Jaco said. "They might not all be gone!"

Pistol in hand, Greg moved into the light, his back flat

against the wall as he moved up the hallway toward the front. Peering through an open door into the main room of the nightclub, he saw papers and the telephone on the floor, an overturned bucket in a pool of water, and several knocked-over chairs—evidence of a brief struggle.

The intruders were gone, along with both Amado and Maria.

Jaco entered the room behind Greg, a length of pipe in his hand.

"They're gone," Greg said. "Where is El Cangrejo?"

"It's a district of Panama City," Jaco replied, tossing the pipe aside. "The financial district, actually. It's just north of here."

"Is there any way to find out where they took them?"

"Possibly. We'll have to clear it with the Wheel." "Wheel" was SEAL slang for their CO . . . in this case, Lieutenant Phillips.

"First things first. We get us out of here, and you to the hospital."

Five minutes later, a Humvee with U.S. Army markings pulled up out front, and half a dozen soldiers wearing full battle gear piled out. Shoulder flashes marked them as members of the 193rd Infantry Brigade, and they wore black MP brassards on their arms. A jeep and an Army ambulance were close behind.

Greg opened the front door. "You the swabbies who called for a lift?" an Army sergeant boomed at them from the street.

"That's us," Greg said. "We need to get back to Rodman ASAP."

"Pile in," the sergeant said, jerking a thumb at the military police Humvee. "And move it! This ain't exactly what you call a friendly neighborhood."

The other MPs had fanned out around the vehicle, setting

up a perimeter, eyes and weapons trained on the surrounding rooftops. A crowd was gathering along the street, and
some of the locals did not look at all pleased.

Not everyone in this part of town, evidently, liked Americans.

As Greg was helping the medics load Jaco into the ambulance, a quartet of PDF soldiers appeared, pushing their
way through the crowd. *"Momentito!"* one called. "Those
two are under arrest! I require that you hand them over to
the proper local civil authorities at once."

"I'm sorry, sir," the MP sergeant replied. "I have already
placed these men under *military* arrest and am required to
transport them back to American territory. If you have a
complaint to file against these men, you should take it up
with the proper Judge Advocate General authorities for the
Canal Zone."

"Don't give me that legal nonsense, Sergeant. I am Captain Hernán Sarmiento of the *Guardia Nacional de
Panama,* we are now on sovereign Panamanian territory,
and I order you to turn those men over to me at once!"

"And I must inform you, Captain Sarmiento, that these
men are American nationals on active duty with the United
States Armed Forces, and as such are subject first to the
provisions of the Uniform Code of Military Justice. If you
have a complaint, it must be passed through the proper
channels. Sir."

Quietly, Greg stepped into the ambulance with Jaco, and
waited, listening. To tell the truth, he wasn't entirely sure
what their legal status at the moment was. Panama City was
part of Panama, not the Canal Zone, which—at least until
U.S. authorities turned it over to the Panamanian people in
1999—was under American military control.

The SEAL part of his training wanted to go to ground
immediately . . . to slip away and go into hiding rather than
depend on the military police.

But they were a long way from U.S. territory then, and Jaco would never make it on foot. All he could do was wait this confrontation out.

"What'd you two guys *do,* anyway?" one of the Army medics asked as he cleaned the mud from around the wound on Jaco's thigh. "Sounds like you two are in a world of shit!"

Greg didn't reply. He was tired, he was angry, and he was annoyed that the Army had come to bail them out rather than fellow SEALs—or, at the very least, the Marines. Like most sailors, he carried a bit of disdain for Army medics, preferring the Navy's equivalent, hospital corpsmen. An unfair bias, he knew, but one that came with his choice of service. He didn't like this medic's attitude, though he and his partner seemed competent enough. The other was already on the radio to the military hospital at Gorgas and talking with a doctor there.

A double thump on the ambulance door made him look back. The MP sergeant motioned him out.

There were eight or ten PDF soldiers present now, and several tough-looking Panamanians in the growing crowd of civilians that might be digbats, none of them wearing friendly expressions. "What's going down?"

"We're moving," the sergeant said. "I finally convinced them that while I have the authority to arrest you, I don't have the authority to turn you over to them for questioning. They're talking to your boss back at the naval station now. If we're lucky, we can get back on U.S. territory before they decide to act."

"I'd like to stay with Jaco."

"Negative. He's going to Gorgas."

"That's an Army hospital."

"It's also the only medical facility down here with inpatient capability. You're coming with me."

"But—"

"Do not give me an argument, mister, or I really *will* put you under arrest." He held up his thumb and forefinger, a half-inch apart. "We're about *this* far from a shooting incident here, and I, for one, don't care for the odds. I know you SEALs are crazy, but if you want our help, you do it my way. Capish?"

He sighed. "Roger that."

He didn't like leaving Jaco, but there didn't seem to be any decent alternatives. "Take it easy, Jaco. We'll spring you from the hospital as soon as we can get a rescue party together."

Jaco grinned. "Don't worry about me. You just stay out of trouble."

He clambered down out of the ambulance. "Who, me? Prudence is my middle name!"

The Panamanian troops watched with glowering expressions as the MP led him to the Humvee and helped him in.

Yeah. If Prudence was his middle name, then Trouble was his first.

Chapter 3

The ride back to base proved uneventful, even anticlimactic after the confrontation north of Paitilla. Picking up the Via España, they headed west through the city toward the Pacific end of the Panama Canal.

From the high, high, spider-work of the Bridge of the Americas spanning the southern mouth of the canal, Greg had a magnificent view of the sprawl of Panama City, from Punta Paitilla to Casco Viejo, tucked in between the azure-blue Bahía de Panamá and the jungle-green wall of the mountains inland. The glass-and-steel towers of the modern city rose like a gleaming forest, giving no hint at all of the desperate poverty in their shadows—or the nearness of war in this tropical ocean paradise. Noriega's declaration that a state of war already existed with the United States was almost certainly a propaganda move to boost his own popularity in Panama, and perhaps a lever in his negotiations with Washington as well.

Noriega probably had no idea whatsoever of the magnitude of the storm about to thunder down upon him and his corrupt regime.

In the meantime, though, Greg knew he had a storm or two to weather of his own. While he was not actually under arrest, technically, the MP unit's orders were not to take Greg back to the naval station at Rodman where the SEALs maintained their base in Panama but to an Army headquarters building tucked in next to the sprawl of Howard Air Force Base nearby.

From the sound of things, the proverbial shit was about to hit the proverbial fan.

The view of the ocean from Howard was stunning, a palm-tufted panorama of the Pacific stretching across the southern horizon. Greg had been intrigued to learn when he'd arrived there that Howard Air Force Base was the only place in the world where—thanks to the twistiness of Panama's geography—the sun actually rose over the Pacific. He decided he was going to need to get down there at zero-dark-thirty some morning to see the spectacle for himself.

Several of the Team Two SEALs Greg had been working with for the past few weeks were waiting for him there, obviously alerted already by the grapevine. Among them was Commander Roger Cahill, the CO of SEAL Team Two, a lean, gaunt man in khaki BDUs.

"Commander," Greg said. He didn't salute as he climbed out of the Humvee, since he was still in civilian clothing. "What's up, sir?"

"You tell me, mister," Cahill replied. He did not sound pleased. "From the smell of things, you and Jaco are in one hell of a world of shit."

"Well, I do need to change my clothes . . ."

"Not talking about that. C'mon. Colonel Hoyt is calling us both on the carpet."

"Huh? Why? The Army doesn't have jurisdiction over the Teams."

"Think again, son. The Army runs everything in the CZ, and the Navy is here on the Army's terms. Colonel Hoyt is one of the Army's key Action Officers down here. Your call for help scrambled an Army quick-response MP team. I think the colonel is going to want an explanation."

Cahill led him into the HQ building, leaving the other SEALs in the reception area at the front. Behind a plastic partition, a small army of men and women in camo fatigues clattered away at typewriters and computer keyboards. Hoyt's office was through a doorway at the far end of a maze of desks, cubicles, and office machines.

Colonel Frederick Simpson Hoyt was a thin, sharp-faced man with white hair and a crisp, no-nonsense manner. "Who the *hell* do you people think you are?" he demanded, when Cahill and Greg entered his office. The place was a tiny, sterile affair, more cubicle than office. The far wall was dominated by a portrait of President Bush, hanging above a rack of bookshelves jammed with dark-bound volumes of military regulations.

"Sir," Cahill began.

"*I'm* talking, Commander!" He stood up, walked around to the front of his desk, and pushed his face to within a few inches of Greg's. "Are *you* the son of a bitch that just tried to trigger World War goddamn Three?"

"I beg the colonel's pardon?"

"My phone's been ringing off my desk for the past half hour. The *comandancia* seems to think we're trying to start a war with Panama! The local police force is up in arms. The Panama National Guard is scouring half of Panama City for two gringos who tried to shoot their way through a government roadblock."

Greg managed an easy smile, hoping to defuse the man's anger. "I thought *they'd* just declared war on *us*. Sir."

"Shut your trap! I don't give a rat's ass what Noriega

says. We are not at war with Panama, not yet! And you, mister, have just done your best to cause an international incident!" He spun, jabbing a forefinger at Cahill. "I told you to keep your damned cowboys confined to base!"

"Sir, with all due respect, my people need to size up the targets they are being ordered to hit."

"Did I or did I not issue orders requiring your personnel to remain on base?"

"You did, sir. I interpreted that order to mean that you did not want off-duty naval specwarfare personnel going on liberty. Jaco and Halstead were not on liberty."

"You interpreted. You *interpreted?* Since when do Navy commanders interpret a colonel's orders? They *follow* them, mister! Or I goddamn know the reason why!"

"Sir, Special Warfare's duty—"

"Do *not* talk to me about your duty, mister." He crossed his arms, scowling. "I do not like 'special forces.'" He sneered the two words. "I do not like the whole idea of 'elite special forces.' So far as I am concerned, they serve only to draw off trained NCOs from regular units, depriving those units of experienced personnel, military budget, and other assets, and do nothing in return to justify the cost of keeping them in place. Furthermore, in my experience, all members of so-called special forces tend to be arrogant, undisciplined, and prone to getting themselves into trouble, trouble from which the regular forces as often as not have to extricate them. *Cowboys*, Mr. Cahill. Goddamn fricking *cowboys!*"

"I'm sure the brass at Fort Bragg would be most interested in your point of view, Fred," a new voice said from the door at Greg's back. "Especially the Army Special Forces. Sorry I'm late, gentlemen."

The newcomer, resplendent in dress whites heavy with colored fruit salad beneath the gaudy gold Budweiser of the

Teams, was a four-striper, Captain John Sandoval, the commodore of Naval Special Warfare Group Two. Several aides accompanied him, making Colonel Hoyt's office suddenly seem quite claustrophobic.

"Captain Sandoval," Hoyt said, his voice cold. "I didn't realize you were on this post."

"Operation Blue Spoon *is* a joint service operation, as I recall," Sandoval said. "Army? Marines? Air Force? And the Navy, too. We all have our jobs to do. And theoretically, we're all on the same side."

"That is beside the point, Captain. This man," he jabbed a finger at Greg, "and his friend managed to terrorize downtown Panama City this afternoon. They were stopped at a routine checkpoint and found to be in possession of unauthorized weapons, while wearing civilian clothing, I might add. Rather than acquiesce to the legal requirements of the Panamanian national authorities, they became involved in a shoot-out, endangering the lives of God alone knows how many innocent bystanders.

"Eluding the Panamanian police forces, they proceeded to break into a closed nightclub and terrorize two members of the staff at gunpoint."

"Sir!" Greg said. "That is not what—"

"Do *not* interrupt me, Chief Halstead," Hoyt said. "I was not speaking to you but to your commanding officer."

"If you're determined to crucify me, Colonel," Greg said, "I might as well get my say in. Those civilians I was supposed to have terrorized were helping us. They were taken away by the PDF and—"

"I am *not* interested in Panamanian affairs! Speak out of turn again, Halstead, and I'll write up the order for a court-martial right here and now!" He glared at Sandoval and began ticking points off of his fingertips. "As I was saying. Unauthorized use of firearms! Assault! Breaking and entering! Kidnapping! Terrorist threats! Conduct prejudicial to good order and discipline! My God, Captain, what kind of a circus are you running down here, anyway?"

"Sounds like a damned entertaining one," Sandoval said. "Chief, I'd like to hear what you have to say about those civilians."

"We overheard the PDF thugs saying they were taking them to the—"

"*If* you people don't mind," Hoyt said, "I am trying to conduct an investigation here. You can discuss local politics on your own time! Captain Sandoval! You must realize that incidents such as what happened this afternoon can only make our mission here more difficult! We are trying to conduct *extremely* delicate negotiations with the Panamanian government, with an eye to having Noriega step down voluntarily in favor of a popularly elected president. Gunplay in the streets is not going to advance our cause with the Panamanian legislature *or* the people!"

Greg was beginning to relax a bit. Hoyt was an officious, bureaucratic idiot, clearly enough, and a dangerous one . . . but a Navy captain held the same relative rank as an Army colonel, and Sandoval was known for taking care of his people.

"With all due respect, Colonel," Greg said quietly, "that is a load of grade-A bullshit. You have only the PDF's word for what happened this afternoon, and you also know they're itching to find out what our timetable is."

"Chief Halstead—"

"As for those negotiations," Greg continued, bulldozing past Hoyt's rising fury, "we all know Noriega's being set up to take a fall, a big one. Even old Pineapple Face knows that much, and he must be going nuts right now trying to figure out what we're up to. Arresting a couple of American servicemen on trumped-up charges might be just the way they could pick up some convenient intelligence on U.S. plans."

"Are you saying Noriega's intelligence service was trying to set you up?" Hoyt asked. "You have no proof of that."

"No, sir, but it's a damned good guess . . . and in intelligence *everything* is guesswork."

"All the more reason for you not to have contact with the locals. Captain Sandoval? I suggest you confine all of your special forces personnel to the post until further notice. The political situation here is entirely too sensitive to allow your cowboys to play bull in the china shop."

Sandoval grinned. "Fred, I'll take that under advisement. In the meantime, I suggest you consult those military regs behind your desk on the specific authority of this office and this department over the personnel of other military services . . . in particular those operating under the jurisdiction of USSOCOM and Naval Special Warfare. Come on, gentlemen."

"Aye, aye, sir." Greg turned to leave.

"I haven't dismissed you, damn it!"

"Oh, yes you have," Sandoval said cheerfully. "Why don't you try getting that stick out of your ass, Fred? It's bad for your posture."

"Have a great day, sir," Cahill said.

"And . . . thanks, Colonel," Greg added. "We really appreciated the lift out of P-City."

Greg pulled the door shut on a sputtering Hoyt and followed the other two back out of the building and into the steamy heat of the early Panamanian evening.

"You tromped on Hoyt pretty hard in there," Sandoval told Greg. "Not a good way to win friends and influence people."

"Sorry, sir."

"I understand the provocation. Still, try to keep a low profile, okay?"

"Aye, aye, sir."

"I assume you have some explanation for what happened?" Sandoval asked Greg, his tone curious, almost matter-of-fact.

"In there, sir?"

"In Panama City, smart ass, this afternoon. The little bit I saw come across my desk sounded like a small riot."

"Chief Jaco and I were stopped at a checkpoint coming out of Paitilla, sir. We were on the point of being arrested, and, well, we sort of resisted arrest, I guess. We broke away and dove into the river."

"Were shots fired?"

"They hit Chief Jaco."

"Did *you* shoot at *them*?"

"Yessir."

"Who fired first?"

"They did."

"I see." Sandoval paused for a moment. "Is it true you two were carrying automatic weapons?"

"There were a couple of Uzis in the car. They were sterile, though, and out of sight. They found them when they searched the car. We tried telling 'em we were Israeli intelligence."

Sandoval smiled. "I doubt that our friends in the Sayaret would appreciate that. Still . . . they didn't see your ID?"

"No, sir. They were sure we were Americans, though. A truckload of digbats apparently picked us up at Paitilla Airfield, then followed us to the checkpoint. Actually, sir, we were trying to evade *them* when we got stopped."

Commander Cahill nodded. "The digbats have been stepping up the pressure lately," he said, "harassing American service personnel, following them, making threats. They've been begging for trouble for months."

"Trying to provoke confrontations, sir?" Greg asked.

"That and keep up a high public profile for Panamanian

consumption. Noriega's trying hard to paint us as the ugly American colonialists, intervening in Panamanian affairs."

"In the vaster scheme of things, I doubt that it matters," Sandoval said. "Whatever Colonel Hoyt might think, things are going down soon, possibly within the week."

"So . . . am I confined to the base, sir?"

Sandoval shook his head. "Of course not. That idiot doesn't have that kind of authority. He just gets his jollies from throwing his weight around. But you'd damned well keep low and out of Hoyt's sights. The man doesn't care for special forces, especially SEALs, and he'll nail your tender white hide to the nearest bulkhead if he can find half an excuse. You read me, mister?"

"Loud and clear, sir."

"Good."

"But . . . a question?"

"Shoot."

"Those two Panamanian civilians, sir. They took us in off the street, helped me patch up Chief Jaco . . . and then lied to throw the PDF off our trail. And they were arrested. Dragged off to something called the 'special detention facility in El Cangrejo.' "

"Your point?"

"Sir! I've heard stories about those so-called detention facilities. Those people helped us. What can we do to help them?"

"Officially? Absolutely nothing. They are Panamanian nationals. We do not interfere in sovereign Panamanian affairs or legal issues."

"Yes . . . sir."

"And if I hear about you taking such action, I will be forced to take appropriate action. And if Hoyt were to catch you, your ass, Chief, would be grass. Do we understand each other?"

"Yes, sir, we do."

"Good." Sandoval looked at Cahill. "I imagine you have some intelligence matters to discuss with this man. Carry on."

"Aye, aye, sir."

They watched as Sandoval and his coterie of aides walked away.

"Need a ride back to Rodman?" Cahill asked.

"I'd appreciate that, sir."

"Good. You can fill me in on what you saw at Paitilla on the way. Dickinson!"

One of the waiting SEAL enlisted men stepped forward. "Yes, sir."

"Pass the word to the rest of the boys. Stand ready for a possible action order."

"Aye, aye, sir!"

"Have you heard anything about Jac?" Greg asked as the other SEALs trotted off.

"Not yet. I'll keep you advised. Talk to me."

During the drive back to Rodman Naval Station, Greg sat in the backseat of the gray Navy-registered Ford and told Cahill what he and Jaco had seen at the Paitilla Airfield. Cahill listened for the most part, making occasional notes on a small pad.

"From what he told me, sir," Greg concluded, "Team Four is making what amounts to a frontal assault on an airfield in order to cripple Noriega's personal plane. That's just a cluster fuck waiting to go down, sir."

"Believe me, Chief, the situation has gone the rounds, both down here, up at Fort Bragg, and back in Little Creek."

"When presented with a military problem, sir, the best solution is usually the simplest and the one that poses the least risk of close combat. A sniper team could take out that plane from the roof of any of a dozen buildings overlooking the airfield. They could do it clean, they could do it quiet, and they could exfiltrate before Noriega's bully boys even realized what had happened."

Cahill gave Greg a sour, sidelong look as he tucked the notepad into a jacket pocket. "I said the situation has been discussed. There are other issues here besides simplicity and stealth."

"Like the Navy getting a big enough piece of the Panama Op pie?" Greg asked. "They're carving this thing up like they did Grenada, aren't they?"

"Chief Halstead," Cahill said with measured care, "this is a damned sensitive time for NAVSPECWAR, hell, for *all* of the military special forces. The Reagan era is over. No more sky's-the-limit budgets for special ops. It's not a matter of getting a big enough slice of pie. It's proving we have any reason to exist at all in a climate where the competition for budget dollars is down to all-out CQB."

Greg chuckled. "I like the image of close-quarters battle in the halls of the Pentagon."

"It's a knife fight, son. Down, dirty, toe-to-toe and no holds barred. The problem is, most of the senior military brass think the way Hoyt does. So far as they're concerned, special forces just skim the money and the best and most experienced personnel away from the regular forces. Their philosophy is that *all* American military personnel should be elite."

"That's ridiculous, sir," Greg said, shaking his head. "The Teams . . . Delta, the Rangers, and the Green Berets . . . Marine Recon . . . they're the best. Hell, the *best* of the best. You need regular troops, too. You can't have a whole army of snipers or AT gunners or combat swimmers, any more than you can have a whole army of clerk-typists."

"That's the theory, and I happen to agree with it. But you and I don't make the rules, and you and I don't allocate budget. Shit, Hoyt's crowd have a point, don't they? Special forces take up way more than their fair share of the military budget. They get the best weapons, lots of ammo for training, and high-cost transport all over the globe. Training, especially. Hell, we're always training."

"And what good is all that training and practice and special-budget crap if they misuse their assets? Throwing Team Four against Paitilla is like using a scalpel to open a fucking jar of pickles."

"*Utilizing* Team Four at Paitilla will provide a high-profile op that will help establish Team credibility and flexibility when employed as a multiplatoon task force on a key military target. There are people in the Pentagon—hell, at Fort Bragg, too—who think the Teams are only good for assassinations and bringing back samples of sand from potential landing beaches."

"Taking an airfield is a job for the Army Rangers. Sir, they're trained for that sort of thing. We're not."

"The subject is not open to discussion, Chief. Team Two is doing pure SEAL-mission stuff. McGowan has Paitilla. He also has his orders."

Greg opened his mouth to say something along the lines of "*Fuck* orders" but bit the words back. That was not an attitude enlisted SEALs voiced to officers, even within the circle of the Teams.

Still, he remembered hearing tales of a SEAL lieutenant j.g. back in 1975, during the *Mayaguez* incident. Cambodian communists had taken an American ship on the high seas and were holding the crew hostage. U.S. Marines had gone in on Koh Tang Island in an op that quickly turned sour. The Marines were evacuated, but they left several of their dead behind.

An admiral on board the *Coral Sea* had had the bright idea of sending that j.g.'s SEALs back to Koh Tang unarmed and under a white flag, to have them recover the Marine bodies off the beach, a suicide mission if ever there'd been one. That j.g. had stood up in a room full of captains and admirals and generals and point-blank refused his orders. That was *not* what SEALs were trained to do.

The man may have saved his career by suggesting a workable alternative—that the SEALs go in stealthily and recover the bodies under cover of darkness. Fortunately, the situation had been resolved politically before further military ops were necessary.

Damn it, someone ought to stand up this time and refuse the orders to assault Paitilla. Unfortunately, Greg didn't have the authority and wasn't even working with Team Four. If he could get an interview with Commander McGowan, who was running the Team Four ops . . .

But his first responsibility was simply to do what he'd been sent down here to do, which was to provide liaison data on the Panama operation with the stay-at-homes of Teams One and Three on the West Coast.

And he felt one other strong responsibility as well. . . .

"Sir?"

"Yeah."

"Just curious. Do you have any idea where that special detention facility might be?"

"The one in Cangrejo? An old warehouse on Calle 61 Este? Negative. And I'd better not hear one word about you going out there looking, either. You hear me, mister?"

"Loud and clear, sir."

"Good." He pulled the car up in front of SEAL headquarters at Rodman. "Chief Callahan should be able to get you what you need. He's got the duty in the armory tonight, but he can put you in touch with some good people."

"Yes, sir."

"Come with me."

Cahill led Greg into the SEAL HQ, taking him past the front desk and outer office and into a locked and windowless briefing room in the back. He walked over to a locker and began punching a combination into the keypad lock.

"Chief . . . you were never in here. And you did *not* see this map."

"Absolutely, sir."

"When you leave this room, you will take nothing with you, except what's in your head. Clear?"

"Yes, sir." What the hell was Cahill pulling off, here?

"Good. I take it you have some high-powered G-2 contacts up at Bragg."

"I have some favors I can call in, certainly."

"You can also talk to RM1 Vazquez. You'll probably find him at the NCO Club. He's Team Two's liaison with the satellite jockeys at NPIC. As you can imagine, we've been requesting a lot of up-to-the-minute high-res imaging of this part of the world. You know, it is absolutely staggering what kind of intel we can get from spy satellites these days. And how *fast!*"

He removed a map tube from the storage locker and pulled out the photographic map inside. It showed a high-altitude aerial view, in black and white, of Panama City, from the canal in the west to Panama Vieja in the east, and inland as far as Lookout Point in the Metropolitan Natural Park. The various districts of the city—La Exposición, Casco Viejo, Balboa, El Cangrejo, and others—were neatly labeled, as were the major streets and landmarks. The map was also divided into a tight pattern of squares—quadrangles—identified by numbers along all four borders of the map.

Cahill unrolled the map on the briefing table in the middle of the room. "I just wanted you to show me where the nightclub was where you two holed up today."

An odd request. Greg had been able to give the street address and the nightclub's name from memory. Silently, he pointed to the spot close by the bridge over the Mataznillo.

"I thought so," Cahill said, nodding. "Excuse me a second," he said. "I'll be right back." He walked out of the room, and for several minutes, Greg was alone with that map.

He didn't need to take notes. The street Calle 61 Este was clearly marked; the map number and the coordinates of a particular quadrangle were easily memorized. Cahill reentered the room. "Okay, Chief. I have to go, now. Meeting with the NAVSPECWAR staff. I have your promise to stay out of trouble?"

"Absolutely, sir."

"Outstanding." Cahill put the map away, relocked the locker, and ushered Greg out of the briefing room, which he locked behind him. "I do not want you drawing any more of Hoyt's fire. Remember that Vazquez can help with specific intel requests you might have while, ah, filing your report."

"Yes, sir."

"I'll talk to you tomorrow. Meanwhile . . . have a *good* evening."

"Aye, aye, sir. I'll do that."

Greg stepped back into the heat of the waning afternoon. By his dive watch it was 1815 hours . . . time for chow, except that he had some work to do first.

And not much time to accomplish it all in.

Chapter 4

El Cangrejo
Panama City, Republic of Panama
2340 hours

The moon, several days past full, was already well into the western sky when Greg and seven companions approached the dilapidated Almacén Calle 61 Este, an imposing structure that did not exactly invite close inspection. The place was surrounded by a high, chain-link fence topped with barbed wire, and several mangy and ill-tempered Rottweilers patrolled the grounds inside. A fenced-in corridor connected the gate on the street with the building's entrance, where several Guardia vehicles were parked.

EM1 Tompkins and TM2 Haines cut through the fence with bolt cutters; Chief Mitchell, Chief Brunner, and BM1 Petrilli stood by with S&W sound-suppressed pistols—called "hush puppies" for their original use in Vietnam—plus Mitchell's canvas bag full of raw steaks.

The rest of the ad hoc strike team—RM1 Vazquez, HM2 Brown, and Greg—stood watch in the alley they'd selected as their ingress point, armed with H&K MP5 SD3 submachine guns with integral suppressors and laser-sighting devices mounted on the heavy barrels. Greg knelt on the pavement, scanning not only the entrance to the street twenty meters away, but the hundreds of illuminated windows in the office buildings rising on all sides.

Nothing like a little clandestine breaking-and-entering smack in the heart of the city's business and financial district, Greg thought. Even this late on a Saturday night, there was plenty of life and activity in the surrounding cityscape.

The SEALs had arrived at the objective in a battered van hotwired from a used-car dealership in Balboa and given plates taken from a junkyard outside of La Cresta. Their weapons and ammo were sterile; there would be nothing linking the United States military to this op . . . *if* everything went down by the book.

"We're in," Tompkins whispered over his throat mike. "Looks clear."

Like shadows, then, the team members began slipping through the hole in the fence. Each wore dead-black utilities, Kevlar vests, ski masks, and combat harnesses. Each wore Motorola comm units and night-vision goggles, though these last were switched off at the moment and riding in the up position. There was plenty of light so far from street and sky.

"No welcoming committee," Chief Brunner whispered. "Be a bitch if we got the address wrong, huh?"

Dogs barked in the distance, around the corner. "Nah," Vazquez replied. "This is the place."

Greg had fed the coordinates he'd lifted from the map at SEAL headquarters to Vazquez, who'd faxed them to a contact in Washington. Two hours later, they'd received a map back over the secure fax line, a satellite photo of the building in front of them. With invasion imminent, the U.S. military reconnaissance services had been working overtime, keeping tabs on thousands of targets and potential targets throughout Panama; potential targets included police and PDF interrogation facilities like this one.

The recon photo had been high-resolution enough to show the dogs in the fenced-in part of the compound, as well as a couple of security guards at the main door and the cluster of Guard vehicles out front. It had actually been taken yesterday, but the SEALs were reasonably certain that this was the facility where Amado and Maria were being held.

Technically, the SEALs were engaged in a recon-in-force. They would covertly penetrate the building and have a good look around; if they couldn't find the two civilians, if they'd in fact pinpointed the wrong objective, they would withdraw with nothing to show they'd been there save an anonymous hole in the fence.

If the two civilians from the nightclub were here, though, the SEALs would assess the situation, and act or not as the situation warranted.

The operation was also, technically, highly illegal. Asshole or not, Hoyt was perfectly correct. The United States was *not* yet at war with Panama, and this op constituted criminal trespass, illegal entry, and destruction of property at the very least. Even so, there'd been no shortage of volunteers for the op. The story of Greg and Jaco's adventure in Panama City that afternoon had spread throughout the Rodman SEAL community. SEALs always took care of their own, and that extended to the people who'd risked their lives for some of their own as well.

The amazing thing was how fast the whole op had come together, from rounding up the personnel to acquiring weapons and a sterile van to receiving the map from Washington to writing up a CYA training request. SEALs and other special forces personnel routinely set up special training exercises in the Panamanian countryside, and this op could—with a bit of mental calisthenics—be thought of as a hostage-rescue training scenario.

That, at least, was how it would read at their courts-martial if this op went sour.

But, hell. If the op went sour, they would have other things to worry about than a lousy court-martial.

A pair of Rottweilers, bristling at their muscular haunches, came tearing around the southeast corner of the building, barking wildly. Mitchell reached into his bag, pulled out a steak, and flung it like a Frisbee, sailing it over the guard-dogs' heads. Brunner and Petrilli, meanwhile, raised their hushpuppies in steady, two-handed grips, preparing to put them to their original use if necessary.

It wasn't. As expected, the dogs were not trained, were not even conditioned to refuse food from strangers, and the steak proved to be a most satisfying diversion. In moments, the dogs were fighting each other over the remaining bloody scraps of meat. Silently, the SEALs moved on.

According to the recon photo, there were only two small windows on the east wall, probably leading to office spaces. Both the front door and the main loading dock for the warehouse were in front, on the north side of the building, but there was a back door as well, opposite the alley, a door not guarded on the outside and presumably kept locked.

Like shadows, the SEALs converged on the back door, three of them dropping into a defensive crouch, their weapons at the ready, pointed away from the building and out into the night. A quick check proved there were no alarms or live circuits; it took Haines perhaps five seconds to open the lock with a couple of picks. It was dark inside, and the SEALs switched on their night goggles and slid them into place.

Each had an assigned task. Petrilli and Brown stood

guard at the door, covering their retreat. The others followed the hallway inside several yards, then fanned out in twos to left, right, and straight ahead when the passageway branched. Greg and Brunner took the middle path, moving quietly. The hall led them past a small warren of offices, storerooms, and restrooms; ahead was the main warehouse floor, dimly lit, labyrinthine with high-piled stacks of shipping crates, chemical drums, and empty wooden pallets.

It wasn't hard to figure out where to go. The shouted demands of an interrogating officer, a man's sudden throat-rasping scream in response, told the SEAL operators all they needed to know. In the lead, Greg signaled his companion. *This way. . . .*

Two men in PDF uniforms stood at the end of the hallway ahead, their backs to the dark-shrouded SEALs. Greg and Brunner moved up behind them in silent unison, reaching around from behind, dragging both men back from the edge of the light, and silencing both with hard, sharp blows to their temples and lowering the suddenly limp bodies gently and quietly to the concrete floor. They dragged the pair down the hall to an empty and unlocked office in the back, used plastic ties to secure both men's wrists behind their backs and their ankles together, and left them on the floor.

"Sleep tight, muchachos," Brunner whispered at the pair. It would have been quicker, of course, not to mention *safer*, for the SEALs to take both soldiers down with their knives or to use killing blows, but lethal force had been ruled out for this op except for certain very specific contingencies. There was no sense in making the inevitable legal repercussions of this night's activities worse than they already were. Breaking and entering on a supposed "training mission" was one thing; murder was definitely something entirely else.

Back at the edge of the light, crouching behind a stack of wooden shipping crates, Brunner and Greg lifted their night-vision goggles back on their ski-mask-covered heads; the scene in the main part of the warehouse was lit all too well by the glare of overhead fluorescents. Within a half-circle of crates serving as walls, a half-dozen PDF soldiers and a couple of men in civilian clothing were participating in the questioning or watching from the sidelines with broad grins on their faces. Both prisoners were naked—standard operating procedure for interrogations in this part of the world. Maria was tied spread-eagle on a set of bare mattress springs on the floor. At least, Greg assumed it was Maria; he couldn't see her face at the moment, which was obscured by the half-naked PDF thug raping her as several of the watchers cheered him on.

Amado was trussed up on what was known within interrogation circles as the "parrot's perch," hung head down by his knees from a horizontal pole, knees apart, wrists bound to ankles, ankles bound to thighs. A large metal washtub full of water on the floor, a set of electrical cables ending in alligator clips, and the end of what looked like a police truncheon protruding from between the prisoner's bloodied buttocks all gave stomach-churning testimony to the nature of the interrogation so far. Amado's upside-down face was puffy, red, black-splotched, and streaked with blood. It looked as if the questioning had been going on for a long, long time.

At the moment, a PDF officer was leaning over Amado, waving an electric cattle prod above his face. *"Dígame!"* the man screamed. *"Cuándo está la invasión Yanqui? Eh? Cuándo!"*

"No sé nada! No más, por favor!" Amado cried, his voice cracking. On the last word, the questioner shoved the

prod against Amado's genitals, turning the plea into a throat-tearing shriek of agony.

"Nighthawks, Nighthawk Three" sounded in Greg's earplug speaker. That was Tompkins. *"One tango down, catwalk on the east side. Clear view of Center Stage."*

"Nighthawks, Nighthawk Five." That was Mitchell. *"In position, west side. Negative tangos. Clear view, Center Stage."*

The interrogator, Greg noted with considerable interest, was the captain who'd been trying to arrest him that afternoon. What was the name? Sarmiento, that was it.

"Nighthawks, Nighthawk One," Greg whispered into his open throat mike. "Closed fist, I say again, closed fist. Take the bastards down."

If he'd ordered "open hand," the SEALs would have continued using less than lethal force. The code phrase indicated a hard takedown, meaning the team was under fire, or they were facing a hostage situation where innocent lives were in danger.

He would think about the morality of the decision later. Right now, all he saw were targets in PDF uniform. He switched on his laser sight, saw a pinpoint of red light dance across Sarmiento's uniformed back and squeezed the trigger.

The H&K's sound suppressor reduced the submachine gun's report to the soft snap of the action. Sarmiento arched up high on his toes, the cattle prod slipping from his grasp as he performed a slow pirouette away from his victim. It was a tight shot; Greg wouldn't have risked it at that angle for fear of hitting the victim, but his H&K's magazine was loaded with 9mm Glaser safety rounds, which meant they wouldn't travel all the way through the body they hit. Greg put a second round into Sarmiento's chest as he spun, then switched targets to a PDF soldier to the right.

Too late. The man was already dropping to his knees, both hands clutching at his back before he pitched face-down into the basin of water. Tiny red pinpoints danced and darted across the kill zone, and each time they came to rest on a Panamanian soldier, the man died. The soft, coughing clatter of silenced weapons rattled out quick and near-silent messages of death.

By this time, several of the PDF troops still on their feet had realized that something out of the way was happening. One shouted *"Cuidado, chicos!"* yanking a revolver from his holster just before a quartet of Glaser slugs slammed into his torso in a ragged line from crotch to throat. The PDF soldier on top of Maria tried to get up, but was knocked partway off the woman by laser-tagged shots coming from three directions. One of the civilians present, a dark-skinned Latino in a white suit, managed to draw a wicked-looking Czech machine pistol from a holster inside his jacket, whirling to face the rear of the warehouse. He died before he could get off a shot, before he could even find a target. The other civilian was already dead.

The entire action took less than three seconds, from first shot to last. "Eight tangos down, Center Stage," Greg said over his Motorola. "Secure the perimeter."

"One, Three. Catwalk, east side, secured," Tompkins' voice reported. *"Moving north."*

"One, Five," Mitchell added. *"We're clear. You're covered."*

Emerging from behind the pallet stack, Greg moved cautiously toward the lighted area, H&K at his shoulder, ready to fire. Amado groaned from his head-down perch and Maria was sobbing wildly, but Greg's first care was to make sure none of the tangos sprawled on the concrete floor posed a threat. Eight for eight, all dead. Only then could he turn his attention to the prisoners.

The code name "tango" generally meant "terrorist" in

this sort of action, but it could also mean "target." The SEALs used the name all the time in training ops, when pretend hostages were freed from pretend bad guys. Somehow, the term dehumanized the enemy, made it easier to target and kill without the distraction of emotion. *Tangos* didn't have a wife waiting for them at home, or kids. They were just . . . targets.

The emotions Greg was feeling had, if anything, helped him in the killing, and now he had to rein them in sharply. Amado was in a bad way, repeatedly half-drowned in the washtub as he hung head-down above it, beaten until his features were barely recognizable, shocked, burned, sodomized with that damned truncheon. *My God,* he thought. *How could anyone do this to another human being?*

"Brown," he called over the radio. "Corpsman front. Civilian casualties."

"On my way."

Greg used his diving knife to free Amado. Brown arrived a moment later, and together they gently lowered the man to the floor. While Brown began tending to Amado, Greg moved over to the mattress springs, where Maria was weeping hysterically. *"Bastardos! Bastardos!"* she repeated, over and over, as Greg rolled the body of the Panamanian soldier off of her legs, then cut the lengths of clothesline that tied her wrists and ankles to the corners of the mattress springs. Her face, arms, breasts, and stomach showed ugly bruises, and her lips and nose were bloody.

"It's okay," he told her. "Maria? *Está bien. Estamos norteamericanos."*

"Quién?" He cradled her in his arms. She seemed to be trying to see past his ski mask, staring up into his eyes. "Americans?"

"You helped me and a buddy out this afternoon," he told

her. "Get that blanket over there for me, will you, Tompkins?"

"Sure thing, Chief."

The other four SEALs in the assault team joined Greg and Brunner in the blood-stained center of the warehouse. "Their security here was piss-poor," Mitchell commented. "No one out front. They were all in here watching the action."

"No reason to expect trouble," Greg replied.

"Shit," Chief Brunner announced. "Shit in a fucking seabag!"

"What is it?"

Brunner was kneeling above the body of the civilian who'd pulled the machine pistol . . . an ugly little Czech Skorpion of a type popular with East-Bloc security and intelligence services. He held up a wallet, flipping open an official ID. "This one is Cuban embassy. Enrique Pérez."

"So's this one," Tompkins announced, checking the other civilian body for ID and papers. "Says here he's Ramón Gutiérrez . . . Cuban embassy, third undersecretary."

"This one's a military attaché," Brunner said. "Ha! In a pig's eye. They're DGI, both of them. Bet you any money."

Cuba's *Directoria General de Intelligencia,* the General Intelligence Directorate, was Havana's equivalent of the CIA . . . and they would be very interested right now in the possibility of an American intervention in Panama. Was the DGI working closely with Noriega? Or simply here as observers?

Shit. Were there Cuban troops in Panama secretly, as there'd been in Grenada?

"Bring the papers," Greg said. "Bring any intelligence-related papers you can find."

"We gonna torch the place?" Vazquez asked.

"Negative," Greg replied. "I have a better idea."

A notebook and pen lay on the floor next to the outstretched hand of one of the PDF soldiers. Greg wrote something on a blank page in the back, tore it out, folded it, and tucked it into the breast pocket of Pérez's bloodstained jacket.

"What'd you write?" Mitchell asked.

"I said we don't like them using our training to torture innocent civilians," Greg replied. "I signed it, 'SM—the Boys.'"

Mitchell snorted. "That'll confuse things, at least."

"Confuse things?" Haines said, then chuckled. "It's fuckin' brilliant!"

"Yeah. I figure by the time the accusations and counter-accusations stop flying, Noriega will be dead of old age."

"The Boys" was the popular *nom de guerre* for the Sayaret Matkal . . . the Israeli special forces unit that had rescued the hostages at Entebbe and performed covert strikes against the terrorist targets worldwide. They were known to be ruthless, highly trained, and very, very good at what they did. While there was no reason to think the Sayaret was operating in Panama right now, it was an open secret that Israeli agents had been training and supplying Noriega's bullyboys.

The message should cause a *lot* of confusion, not only in Panama City but in Tel Aviv as well. Greg knew that the CIA and various military intelligence agencies operating in Central America were concerned about the Israelis providing training for the PDF. Maybe this would help screw up communications there. Noriega was already suspicious of damn near everybody. That one brief note could do a world of good, so far as the U.S. was concerned.

"Let's get these two out of here," Brunner said.

"Petrilli," Greg called over his Motorola. "Sitrep."

"Back door's clear, Chief. No bad guys."

Both of the freed prisoners were wrapped in blankets found on the floor nearby and carried out the back door. The rest of the team formed a living wall around them, watching ahead, the flanks, and behind all at once as they slipped from the back door and stepped out through the hole in the fence. Tompkins retrieved the van, backing it into the alley so that they could load the two on board through the back doors.

After that, it was a quick, silent ride back to American Canal Zone territory and Gorgas Army Hospital.

"This is *highly* irregular, Chief," the head nurse at the hospital ER said, twenty minutes later. An Army medic was taking Amado's blood pressure. "I mean, if we have no record in the computer, and neither of them has identification on them . . ."

"*Trust* me, Lieutenant," Greg said in his best old-hand know-the-ropes manner. "They're both government employees. They just started work with our group today, and the paperwork hasn't come through yet."

"If they're civilian employees with the Navy, they should have proper ID."

"Ma'am," Greg said patiently "If they had any ID, the bastards that did this to them took it."

"That's right," Vazquez added. "Hey, I'll bring all the paperwork down here first thing in the morning. But right now, damn it, they're *hurt!*"

"You're healers here," Greg said as a white-coated doctor banged through the double ER doors. "Now *heal,* damn it. Or are you going to let them both bleed to death right here in the ER?"

The doctor stepped between the two side-by-side gurneys, pulling up eyelids first on Amado, then on Maria. "Jesus," he said. "What happened, a car crash?"

"Worse, sir," Greg told him. "Noriega's thugs happened.

They worked them both over pretty hard. We thought they needed immediate medical attention."

"You thought right. Give me their vitals."

"Male patient, BP one-oh-five over thirty. Temp one-oh-one point two. Respiration shallow at twelve. Female patient, BP one-twenty-eight over seventy. Temp ninety-nine point six. Respiration twenty."

"Bleeding?"

"Superficial for both. Cuts and bruises."

"The guy's got internal bleeding if that BP is any indication. Nurse? Cross and type for two unit, both patients. X-rays, skull and spinal, full series. And blood gases. Stat."

"Yes, Doctor. But . . . we don't have any records on their being base employees."

"Just do it, Lieutenant. Like the man says, we're healers, and these two need healing."

"Yes, sir."

Greg relaxed a little. They were pulling a bit of a scam, here. There were thousands of Panamanian civilians employed by the U.S. military working on-base in the Canal Zone, from janitors and drivers to clerks, secretaries, and technicians of all kinds, and those civilians had the right to medical care at Gorgas as part of their employment packages. But civilians not so employed had no business being at Gorgas at all.

But, damn it all, Greg was damned if he was going to rescue these two in an all-out gunfight, then see them vanish from a civilian hospital. The PDF had long arms, longer memories, and plenty of motive to track these two down. The first thing they would do once they found the El Cangrejo warehouse facility raided was start questioning every civilian hospital in Panama City.

They would have eyes and ears inside Gorgas as well, and sooner or later they'd get around to checking here. But Greg thought they'd have a bit of time before that happened. And the SEALs would have their tracks covered by morning.

The doctor was carefully examining Amado's face, neck, shoulder, arm. He took special note of the bright red rope burns around his wrist, then turned and checked Maria's wrist as well for the telltale marks. "Hm," he said. "Just how do *you* people come into the picture?"

"We were just passing by," Greg said. "We heard screams and checked it out to see if we could help."

There were just the two of them in the ER, Greg and Vazquez, and they'd left their weaponry and other equipment in the van, but they both still were wearing their combat blacks, a sharp, even disturbing counterpoint to the crisp white of the doctor and the ER nurse. The doctor looked up and eyed them with an expression that suggested he was working on the question of whether they were liars or lunatics.

"Passing by, huh? What were you doing there?"

"Just happened to be in the area, sir."

"This wouldn't have anything to do with a Navy SEAL who came in here this evening with a bullet wound in his leg, now, would it?"

"I really couldn't comment on that, sir."

"What are you? Team Four? Or Army SF?"

"Uh, actually, I'm with Team Two."

The doctor nodded. "That tells me a *very* great deal. I worked with your people for a while at Fort Bragg. Team Six. Lots of running injuries, knees and ankles. And the occasional case of hypothermia." He was palpating Amado's belly now, an intent expression on his face. "Well, however you came to find these two . . . they'll be okay."

"Thank you, sir. Uh . . . doctor?"

"Yes?"

"If I were you, I'd request a special guard for these two.

Noriega's thugs will be looking for them, and I'd be willing to bet they'll be looking here pretty soon."

"I'll speak to the provost marshal."

He continued his examination, while the medic drew blood from Amado's arm, carefully inserting and filling several rubber-capped glass bottles in the Vacutainer cuff and the needle he'd already slipped into a vein. The doctor seemed uninterested in further conversation, so Greg jerked his head toward the door and the two slipped out. They passed the nurse as they joined the other SEALs in the waiting room. She gave them all a hostile glare but hurried on into the ER without further comment.

"How are they?" Mitchell asked.

"The doctor says they'll be okay," Greg said. "You find out anything about Jaco?"

Brunner nodded. "They didn't even admit him. Bandaged him up, shot him full of antibiotics, and sent him back to Rodman. He's fine."

"You got all of that out of that white-starched Valkyrie?" Haines asked. "I'm impressed."

"Actually, no." He nodded toward another Army nurse at the ER reception desk. "I talked to Mary-Jo while you were in there. She was happy to look up the record."

"He also has a date with her next Saturday," Tompkins said, shaking his head in disgust. "Ain't right, an enlisted man making it with an officer and in less than ten minutes, too!"

"Some of us," Haines replied, "just got it."

"Well," Greg said, "we'd best get back to Rodman. I have a feeling we're going to get it, if news of this gets out."

"What do you mean *if*?" Mitchell said. "That son of a bitch Hoyt's gonna be all over us after this one."

"Yeah," Petrilli added. "The PDF and the DGI, hey, that's all in a day's work, right? But Colonel Hoyt—"

"Is a pencil-necked snub-dicked circus geek with delusions of adequacy," Greg said, completing the thought. "Leave him to me."

"Cool," Brunner said. "He's all yours."

Greg wondered just what it was he was going to do with an Army colonel.

Chapter 5

Howard Air Force Base
Republic of Panama
1015 hours

"What the *hell* is the meaning of this, mister?" Colonel Hoyt waved a sheet of neatly typewritten paper above his desk. His face was a mask of white fury. Even President Bush, watching from his place of honor on the wall behind Hoyt's back, appeared to be faintly disapproving.

"It is, sir," Greg replied calmly, "a formal mission intent order. DOD Twenty—"

"*Don't* you give me that crap! You are in one hell of a lot of deep, hot water, sailor. Your Navy career has just come to a dead stop. *I'll* see to that!"

"Sir, I fail to see what the problem is."

"*This* is the problem!" Hoyt yelled, slamming the offending form down on the desk, the crack as the palm of his hand hit the wood ringing off the walls of Hoyt's office. "What the hell is this garbage about 'unless otherwise directed'? . . ."

"'Unless otherwise directed,'" Greg said, repeating from memory, "elements of SEAL Team Two currently assigned to SEAL Headquarters, Rodman Naval Station, will

70

conduct an antiterrorist hostage-rescue exercise in an off-base setting in or about the environs of Panama City. This exercise is for the purpose of sharpening the hostage-rescue and surveillance skills of Team Two members attached to Rodman, in order to—"

"I *know* what it fucking says!" Hoyt screamed. "You wrote up a mission intent without clearing it through my office first!"

"But we did inform your office, sir. As a special courtesy, in fact. We weren't *required* to tell your office about our training routine."

That was true, so far as it went, though the Army authorities did need to know about any major operation, whether for training or otherwise, on sovereign Panamanian soil. The question revolved around what constituted a "major" operation.

"You . . . were . . . confined . . . to . . . *base!*" Hoyt said, punctuating each word with a stab of a forefinger aimed squarely at Greg's face.

"Sir, with respect, my understanding was that we were confined to base during off-duty hours. Last night we were on a training evolution, as is explained in that advisory. Knowing that you would have an interest in the operation, we made sure to send your office a copy of that mission advisory. Unfortunately, you weren't here at the time, so I made sure a copy of this was turned in with your night adjutant."

"Of course I wasn't here, you idiot! It was after hours! I'd already gone home for the evening! How the hell was I supposed to see this thing before this morning?"

Greg suppressed a smile. He'd employed an old trick, one evolved by SEALs during Vietnam. It was called "UN-ODIR" from the opening words of the mission intent— "Unless otherwise directed." It had been used to good purpose in Vietnam, when SEAL operators had needed to mount missions in-country, and commanding officers farther up the line were becoming increasingly nervous about SEALs accidentally or deliberately violating the myriad lines on maps, regulations, and rules of engagement woven around the American military forces like suffocating nets.

The problem was that once a mission plan was submitted to headquarters, it was a near-certain bet that those same plans would be in enemy hands before nightfall. South Vietnamese soldiers worked at every level of the military command structure in Nam, and there were lots of North Vietnamese moles, sympathizers, or mere opportunists in the infrastructure. No plan was secure if it went the route up through channels. *No* plan.

And nine times out of ten, proposed missions were scotched by higher authority anyway. The brass had always feared that the wrong target might be hit. That the op might bring down unacceptable collateral damage and some bad press. Or the plan might just be deemed too risky, too likely to result in yet more body bags going back to the World at a time when success or failure, and the rise or fall of military careers, was determined by body counts.

Too many local COs didn't want to risk an op that subjected them to the risk of failure and possible censure. Greg had been there as a raw newbie SEAL, had seen the dithering, the indecision, the downright stinking *fear* of the REMFs.

The solution was clear, so far as Team operators were concerned, a solution evolved by several different SEAL units in Vietnam. In order to overcome both bureaucratic mismanagement and enemy intelligence, individual SEALs had come up with the concept of UNODIR, writing up the plan for their intended mission and turning it in, but doing it so close to the mission jump-off time that no one up the convoluted chain of command or at headquarters would have the time to say no . . . or get a copy of them off to the local communist cell leaders. By the time the orders reached the right people—or the wrong ones, for that matter—the SEAL strike force was long gone, off and on its way.

It was a great ass-covering maneuver, so long as the commanding officers involved didn't catch on. Generally they didn't, since most SEAL missions were successful . . . and therefore damned hard to criticize without the CO in question looking like an asshole.

Greg was beginning to believe, though, that Hoyt didn't care what he looked like. He was one of the Army's Action Officers in the zone, and he did *not* like his authority being challenged.

He'd been confident of his ability to handle Hoyt; he was beginning to think he'd bitten off a bit more than he could chew.

"I know what you're pulling here, Halstead," Hoyt growled. "Don't think I don't! That little blue ribbon of yours isn't going to get you out of hot water this time. Your ass is by the Lord Harry *mine!*"

"Yes, sir," Greg said. Perhaps if he pulled the meek, well-behaved, good-little-tin-soldier routine. Don't give the guy anything to attack. "Whatever you say, sir."

Hoyt glowered, daring Greg to come back with an argument, an insult, a smart-ass comment, anything he could nail. Greg decided he simply wasn't going to give the man the satisfaction. It was clear there was nothing he could do to deflect Hoyt from his current crusade, which at the moment seemed to involve nailing Greg's hide to the nearest bulkhead.

"You damned specwar cowboys are all the same! Stealing funding from the services that need it, pouring it into half-assed stunts better suited for Hollywood than the military."

"As you say, sir."

"Just what the hell were you playing at last night? My

phone's been ringing off the hook all morning! Someone carried out a raid of a Panamanian police station! Masked raiders, with high-tech infiltration gear! At least twenty PDF soldiers were killed! What do you have to say about that?"

"I really can't say anything about it, sir. We did *not* raid a police station, and we did *not* kill twenty PDF soldiers last night." He shrugged, spread his hands, and did his best both to look and to sound sincere. "Just where are you getting your information, sir?"

"I'm asking the questions, soldier!"

Greg was currently wearing his chief's khakis and was most obviously a sailor, not a soldier. Hoyt's excitement was getting the better of him, and he was starting to sputter. Greg wondered, with almost idle curiosity, if the man was going to give himself a stroke on the spot and solve the whole problem, at least insofar as the Navy was concerned.

Ah, but no such luck. Hoyt reached for a pen, pulled a form from his desk, and began writing in a small, tight, neatly precise hand. "I am putting you under close arrest, mister," he said, his voice dropped from storm and fury to cold deadliness. "I am further authorizing your immediate return to Fort Bragg for trial. We have no room in here in the zone for insubordinate smart-asses who think they know it all . . . or for Wild-West cowboys who go off half-cocked. You are going to be *out* of here on the very first available military transport!"

"You're absolutely right, sir."

"What the fuck are you playing at?"

"Me, sir? Absolutely nothing, sir. I am showing all due respect to the uniform of a commissioned officer of the United States Army."

Hoyt's face purpled again. "Meaning you have no respect for me, of course. I know insubordination when I hear it."

"Sir, I assure you I have and have had all due respect both for you and your position."

Hoyt reached out and stabbed a button on the intercom on his desk. "Sergeant-at-arms! Get in here!"

An Army sergeant in khaki dress uniform, with white helmet, brassard, gun belt, and a black MP armband, entered the room. He was, Greg recognized, the equivalent to a Navy master-at-arms—basically a senior police officer.

"Mr. Halstead is under close arrest," Hoyt said. "Put him in the stockade."

"Yes, sir!" He saluted the colonel, and Greg smiled. Navy and Marine custom dictated that personnel be uncovered indoors and, therefore, not salute.

He felt a little as though he'd stepped through the magic looking glass. There were bureaucratic assholes like Hoyt in every branch of the service, but it was rare to meet one as royally puckered as this one.

The stockade—the Navy called it "the brig," but this was the Army's jurisdiction, after all—was a bleak place of institutional concrete block, green paint, and steel bars. He was processed with grim efficiency, then placed in a common holding cell with a half-dozen other offenders. The bars of the sliding cell door clanged shut, and Greg nodded at his new roommates.

"Hey, get a load of the sailor boy," a sergeant on one end of one of the cell's two benches said, snickering. "Where's his cute widdle tidy-whities?"

"Fuck you, too," Greg replied cheerfully. "Move over."

"Mebee he don't want to, faggot," another sergeant growled from the other side of the cell. That one was big, with tattooed arms like a wrestler's showing beneath rolled-up khaki sleeves, and a large and drooping paunch.

Greg felt the shift in focus and in hostility permeating the cell.

The two sergeants were trouble, big, prickly, and mean. He knew the type. They had the feel of thugs who didn't give a damn, of not-too-bright bullies who would pick a fight just to prove who was toughest. The other four, a corporal and three privates, watched with large and frightened eyes. Greg's guess was that those four were in on some minor charge—drunkenness, maybe, or being AWOL—but that the sergeants were real trouble.

The big sergeant moved closer, arms held out from his sides, fingers clenching and unclenching.

"Chill," Greg said. He felt the bars of the cell at his back. There was no retreat. He would talk his way out of this, or fight. "I wouldn't want you to hurt yourself."

"Fuck you, faggot. I can take you apart without breaking a sweat."

Greg glanced to the left, checking the guard station on the far side of the holding tank area, next to the door. An MP sat at the desk, his feet up, closely studying the centerfold of a *Playboy* magazine.

"Guard!" he called. "There's trouble in here!"

The MP glanced up, then shrugged. "Sort it out among yourselves. I'm busy."

"Mommy's not here to help you, faggot," the sergeant said. "I'm gonna mop the floor with your ugly face."

"Why would you want to?" Greg said, keeping his voice calm and friendly. "You won't prove anything by beating up *me*."

"And mebee I'll just do it for fun." The sergeant smacked right fist into left palm and advanced, a sudden grin rearranging his face.

Navy SEALs were trained to use a variety of weapons, including their own bodies. In training they were drilled extensively in the basics of Hwrang-do, and over the past few years Greg had studied several other martial arts forms, including T'ai Chi and Shaolin Kung Fu. He dropped into a stance, center of gravity low, drawing in a deep breath, feeling chi energy flood his being, feeling the grounding with the earth. His left foot came up onto the toe—Cat Stance. His hands opened and hardened—Tiger Claw. His gaze locked not on his opponent's eyes, but at the V of his shirt beneath his throat, allowing him to be aware of the man's entire body.

The sergeant's eyes widened, and he stopped almost in midstep. "Oh, *shit,*" he said, and he took a step backward. "*Shit,* you're one of *them!*"

"You have a problem?" Greg asked. His attention remained fixed at the top of the man's sternum.

The sergeant's beefy hands came up, open, palms out. "Hey, all in fun, Mac. Right? I ain't got no beef with you."

"I'm cool," Greg said, but he didn't relax.

"I was just foolin', Mac." The sergeant backed up to his place on the bench to Greg's right and sat down. "Really!"

Evidently, the guy had run into a martial arts expert once before, and he must have come out of that encounter second best. Maybe he wasn't as stupid as he looked, and he *was* trainable.

Greg relaxed from the Tiger Claw position but kept his full attention on the man.

"What're you?" the other sergeant asked from the opposite bench, to Greg's left. "Special Forces?"

"He's Navy," the corporal said. "Must be a SEAL."

"How about it, Mac?" the sergeant on the left said. "You a SEAL?"

"Look at that trident on his chest. He's a freakin' SEAL, all right."

"Think you're real tough stuff, don't ya?" The sergeant to the left stood suddenly, and Greg turned to face this new threat. He sensed more than heard the movement behind him, as the heavy-set sergeant lunged from his bench at Greg's back. Greg dropped and snapped his right foot out and back, catching his attacker's kneecap, snapping it out from under him. The man shrieked and stumbled, falling forward into a snap-blow hard across the side of his head from Greg's right forearm. The man fell, a dead weight slamming on the concrete floor.

Greg was facing the sergeant to his left before the other man was down. "Hey, easy, man," the sergeant said, raising his hands. "I just stood up, is all."

"Why don't you sit down?" Greg said and helped him, pushing him back as he kicked the man's feet out from under him with a leg sweep. The guy sat, hard, his head slamming against the bars at his back.

The whole exchange had taken only a few seconds. Greg turned and looked at the others. "Anyone else want some action?" he asked, his voice level.

"No way, Chief," the corporal said. "Those guys were trouble from the git-go. You've done us a real favor."

Greg glanced at the guard desk. The guard was gone, the *Playboy* with him. Apparently he didn't care much what went on in the tank, so long as he wasn't disturbed.

"What happens when those two wake up?" a private asked, nervously.

"They'll behave," Greg said with a shrug. "Or else I'll just have to put them to sleep again."

His remaining cellmates were quick to fill him in. All four were drunk-and-disorderlies, rounded up by the MPs the night before when their drinking binge in Panama City had gotten a bit louder and more rambunctious than usual. The two sergeants though, had been brought in that morning, both charged with possession of narcotics—cocaine, to be specific.

The Army had come a long way with its drug problems since Vietnam, but that didn't mean the problem was solved, especially in a place like Panama where the big Colombian cartels practically owned some parts of the country and used countless coastal villages, inland air-fields, and private warehouses as part of their vast trans-shipment network between South and North America. There were tons of cocaine available if you knew who to talk to . . . and lesser amounts of just about everything else.

Drugs were a large part of what was keeping Noriega in power—not to mention making him one of the richest men in the Americas. The arrest of two Army sergeants gave a hint of just how corrupting and insidious the drug trade's influence was within Noriega's realm.

Groaning, both sergeants came around some minutes later. Neither seemed particularly anxious to continue the festivities. Both found a corner of the cell as far from Greg as they could manage and sat on the floor nursing their bruises.

Time dragged with agonizing slowness, measured out by a large clock on the concrete block wall above the guard desk. When the guard returned some time later, he continued to ignore the prisoners. Greg began to wonder when Hoyt would make good on his promise to ship him back to the States.

Greg wasn't particularly worried about his arrest. Hoyt was a narrow-minded bureaucratic idiot operating well out-side the boundaries of his authority. Everything would be straightened out by the time he reached Fort Bragg—assuming Commander Cahill and SEAL Team Two didn't intervene first. Heaven help Hoyt if *that* happened.

But Hoyt's intransigence threatened to disrupt Greg's intelligence-gathering mission in Panama . . . not to mention all specwar ops in the region. Somehow, Greg had to get word of his arrest to Cahill.

When the guard returned to his post, a good twenty minutes later, Greg called out to him. "Hey! Corporal! I get a phone call, right?"

"You've been watching too many cop shows, Chief," the

man said with a grin. "You get to talk with a JAG lawyer
later. *Maybe.*"

Greg sat down again and tried to relax, a task all but impossible as the clock ticked away. The two sergeants
watched him with dark eyes from the far corner of the cell.
Getting any sleep in here, even a quick nap, wasn't a good
idea. He had nothing to do, really, but think.

He found himself thinking a lot about Wendy. Damn it
all. He still missed her, missed her more than ever now after
more than a year of separation.

This was their second separation in the past seven years.
The first had begun the night she'd walked out on him back
in '82, when he'd told her he was going back into the
Teams. She'd returned a week later; Mark needed two par-
ents . . . *especially* if one of them was going to be gone half
the time on some deployment or other to who knew what
Godforsaken corner of the world. They'd agreed to tough it
out until Mark was grown and on his own. Privately, Greg
had assumed—hoped, really—that things would smooth
over by the time Mark graduated from high school.

They hadn't. They'd had a hell of an argument a year
ago, just after Mark joined the Navy, and she'd walked out
once again.

She'd not come back.

He had seen her several times and talked to her by phone.
She'd not served him with papers yet, after all, so maybe
there was still hope. Maybe.

Damn, if she could just hang on until his retirement . . .
just ten more years. Then Greg could get out after his thirty,
and they would start to live the way they were supposed to
live.

Greg knew the chances of them being reconciled weren't
good, not at all. The last time he'd talked to her, by phone
just before leaving for Fort Bragg six weeks ago, she'd
sounded damned bitter. She blamed him for Mark's deci-

sion to volunteer for SEAL training, and she accused him of going back on his word.

Greg had been determined to talk her into seeing reason, but then the crisis in Panama had flared, and he'd gotten his orders—first to Fort Bragg to work with SOCOM's intelligence section, then to Panama.

And once again his private life had gone on hold.

Still, he'd been able to convince her to get together with him again. Christmas. He'd be back in California for Christmas. He would meet her in San Francisco, maybe take her out to dinner. They would talk, really talk, and maybe get this thing worked out once and for all.

Was it worth it? Hell, how was a guy supposed to weigh things like that? An old, old saying held that if the Navy had wanted him to have a wife, they'd have issued one with his seabag. Deployments to sea or to overseas duty stations were hard on all Navy wives; it was a thousand times worse for the wives and girlfriends of SEALs, men who might be called out at any time of the day or night, to vanish for days, weeks, or months at a time and return unable to talk about where they'd been or what they'd been doing.

More than once in the past years, Greg had considered getting out. He'd put in twenty years already. He could retire on that.

But there was some part of him, deep, deep down inside . . . a part that had found brotherhood and family with the men who'd been through BUD/S with him, who'd served with him, who'd fought alongside him and sometimes died alongside him.

How could he possibly turn his back on them, even for Wendy?

"Halstead!" a voice snapped, cutting through his increasingly muddied thoughts. "Halstead, front and center!"

An Army captain stood at the holding tank door, keys in

hand. Behind him stood the holding tank guard and the gaunt, familiar form of Commander Cahill.

He came to attention. "*Sir!* Chief Halstead reporting, *sir!*"

"Grab your gear at the cage out front," the captain growled. "You've been sprung."

"Thank you, sir."

"Don't thank me, Chief." The captain slid the cell door aside, letting him step through. "Thank Noriega."

"I beg your pardon?"

"Things have hotted up since yesterday, Chief," Cahill told him. "Hoyt's agreed to release you. Reluctantly, but your arrest has been rescinded. The orders have already gone through."

"I knew you'd come through, sir. Thanks!"

"Bullshit. I didn't have a damned thing to do with it. I was still trying to find out where you were when Hoyt called me and told me to come pick you up. Things are going to hell here, Chief . . . but maybe you're not aware of that yet."

"Why? What's happened?"

"We're going to war. Hoyt phoned Fort Bragg to dump you in their laps, and they dumped you squarely back in his. Ordered him to let you get on with what you're supposed to be doing. I think his ears are still burning."

"Couldn't happen to a nicer guy," Greg said. At the cage in the next room, he signed for his personal possessions—wallet with fifty-two dollars and two credit cards, belt, notebook, and pen. "So what *is* going on?"

"Come on. I'll fill you in on the way back to Rodman."

TM2 Jablonsky was waiting outside with a car from the Navy vehicle pool. Cahill and Greg got into the back, while Jablonsky drove.

The situation had indeed worsened. Yesterday, sometime before Greg and Jaco's encounter at the bridge, an American Marine lieutenant had been shot dead at a PDF road-block. Two other Americans, a Navy lieutenant and his wife, had witnessed the shooting and fled, but PDF troops had captured them and taken them to a local headquarters for "questioning." The lieutenant had been severely beaten, his wife roughly fondled and threatened with rape. After several nightmare hours, the couple had been released.

In response, the National Command Authority—that meant the president and the secretary of defense—had directed the execution of Operation Just Cause, an American invasion of Panama.

It would take several days, of course, for the U.S. military to mobilize and deploy, though lots of men and equipment had already been flown into Panama in anticipation of hostilities breaking out.

"SEAL Two and SEAL Four have been ordered to execute their operational plans," Cahill said as they entered the Rodman Naval Station grounds and drove toward the SEAL HQ. "Unfortunately, Chief Jaco was on the assault team for Two's part of the festivities, and he's going to be out of action for a few days. I've got plenty of guys eager to take his place . . ."

"But I've been practicing with the team, sir," Greg said. He resisted the impulse to raise his hand with a wild "Pick me! Pick me!"

"Are you volunteering?"

"Yes, sir. Damned straight, sir." He thought about Wendy . . . then pushed the thought away. *She'll understand. She's got to . . .*

But it looked as though he wasn't going to be going home for Christmas after all.

Chapter 6

Balboa Bay, Panama Canal
Panama City, Republic of Panama
2340 hours

Greg lay in the rubber duck—a SEAL Combat Rubber Raiding Craft or CRRC—trying to ignore the cloud of bloodthirsty mosquitoes swarming around his head and hands. Waiting under impossibly uncomfortable positions was supposed to be a SEAL specialty, but that didn't mean the SEALs themselves liked it. Long hours of training in BUD/S had taught them to endure discomfort, but all Greg could think about was the op as he awaited the order to go.

The ten SEALs of Task Unit Whiskey were afloat in two CRRCs among the tangled roots and stinking mud flats of a mangrove swamp on the east bank of the canal, perhaps a mile and a half north of the Bridge of the Americas, and a mile across Balboa Harbor from the Rodman Naval Station. South, only a few hundred meters across the black water from their hiding place, was their objective.

SEAL Team Two was tasked with crippling the *Presidente Porras,* a sixty-five-foot PDF patrol boat used by Noriega as his personal yacht. The craft was tied up to Pier

18, a floating concrete dock at the eastern bank of the Panama Canal's Pacific entrance.

The tactical situation was a strange one, with U.S. and Panamanian facilities in such close proximity to one another. In some cases, such as at Howard Air Force Base, the Panamanian assets and buildings were actually intermingled with those controlled by the U.S. military.

In this case, the target was actually under the guns of the American naval station. A U.S. fire-support team at the base was manning .50-caliber heavy machine guns equipped with powerful night-vision devices, 60mm mortars, and grenade launchers, all preregistered on various Panamanian targets across the canal. Task Unit Whiskey would have plenty of firepower supporting them, should heavy-hitting backup be necessary.

H-hour for the invasion was 0100 hours, 20 December . . . but for the SEALs of Teams Two and Four, Operation Just Cause got under way some hours earlier. Task Unit Whiskey had entered the water at Rodman at 2300 hours and zigzagged across the black canal in two CRRCs, their motors barely purring.

Already, the op had departed from the carefully crafted and orchestrated plan approved by SOCOM days before. To begin with, the jump-off from Rodman had been abruptly moved up thirty minutes from 2330 to 2300—always a bad sign suggesting that events were proceeding outside the strike force's area of control. Then, and far worse, halfway across the canal the outboard motor of one of the CRRCs had died, resisting every effort to restart it. Evidently, the powerful little thirty-five-horsepower outboards were not designed to run at such low speed, and the strain had burned out the engine. The team had a spare along, but Commander Cahill, in the lead rubber duck, had elected not to use it. There were PDF patrol boats abroad on the canal this night, and the chances of making noise and being discovered were just too damned high.

Instead, Cahill had passed a line to the second rubber duck and towed it with his own. They'd made it to the mangrove swamp by just past 2330 hours without being spotted.

Greg was in the lead CRRC, with Commander Cahill, who'd insisted on a seat in this operation even if commanders were supposed to run covert ops from a desk. Also aboard were Lieutenant Richard Douglas, the Wheel of Team Two's Third Platoon, plus Chief Mitchell serving as coxswain, and TM2 Haines manning an M-60 machine gun. In the other boat were Chief Brunner, EM1 Tompkins, RM1 Vazquez, BM1 Petrilli, and HM2 Brown.

"Heads up," Cahill whispered suddenly. He was touching the earpiece of his radio, listening intently. "Change in plans."

"Aw, Christ!" Mitchell said quietly. "I knew it! The REMFs got cold feet!"

"Negative," Cahill replied. "They've just moved H-hour up by fifteen minutes. Possible security leak. The curtain goes up at oh-oh-forty-five hours."

Greg pulled back the Velcro strap on his watch, checking the time—2345 hours—then swiped quietly at the formation of mosquitoes jockeying for position in the chow line on the back of his hand. That made it just an hour to go until the invasion started. The SEALs' timetable should not be affected.

"Okay, team," Cahill said. "Let's do it."

He wondered how Team Four was doing at Paitilla.

Off Paitilla Airfield
Panama Bay, Republic of Panama
2345 hours

Lieutenant Commander Tuohy was also bobbing about in a black rubber duck, motoring quietly across the choppy waters of Panama Bay. There was light enough from the city's waterfront half a mile to the north for him to see the other CRRCs in the formation, motoring *en masse* toward Point Paitilla.

He hoped to hell the PDF wasn't paying close attention to the waters of the bay.

It was, Tuohy thought, more like a typical Ranger op than anything ever tried by the SEALs, even during the glory days of Vietnam. Sixteen rubber boats, carrying fifty men from SEAL Four's Golf, Bravo, and Delta Platoons, had been dropped off in the bay by Navy patrol boats about a mile off the point where Paitilla Airfield ended at the water's edge. SEALs were used to operating in small combat groups—eight-man squads, or sixteen-man platoons, at most. A three-platoon assault was unprecedented in the history of SEAL team warfare.

But then, there was a lot about this invasion that was unprecedented. Among other things, it was the largest single airborne operation since World War II. Throughout Panama, various special-forces units were targeting twenty-seven different objectives, all of them scheduled for an H-hour of 0100. SEALs had only two of those objectives—Noriega's Learjet at Paitilla, and his yacht at Pier 18. Elsewhere, Army Rangers would be parachuting onto airfields; Army Green Berets would be throwing out blocking forces, closing roads, and searching for Noriega himself; Delta Force was going into Modelo Prison in downtown Panama City in an attempt to rescue an American citizen, Kurt Muse, and after that they would be joining the hunt for Noriega.

It was a massive operation on a grand scale. Tuohy knew the three-platoon assault on Paitilla was risky, but it was also intensely exciting. It was, in fact, nothing less than history in the making.

After inserting into Panama Bay and forming up, the

SEAL Four assault force had begun making the final seaborne approach to the airfield. The end of the airstrip was just visible now, a black line at the surf's edge a hundred yards ahead.

"All units," Tuohy whispered into his lip mike. "Anchor and hold position. Deploy combat swimmers."

The water was shallow here, just off the end of the runway. Combat swimmers clad in black wetsuits, combat harness, fins and masks, and carrying H&K submachine guns, rolled off one of the rafts and silently began swimming toward the shore. They would perform a quick beach reconnaissance, then signal the rest of the assault force in.

Minutes passed, with no sound but the far-off hiss of the surf.

"Armada, Armada, this is Home Plate," sounded in his radio earpiece. "Come in, Armada."

"This is Armada," he replied, whispering into the needle mike at his mouth. Shit! What now? He already had swimmers on the way to the beach. If they were calling off the op now . . . "I copy."

"Armada, we have two advisories for you," the voice said. "First, H-hour has been moved up, repeat, moved up, by fifteen minutes. Please repeat. Over."

"H-hour has been moved up fifteen minutes, roger," Tuohy said. So the invasion was set to begin now in less than an hour, instead of in an hour and a quarter. Why the change? Somebody higher up the command ladder must be jumpy about something.

"Advisory two," the voice in the ear piece continued. "We have a report of a PDF helicopter taking off from Colón a few minutes ago, and they have given Paitilla as the end point on their flight plan. There is a possibility, repeat, a possibility that Pineapple is aboard that aircraft and that he is headed for your objective. Over."

"Copy that, Home Plate. An aircraft may be en route to the objective, and Pineapple could be on board. Over."

"Confirmed, Armada. Good luck. Over."

"Roger that. Over."

"Home Plate out."

Tuohy thought a moment, then signaled the other CR-RCs over the platoon channel, directing them to up anchor and open up their throttles at dead slow. There was a new sense of urgency pushing them ahead now. Not only was the invasion set to begin at 0045 hours instead of 0100, but Colón was only thirty-five miles away, at the Atlantic end of the canal. If Noriega was indeed aboard that helicopter, and if he was headed for Paitilla, it could be that he'd gotten wind of the invasion and was going to try to escape on board his Learjet—the very eventuality SEAL Team Four was trying to prevent.

The belly of the CRRC scraped sand and gravel, and the SEALs on board spilled out into the tumbling surf. Tuohy gripped his H&K and crouched at the water's edge, using the submachine gun's night scope to penetrate the darkness ahead. The airstrip was quiet—and appeared deserted. So far, there was no sign that the flotilla had been spotted

All around him, other rubber ducks were grounding on the beach, the SEALs onboard rising and moving forward. The combat swimmers were already crouched at the near end of the runway, scanning the area ahead. The hangar buildings were at the far end of the runway, perhaps 1,200 yards away. Tuohy thought once again that the op would have been better off with a sniper team on one of the skyscrapers close by the airfield holing the Learjet's tires and fuel tanks or putting a rufus round into an engine intake.

Theirs not to reason why, he thought, recalling the Tennyson poem about a doomed cavalry charge. *Theirs but to do or die.*

Screw that. The op still had an excellent chance of success . . . *if* the SEALs could make it to the Learjet's hangar unobserved. They would take out the guards, then secure the jet and hold the perimeter until the Army could relieve them. Nothing to it.

Quietly, Tuohy reminded the gathered SEALs of the mission ROEs, the Rules of Engagement. They were to maintain the element of surprise, taking down guards or airfield personnel quietly and, if possible, nonlethally. When fired upon, they would fire back, but they were to check their fire . . . meaning they should be careful about accidentally hitting buildings around the airport that happened to lie in the line of fire with legitimate targets. A pitched gun battle in what amounted to downtown Panama City was bound to cause what the Defense Department was pleased to call "collateral damage," but the idea was to keep that damage—and civilian casualties—to a minimum.

Perhaps the strangest rule for the evening involved the aircraft at Paitilla. There were a number of hangars at Paitilla Airfield, many housing aircraft belonging to Panama City's rich and elite. The orders from the Defense Department stated quite clearly that excessive damage to "civilian assets" was to be kept at a minimum. In fact, even Noriega's Learjet, the SEALs' primary target, was to be disabled, if possible, without damage. Tuohy remembered a briefing session a few weeks ago where one general had rumbled on and on about not wanting to have to buy the Panamanian government a new Learjet after the invasion was over.

It made no sense to Tuohy, any more than it did to the other SEALs gathered at the end of Paitilla's tarmac. Most of those multimillion-dollar private jets belonged to drug lords living in Panama, to Noriega's wealthy cronies in government or the PDF, or to *both* where the two were one and the same.

But orders were orders, and these orders forbade the use

of rufus rounds or anything else that did more than damage the Learjet's tires. Golf One would move in, secure the hangar with Noriega's jet, and slash the tires if necessary. Golf Two would drag other aircraft out of nearby hangars and position them on the runway, blocking flights in or out.

And then they would sit tight, and wait for the dawn . . . and relief.

Following their carefully choreographed op plan, the three platoons formed into four groups—Lieutenant Casey's Golf One and Lieutenant Phillips's Golf Two ahead and to the center, to right and left, on point; Bravo Platoon, under Lieutenant j.g. John Connors, on the left rear flank and Delta on the right rear.

Lieutenant Commander Tuohy gave the order. *"Move out!"*

Tuohy himself would remain there, at the infiltration point, along with two Air Force controllers and several SEAL corpsmen. The SEALs were setting up a small emergency casualty station, just in case. The Air Force controllers were supposed to open communications with an AC-130 gunship orbiting above Paitilla. If things got too nasty that evening, the SEALs would be depending on the gunship and its devastating arsenal of high-tech weaponry to put down a curtain of fire between them and any pursuit.

Had they covered everything? Had they *missed* anything?

Tuohy couldn't help but feel a certain nagging worry, a feeling that events were already rocketing ahead out of his control. As a SEAL officer, he'd been trained to lead small groups of men—eight-man squads or sixteen-man platoons—and he'd been trained to lead them from the front, not to crouch in the rear trying to watch everything at once.

One of the Air Force sergeants was whispering softly in the darkness. "Come in, Nighthawk. This is Armada. Come in. Over."

"Anything?" he asked.

The Air Force controller shook his head. "No, sir. We're not getting through."

Great. *Perfect.* Things had started to go wrong already and in a big way. If they couldn't talk to the Specter gunship overhead . . .

The AC-130 mounted a truly impressive broadside: one 40mm cannon, two 20mm cannon, two 7.62 Gatling mini-guns, a 40mm grenade dispenser, and—a real monster—a 105mm howitzer, all aiming out of the left side of the aircraft. The gunship also carried no fewer than five high-tech communications systems, allowing the aircraft to stay in close touch with friendly forces on the ground.

But, damn it, the SEALs had to be able to talk with the Specter to call that fire down.

Still, there was no sign of the enemy. Thank God. Maybe this was going to be the walk in the park the mission planners had assured him it would be.

Briefly, he wondered how Team Two's Task Unit Whiskey was doing with Noriega's yacht.

Balboa Bay, Panama Canal
Panama City, Republic of Panama
2355 hours

Greg pressed his swim mask tight against his face, clamped the mouthpiece of his Draeger rebreather unit tightly between his teeth, and rolled over the side of the CRRC. The water temperature was fifty degrees, a little on the chilly side, but his wetsuit would keep him warm for the swim in to Pier 18. The rebreather he wore provided a steady flow of oxygen without giving off noisy or highly visible bubbles. He carried a twenty-pound Hagensen Pack slung over his shoulder by its long, canvas straps.

BM1 Petrilli followed him into the cold and ink-black

water a moment later. Between midnight darkness and the silt suspended in the water, visibility was limited to a few feet or less, but Greg could see Petrilli's black silhouette as it moved against the surface.

Because of the failure of the outboard on one of the CR-RCs, Cahill had motored the two designated swimmers out to the final insertion point in the one working rubber duck, 150 yards north of Pier 18, and now was returning to the mangrove swamp to pick up Brunner and Tompkins, the other two swimmers. He would bring them back to the drop-off waypoint, then tow the disabled CRRC back across the canal to Rodman. The four SEALs would be on their own, then. After planting their explosive Hagensen Packs, they would box their way out of the pier area, then swim south-west toward the Bridge of the Americas where a pair of waiting Navy PBRs would pick them up.

With only one duck available for the insertion, of course, it would take longer for all four swimmers to assemble at the objective, but that shouldn't be a major problem. They'd trained for this op in teams of two, allowing for the possibility that one of the teams might become lost on the way in. The only absolutely reliable fact of any combat mission was the certainty that the infamous Murphy would, sooner or later, pay them a visit.

The water around them was completely black, with only a faintly glowing trace of diffuse, silvery light swirling about on the underside of the surface. Greg and Petrilli dove to a depth of twenty feet and leveled off there, checking their wrist compasses for direction before beginning their swim. They would have to watch their depth carefully. Draeger units provided oxygen at the same pressure as the water around them. The deeper they went, the higher the pressure. At depths greater than about thirty feet—two atmospheres—oxygen became a deadly poison.

For that reason, Draegers were used strictly for shallow

approaches to a target. Their advantage lay in their stealth. There would be guards on that pier and on board the *Presidente Porras* as well, and there might also be underwater microphones listening for the approach of frogmen. Draeger gear was utterly silent, where open-circuit scuba gear gave off telltale clouds of bubbles as well as a characteristic gurgling sound with each exhalation.

Greg checked his diving watch. Midnight, on the nose. Another forty-five minutes to go until the official beginning of the war. In one sense, the mission had already been compromised to some extent by the last-second change of time for H-hour. The four Mark 138 Mod 1 Hagensen Packs carried by the SEALs, each containing twenty pounds of C-4 explosives, Mark 39 arming devices, and Mark 96 detonators, had been armed back at Rodman before they'd set out. The idea had been to make the actual op simpler and safer by eliminating the need for the SEALs to arm the explosives in the water. The timers all had been preset for 0100—the original time for H-hour.

Still, that shouldn't make a critical difference. It would take time for the *Presidente Porras* to clear away and fire up her engines, even if Noriega was already onboard. So long as the SEALs reached their target before the *Porras* actually pulled away from Pier 18, the Panamanian presidential yacht wouldn't make it very far.

In the midnight blackness of twenty feet down in the oily waters of the bay, all was silent. Sound carried exceptionally well under water, and the area around a marina or naval facility was usually fairly noisy with the clank of chains, the throb of boat engines, the rasp of cables . . .

The sudden barrage of noise startled Greg, making him pull up short. Petrilli nearly bumped into him. It sounded as though a dozen heavy boat engines had all started up almost simultaneously, a dull, pulsing rumble that seemed to come from every direction. What the hell was going on?

They'd just resumed their swim when a loud bang sounded through the water, an almost metallic ringing that hurt the ears. That had been an explosion . . . and an underwater explosion at that. It sounded like . . . hell, it *sounded* like someone had just dropped a hand grenade into the water.

If that were true . . .

Greg clasped Petrilli on the shoulder, signaling a halt. Carefully, he let himself drift upward, until his face mask just broke the surface. What he saw turned him colder than the water around him.

The night sky over Panama City was alive with tracers, long, arcing lines of moving stars aglow with yellow, green, and orange hues. The unmistakable stutter and crack of gunfire, punctuated by the deeper rumble of explosions, thundered and rumbled in the distance. Closer at hand, dozens of boats at the dock area up ahead were starting their engines. The *Porras,* now lay only a few dozen yards away, looming against the city-glow behind her. Greg could see a lot of activity on board. Panamanian sailors were moving along the deck, and others were gathered on the pier alongside.

By Greg's diving watch, it was still thirty minutes before H-hour, the *new* H-hour. The war had begun ahead of schedule.

Somehow, Noriega's forces had gotten wind of the operation . . . or maybe someone had just gotten trigger-happy, shooting at shadows. One way or another, Old Man Murphy had put in his appearance as expected, big time.

The question now was whether the assault on the *Porras* had been compromised. Hovering just beneath the surface of the water, Greg watched the movements on board the presidential yacht. Whatever they were doing up there, they didn't appear to be aware of the SEALs moving in for the attack. Good.

Petrilli was station-keeping next to Greg. They ex-

changed glances through their masks, and Greg gestured
toward the target. Petrilli nodded.

They would push on, gunfire or no gunfire.

Submerging to twenty feet once more, the two SEALs
began moving toward the *Porras*, using slow, almost lan-
guid strokes of their swim fins. Pier 18 was a concrete
structure extending from the shoreside dock, supported by
heavy pilings. The *Presidente Porras* was tied perpendicu-
lar to the pier, bow-on, nestled between two boats belonging to the Panama Canal Commission. Greg and Petrilli
swam up to the pier, surfacing beneath it, shielded from
view by shadow and by the algae-slimed pilings. They
could hear the pounding of boots on the pier above their
heads, hear the shouts in Spanish as the PDF soldiers called
to one another.

With a thunderous roar, the engines of one of the commission boats fired to life, churning the water astern. As
Greg and Petrilli submerged again, they could hear the entire harbor coming to life beneath the surface—the roar and
pulse and throb of marine engines. The Panamanians were
evidently starting up all the boat engines they could, hoping
to discourage frogmen from approaching any Panamanian
boat.

And then a savage, sharp crack sounded close by, a hammer of sound that left Greg's ears ringing. Then another
blast . . . and another after that. Shit. Those were definitely
hand grenades and pretty close by, too, though far enough
off that Greg knew they weren't being aimed at them. The
PDF troops ashore must be tossing them into the bay at random to discourage an undersea assault.

No matter. The soldiers overhead still didn't know the
SEALs were at the scene. They merely feared their presence and with damned good reason. Together, Greg and
Petrilli swam beneath the dark hull of the *Presidente Porras,* ignoring the chaos breaking loose around them.

With a roar as loud as any of the grenades, the *Porras*'s engines boomed to shuddering life. Beneath the vessel's keel, there was a slight stirring of the water and the thirty-one-ton vessel tugged impatiently at her moorings, but no immediate danger.

Only a few feet separated the yacht's keel and the muddy bottom, but it was sufficient for the two SEALs. As the waterfront came to life, he and Petrilli got to work.

Paitilla Airfield
Panama Bay, Republic of Panama
2359 hours

Lieutenant Tom Casey, the CO of SEAL unit Golf One, didn't like this, not one bit. Between the airfield lights bathing the runway and the towers of the skyscrapers of downtown Panama City looming to north and east, he felt as nakedly exposed as a cockroach on a dinner plate. Right now, he wished he were on one of those brightly lit apartment balconies, peering down the scope on a .50-caliber sniper rifle. Why the brass had elected to take *this* route, with fifty SEALs in a John Wayne-style ground assault, was beyond him.

But they were here and they would carry out their mission. At least they still seemed to have the element of surprise.

Casey and the SEAL assault force were only about a quarter of the way up the 1,350-foot runway when all hell broke loose, the element of surprise dissolving into the might-have-been. The SEALs went to ground, clutching at asphalt as the sky lit up with tracer fire and searchlights. Somewhere, an air raid siren began its eerie wail. Closer at hand, automatic gunfire barked and chattered. The war had obviously begun, and begun way ahead of schedule.

None of the fire seemed directed at the SEALs, however. Casey checked left and right but saw no motion, no indication that they'd been spotted. So far, so good, then. They would continue the op, even though their chances of carrying out a surprise attack had just been completely shot to hell.

"Go!" he snapped over the tactical radio. "Keep moving!"

They rose from the pavement and began jogging up the runway. Judging from the number of tracers arcing through the night, someone had spotted American aircraft over the city.

And that wasn't good.

Movement snatched at Casey's awareness, a glimpse of shadows running in the dark. Shit. That was too far off to the side of the runway to be part of the assault force. It looked as if someone was running behind the warehouses and hangars near the head of the runway. Raising his rifle, he peered through the heavy nightscope, peering into a night suddenly brightened in glowing masses of green and yellow on black. It looked as if a force of PDF troops, a *large* force, was running toward the same hangars the SEALs were closing on.

"Hostiles!" he snapped over the radio. "Ten o'clock! *Hump* it!"

So now it was a race, and one with a deadly finish. Those PDF troops were running toward the hanger where Noriega's Learjet was stored. If they made it there first, the SEALs would find themselves having to assault a defended position, a very different, far more difficult and costly tactical proposition than simply holding it.

The SEALs were only thirty yards from their objective when an amplified voice boomed out of the darkness ahead. *"Alto!"* Then, in English, "What are you men doing here? You will surrender at once!"

"You surrender to us!" Petty Officer Morida, one of the SEALs, called back.

Casey used his rifle's nightscope to probe the darkness of the open hangar. He could easily make out the shape of the Learjet parked inside, its rounded nose brightly illuminated by the lights from the airfield tower and terminal. He could also see the forms of several soldiers scrambling for cover, including a couple of men with rifles crouched behind some fifty-five-gallon drums close by the far wall. They were aiming their weapons, it seemed to Casey, directly at him.

Shit! An ambush!

"Throw down your weapons!" the PDF officer called. "You are our prisoners!"

"Fuck you, asshole," someone near Casey said.

"Golf One!" Casey called over the tactical channel. "Shift right! Take cover!" They needed to get out of the line of fire, to get clear of this ambush kill zone. There was a light aircraft on the runway to the right that might provide some cover. Some of Golf One's SEALs were already there.

And then time ran out. One of the Panamanians opened fire, perhaps anticipating his commander's orders a bit too quickly. Suddenly, muzzle flashes flickered and winked from three sides—from the hangar and from each flank—a storm of full-auto gunfire.

The SEAL assault force had just walked into Hell.

Chapter 7

20 December 1989

Presidente Porras, Pier 18
Panama City, Republic of Panama
0011 hours

Five minutes after Greg and Petrilli reached Pier 18 and their objective, two more black shapes materialized out of the midnight waters of Balboa Bay, burdened by Draeger gear and Hagensen Packs. Brunner and Tompkins joined them with a thumbs-up greeting. There'd been some initial concern about the possibility of PDF frogmen on underwater patrol, but that threat had largely been discounted early on. The PDF didn't have units to match the SEALs in training or equipment, nor were they likely to be mucking about down here in the middle of the night when their buddies topside were tossing grenades into the water. Nonetheless, Greg was glad to see the other two SEALs. It made him and Petrilli feel just a little bit less lonely.

Visibility was so bad it was almost impossible to see them anyway, save as half-glimpsed shapes moving against the glare of light from the surface. The water was muddy, especially with the *Porras* racing her engines and stirring up the fine-grained bottom silt beneath her keel.

They didn't need to see, however, save to positively identify the target from the sheltered waters beneath the pier. The two combat swimmer teams operated independently of each other, the idea being that either could carry out the mission on its own if the other ran afoul of trouble on the way in. Greg found a spot on the keel about a third of the way forward from the whining screws, sliding his hand along the aluminum hull. Idiots. The *Porras* had only been in service seven years, but her hull was rough to the touch with weed, barnacles, and encrusted marine algae. Didn't the bastards ever haul these things out of the water for a scrapedown and paint job?

He pulled his Mark I SEAL knife and used it to scrape a clean patch onto the hull. There was a wonderful irony in the fact that the PDF troops on board were running the engines to keep frogmen away . . . and thereby providing the perfect cover for the SEALs as they scraped clean patches on the hull with their knives.

Greg was glad that an earlier plan to cripple the *Presidente Porras* by fouling her screws with cable had been dropped in favor of a simpler and more direct approach. Throwing a cable over those screws while they were turning would have been difficult, even suicidal.

They knew their target very well indeed, having studied her for long hours during the op planning stages. Swiftships of Morgan City, Louisiana, had provided detailed specs and blueprints for Noriega's presidential yacht, and the SEALs had practiced with identical craft in rehearsals at Eglin Air Force Base in Florida.

The *Presidente Porras* was actually a patrol boat, sixty-five feet long and with thirty-one tons displacement. She had a single deckhouse with an awning extending aft, with a single 12.7mm machine gun mounted in a gun tub on the aft deck. Her two props were driven by twin GM 12V71 TI N75 diesel engines generating 1,020 horsepower, and she could manage a top speed of twenty-three knots. She had an aluminum hull, could carry six tons of diesel fuel, and was manned by a crew of eight.

The *Porras* had one sister craft in the Panamanian navy, an identical vessel named the *Comandante Torrijos.* It was the *Presidente Porras,* however, that Noriega maintained as his personal yacht. She was his getaway vessel in case things got too hot for him in Panama City. She could easily make the run east and south along the coast to reach sanctuary with Noriega's drug-smuggling buddies down in Colombia.

Her aluminum hull meant that they couldn't attach magnetic limpet mines. Though there was a kind of powerful underwater adhesive developed for SEAL ops like this, the combat swimmers had opted for a simpler suction attachment device which gripped the hull tightly with the throw of a lever. The hull needed to be relatively smooth, however, and free of marine growth. It took less than a minute to scrape a small patch clean and attach the Hagensen Pack.

But there was a small problem now. Mission planners had assumed that the war wouldn't be starting until the original H-hour of 0100. The early outbreak of hostilities meant the war would be almost an hour old by the time the preset arming deuces in the Hagensen Packs finally went off, and there was no way the SEALs could reset them. The idea of presetting the detonation times had been to simplify things for the combat swimmers during the op—SEALs working in near pitch-darkness, in cold water, under the pressure of completing their mission and getting clear of the target. Setting timers by feel was a great way to encourage a premature start to the war, and to guarantee several SEAL casualties.

As long as Panamanian divers didn't come down to check the hull, the 0100 settings shouldn't matter. And if Noriega arrived on board his yacht at a quarter till for a quick middle-of-the-night cruise . . . how bad was that?

Greg threw the locking lever, then tugged at the pack to make sure it was firmly attached. Nope, that baby was going nowhere. He checked his watch, barely visible by its own glow in the murky water. It was thirteen minutes past midnight.

Petrilli touched his arm, a signal that he'd finished attaching his pack as well. Together, the two SEALs swam out from beneath the *Presidente Porras*. At this point, the water was too muddy for him to see Brunner or Tompkins but, according to the mission plan, the two teams were operating as completely separate units.

The muffled commotion on the pier, the throb of the *Porras*'s engines, the occasional flat underwater crack of hand grenades faded into the night behind them as they flippered out into the bay. Mission accomplished, and without a hitch.

Now all they needed to do was get the hell out of there.

**Paitilla Airfield
Panama Bay, Republic of Panama
0015 hours**

Lieutenant Tom Casey dropped to the pavement of the runway as full-auto fire chattered and snapped through the air on all sides, the oddly flattened rattle of AK-47s echoing off of the surrounding buildings. All around him, the other eight men of his command were going down. Chief Donald McFaul was punched backward by a round that caught him squarely in the head, killing him instantly. Petty Officer Tilgman lay sprawled on the tarmac, unmoving in a pool of blood that looked tar black in the runway lighting. All around him, other SEALs lay wounded, mowed down by that savage crossfire.

As he'd been trained, Casey tried to ascertain the situation, moving from man to man, checking their condition.

It didn't take long for him to realize that of the ten SEALs of Golf One, he was somehow the only man left untouched. He had two dead . . . and the other seven all were wounded, some of them badly.

"Golf Two, this is Golf One!" he called over his radio. "I've got a situation here!"

In terse, hard words, he described it. Normal procedure at this point would have called for him to pull his command back while Golf Two provided covering fire . . . to pull back taking all dead and wounded along. SEALs *never* left their own behind, whether wounded or dead.

But, damn it, one man couldn't carry out eight all by himself!

"Sit tight!" Phillips told him. "I'll send you some help! Over!"

"Roger that!"

Lieutenant Phillips and Golf Two were on the tarmac perhaps a hundred yards to the left. They'd stumbled into a group of armed civilians—probably drug-trafficker guards, in fact—and taken them down in utter silence, leaving them bound in plastic slip-ties. Now, though, as bullets swept across the tarmac, they turned the full weight of their considerable firepower on the hangar that housed Noriega's Learjet. According to the original plan, Golf One was supposed to take up a support position while Golf Two went in to slash the target aircraft's tires. This time, though, it was Golf Two providing the covering fire.

Casey added his H&K to the fusillade of automatic fire, loosing brief, carefully aimed bursts into the darkness of the hangar. Through his nightscope, he saw one PDF gunman pitch back from behind the cover of his fifty-five-gallon drum and slam into the concrete-reinforced wall of the hangar. Those drums, though, appeared to be filled with concrete, making them ideal cover for the ambushing forces.

And gunfire was coming in at the SEALs from at least three directions. Looking up, beyond the terminal, he could see people gathered on balconies of the high-rise condos near the airfield. He was willing to bet a month's pay that some of those spectators were PDF officers—some of them were reported to be doing *very* well indeed in Noriega's organization—and that they'd come out when the shooting started and seen the SEAL assault force on the runway.

One of those balconies, he knew, belonged to a couple of Team Four SEALs who'd rented the place just the day before and who were using it as an observation post for this mission. They must have a great view of the ongoing firefight; why in the *hell* couldn't a couple of SEALs have been tasked with taking out Noriega's jet with a .50-caliber sniper rifle?

Theirs not to reason why . . .

Shit.

Two men from Golf Two reached Casey's position. "Let's get these men out of here!" he shouted, straining to be heard above the thunder of automatic gunfire.

The weight and accuracy of SEAL weaponry was gradually beginning to turn the tide of battle in the Americans' favor. The rest of Golf Two's SEALs were lying flat on the tarmac to Casey's left, pouring a furious hellstorm of fire into the hangar and the surrounding buildings. A moment later, Lieutenant j.g. Connors's Bravo Platoon came up from the rear, dropping to the pavement between the Golf elements.

"Grenades!" Lieutenant Phillips shouted. "Hit 'em with grenades!"

"What about the ROEs?" Connors called back.

"*Fuck* the ROEs!" Casey yelled. Their operational orders limited them to 5.56mm and 7.62mm small-arms fire, but they could peck away at those cement-filled barrels until doomsday without hitting the ambushers behind them.

But a couple of forty mike-mikes in there might do the trick.

Lieutenant j.g. Connors rose to one knee from the tarmac, lifting his M-16 to his shoulder, his finger on the trigger of the M-203 grenade launcher mounted beneath the rifle's barrel and ahead of the magazine. Before he could fire, however, an AK round slammed into his head squarely, knocking him backward in a bloody, lifeless sprawl.

But a number of other SEALs in Bravo were carrying M-203s, and in another moment, 40mm projectiles were arcing through the night to explode in and around the hangar.

So much for the ROEs about not damaging aircraft.

Screams sounded from inside the hangar. More grenades burst inside, spraying shrapnel across the cement-filled barrel barricades. The Learjet was holed in several places by shrapnel, but still there was no guarantee that it was crippled, and there was damned little chance now of capturing the aircraft as originally planned.

"Golf One, this is First Tee!" sounded over his radio. "Do you copy?"

"Copy, First Tee," Casey replied. That was Lieutenant Commander Tuohy, back at the sea end of the runway.

"Golf One, we have reports of hostile armored cars approaching your end of the objective. Do you see any in your area? Over!"

"Negative," Casey replied. "Negative on the armored cars. But we're taking damned heavy fire here! My whole squad is down, dead or wounded! Bravo Platoon's wheel is down. We're in serious trouble!"

"Roger that, Golf One. Try to pull your people back to the insertion point."

"Copy, First Tee. We're working on it."

Armored cars? Shit. That was all they needed. The PDF didn't have much in the way of armor, even light stuff, but even a digbat pickup truck with a machine gun over the cab would be a bit more than the nakedly exposed SEALs could handle just now.

But that did give him an idea.

None of his people was able to fire. Crawling on his belly, he made his way across the runway to one of the Bravo element SEALs. The man was firing his H&K, but slung across his back was the stubby tube of an AT-4.

"Johnson!" he shouted.

"Yessir!"

"Use your AT! Take out that plane!"

Casey was taking a gamble, and he knew it. The assault force had a limited number of AT-4s, brought ashore in case the assault ran afoul of PDF armor. If there was any armor in the area, they would need every one of the light antitank weapons they could muster.

On the other hand, Armada's primary mission was taking out Noriega's jet. The SEALs were pinned down and might well be forced to retreat without reaching their objective, and there was no guarantee that 40mm grenades lobbed at the hangar would cripple the aircraft.

Spending an AT rocket on the LearJet would finish the mission in a most satisfying and spectacular manner . . . and might even warn off Panamanian armored vehicles that might be tempted to join the pitched battle at Paitilla.

Johnson grinned at the order. "Aye, aye, sir!" He set the H&K aside and unslung the AT-4, a short, stubby tube holding a single antitank rocket. Dropping the tube across his shoulder, Johnson sighted in on the Learjet just thirty yards away. Casey checked the weapon's back-blast radius, then slapped Johnson's shoulder. "You're clear!"

The AT-4 fired, sending a dazzling, burning flare streaking across the tarmac and into the hangar. There was a flash and a hellishly loud bang, and the Learjet crumpled, its midsection engulfed in a roiling orange ball of flame.

"That'll teach the bastards!" Johnson said, dropping the spent AT tube.

"Good shot. C'mon. Help me get some of these people the hell out of here."

Awkwardly, still flat on their bellies, the two SEALs began crawling across the tarmac toward the scattering of bodies in the ambush zone. Casey reached Rodriguez, rolling the badly wounded SEAL onto his back and checking the man's injuries. A gaping hole in Rodriguez's stomach was soaking his combat utilities with fast-welling blood. Casey packed the wound as best he could with rolls of gauze from his first aid pack, but there was little else he could do here. Rodriguez needed medical help, and fast.

Grabbing the man's combat harness, Casey began dragging him along the pavement, a few painful feet at a time. Kalashnikov auto-fire cracked and snapped around him. Away from the hangar area, the surrounding light dropped off enough to give him a feeling of protection. The darkness wasn't complete, but he felt a little less bug-on-a-plate visible partway down the runway.

Although isolated rounds continued to cut the air overhead, Casey was at last far enough from the PDF shooters that he could stand, lifting Rodriguez in an awkward fireman's carry and hurry him the rest of the way to the SEAL command post. SEAL corpsmen hurried up to him to take Rodriguez from his shoulders. Nearby, the two Air Force communications specialists were hunched over a backpack radio set up on the tarmac, repeating the same call over and over. "Nighthawk, Nighthawk, this is Armada. Do you receive, over?"

Lieutenant Commander Tuohy was using his strap-on Motorola to talk to the mission overwatch back at Rodman. "Confirmed, Clubhouse," he was saying, his voice dead-steady and surprisingly calm. "We have three KIA, repeat, three KIA, and at least seven WIA. We are taking heavy fire at the hangar, and we cannot patch through to Nighthawk. We are in urgent need of gunship support and helicopter medevac. Over."

Tuohy might have been ordering take-out, he sounded so matter-of-fact, so *professional* was his manner. Casey couldn't hear the reply, of course, but Tuohy continued, "I copy, Clubhouse. However, I do not, repeat do *not* intend to withdraw." Another pause. "General, my orders were to seize the airfield and hold it until relieved. Those remain my intentions. Over." Another pause. "Roger that, Club-house. We'll keep you informed. And try to get us an alter-nate channel through to Nighthawk, okay? Armada, over and out!"

This far from the hangar area, the sounds of battle were muted by distance. Casey could clearly hear the steady drone of a large aircraft somewhere in the darkness over-head, slowly circling.

Tuohy's eyes met Casey's. "Lieutenant Casey! What's the situation in there?"

"Damned tight, sir. Where the hell's our air support?"

"We haven't been able to raise them," Tuohy replied. "They're up there, but either we were given the wrong freaks, or there's a mechanical fault."

Casey looked up into the sky, trying to place the drone of the AC-130 overhead. Gunfire continued to rattle and echo throughout the city, and streams of antiaircraft fire seemed to be searching for the intruder. A pair of strike aircraft—probably F-15s out of Howard by the sound of them—thun-dered low across the bay out of the south, hurtling toward some unknown mission north.

There was an ironic contrast there. War had begun in all its furious, bloody clamor, the full might of the combined arms of the United States of America descending *en masse* upon this one, tiny country. The U.S. obviously held the technical edge over the PDF, as well as undeniable superiority in numbers and in training. AC-130 gunships, F-15s, radical innovations in guided "smart bomb" technology, the SEALs themselves with night-vision gear and sophisticated electronics. There were even rumors that the Air Force was flying the new F-117 strike fighter this night, its first use in combat. The so-called stealth aircraft was supposed to be all but invisible to radar, able to fly into a hot combat zone to take out enemy defense radars and antiair assets without being seen.

And yet for all the wonders of technology fielded in Panama, it still came down to CQB—Close Quarters Battle—and the skill and determination of individual men. All of the high-tech gizmos in the world couldn't take—and hold—an enemy airfield.

"Where are you going?" Tuohy asked him as Casey turned away.

"Back to the hangar, sir." He jerked a thumb over his shoulder at the blaze of light down the runway. Muzzle flashes winked and flickered, accompanied by the continued crash of battle. "Some of my people are still in there."

"Roger that. Good luck."

"We'll need it, sir. Just get us some support! Sir." Accompanied by two SEAL corpsmen and the men from Golf Two, he hurried back toward the firefight.

One of the Golf Two SEALs looked up as a heavy aircraft droned serenely overhead. "Where the *fuck* is that gunship?"

Balboa Harbor
Panama City, Republic of Panama
0028 hours

Greg continued to swim steadily through the ink-black water, guided only by the faint glow from his wrist compass. He and Petrilli were working their way south through a forest of seaweed-coated pylons, bollards, and pier supports, hoping to stay clear of the center of the harbor where the Panamanians seemed to be concentrating their search-and-destroy efforts.

It had taken only a few minutes for him and Petrilli to finish attaching their Hagensen Packs to the hull of the *Presidente Porras,* and they'd swum clear at 1213 hours. A little more than half an hour to go before the timers went off.

By this time, Greg was certain that the PDF defenders had somehow gotten wind of the SEAL attack and were making the maximum effort to find and kill them. Had the PDF troops at Pier 18 guessed the target of the underwater assault and sent divers down to check the *Porras*'s keel for explosives? Well, that was beyond Greg's control. They would know the worst at 0100.

Of greater concern at the moment were the PDF harbor patrols. Small boats were zigzagging across the east side of the canal, randomly dropping hand grenades in an attempt to depth-charge any U.S. combat swimmers in the area to the surface. So far, most of the blasts had come from farther north, in an area on a direct line across the canal from Rodman to the pier area at Balboa. That made sense tactically. If swimmers were coming all the way across the canal from the Rodman SEAL base, or if they were swimming home, that's where they would be found.

In fact, during planning, the SEALs had considered swimming the mile across from Rodman to Pier 18. That approach had been rejected, however, because there was a chance that the PDF would open the drainage locks for the canal to the north as a defensive measure. If that happened, any combat swimmers would find themselves being swept south and out to sea on a twelve-knot current. Not good.

But the SEALs had elected to make their approach on the surface, in the CRRCs, then E&E south through the pylon

forest, well clear of the expected line of approach or withdrawal. Once clear of the piers, they would strike off toward the southwest, aiming for a fuel dock and a waiting
PBR beneath the Bridge of the Americas.

Don't be where the enemy expects you to be. That was
one of the prime tenets of warfare—especially warfare such
as this, where success depended on stealth, surprise, and
the unexpected.

A sudden blast roiled the water nearby, the concussion
hammering against Greg's eardrums. Shit! That had been
close! Had they been spotted?

He reached out to his left and touched Petrilli's shoulder,
the prearranged signal to halt. The two men waited, listening . . . but there were no more blasts, and none of the
sharp, chirping sounds of bullets striking the water. A random toss of a grenade off the pier, perhaps?

As he hovered in the black water, Greg remembered
hearing stories of the UDT—the Navy's Underwater Demolition Teams of World War II, the unit from which the
SEALs had been created almost three decades before. He
remembered some of the old hands during his tours in Vietnam talking about raids and reconnaissance missions onto
Japanese-held islands. In daylight, you could see the bullets
fired at you from the beach, silver arrows of turbulence driving down into the water at an angle, penetrating several feet
below the surface before the bullet slowed, then sank toward the bottom. Some of the UDT swimmers had actually
caught falling bullets that way and kept them as souvenirs.

This type of combat was far different, groping about in
pitch blackness, not sure whether or not the enemy knew
where you were, not sure if those grenade blasts were pre-
cautionary . . . or aimed directly at you.

Another thing. It was *hot.* The SEALs had elected to
wear their wet suits on this op, even though they could have
completed the mission in the 50-degree water without

them. That decision had been a crapshoot, actually. When the mission was being planned, weeks before, there'd been no way to predict that far in advance how warm or cold the water in the canal would be, and so their training sessions back in the States had been carried out with wet suits. They could have decided to leave the wet suits at Rodman for this op, but SEAL doctrine warned that the fewer elements changed between rehearsal and the real thing, the better the chances of success. They'd practiced placing explosives on a target boat's hull wearing these damned things, and they'd carry off the actual mission wearing them.

But damn, Greg was beginning to overheat. Wet suits kept the wearer warm by allowing a layer of water warmed by body heat to serve as insulation between skin and cold. As he worked, the water in his suit approached body temperature, making him feel as though he were working inside a sauna.

No sign of close pursuit. No more grenades nearby. Maybe they'd gotten clear.

He signaled Petrilli again, and the SEALs continued their swim.

Paitilla Airfield
Panama Bay, Republic of Panama
0035 hours

By the time Casey made it back to the hangar area, the battle had nearly dwindled away completely into uncertain stillness, a stillness broken only by the sounds of battle in the distance and by the occasional crack of a sniper's rifle close by. With a gaping hole blown clear through Noriega's jet, there'd been no need for the PDF to keep defending the thing, and the enemy had pulled out, dragging their wounded with them. Golf Two had pushed ahead, entering the hangar and reporting that it was clear of PDF troops.

The last of the wounded men had been evacuated to the command post. The remaining SEALs had dropped into a defensive perimeter around the hangar. Although the sounds of battle continued to rattle among the skyscrapers north of Paitilla, none of the shots seemed to be aimed at them. Casey took up a position inside the ring of SEALs, just outside of the hangar.

Eight PDF bodies remained inside the hangar, dragged out from behind the impromptu barricades and laid in a row. Judging from the number of bodies—and the intensity of the fire that had greeted the SEAL force—Casey guessed that there must have been at least twenty Panamanian soldiers there, possibly more. The SEALs had been lucky . . . and skillful. Twenty well-entrenched defenders could have held off a small army all night, and the ambuscade had been set up to do just that. SEAL firepower—and willpower—had broken the ambush, but it could so easily have gone down worse.

SEALs were not meant to engage a dug-in foe in a pitched battle. Paitilla Airfield might have been a victory, but if so, it was a victory forged in Hell.

Chapter 8

20 December 1989

Balboa Harbor
Panama City, Republic of Panama
0041 hours

Greg swam with steady strokes of his swim fins through the dark water, following his compass to round the mass of land called La Boca—"the Mouth," referring to the southern mouth of the canal. It had been some minutes since he and Petrilli had heard the thuds and bangs of hand grenades tossed into the water. Since that time, they'd worked their way clear of the forest of pilings near Pier 18, swimming west and then southwest along the La Boca shore before striking out into deep water, making for the Bridge of the Americas. Both SEALs were moving more deliberately now. Overheating and exhaustion were taking their inevitable toll, dragging at their legs, slowing their progress.

The explosions might have abated, but the bay was far from silent. Thumps, clangs, and thuds continued to reverberate through the water, and he could hear the far-off throb of boat engines. He wondered again if the PDF had discovered the explosives planted beneath the *Presidente Porras*. He glanced at the luminous dial of his dive watch. Another nineteen minutes before they knew. . . .

They were into the home stretch of their swim now, however. Though they couldn't see it from their cocoon of wet darkness ten feet beneath the surface, the Bridge of the Americas must lie just ahead. If Greg's steady count of flipper-strokes from the last waypoint was accurate, the fuel pier that was their objective now lay less than five hundred yards ahead. An easy swim.

Odd. He thought he heard . . .

Yeah, he was sure of it now. He could hear the low-pitched hum of a boat's propeller . . . and it was steadily growing closer.

Determining distances underwater by sound alone was always tricky. Even directions were uncertain, especially when the sound waves tended to reflect off the bottom or from the hulls of boats in the water, spreading out and converging in unexpected ways to make it seem that the noise was coming from all directions.

But it felt as though the sound was coming from the north, that it was fairly close, and that it was bearing down directly on the two SEALs. He felt a touch on his arm, sensed Petrilli's black shadow hovering at his side. Petrilli heard it, too.

Now the sound was *much* closer, bearing down on the SEALs like an avalanche of throbbing noise. Was the boat coming directly toward them or slightly ahead or behind? It made a life-or-death difference. Greg and Petrilli could easily try to swim out of the boat's line of travel and find themselves instead moving directly into its path.

Which way?

There was only one sure way to go to keep from being run down, and that choice itself offered its own danger. Greg grabbed Petrilli's wrist and jerked it down, hard. Together, the SEALs dove, swimming straight down into the inky depths.

Twenty feet, by Greg's depth gauge. Twenty-five . . . thirty . . .

Draeger rebreathers provided pure oxygen at ambient pressure, which meant that at thirty-two feet down, they were breathing oxygen at two atmospheres. At that pressure, oxygen became poisonous, and the deeper they dove, the more toxic it became.

The boat was almost on them now. Greg could feel the pressure of the oncoming bow wave. The craft was big—at least thirty or forty feet long, and propelled by twin screws. Thirty-five feet down, now . . . forty. At forty-five feet, he leveled off, hovering in darkness. This deep, he was breathing oxygen at almost two and a half atmospheres, deadly if he kept it up for long. Full-blown oxygen poisoning could cause convulsions that almost invariably led to drowning. He tried to keep his breathing shallow and steady and very slow, fighting the urge to gulp down breaths in time with his pounding heart.

He felt the boat pass overhead, moving fast, the pressure wave off its hull a roiling, powerful surge through the water. Had the people on that craft spotted them somehow, possibly with a fish-finder sonar unit? Or was the passage over the SEALs' location simply happenstance? If hand grenades started showering down from above in the passing boat's wake, they would know they'd been seen. Otherwise . . .

The pressure wave grew stronger, a powerful hand pressing him down, trying to drive him deeper still. Then he felt the turbulence from the twin propellers, a churning beat pounding through the water simultaneously lifting him higher and pushing him down.

And then the throb of the screws was dwindling.

Greg and Petrilli continued to hover in the darkness for long moments as the engine noise faded into the south, toward the La Boca shore.

They waited minutes more, delaying their ascent in case the boat swung about for another pass or was being followed by other marine craft. Finally, though, the two men allowed themselves to rise slowly to the surface. Greg couldn't detect any of the initial symptoms of oxygen poisoning—blurring vision or shortness of breath—but that didn't mean they hadn't been affected. They would need to have themselves checked out by a Navy doctor once they were back at Rodman.

He broke the surface. Petrilli surfaced nearby a moment later. The sky was overcast, faintly lit to the northeast by the glow of Panama City's lights. The sound of gunfire continued to rumble in the distance. A lot of people were shooting at each other over there.

Petrilli spat out his Draeger's mouthpiece. "Whaddaya think, Chief?" he said, bobbing slightly in the gentle swell from the open ocean to the south. "Was that the goddamned *Porras* that just tried to run us down?"

Greg rotated in the water, pushing his swim mask up on his head and staring into the darkness to the south. He could see lights on the Bridge of the Americas in that direction, just emerging from the night, but nothing like the running lights of a boat. Maybe they'd turned off to east or west, or else they'd been going flat-out, and faster than Greg had thought.

Yeah, it was possible. The boat that had just thundered overhead had been traveling from the general direction of Pier 18—from the Balboa waterfront, in any case—and had vanished around the curve of La Boca, heading south toward the open ocean beyond the Bridge of the Americas. It was just possible that Noriega had arrived at Pier 18 and was escaping Panama City now on board the *Presidente Porras.*

The big question, of course, was whether the Panamanians on board had discovered the Hagensen Packs and removed them before leaving the pier . . . or if the explosives were still attached to the patrol craft's keel.

There was no way to know until the explosives detonated, *if* they detonated, in another ten minutes.

He dropped his mouthpiece. "Might have been," he said, replying to Petrilli's question.

"If it was, maybe Pineapple Face is on board. Man, is he ever gonna be in for a surprise! He'll end up *flying* to Colombia instead of going by boat!"

"Unless they found our handiwork," Greg said. "Well, if that was the *Porras,* there's nothing we can do about it either way. Our job is done."

"Yeah!" Petrilli said. "Destruction, chaos, and despair. Our job here is done!"

Greg chuckled at the old joke, then reseated his mask over his face. "Let's get the hell out of here," he said. "We're almost home to a shower, dry clothes, and a hot cup of coffee."

"Make mine a cold beer," Petrilli said. "I'm so freakin' hot I feel like I've been running marathons in the sun all day!"

Underwater again, swimming at a depth of ten feet, the two SEALs made steady progress south. Surfacing once more ten minutes later, they could see the spider-work traceries of the Bridge of the Americas towering above them less than a hundred yards ahead. Lights glared off the bridge structure, painting a gaudy and dazzling display across the night, reflecting off the water in shimmering, wave-ruffled bands.

Greg checked their course off the angle of one of the massive pylons. They adjusted it slightly, and within another few minutes they could see the fuel pier that was their destination.

Long, low, afloat on massive pontoons, the pier was the terminus of fuel lines running along the seabed west from La Boca. In the shadow of the Bridge of the Americas, this was the southern mouth of the Panama Canal, gateway to the Pacific Ocean. Seagoing vessels of all sizes passed this point by the hundreds every day, and some skippers chose to top off their fuel tanks there at the strategically placed fuel pier before proceeding on to Hawaii, the Far East, or the ports of California far to the north. It also served as a base and refueling point for the professional pilots who, by law, guided all ships through the canal.

At the moment, several small patrol boats were moored there, but all appeared blacked out and deserted. Two, though, showed distinctive profiles silhouetted against the pier's lights, a pair of Navy PBR patrol craft, high-powered SEAL boats dispatched from Rodman to await their arrival. As the SEALs swam closer, Navy personnel on board waved greeting.

A SEAL lieutenant j.g. was waiting on the afterdeck of one of the boats as Greg put his hands on the swim ladder. "Permission to come on board, sir," he called up from the water. Several other SEALs were on board in full combat dress, while others guarded the fuel pier.

"Permission granted," the j.g. called back. "Welcome aboard!"

Greg clambered up the ladder and stepped dripping onto the deck. He saluted the officer, then the ensign hanging from the flagstaff aft. "It's good to be on board," he said, as Petrilli climbed out of the water behind him.

Brunner and Tompkins were there as well, divested of Draeger gear and combat harness but still wearing their wetsuits. "About time you guys showed up," Chief Brunner said. "What kept you? Hot date with the local girls?"

"Not quite. We had to go deep to keep from being run down by someone in a hell of a hurry. Did you guys see a fair-sized twin-screw vessel tear past here a few minutes ago?"

"Negative," Brunner said. "He must have veered off. It's been pretty quiet here."

"Except for the show over in Panama City," Tompkins added. East and northeast, the sky was still lit by the city's lights, and occasional streaks of tracer fire still drifted above the horizon, accompanied by the far-off rumble of small-arms fire.

"I take it you boys completed your mission, though," the j.g. said. "No problems?"

"None to speak of, sir," Greg replied.

"Yeah," Petrilli said. "We'd just like to know if that was the *Porras* that ran us down . . . maybe with old Pineapple Face on board."

"Well, we'll know in a moment," Greg said. He looked at his watch.

Zero-one hundred hours, exactly.

To the northeast, behind the low rise of La Boca, a bright flash illuminated the sky. A second flash, not as bright, followed the first, followed by the orange glow of a fireball rising above the silhouetted headland.

Seconds later, the sound reached them, a deep, heavy, double boom softened by distance but still almost palpable.

"Hoo-yah!" one SEAL yelled, and others cheered.

Greg felt none of the elation, however. He was tired, on the ragged edge of exhaustion. All he could really feel now was relief—relief that the op was over; relief that the mission had been a success; above all, relief that they'd all made it back in one piece.

. It had been a classic Navy SEAL op. Four highly trained operatives with a lot of high-tech muscle had swum unobserved deep into hostile territory, planted explosives on a target under the noses of enemy troops, and swum out again without ever being seen. The irrepressible Mr. Murphy had been very much in attendance, and plenty that could have gone wrong had done just that. Jaco's incapacitation, the CRRC engine conking out, the time of the op being hastily moved up, the war itself breaking out ahead of schedule, any one of those complications could have resulted in a very bloody and messy end to the op or, at the very least, forced them to abort the mission.

The fact that the blast had occurred back at Pier 18 and not off to the south meant that the *Presidente Porras* had still been at the dock when the explosion had gone off. The boat that had so narrowly missed them must have been another vessel, possibly a harbor patrol craft, possibly the *Porras*'s sister craft, the *Comandante Torrijos*.

Meaning, most likely, that Noriega was still at large, unless one of the other Special Forces units deployed to catch him had gotten lucky. That didn't matter. SEAL Team Two, with one unofficial tag-along from Team Three, had carried out their mission, and that was all that mattered now.

The rest of the war was now SEP—Someone Else's Problem.

Paitilla Airfield
Panama Bay, Republic of Panama
0130 hours

Lieutenant Commander Tuohy walked over to the area designated as a casualty station. Gunfire continued to crackle and snap throughout the city as the war got under way in earnest, but the airfield remained silent. The SEALs had finished rolling a number of light aircraft out onto the runway, effectively blocking it so that no one could land or take off, but leaving an open space near the main hangars for incoming helicopters. Then they'd settled down to wait.

The mission, Tuohy thought with grim pessimism, was falling further and further away from the carefully planned time curve established back at Fort Bragg. First, the SEALs had found themselves playing catch-up, behind the clock and racing to make up lost time—never a good way to start a war. They'd lost the race, too; the enemy had spotted them with time enough to assemble a hasty ambush, catching the SEALs in a deadly crossfire.

And almost nothing since had gone right. The failure to communicate with the AC-130 orbiting overhead . . . the deaths of three good men and the wounding of nine more . . .

And now the medevac choppers were late.

The plan called for medical helicopters to be waiting on the ground at Howard, ready to lift on an instant's notice. Howard Air Force Base was an easy ten minutes' flight from Paitilla. He'd called for them an hour and a half before.

Where the hell were they?

The wounded SEALs had been dragged into the makeshift aid station, lying there on blankets scavenged from one of the hangars, and the SEAL corpsmen were working hard to keep the most badly wounded among them alive. Eight of them were doing okay, but one, TM2 Rodriguez, was in a bad way, bleeding heavily. He might well not make it.

One corpsman, an HM1 named Peters, had moved away from the others, slumping to the tarmac with his back to the hangar casement. The man looked utterly spent.

Tuohy walked over to him. "Peters? How's Rodriguez doing?"

Peters looked off to his left, where two other corpsmen were working over the still form of the badly wounded SEAL. "His golden hour was up a while ago," he said with a shrug. His voice was flat, almost without emotion. "I don't know if we can hold on to him or not."

"Shit." The so-called golden hour was the magical sixty minutes after a man was badly wounded. Get to him in that time, stabilize his condition, and you had a good chance of saving his life. If you couldn't get him back to a rear-area surgical unit in that time, though . . .

"Where the hell is the medevac?" Peters asked, feeling flooding back into his words. "Medevac choppers were supposed to be ready at Howard, to roll!"

"They're being held on the ground," Tuohy replied. "Heavy air traffic." The explanation, glib enough when it had come through on the radio an hour earlier, seemed so lame now. Helos would be coming in low, almost on the deck, across Panama Bay, and well below the operational altitudes of any aircraft engaged in alpha strikes against targets in or near the city.

"We can't stop the fucking bleeding, sir," Peters said. "He needs surgery. He needs more than we can give him here. Did you tell them?"

"I told them. Hang in there."

"Don't tell me that, sir. Tell *him*." Peters rose to his feet and returned to the tableau, where the corpsmen battled silently to save Rodriguez's life.

No Rangers, and no medevac chopper. What the hell was going on?

Torpedoman's Mate 2nd Class Isaac Rodriguez, the nephew of a Green Beret Medal of Honor winner, had completed his post-BUD/S probationary period during the flight down from Little Creek. He'd worn the SEAL trident for one week.

He died minutes later, as the corpsmen fought to drag him back.

Rodman Naval Station
West of the Panama Canal
Republic of Panama
0745 hours

Greg walked up to the office door, banged on it three times, then pushed it open and stormed through. He was wearing dry dungarees, having changed out of his wetsuit hours earlier, but smears of black camo paint still streaked his face. He was tired, as tired as he'd ever been since Hell Week in BUD/S, but the fury surging through his body now kept him on his feet, kept him focused, sharp, and on course.

Roger Cahill looked up from the map he was studying with Captain Sandoval and several other officers, some in Navy uniform, one a major in Army camouflage BDUs. "What the hell do you want?" Cahill demanded.

"Sir! There's some scuttlebutt going around the base," Greg said carefully, "to the effect that our SEAL Four people are still at Paitilla, that they were supposed to have been relieved hours ago. Is that true? And if it is, why the hell haven't they been pulled out?"

"Take a number, Chief," Cahill said, his voice raw with exhaustion. "You're only about the tenth SEAL to come barging through that door this morning."

"And the scuttlebutt?"

"It's true. The Rangers are being held back."

"Goddamn! Why?"

"Because Colonel Hoyt suggested that they be held in reserve for another operation. They've been seconded to General Fitzpatrick."

"Hoyt!" That narrow-minded, pencil-necked, hidebound bastion of shortsighted, brass-polishing idiocy! "The word is that they've taken heavy casualties."

"You people did a hell of a job last night, son," Sandoval told him. "SEAL Four is doing their job. Hang tight and let them do it."

"Shitfire," the Army major said with a wry grin. "It's Grenada all over again. Those boys just hit a rough bit, is all, and they want to get our attention."

"We do *not* know that, George," Sandoval said. "And what they say happened on Grenada just flat didn't happen. I know. I was there."

"So was Tuohy, wasn't he? I think he's yanking your chain, trying to get a quicker response."

Greg felt a flash of anger, quickly suppressed.

The U.S. Navy SEALs had been deeply involved in the Grenada op, though their contribution had turned out to be somewhat controversial. One particular mission had been the raid to rescue the island's governor, Sir Paul Scoon, from house arrest, and to prevent him from being used as a hostage. Elements of SEAL Six, the Teams' high-profile antiterrorist unit, had managed to secure Scoon in Grenada's Government House, but then found themselves surrounded by Grenadan forces.

The controversy arose from exactly what had happened during the next, wild few hours. With several wounded men, the SEAL commander had transmitted numerous requests for assistance. Those requests had become more and more urgent as time went on. Some critics of the SEALs and of special warfare operations groups in general claimed that the SEAL commander had lied about the condition of his men in order to get a quicker response.

The crack about Tuohy being there actually referred to his participation in *another* operation at Grenada—a parachute jump by twelve Team Four men into rough seas off Point Salines. That op had been a total washout. Four SEALs had died that night, drowned in eight-foot seas. After repeated attempts, the Team Four men had had to be rescued, without making it ashore or accomplishing their mission of planting homing beacons for a Ranger assault.

The major seemed to be combining elements of the Grenada disasters, insinuating that Tuohy was exaggerating the seriousness of his situation.

"Sir!" Greg snapped. "That is un-goddamn-called for! Tuohy is a good man!"

"As you were, Chief," Cahill warned.

Greg took a deep breath. He was perilously close to insubordination now, and he knew it. "The Teams do *not* leave their people behind," he said after a moment. "Ever. If there are wounded ashore, we need—"

"*You* need to tend to your own duties, Chief," Sandoval said. "McGowan's people are being taken care of. Leave it at that."

"But—"

"That's an *order,* Chief."

Greg forced himself to stop, to come to a rigid attention. "Yes, sir."

"You will be informed of events as they develop," Cahill said. "Meanwhile, you and your people, stand down. Get some sleep. You look like hell."

"Aye, aye, sir." Greg was so furious that he scarcely trusted himself to speak. Keeping his anger under rigid control, he added, "If, sir, there is a need for Team members to effect a relief or a recovery of our shipmates at Paitilla, I wish to volunteer."

"We'll keep that in mind. Dismissed." The officers had already returned their full attention to the map. There was nothing further Greg could do here.

Hoyt! That bastard. Was this some petty scheme to get back at the SEALs for loss of face? Or just another JANFU . . . a Joint Army-Navy Fuck-Up?

Greg didn't know, but he was sure as hell going to find out.

Paitilla Airfield
Panama Bay, Republic of Panama
0820 hours

Dawn in Panama had come at just before 0600. Standing in the control tower above the hangar containing the ruin of Noriega's jet, Tom Casey shaded his eyes and peered past the backlit loom of nearby condos and apartment buildings at a patch of ocean dazzlingly silver and alive with sun-dance, just beneath the rising sun.

"Panama City," he said. "The only place in the world where the sun rises over the Pacific and sets in the Atlantic."

"Everything's bass-ackward here," Tuohy replied. He sounded bitter. He was taking the high casualty count hard, Casey thought—especially the death of young Rodriguez. "The criminals run the country and war is fought by ROEs."

"Yeah, it's like Vietnam all over again," Casey said. "Combat by the rules, and you will *not* color outside the lines."

The control room was the typical traffic controller's aerie, a circular space with slanted windows all around, with consoles mounting radar screens and communications gear. One windowpane, the western one overlooking the airfield and Noriega's private hangar, had been shattered by gunfire. On the floor, beside an overturned chair and with shards of glass scattered across the camouflage uniform, lay the corpse of a PDF soldier. Most of the left side of the man's head had been blown away. The right eye remained open, staring blindly at the ceiling. A pair of SEAL enlisted men, a sniper team, stood on the other side of the room, studying the buildings around them with binoculars.

Casey stepped across the body and gingerly brushed some of the glass off the console, then propped his hip against the cleaned area. "So, Boss," he said. "You think they'll take it out of our pay?"

Tuohy gave him a wry look. "I doubt it. But would you believe that idea was actually circulating during the op planning?"

"Shit. I thought it was just the private planes they were worried about."

"That was their number-one concern," Tuohy said. "There were a few congressmen on the Armed Forces Appropriations Committee and some assholes in the State Department who wanted to be absolutely certain our operation here did not damage private property . . . and that meant the private jets owned by rich Panamanians. Government officials, Noriega's cronies and mistresses, drug lords, that sort of thing. But there was a lot of worry later on about collateral damage to the buildings near the airport."

Casey waved a hand at the shattered control tower window. "Oh. Like that?"

"Yeah, like that. I think they don't want to have to buy new planes or buildings to replace what we destroyed, once Noriega is out and a new government is in power."

"It's a war, dammit," Casey said lightly. "Windows get broken."

"Explain that to the fucking politicians who sent us here," Tuohy replied.

The PDF soldier on the floor had been taking up a sniper's position in the control tower four hours earlier, a hide with a perfect line of sight down into the SEAL perimeter around the hangar. One of the Bravo element SEALs on perimeter watch had spotted him through a starlight scope and taken him down with a burst that had smashed through the window, killed the soldier, and punched holes in the ceiling beyond.

"I think we've already explained things pretty clearly," Casey said. "With bullets of one syllable. We're just here to do our job."

"Job." Tuohy snorted the word. "This isn't war. It's politics."

"War is politics inflicted on the other guy with a very big stick."

"Maybe," Tuohy said. "Let's get back to the perimeter."

They left the two enlisted SEALs in the control tower and made their way back down the zigzagging stairs to ground level. Outside, beneath the bright, early-morning tropical sky, the SEAL assault force remained alert and ready to repel an attack from any direction. About half of the men crouched or lay behind makeshift barricades along a perimeter encompassing the hangar and several smaller buildings, weapons pointed outward, on watch. Some stood guard over the light aircraft that had been rolled into blocking positions. The prisoners taken the night before were almost certainly hirelings for a drug cartel, and Tuohy was concerned that some of them might try to reclaim their property and escape by air.

The rest of the SEALs sprawled in the circle's center, catching some badly needed sleep. A few, the SEAL corpsmen, the Air Force liaisons, the SEAL radiomen, continued their duties in a central area designated as an HQ. One SEAL stood guard over the half-dozen dirty-looking civilian prisoners.

Commander McGowan was sitting on the ground next to the radio operator. He had come ashore early this morning with Fourth Platoon to reinforce the shore party.

"Anything yet, sir?" Tuohy asked him.

"We have a clear channel to Rodman," the SEAL officer replied. "And we are in contact with Howard. They've both been promising us our relief, but nothing's on the way yet."

"Shit," Tuohy said. "What's the delay? More heavy air traffic?"

"Maybe," Casey suggested, "we've all been transferred to the infantry, and they just haven't bothered to tell us."

Still no relief. That was bad news indeed. SEALs were simply not suited to the role of combat infantrymen, assigned to hold the ground they'd captured in the night.

Hell, it shouldn't have been SEALs assaulting a freaking airport in the first place. SEALs were at their best in quick, silent in-and-out raids, the sort where they could do their dirty work and be gone before the enemy even knew they were there. To have those same SEALs hold a fixed position in broad daylight was sheer insanity. The assault force was packing a lot of firepower, true, but the ammunition supplies for that firepower were sharply limited. And not just ammo was in short supply. They didn't even have canteens or MRE rations along.

They wouldn't have needed them, either, not when the Army Rangers were supposed to relieve them before dawn.

But here it was—dawn, and the Rangers were not yet on the way.

The ongoing battle continued to thunder and echo from the heart of Panama City, and the SEALs could see several clouds of black smoke hanging like ominous, ragged stains against the tropical sky. Several times, Army helicopters flew past the airfield, skimming rooftops, but too far off to signal.

Of the big AC-130 that had been supposed to provide pinpoint cover fire for the SEALs the night before, there was no sign. Evidently, it had left the area, but there was still no word as to why communications with the Air Force plane had failed, or news as to whether or not it would be back. At the moment, Casey thought, he would prefer a flight of those helicopters circling in the distance—Cobra gunships could go anywhere, pop up on a target from behind a building, and lay down a deadly accurate barrage of rockets or machine-gun fire.

"I still think you should have been wheel on this op, sir," Tuohy told McGowan. "I didn't want this. *Any* of it."

"Yeah, well, you've got it. I think I'll be of more use back at Rodman, trying to pry those Ranger helicopters off the tarmac." McGowan clapped Tuohy on the shoulder. "You're doing a hell of a job, son. Keep it up."

McGowan, Casey knew, had originally been slated to

take operational command of the Paitilla raid, but Commodore Sandoval had stepped in just before Team Four's deployment to Panama, placing Tuohy in operational command, with McGowan in an oversight role in a PBR off the coast. The official word was that McGowan had no combat experience—"Zero operational experience," in the commodore's words, while Tuohy had been in combat in Grenada.

Scuttlebutt within the Team said it was because McGowan was not, as they said, a "real-deal SEAL." He'd been a member of the Navy UDTs, the Underwater Demolition Teams, the unit formed in WWII out of which the Navy SEALs had been created in 1961. In 1983, the UDTs had been folded into the Navy SEALs; the two had increasingly similar missions and training, though the SEALs had more specialized weaponry training after graduation from BUD/S.

UDTs 11, 12, and 21 had been deactivated. In their place, SEAL Teams Four and Five had been created, mostly utilizing former UDT personnel. There was still some thought within the Navy special warfare community that the former frogmen weren't *real* SEALs.

Which, of course, was patently ridiculous. The UDT frogmen had never been as high-profile as the post-Vietnam SEALs tended to be, but they were every bit as well trained and as motivated. McGowan might lack combat experience, but Tuohy's deployment to Grenada scarcely counted. If anything, Casey thought, that particular clusterfuck should have counted *against* Tuohy.

In Casey's mind, a likelier explanation for the swap was the fact that Commander McGowan had not liked the idea of a large-scale frontal assault on Paitilla, while LCDR Tuohy had supported it. Since the big-assault boys had carried the day in planning, it was logical for them to want their own people at the operational helm.

Once again, Casey thought with a mental snort—*politics*. . . . the surest way Casey knew to scramble priorities, to divide assets, focus, and efforts, and in general to turn a military victory into defeat.

Chapter 9

Paitilla Airfield
Panama Bay, Republic of Panama
0625 hours

Thirty-seven hours. Thirty-seven *fucking* hours, and *still* their relief hadn't shown up. Lieutenant Commander Tuohy was beginning to wonder if the rest of the military had simply forgotten about the little band of SEALs holding on to Paitilla Airfield.

He paced along the perimeter, checking with the SEALs on watch, trying to keep up spirits that were becoming frayed and ragged after a full day and a half. The sounds of battle had subsided late the first day . . . yesterday, and last night had been fairly quiet, a quiet broken only occasionally by the crack of a sniper's shot or the sudden rattle of gunfire from a sentry startled by shadows. Paitilla seemed to have been relegated to a backwater of the war.

There was no immediate threat to the SEAL position. The entire Paitilla region appeared emptied of PDF and civilians alike.

But four good men were dead in an operation that simply shouldn't have been mounted in the first place.

Morale within the perimeter was becoming a real problem—an unusual one for SEALs. The casualty tally now stood at twelve—four dead, eight wounded—the highest number of SEALs casualties during a single engagement ever. The only other single loss to even come close was the drowning death of four Team Six SEALs during Operation Urgent Fury, the invasion of Grenada.

Tuohy had been in Team Six then. He'd been there, a part of that mission, though not in command.

He still had nightmares about that op, sometimes . . . of running down the open tail ramp of the C-130 Hercules and launching himself into darkness with eleven other SEALs. He remembered that wild parachute glide in the wind, remembered hitting the water too hard and losing much of his equipment, remembered his parachute reinflating on the surface and dragging him along, threatening to pull him farther out to sea. Only some fast and desperate work with his SEAL knife, cutting away the chute rigging, had saved him.

The wind had been lashing the night at a stiff twenty knots. The jump was supposed to have taken place at dusk, with light enough remaining to see by, but scrambled orders and SNAFUs up the line had delayed the jump by six full hours.

The jump had been badly scattered by the wind and darkness. He'd managed to rendezvous at last with seven of the other SEALs, but four men—MM1 Butcher, QM1 Lundberg, HT1 Morris, and EMC Schamberger—had never been found. One of the two small boats dropped with the SEALs had been lost as well. It had taken hours to reassemble, find the remaining boat, and make their way to their first objective—the Spruance-class destroyer USS *Sprague*.

One of the nastiest ironies of that night, Tuohy thought, was that the deaths of the four SEALs had probably been unnecessary. The idea had been to parachute into the sea near the *Sprague* on 23 October, two days before the invasion. They would rendezvous with the destroyer, go on board, and pick up a four-man Air Force Combat Control Team. Only then would they motor the forty miles from the destroyer to Point Salines, where they would go ashore and mark LZs for the Rangers. They could just as easily have rendezvoused with the *Sprague* by helicopter—she had a helipad aft for LAMPS ASW helicopters—or they could have fast-roped to her deck. Things would have been a bit touchy in a twenty-knot wind, sure, but the destroyer's helipad crew was trained and skilled at bringing in helicopters even in gusting winds, dark, and rain. It would have been a damned sight safer than jumping blind into the night-shrouded ocean.

Despite the loss of one-third of their number, the SEALs had continued to attempt to complete their mission, though the single remaining whaleboat was dangerously over-loaded. On the way in, they'd spotted a Grenadan patrol boat and cut power. In the high seas, though, the boat had broached to and nearly swamped, and the 175-horsepower outboard had died and they'd not been able to restart it. The outgoing tide had dragged them farther and farther out to sea, and they'd finally called for a rescue.

The following night, the night before the scheduled inva-sion, they tried again, even though the mission was by then a full twenty-four hours behind schedule, but the unrelent-ing Murphy had struck again. On the run into the beach, their boat had capsized in the heavy surf, and the Air Force controllers had lost all of their beacon gear. Once again, the men were swept out to sea by the powerful tide, and only through great good luck had they all been recovered.

But the mission had ended in complete and utter failure.

"Whaddaya think, sir?" One of the Bravo element SEALs, BM2 Hoskinson, called to him, interrupting his increasingly black thoughts. "Are they ever comin' for us or not?"

Tuohy stopped and looked at the young SEAL, crouched behind a makeshift barricade of fifty-gallon drums and coils of steel cable. The man had only recently joined Team Four after completing his BUD/S training at Coronado and his six-month apprenticeship at Virginia Beach. He'd been in the same BUD/S class as Rodriguez.

"They'd damn well better, Hoss," he said, making the words a growl. "The brass hats don't want the whole Team gunning for them, do they?"

Hoskinson laughed. "You got a point, sir."

Tuohy wished it were that simple.

He continued walking the perimeter, checking positions, chatting lightly with the SEALs holding them.

There'd been a lot of analysis after Grenada, a lot of finger-pointing and faultfinding. A board of inquiry had cleared Tuohy of any responsibility for the deaths of the four SEALs, and even added a commendation to his personnel file, to the effect that he had carried out his duties in the best and highest traditions of the U.S. Navy on that deadly night.

But then, *everyone* had been getting commendations for Grenada. Hell, they'd been passing out medals like candy at Halloween after that one. The invasion was a public relations coup, a major propaganda victory over the communists, a proud declaration that the United States was no longer on the retreat in the Cold War. Too, Grenada had been the ideal opportunity for career officers in all of the services to get their tickets punched—to have it noted in their records that they'd been in combat and hence were eligible for promotion. There had been no failures at Grenada . . . and if some of the operations hadn't gone as smoothly as others, well, the facts could be swept under the carpet easily enough. Damn it, the invasion of Grenada had been a *win*. Hey, with a high-visibility PR victory like Grenada, you couldn't admit that some of the individual ops had gone down a little less than perfectly, could you?

But the truth of the matter was that the Navy SEALs had lost a bit of their luster on that op, no matter how bright a coat of paint the high-ranking brass slapped over it. There were critics—generals and admirals at the Pentagon, at Fort

Bragg, on the Joint Chiefs—who were now voicing the idea that the SEALs were obsolete, a needless drain on scarce appropriations resources, a force useful in Vietnam but rendered ineffective by the realities of modern warfare.

A loud crash and tinkle of shattering glass brought him back out of his dark and circling thoughts. At first he thought PDF snipers might be about to open fire, smashing out the window of one of those nearby condos . . . but the area still seemed peaceful. Walking toward the source of the sound, he rounded the hangar casement and found two SEALs standing in front of a coin-operated candy dispenser. One of them had smashed in the glass front with the butt of his M-16, and they were helping themselves to the candy bars spilling onto the pavement.

"What the hell are you two doing?" Tuohy demanded. Violation of the standing orders against damaging civilian property was a court-martial offense. Technically, he could arrest these two for looting. "That's civilian property!"

"Damn it, Commander," one said, holding up a fistful of chocolate. "We're *hungry!* These are the only rations we've seen out here!"

"Yeah," the other said. "If the Navy ain't going to feed us, we're on our own, right?"

Tuohy opened his mouth to blast them both for willful disobedience, then thought better of it. "Shit," he said. "Give me one of those . . . and tell the others to help themselves."

"Aye, aye, sir!" They laughed, and for a moment, low morale was held at bay.

It wouldn't last for long, though.

Peeling the wrapper off his candy bar and taking small, savoring bites, Tuohy continued his prowl along the perimeter. It was ironic. When he'd been brought in by Commodore Sandoval to replace McGowan, he'd been excited by the chance, thrilled by the sheer scope and glamour of the whole operation. The last thirty-some hours had changed his mind.

Like most in the Navy Special Warfare community, Tuohy had looked at the invasion of Panama as a chance to prove that the Teams still had what it took. They'd been superb in Vietnam, waging small-unit guerrilla tactics against the VC and North Vietnamese. Since the 1970s, SEAL units had carried out literally hundreds of covert ops, sneak-and-peek insertions into communist bastions all over the world; raids on terrorist camps; surveys of hostile ports, shipyards, and beaches; take-downs of drug production facilities; antiguerrilla ops in a dozen different beleaguered nations from Indonesia to El Salvador to Lebanon . . . in short, everything they'd been designed to do. The vast majority of those black ops had come off successfully, with no casualties, usually without any gunplay or the enemy ever even knowing they'd been there.

But, of course, the nature of those operations was such that they would remain in the shadows, unknown, unsung. What the public *heard* about were the failed ops, specifically Grenada. Several mass-market paperbacks had been published almost before Operation Urgent Fury had been declared a success, all poking holes in what they claimed was the SEAL myth. Military and media pundits alike discussed the SEAL role in Grenada endlessly, pointing out the failures, ignoring the successes, and calling into question the very need for the Teams. The SEALs desperately needed a good, solid success in Panama if they were to regain their reputation, more, if they were to keep their share of the funding.

Trouble was, there were too many people—non-SEAL people—trying to write SEAL operational orders these days. In Vietnam, the SEALs had had to follow orders, certainly, but they'd had a high degree of freedom in operating within those orders . . . or they'd been able to create that freedom when they needed it, using the "UNODIR" dodge or simply by not keeping people farther up the command ladder fully informed, submitting *results* instead of plans.

The modern SEALs were too large, too structured, too tightly tied in with the military command and logistical systems to pull that sort of con nowadays. At Grenada, they'd found themselves under orders to carry out a needlessly complex multiphase operation in the teeth of darkness, high winds, and rough seas. They'd tried to carry on—God, how they'd tried! But that was one time when the powers that be were simply asking too much.

And now, at Paitilla, history was repeating itself. The assault on the airfield had been too big, too complex, too vulnerable to equipment malfunction and confusion. Hell, the SEALs, good as they were, simply had no business trying to carry out an op like this, not one involving a pitched battle for control of an airport. Tuohy had supported the large-scale attack earlier in the planning, true, but since then . . .

Yeah, a man could change his mind.

A new thought arose, a distinctly unpleasant one. What about his own career? This made two combat ops, now, in which he had had a major role—and which had ended with four good men dying. It was a morbidly selfish thought, he knew, but it was there nonetheless. He could easily be remembered as a jinx wheel, the SEAL commander who always lost men on combat ops.

Damn, this was not going to stop here, either. The other day, Commander Cahill, Team Two's CO, had talked to him in his office back at Rodman about how Chief Jaco from Team Two and another SEAL, the liaison from the West Coast, had scoped out Paitilla a week ago. Cahill had said that their report would be dragging up all the old issues about the Paitilla op again, with special emphasis on how all they'd needed to do was put a sniper in one of those buildings over there . . .

And Tuohy was on record as having urged the large-scale op. Damn it, it had seemed like such a good idea at the time, a way to help the Teams define their mission in a changing world and a means of advancing his career.

Shit . . . shit . . . *shit!*

He completed his circuit of the perimeter, then made his way back to the makeshift HQ at the circle's center. The Air Force technicians had long since given up with their equipment, but a SEAL radioman was maintaining contact with McGowan, who'd returned to Rodman yesterday. The worst problems the assault force had to deal with now, it seemed, were monotony and hunger. Water was free for the taking from any of a number of outdoor spigots, but the only food to be found was in those damned candy machines.

He wondered if they would be gigged for damaging civilian property when this was over. Yeah, just the absolutely *perfect* end to a perfect op! He would tell the inquiry board that he'd ordered his men to bust the machines. He didn't mind taking the rap, not when his unit was being beached high and dry.

Where the hell was their support? First no AC-130 gunship, then a late medevac, and now no Rangers. This was goddamn freaking ridiculous.

"Get me Commander McGowan," he snapped, walking up to the radioman on duty.

"Channel's open, sir."

He picked up the headset with attached lip mike. "Home Plate, Home Plate, this is Armada. Do you copy? Over."

"This is Home Plate," McGowan's voice replied. There was a lot of interference, a rattling thunder almost masking the words. "Go ahead, Armada!"

"We're at thirty-seven hours and counting, Commander," Tuohy said, not bothering to mask the anger in his voice. "Where the hell is our relief?"

"On the way!" was McGowan's answer. "We lifted off

from Howard a couple of minutes ago. We should be there inside of ten minutes!"

The news disarmed Tuohy's anger, at least momentarily. "Relief force is on the way!" he called out to the others. The SEALs nearest him vented a ragged cheer.

"That's good news, sir," he said into the mike. "We'll be expecting you. Over and out!"

It was an indication, though, of just how paranoid Tuohy was feeling at the moment, that he didn't allow himself to really begin to believe until he heard the far-off *whop-whop-whop* of approaching helicopters.

A *lot* of approaching helicopters. He moved out from behind the hangar casement to a point where he had a clear view to the west. There, just above the azure blue of Panama Bay, a scattering of tiny black dots was visible against the sky. Seconds passed, the noise growing louder, and the individual dots began resolving into aircraft, bug-faced, front canopies gleaming in the morning sun. They looked, Tuohy thought, like a flight of dragonflies, their movement made ponderous at first by distance and perspective, but becoming more and more agile as they drew close to the far end of the runway.

A pair of Apache attack helicopters clattered over the hangar area first, circling, checking for hostiles. The Black-hawk transports came in next, skimming just above the runway, flaring nose-high at the last moment and settling in for landing.

The rotor wash from the descending aircraft blasted across the runway, raising a whirling cloud of dust that sent several SEALs ducking for cover. A light Cessna parked on the runway tipped wildly as the gust caught it under one wing, then lifted high and flipped over. Several more small planes were scattered like toys in a windstorm as the first Blackhawk lightly touched down and Army Rangers began piling out.

So much, Tuohy thought, for protecting civilian property at the airfield. In ten seconds, those Army helos had caused more damage than had the entire firefight. Compared to this, a smashed candy machine was nothing.

An Army captain trotted toward him. "You guys know how to make an entrance," Tuohy told him. "Welcome to Paitilla."

"You the man in charge?"

"That's me. What the hell happened, anyway?"

"What do you mean?"

"Why'd it take you so long to get here? We were supposed to be relieved thirty hours ago."

The man shrugged. "Hey, I don't call 'em. I know we were supposed to deploy two nights ago, but then the word came down that the op had been delayed. They had us up north yesterday, chasing rumors. We only got the go-ahead to come relieve you guys maybe half an hour ago."

Suddenly, it just didn't matter any longer. "C'mon, Captain," he said. "I'll show you around."

"Right. You'll need to get your people organized to go out on the helos."

"And about damned time, too."

For the SEALs of Team Four, the war in Panama was at long last over.

25 December 1989

**Playa de las Suecas
Isla Contadora, Republic of Panama
1410 hours**

Christmas Day.

The afternoon sun glared down on the water to the south, where gentle rollers surged in from the ocean, breaking on a beach of velvet sand. A Spanish version of "O Holy Night" was playing on a boombox nearby, and the snack-shop at the top of the dunes behind them was decked out in red and green. Christmas in the tropics always seemed a bit surreal to Greg, even though he was from California himself and rarely had to contend with a proper white Christmas. Somehow, eighty degrees on a sunny beach scattered about with small groups of naked people just didn't quite cut it as a proper reflection of the holiday season.

The Playa de las Suecas—the name translated rather pleasantly as the Beach of Swedish Women—was tucked away on the southeastern coast of Contadora, a 1.2 square-kilometer island perhaps seventy kilometers southeast of Panama City. There were twelve beaches on the island. Best known, perhaps, was the Playa Ejecutiva on the island's north side, which lay beneath the brooding presence of the mansion that once had belonged to the shah of Iran after the revolution that drove him from power. Contadora was a literal paradise. The place was a popular playground for rich European and North American *touristas* visiting Panama. The snorkeling and diving were superb, the surfing good, the scenery magnificent.

But the off-duty SEALs had flown down the day before for other reasons than the snorkeling. They'd come for the scenery, right enough, but it wasn't the deep blue Pacific or the rocky bluffs that interested them. Playa de las Suecas was the only legal nude beach in Panama.

Greg had joined the party at Brunner's suggestion—less for the brown, naked bodies baking under the tropical sun, however, than to stay well clear of Colonel Hoyt and his vendetta against special-ops forces. There was a lot of bad feeling right now between the SEAL community and some of the Army staff personnel—those who, like Hoyt, felt that special forces were a waste of resources, military appropriations, and trained men. While most of the SEALs were staying put at Rodman, some had elected to make themselves a bit scarce around the U.S. bases on the mainland.

"Man, oh, man, will you get a load of *her!*" Petrilli said, nodding toward a startlingly attractive woman walking up the beach wearing sunglasses and sandals and nothing else.

"Nice," Tompkins said. "*Real* nice. Natural redhead, I see."

"I hope she has plenty of sunblock on," Brown commented. "Something with an SPF of a couple of million or so. With that skin she'll be burnt to a sizzling brown crisp before she makes it across the beach."

"If she doesn't," Tompkins said, "maybe we should offer to smear some on. Wonder where she's from?"

"Don't know," Greg said. "It's kind of bizarre, though. Don't these people know there's a war on?"

"Oh, really?" Brunner said, lying back on the sand and stretching out full-length, his hands clasped behind his head. "A war, huh? That's good to know. Anyone I know?"

"Yeah," Petrilli said, continuing to stare at the redhead's nicely shifting buttocks as she walked past the small group of SEALs, "Wake me when it's over. Man, I must be dreaming!"

"Your dream girl has a friend," Brunner said, laughing. The redhead had just been joined at the top of the beach by an athletic-looking man who swept his arm behind her and led her on a path leading away through the dunes.

"Too bad, Pet. Maybe he wants some sunblock, too."

Ignoring the banter, Greg let his gaze drift across the entire sweep of the beach. It was actually fairly crowded, with perhaps a hundred sun worshippers gathered on the tan sands or frolicking in the roll and tumble of the Pacific surf. Normally, he'd been told at the resort activities desk up the road, Contadora's beaches weren't this crowded, but there was always a big influx around the major holidays.

And today was Christmas.

Merry Christmas.

He wondered what Wendy was doing right now. Having Christmas dinner with her mom, he supposed. Damn, he missed her.

From the look of it, the war certainly didn't seem to have daunted the tourists at Contadora. Most would be Europeans; the U.S. State Department had warned off the American tourists when things started turning ugly with Noriega. Flights in and out of Panama City's airport had been stopped, of course, when Task Force Red had taken down Torrijos International Airport and Rio Hato during the first hours of the invasion.

But now, in fact, the war was all but over. By the end of D-day, the 20th, the Army's Task Force Bayonet had secured the *Comandancia*, Fort Amador, and PDF sites throughout Panama. Other task forces had secured a hundred other sites, including Panama Vieja, Renacer Prison, and the vital Madden Dam, which controlled the water levels in the Panama Canal. A Marine task force, Semper Fi, had gained control of the Bridge of the Americas over the canal and the Panamanian portions of Howard Air Force Base. On the twenty-first, the Panama Canal had been reopened for daylight operations, American nationals had been rescued from the Marriott Hotel in downtown Panama City, and Task Force Bayonet was gaining control of the rest of the capital.

By the twenty-third, Torrijos Airport had been reopened, and most military operations in the Canal Zone were aimed at maintaining stability and order, with military forces rounding up and disarming the remaining roving bands of digbat and PDF troops. Special Forces and the newly arrived 2nd Brigade of the 7th Light Infantry had redeployed to the western portion of Panama, in part tracking down drug cartel members and the Noriega government still at large.

Of Noriega himself, there'd been no trace during the invasion. Units sent to arrest him at several different locations all came up empty, one apparently missing him by scant minutes. Only early on the day before had he finally surfaced—at the Vatican embassy, seeking asylum with the papal nuncio—and U.S. forces had already moved to bottle him up and demand his surrender. Greg and the other SEALs had gotten the news yesterday, before they'd caught the helicopter transport to Contadora.

One thing was immediately clear, and Greg was already making mental notes on that fact for the report he would write for Fort Bragg and for SEAL Team Three. The Navy SEALs had been engaged in two operations—not counting the strictly unofficial hostage rescue of the previous week, which had not been a planned part of Just Cause. One had been mounted along the lines of traditional SEAL ops, a small team slipping in, planting explosives, and slipping out. That op had proven to be a complete success. Eyewitnesses had seen the *Porras*'s two diesel engines hurled high into the air by the blast, which had blown Noriega's yacht to bits, yet spared the Canal Commission boats tied to the dock to either side. Greg's fears at the time that the SEAL combat swimmers had been spotted had proved groundless. The shooting had broken out early when Panamanian units opened fire on American troops moving up to their invasion jump-off positions near the Pier 18 waterfront, not because the swimmers had been seen. As he'd thought, the grenades tossed into the waters of Balboa Bay had been a precaution only, not an attack against known targets.

The other operation, employing the SEALs in large-unit assaults against a defended position, had ended in success but at a grievously unacceptable cost. Four dead, eight wounded . . . and considerable collateral damage to the airport facilities. For SEALs, who considered an op to be technically a failure if gunfire was employed, the Paitilla op had been a cluster fuck from the word go. The SEAL and Navy Special Warfare communities would be putting Paitilla under the microscope for a long time to come, trying to learn what had gone wrong and how to prevent a repetition in the future.

Another victory like Paitilla, Greg thought, paraphrasing Pyrrhus, the ancient Greek general who'd lent his name to the term Pyrrhic victory, *and the SEALs are finished.* Already tight in the ongoing competition for funds and equipment, the Teams might easily be phased out by big-unit generals and admirals who would see Paitilla as proof that the SEALs couldn't hold their own on the modern battlefield.

And there was also the matter of the rumors . . . the scuttlebutt already circulating among enlisted personnel back at Rodman, that Tuohy had panicked and called for help when he didn't need it, and, conversely, that the Ranger relief force had been deliberately withheld by officers who remembered the incident at the Government House in Grenada and thought that the SEALs there had behaved in something other than the best traditions of the American military.

All nonsense, of course. But the powers that were, Greg knew, were going to be looking at the Teams very closely in the future, especially when another war came along.

He found himself thinking about Mark, his son, just about to begin his BUD/S training back at Coronado.

What role would the Teams have when *he* found himself in battle?

"Jesus!" Petrilli said, soul-felt reverence in the name. "Get a load of that blonde!"

The woman emerged from the surf just a short way down the beach from the watching SEALs. Utterly unselfconscious, she walked to a blue towel on the sand nearby, picked it up, and began drying herself.

"I'll bet *she's* Swedish," Tompkins said. "You can tell. Look at that hair!"

"Or German."

"Ah, you're both nuts," Brunner said. "What you gentlemen see there is one hundred percent *woman,* and it doesn't matter what country she's from."

"Yeah," Tompkins said. "All woman, no clothes."

"No tan lines," Petrilli said. "What about you, Twidge? Whatcha think? We haven't heard out of you all afternoon! Get with the program, okay?"

"I think," Greg said slowly, "that you should all put your tongues back in your mouths and your towels over your laps, so that you stop sharing so much information on the state of your hormones."

"Shit, Twidge," Tompkins said. "That's easy for you. You're married."

"So are you, Tompkins," Brown reminded him.

"Oh." He continued to watch the nude blonde as she finished drying herself, then spread out the towel and sat down on it a few yards away, looking out at the ocean. "Oh, yeah. Doesn't mean I can't look."

"Geeze," Greg said irritably. "Grow up, people. Bodies are bodies. It's no big deal."

Memories of Wendy seemed to rise like an incoming tide, and Greg lay back on the sand, eyes closed. *God,* he missed her.

God, he wanted her back.

Chapter 10

Headquarters
Naval Special Warfare Command
Coronado, California
1415 hours

Greg rapped three times on the door.

"Enter."

He stepped through the door and closed it, shutting off the clatter of computer keyboards and the bustle of naval office workers, military and civilian. Admiral Charles Weatherbee looked up from his broad, oak desk, his notorious frown prominent. His swivel chair was flanked by American and Navy flags, and a large portrait of President Bush graced the dark-paneled wall at his back. Other walls bore framed prints of events out of Navy history.

Three other officers were in the room as well, a captain, a commander, and a lieutenant commander. The captain was Captain Roy R. Scott. The lieutenant commander was Phil Bailley, on Scott's staff. He didn't know the other man.

He came to attention. "Master Chief Greg Halstead, reporting as ordered, sir."

"At ease, Master Chief." Weatherbee's voice was a raspy growl. "I gather you know Captain Scott and Commander

Bailley. This is Commander Driscoll, on my command staff. I've asked these gentlemen to join us here today."

"Yes, sir." He knew Bailley personally and Scott by reputation. Scott was a SEAL serving as commander of NAVSPECWARGRU-One, the headquarters unit for all of the West Coast SEAL Teams, SEAL Delivery Team, and Special Boat Squadrons. Weatherbee was commander of Naval Special Warfare Command here in Coronado and was, hence, the senior SEAL in the Navy. All three men wore the trident insignia of the SEALs on their dress whites, just above impressive racks of ribbons.

"Do you know why you're here?" the admiral demanded.

Greg glanced at the other three officers. The setting, while reasonably informal, was a bit reminiscent of the setting for a special court-martial, where a judge presided over three or more senior officers to try serious offenses by military personnel. He hadn't actually been accused of anything . . . at least, not yet. Still, he had a pretty good idea of what this was about.

"No, sir. I don't."

"Are you happy as a SEAL, Halstead?"

The question took him by surprise. "Uh, yes, sir. Very much so."

"You've been a SEAL for . . ." He looked down at the open personnel folder before him.

"Twenty-two years, sir. Pretty near."

"And twenty-three in the service. And are you aware, Master Chief, of your responsibilities to those in authority over you?"

"Yes, sir."

"Including supporting those in authority over you publicly, even if you, personally, disagree with their policy?"

"Yes, Admiral. I'm aware." He started to say something more, then decided to sit on it. He had the feeling he was in the middle of a minefield here.

"You were going to say something more, Master Chief?" Scott asked.

"Only—with respect, sir—that that responsibility goes both ways, up *and* down. I also have the responsibility to speak up if I note something seriously wrong in the chain of command, a problem that isn't being addressed, a short-coming that—"

"*Don't* lecture us on responsibility, Master Chief," Weatherbee said, his face darkening. "I wish only to know that you are aware of your place within the chain of command and what your duties are."

"Yes, Admiral. I'm very aware. Sir."

"Good. Last week, you attended a conference in Little Creek."

"Yes, sir." That had been the annual meeting of the Fraternal Order of SEAL/UDT, a gathering of some hundreds of Team veterans, both active and retired.

"And who was the keynote speaker there?"

Greg sighed. He knew where this was going, now. "Captain John Sandoval, the commodore of Naval Special Warfare Group Two."

"And what happened there, Master Chief?"

"The Commodore gave a speech, sir."

"And? . . ."

"He was booed off the stage, sir."

"Don't you think that's a bit unusual, Master Chief? A senior captain, a commodore, no less, the commander of all East Coast SEALs, treated with that kind of disrespect?"

"I believe, sir, that the disrespect was on his part, that Captain Sandoval failed in his responsibility to the men he commanded. Especially the members of Team Four and the four men who died at Paitilla. He showed, in my opinion, considerable disrespect for the SEALs at that conference by blatantly minimizing what happened in Panama and by glossing things over to the point that he actually told the audience that—"

"People die in combat, Master Chief," Weatherbee said, interrupting. "Military personnel, *all* military personnel, are expected to offer their lives in the service of their country, if need be."

"I don't question that, sir. I never have."

"But I'm given to understand that you were on your feet with the rest of those men, booing Captain Sandoval until he was forced to conclude his remarks and leave the stage."

Me and about two hundred other guys, yeah, he thought. But he said, "Yes, sir."

"Exactly what was it in Captain Sandoval's speech," Scott said, "that set the audience off?"

Admiral Weatherbee shot Scott a sharp and glowering glance but said nothing. Obviously, he wished to stay away from Sandoval's responsibility in the issue.

"He did not once mention the SEAL casualties at Paitilla Airfield, sir. He addressed the group as though nothing had happened, as though everything had gone completely and perfectly according to plan. We started booing, sir, when—"

"You showed monumental disrespect to a senior officer, Halstead," Weatherbee said.

"Yes, sir. That senior officer had the golden, unmitigated gall to stand up there and tell us that everything worked perfectly, that there were no lessons to be learned from the SEAL operations in Panama." There. He'd said it. "You're damned straight we booed him off the stage. Those four men should *not* have died. By ignoring the mistakes that were made, by doing his damned best to cover up those mistakes, he was showing monumental disrespect to those four men and to every man who's pinned on a Budweiser. Including you, sir."

"Master Chief, it's my business whether I feel that someone has shown disrespect to me or not. Not yours." He shook his head, leaning back in the chair. "It seems to me you are taking this thing entirely too personally. Do you have some personal problem with Commodore Sandoval? I know you worked with him in Panama."

Greg remembered Sandoval coming in and taking his part against Colonel Hoyt. "I didn't work with him, exactly, Admiral. But I did talk to him."

"And what did you talk to him about?"

Best not to go into the affair with Hoyt. That could stir up a real hornet's nest. "In my capacity as a liaison for the West Coast SEALs, sir, I told him that I felt the use of a large SEAL force in what amounted to a frontal assault on the Paitilla objective was a mistake. That there were other ways to accomplish the mission objective without risking so many men. Sir."

"And what was his response?"

"That the Panama operation was a high-profile op for the Teams. That the Teams needed to demonstrate that they could work with other branches of the service in a modern combat situation. I believe he said something to the effect that the Paitilla operation would establish credibility for the Team with senior planners in Washington, by proving we could be employed as a multiplatoon task force against an important target. And he told me that the decision was not open to further discussion."

"That sounds perfectly reasonable to me," Weatherbee said. "The Navy, the Teams, are not democracies. We cannot allow enlisted personnel to dictate strategy, tactics, or doctrine. Do you follow me, Master Chief?"

"Yes, sir. May I remind the Admiral, sir, that the United States armed forces do not accept 'I was just following orders' as a valid excuse? I think My Lai was an excellent case in point."

My Lai was the infamous incident in Vietnam in 1968, where an inexperienced company of U.S. Army soldiers had killed several hundred Vietnamese civilians, many of them women and children. The investigations and courts-martial that had followed the affair had amply demonstrated that the American fighting man was not only expected to question orders that were illegal. He was legally responsible to do so.

"We are not discussing ancient history, Master Chief. And there is no question that Sandoval's orders were legal, in every sense of the word. To be blunt, the orders were not even his. He simply had overall responsibility for the operation, as CO of the East Coast teams."

"Yes, sir. The responsibility was his." He decided not to point out that Admiral Weatherbee, as Sandoval's direct superior officer, was also, ultimately, responsible for whether or not those orders were given and carried out. "Sir, perhaps I can put it this way. As a senior petty officer, I consider it my responsibility to point out to my commanding officers possible problems or oversights of which they may not be aware. I understand that it is my responsibility, as an NCO, to make recommendations, to protest, if necessary, orders that appear to me to be illegal, reckless, poorly organized or thought out, or badly planned.

"Commodore Sandoval might not have written those orders, but he sure as hell signed off on them. I made recommendations, as was required of me by *my* orders, and I pointed out what I felt were shortcomings in the operation as originally planned. Commodore Sandoval chose to disregard those recommendations—as was his right, certainly—and as a direct result, four good men were killed. It was, sir, in technical terms, a cluster fuck."

"You will watch your language, Master Chief," Commander Driscoll warned.

"Aye, aye, sir. But the operation was poorly conceived

and poorly planned, and the worst of it was, two men with a sniper rifle could have carried out that mission in relative safety. To insist on the large-scale assault with men who were not trained for that sort of op was sheer, pig-headed stupidity. Sir."

"Master Chief, that is enough!" Weatherbee bellowed. "I am being more than patient with you, and I am taking into consideration both your excellent service record and the fact that you are the recipient of the Medal of Honor. But you are overextending yourself. We are *not* here to debate the merits of the Paitilla operation but, rather, to look at your actions since that time, actions that seem calculated to undermine the authority of a senior SEAL officer."

"It is not my intention to undermine anybody's authority, Admiral. I'm simply pointing out that it *is* my job to call attention to idiot mistakes being made by my superiors."

"Master Chief!" Driscoll shouted. "That is uncalled for!"

"Yes, sir. Sorry, sir."

"Mistakes are made in wartime," Weatherbee said, his voice calm. "In combat, victory goes to the side that makes the fewest blunders. That is a basic axiom of war."

"Yes, sir. And it is our responsibility to keep our side's blunders to a minimum, I would think."

"*Don't* interrupt me. What I wish to address this afternoon has nothing to do with Paitilla. It does have to do with your undermining a superior officer's authority. That is an extremely serious offense, as I'm sure you are well aware. It *could* be a court-martial offense. It is my hope to settle this without recourse to legal procedures, however, especially in light of your record."

All of which meant either that they didn't want the bad publicity of court-martialing a Medal of Honor winner or that they didn't want the public to know just how badly screwed up the Punta Paitilla operation was . . . information that would become public should he be charged and brought to trial.

"Thank you, sir," he said.

"In fact, Master Chief," Weatherbee said, "I'm not that concerned about the booing incident. You were one of several hundred men, after all. What I am trying to establish is whether or not you have some sort of personal vendetta against Commodore Sandoval. If you do, I assure you that the Navy, and the SEALs, have absolutely zero tolerance for that sort of thing. Do you read me?"

"Yes, sir." He took a breath. "Sir, to tell the truth, I *liked* Captain Sandoval. He was a good man, and he stood up for me when I needed it."

"Meaning your contretemps with Colonel Hoyt, one of the Army's action officers in the Canal Zone. I am aware of that."

"Then you must be aware that Captain Sandoval intervened on my behalf. I have no reason to dislike him personally."

"Good." Weatherbee reached into a manila folder and extracted a document—several pages of computer printout. "I wonder if you recognize this?"

Greg couldn't see the heading, but he was sure he knew what it was. "Yes, sir."

"Five days ago, immediately after your return from Little Creek, you wrote this, this *epistle*, and sent it up the chain of command."

"Yes, sir."

"Your letter has been creating quite a stir."

"Sir," Captain Scott said.

"What?"

"I concurred with that letter and everything in it. It was I who passed it on up from my desk to yours."

"I know that, Captain. I am, in fact, grateful for bringing

this thing to my attention." Weatherbee looked back at Greg. "Are you aware of how seriously you have challenged naval command authority and the chain of command in this document?"

"It was my intention, sir, to make clear within the SEAL community and the chain of command that mistakes were being made, that mistakes were being covered up, and that these policies were detrimental to the Teams, to the U.S. military, and to the United States. Sir."

"Bullshit. A noncommissioned officer does not discuss policy. Understand me?"

"Yes, sir. I was not aware that I had done so."

"Commander Driscoll."

"Yes, sir."

He handed Driscoll the sheaf of papers. "Would you read this, please? Aloud."

"Yessir. Ah, the letter is addressed to the commander of SEAL Team Three, to the commander of Naval Special War Group One, and to the commander of Naval Special Warfare Command, as well as to SEAL Command of U.S. Special Operations Command, at Fort Bragg. It is dated 7 January 1990 and is titled 'Accountability for the Deployment of Special Warfare Personnel in Combat.'"

Driscoll cleared his throat, then began reading.

Throughout the history of naval Special Warfare, our community has won a reputation for being able to operate well within unique combat environments, a reputation that is very well deserved. We are trained to enter those combat environments, carry out complex and dangerous missions, and walk away from the operation with few or no friendly casualties. Many people now believe that Operation Just Cause, in Panama, has shattered that reputation. At Paitilla Airfield, on the night of 20 December 1989, elements of SEAL Team Four suffered a casualty rate of twenty-five percent, including four KIA. That is a far higher casualty rate than is typically suffered by ordinary ground troops.

It is widely believed that much of the responsibility for these casualties lies with a so-called "army green mentality" that is being forced upon those officers overseeing the development and execution of naval doctrine. It is also widely believed that "special operations forces," including the Army's Green Berets, Delta Force, and Rangers, and the Navy SEALs, are typically and routinely given the most difficult tasks in modern combat situations.

This is, simply stated, not true. From the very beginning of our training, we are taught that we plan and operate to win. It is part of our training and part of our heritage to acknowledge both the need to fight again another day and that we are not trained to make headlong charges against enemy bunkers.

Unfortunately, there appears to be a new philosophy emerging among those of our leaders who have never themselves been in combat or who are unfamiliar with special operations. This philosophy has been seeping down through the chain of command to infect even combat-experienced officers who, frankly, should know better. This philosophy states that we are expendable and that our training enables us to take on the very toughest combat scenarios, scenarios in which we would not dare send in ordinary soldiers.

In fact, exactly the opposite is true. Because we are better trained and more experienced in operating under difficult conditions or in dangerous combat situations, it is imperative that we plan and carry out our missions in such a way that we preserve such high-value personnel.

Reviewing the mission carried out against Punta Paitilla Airfield during Operation Just Cause, it is clear to the most casual observer that our leaders delivered SEALs on the ground into an unfair role, one in which high casualties were almost certain, and where the possibility of mission failure was quite high.

The SEAL objective at Paitilla Airfield was to prevent General Noriega from using his private aircraft to flee the country, nothing more involved than that. This could have been easily and economically carried out by a minimal number of SEALs, using some of the advanced weaponry and technology that we have been developing and procuring—at great expense—over the past decade. Specifically, a sniper team situated in a nearby high-rise building could have disabled Noriega's plane without giving away their position, without attracting attention, and without risking undue casualties.

Instead, the SEAL leadership in Panama sent in too many men, men not accustomed to working in such large units, and they sent them in against a heavily defended objective when it was absolutely unnecessary to do so. These leaders must be held accountable for their decision to employ their men in a capacity for which those men were not trained, equipped, or properly supported. They must not be allowed to lead the fine young men who comprise our Teams into such costly and completely unwarranted situations ever again.

Gentlemen, we must learn from our mistakes, and we must learn from the costly blunder at Paitilla and not allow that operation or its consequences to be hidden away by a cover-up within our community. We must adapt our training programs to emphasize the

*fact that most objectives can be met without loss of
life. We must emphasize throughout our community
and in our relations with other military branches that
the planning and execution of our missions are based
on solid common sense and that it takes into account
the value of our personnel. The Navy spends an estimated $80,000 training each new SEAL. We cannot
squander these resources.*

*More important, we cannot allow what amount to
intra-service political considerations or internal politics to dictate our mission planning or to place the
lives of our men at needless risk. To do so is crimi-
nally irresponsible and violates the covenant of mu-
tual trust between both enlisted and commissioned
SEAL personnel in the field and the men who give
them their orders. . . .*

"That's enough, Commander," Admiral Weatherbee
said. He'd been leaning back in the office chair, eyes
closed, listening, as Driscoll read the letter. "Master Chief,
those are extremely strong words."

"No, sir. I don't think they're strong enough."

"Halstead," Weatherbee said, with the air of someone
who has been patient but who is fast becoming exasperated,
"you do not know what the hell you are talking about. The
operation at Paitilla was meticulously planned and orchestrated. Our intelligence was excellent.

"In short, the Paitilla operation was good. It was well executed and resulted in the successful completion of the mission. While the team suffered casualties in combat, they
were not the only casualties suffered in Operation Just
Cause. For your information, special forces carried out a
wide variety of missions during Just Cause. In addition to
some five hundred naval personnel, including the SEALs,
there were over twenty-eight hundred Army special forces

personnel involved, including three battalions of Rangers, and a Delta Force operation to rescue an American citizen held at a Panamanian prison. All of these men were given dangerous assignments, which they carried out with one hundred percent success. The dangerous nature of their missions is actually belied by the low number of casualties—eleven killed, total, and 129 wounded. Considering the full scope of Just Cause, it is astonishing that casualties among special warfare forces were that light.

"You don't know the first damned thing about the planning and intelligence that went into this operation, and here you are writing letters to everybody you can think of. I remind you, Halstead, that enlisted men—even master chiefs—do *not* set policy, do *not* establish doctrine, do *not* question the decisions of their superiors, do *not* undermine the authority of those superior officers through gossip, innuendo, or hate mail, and they do *not* stab their brother SEALs in the back with malicious crap like this. Am I making myself clear?"

"Yes, sir. Crystal clear, sir."

"You do not name either Commodore Sandoval or myself in this document. You are very, *very* fortunate that you did not. If you had named names, I would be forced to order the convening of a general court-martial, charging you with insubordination and conduct prejudicial to good order and discipline.

"You are also extremely fortunate that Captain Scott, here, has intervened on your behalf. He has told me, at some length, in fact, that you were operating within the purview of your orders. I have a different interpretation of those orders. You were expected, as Team Three's liaison with the Panama operation, to observe the implementation of operational orders, *not* to criticize them.

"Now, it has come to my attention that there were quite a few irregularities in your conduct prior to, during, and since the outbreak of the war. I am informed that, among other possible charges, you were involved in an incident with Panamanian defense forces during which shots were fired, and after which the Army was required to enter civilian territory to recover you, presumably before the incident escalated into open warfare. I am informed that you and other SEAL personnel took part in an unauthorized and highly illegal military operation against elements of the Panamanian defense forces on behalf of Panamanian civilians, that shots were fired, and casualties were inflicted on PDF soldiers and foreign nationals . . . specifically Cuban nationals operating under diplomatic immunity. And I am informed that you demonstrated insubordinate behavior toward a senior officer of the United States Army.

"I also find that, once the war had actually begun, you took part in a SEAL Team operation in a . . . well, let's say a highly unorthodox manner. You were still assigned to Team Three and had no business joining a mission being carried out by Team Two.

"And, finally, after the conclusion of hostilities, you have engaged in insubordinate behavior directed against a senior-ranking officer of the U.S. Navy and have written letters to members of the chain of command blatantly criticizing the leadership of the naval Special Warfare community for errors in judgment and—your words, Master Chief—for criminal irresponsibility."

"Yes, sir." He didn't add the question he most wanted to throw at Weatherbee. *What's your damned point?*

"Essentially, Halstead," he said almost as though he'd heard the unspoken question, "we want your guarantee that this inappropriate behavior is going to stop. Now."

"Admiral," Halstead replied, looking the man straight in the eye. "I stand behind that letter, and everything I said in it. My concern, my only concern here, is the good of the Teams. What's happening within the SEAL community, within the SEAL leadership, is weakening the Teams. If we let Paitilla be swept under the rug, we're setting ourselves up for an even worse disaster later on. Damn it, sir, we're guaranteeing that more of our good, young men are going to become casualties of war . . . no, casualties of idiocy. They're going to die for no good reason, and that could destroy everything we've created within the Teams."

"I hear your concern. Now hear mine. This letter undermines the authority of your superior officers, and it undercuts the entire special warfare chain of command. You *will* write an apology and a retraction. You will *not* write such a letter again." He patted the service record in front of him. "Believe me, son, we have way more than we need to hang you from the nearest mainmast. I do not wish to exercise the option of a general court . . . but I will do so if you make it necessary. Count on that!"

Greg hesitated for a long moment. *Damn* them all! They were going to make him eat the proverbial crow, and they were going to insist that he like it.

No. This was too important. . . .

"Greg," Captain Scott said. "Give them what they want. I'll make that an order if I have to."

"Sir, this is not right!"

"And what are you going to prove if they drum you out of the Navy? Or put you in prison for three years? They could do that. And they will."

"They don't want this story going into a court record, Captain. They don't want Paitilla to become general knowledge!"

"Is that a threat, Master Chief?" Weatherbee wanted to know.

"No, sir. It is a statement of very simple fact."

"Well let me give you a simple statement of fact. If you fight this, you will lose." He spread his hands. "You think I'm the ogre, here, but believe me, even an admiral can be made into a messenger. I have my orders in this regard. And now, so do you."

I was just following orders!

"I'll write the apology, Admiral. I will not retract what I said, however. What I said was the truth as I see it, as I understand it."

Weatherbee considered this a moment.

"Have the apology on my desk at zero-eight hundred tomorrow morning. We'll see about the rest."

"Aye, aye, sir."

"Dismissed!"

He came to attention, then turned to leave.

"Oh . . . Halstead?"

"Yes, Admiral?"

"I gather your son just started BUD/S."

"Yes, sir. Class 9001."

"Congratulations. I know he'll be a credit to the Teams."

And Greg walked away from the naval Special Warfare Command headquarters wondering if he'd just been given a subtle threat.

Chapter 11

4 February 1990

BM/S class 9001
U.S. Navy Amphibious Training Center
Coronado, California
0001 hours

The lights came on, harshly, jarringly, impossibly bright.

"Aw*right* you tadpoles! *Outa* them racks! *Move-move-move!*"

A metal garbage can hurtled down the center of the barracks, clashing and clanging on the tile floor and careening off the concrete-block wall next door to the senior proctor's hutch. A couple of assistant instructors followed it down the aisle at a trot, one using a pair of garbage can lids as cymbals, the other smacking the steel uprights of bunk beds—"racks" in the Navy's vernacular—left and right.

"That's it! *No* more life of luxury. *No* more beauty sleep! *No* more lazy loafing! Hit the deck, you slimy-assed tadpoles! *Move-move-move-move-move!*"

"Now reveille, reveille, reveille" blared from the 1MC speaker mounted on the wall, adding to the cacophony. *"All hands on deck. Class Ninety-oh-one, commence Motivational Week. That is, commence Motivational Week."*

BM3 Mark Halstead had rolled out of the top bunk of his

rack and hit the cold deck barefoot almost with the first screamed order and was already tugging on his dungaree pants. He hadn't been asleep—not really. He'd hit the rack two hours earlier, all too aware that the next day would be the first day of "Motivational Week." His dad had told him all about BUD/S, of course, and he'd told him plenty, plenty about Hell Week.

Mark knew he would soon be desperately in need of rest, but he'd been too excited—and too damned scared—to sleep.

In the darkness outside the barracks windows, an explosion rocked the night, followed by the ear-hammering chatter of a machine gun. "Move-move-move-move!" an assistant instructor was screaming. "Outside! C'mon, you tadpoles! On the grinder! Fall-in-fall-in-fall-in!"

Through a banging, screaming, shrieking, clattering, booming chaos of noise, Mark crowded with the other SEAL recruits through the barracks door, chivvied along by the assistant instructors like sheep herded by yapping sheepdogs. Sleepy, dazed, half-dressed sheep. Most of the recruits wore nothing but their Navy-issue boxers and green T-shirts. The "grinder," the paved drill field behind the barracks, was bathed in harsh light from overhead poles.

More drill instructors awaited them as they tumbled out of the building. One stood by the door itself, casually holding an M-60 machine gun with a long belt of linked ammo trailing over his shoulder. He continued to blast away with the weapon, aiming into the sky. Another explosion went off nearby. Damn! Those were live charges! The concussion left Mark's ears ringing.

"Fall-in-fall-in-fall-in! Toe the line! Move-move-move-move-move!"

Mark had just reached the painted line on the grinder—he was among the first half-dozen to do so—when another class proctor bellowed, "Too slow! Too slow! Hit the deck! Gimme push-ups! Now-now-now!"

Most of the forty-eight recruits remaining in the class hadn't even reached the line, yet. Some were still coming out of the barracks, urged along by screams and imprecations, machine-gun fire and explosions. Mark dropped to the pavement and started doing push-ups, but before he'd done ten, Weyer, the chief drill instructor, was screaming again. "On your feet! On your feet! Fall in! Fall in!"

Except that other instructors were shouting contradictory orders. "Columns of two! Columns of two!" "Down on the deck! Gimme fifty!" "Fall in! Toe the line!" *"Hit the god-damn deck!"* *"Move-move-move-move-move!"*

In seconds, an already disorderly rout became total and complete chaos, and still the gunfire and explosions—some of them coming over the outside loudspeaker system now—shattered the quiet of the southern California night.

"The idea is to start you off with as good a simulation of warfare as they can manage," his dad had told him, during his last leave a year ago. That was when Mark had told him—and Mom—that he was going to join the Navy and he was going to be a SEAL. *"And they're good at it. Confusion. Shouting. Noise. Proctors running around screaming their heads off. Proctors in your face, screaming orders that don't make sense. Battle is total chaos, and they try to inflict as much of it on you as they possibly can."*

Mark had questioned his dad closely about Basic Underwater Demolition/SEAL training, or BUD/S, with special attention to Hell Week. He'd learned a lot and he thought he knew what to expect, but he wondered now if knowing what was coming was just going to make it harder to get through. Mark had always been high-strung, a worrier, and the anticipation, the sheer, raw anxiety of waiting for the hammer to hit, could be as wearing on him as the actual blow.

He stood at attention, now, his eyes fixed forward. One

thing that his father had told him about was now no longer in evidence—the Bell.

The Bell was a relic from the late '60s, a big, brass ship's bell mounted on a post next to the grinder for DORs, or "Drop On Request." Inscribed on the thing were the words, HE WHO RINGS THIS BELL WHILE COVERED SHALL PUSH OUT 54 BEFORE HE IS RECOVERED. The bell had been a gift from Class 54. If a tadpole had had enough, if he wanted to quit, all he needed to do was walk up to the post, place his feet in the big, green painted frog's feet on the pavement, ring the bell three times, and shout "I quit!" Nearby, against the barracks wall, would be a double line of trainee helmet liners, one for each man in the training platoon who'd already given up. During Hell Week, they made it real easy to quit, assigning a couple of tadpoles to "run the Bell" with the class everywhere it went, a constant reminder that any recruit was just that far away from a hot shower, dry clothes, hot food, and eight blissfully uninterrupted hours of blessed, blessed sleep.

It was a nice touch, he thought, a final bit of psychological torture added to the week from Hell.

It was also by now something of a legend within the Teams, a mark of pride among those recruits who toughed it out and stayed the course.

But the Bell was gone, and there'd been no explanation. He wondered what had become of it. Scuttlebutt within the training platoon had it that they—the mysterious "they" who dictated every aspect of a recruit's life—had opted to get rid of it.

Well, there would be plenty of opportunities for the quitters to quit. The Teams were famous—perhaps *infamous* was the better word—for having the toughest training course in the world. The average dropout rate was something like 60 percent. Class 9001 had started out four weeks ago with seventy-five recruits. So far, twenty had flunked out, missed making their quals, or simply given up. Five had been "rolled over" to a following class, and two more had been dropped for injuries sustained in training—a sprained ankle and a broken wrist.

Some classes had reached graduation with only 5 percent of the recruits remaining, and one well-remembered class, number 78, had evaporated completely along the way, graduating no one at all.

But the idea was that since combat was the toughest experience men could face, the training had to be as tough as human ingenuity could make it. If the program was hard on recruits, if it had impossibly high levels of attrition, if it was goddamned unfair, so be it. The program's strength lay in the fact that those who graduated knew they'd been through hell, knew that the men they served with, that even the officers leading them, all had been through that same hell as they. It was a philosophy that had stood the SEAL Teams in good stead since 1962 and the Navy UDTs for another twenty years before that.

Get rid of the Bell? The emblem of just how tough BUD/S was? The Bell, hated by SEAL recruits, was beloved by the SEAL community at large.

What the hell were they thinking of?

"Form up! Form up! Column of twos! Sound off! Hoo-yah!"

"Hoo-yah!" The SEAL war cry echoed off the surrounding buildings.

"Boat crews, man your boats! Double time! Forrard . . . *harch!*"

Somehow, the proctors had managed to bully, shove, and nag the SEAL recruits into line and had them setting off now at a steady jog, off the grinder. Their boats—their "rubber ducks"—rested in racks nearby.

Each BUD/S class was divided into seven-man boat crews. Each crew had its own rubber duck, a twelve-foot inflatable raft properly known as a Combat Rubber Raiding Craft, or CRRC, or alternatively as an Inflatable Boat, Small, or IBS. One rubber duck could carry seven SEALs and a thousand pounds of equipment, propelled by oars or by a 7.5 horsepower outboard motor mounted aft.

Each boat crew was fully responsible for its own duck . . . which meant they carried it with them everywhere, cleaned it, cared for it, and posted one of their number as a guard at all times. Drill instructors liked nothing more than to discover an untended, unguarded rubber duck, and some of them possessed absolutely malicious senses of humor. . . .

"Boat crews! Raise your boats!"

"Hoo-*yah!*"

Mark was assigned to Boat Crew Five. He stepped in with the others in his crew, heaving the thing into position overhead. A rubber duck, fully equipped except for the motor, weighed 289 pounds. That is, it weighed 289 pounds when it wasn't filled with water . . . or sand . . . or with a proctor standing in it, bellowing imprecations at the recruits trying to keep it up and balanced. This time, though, they were carrying just the boats, without passengers or cargo . . . and a good thing, too, since they were now required to run through sand and darkness, through the dunes and down the beach to the ocean, all the while holding the CRRCs above their heads. If they'd been carrying instructors as well, more than one would have stumbled and put their instructor overboard, and God help the crew that committed such a sin!

One boat crew, Number Three, currently had only six men, which put them at a disadvantage in competitive boat events. But this was BUD/S, and as they frequently heard, "The only *easy* day was *yesterday!*"

No excuses allowed.

"Move-move-move, you maggots! You think we have all day? Now beach your boats! Into the water! *Move-move-move-move-move!*"

Mark allowed the flood of orders to sweep over him, riding them out, obeying what he could, enduring the name-calling and derision when he missed. After carrying their rubber boats down to the water's edge, they were required to leave the boats behind and charge out into the rolling surf.

"Okay, maggots! About face! Fall in line!"

In water up to their waists, with two-foot rollers surging past them, the BUD/S recruits stood in a ragged line, trying to maintain formation as the water shoved and buffeted them with each crashing wave. Mark stood at attention with the others, soaking wet, now. The stars were bright and cold in the night sky, the drill instructors only dimly visible on the beach. The water was cold—a near-constant fifty-five degrees all year, not cold enough to induce hypothermia but chilly enough to leach the strength from muscle and bone.

"Let me hear you sing!" boomed from the beach. "The water is my friend!"

"The water is my friend!" the recruits chorused back.

"Again!"

"The water is my friend!"

"Again!"

"The water is my friend!"

"Awright! Hit the beach! Move it! Move it! I do *not* have all day!"

When they scrambled back onto the beach, the night breeze chilled worse than the water. After a few hours of this, in and out of the ocean, hypothermia *would* set in, leaving the recruits miserable and shaking, teeth chattering.

Yeah, Dad had warned him about that, too.

"O-*kay,* tadpoles! Let's have us some sugar cookies!" Weyer, Mark thought, was positively in his glory, striding about the beach, hands on hips, his crookedly malevolent grin, invisible in the darkness now, still very evident in his voice. "Down on the deck! Now! Now! Now roll . . . *roll!* Let's make some sugar cookies!"

Wet recruits rolling in the sand resulted in wet recruits thoroughly encrusted with sand, "sugar cookies" in BUD/S terms. Suddenly, each and every move chafed and rasped and burned as sand collected in every crevice, at every joint, beneath every fold of skin and proceeded to rub the victims raw.

"Boat crews! Man your boats!" And this time, there was an instructor or assistant proctor standing in each of the seven boats. The soaked and sand-covered tadpoles struggled to lift the boats over their heads, as their passengers yelled and fumed and belittled their every effort, all the while lurching from side to side in gleefully malicious attempts to unbalance the trainees and make them fall.

They started with a six-mile run.

Arms straining against the uneven weight and bulk of the CRRC above his head, Mark jogged across the sand in close formation with six other recruits. He couldn't see the stars any longer; they were blocked by the rubber raft overhead. He kept his eyes on the back of TM1 Walker, the recruit immediately in front of him, and kept jogging.

This is what you signed on for. . . . This is what you signed on for. . . .

The words, repeated over and over and over in his head, the emphasis of a left foot hitting the sand punctuating every other word, became a kind of cadence, steadying his run, measuring his pace, lulling his mind into a place where he didn't need to think, didn't need to feel.

This is what you signed on for. . . . This is what you signed on for. . . .

He was terrified of Hell Week. He'd always been terrified of it, terrified of the possibility of failure, of not having what it took. In part, of course, he didn't want to disappoint his father, though that particular motivation wasn't as strong as Mark himself had expected it to be. There could be no thought of actually *competing* with his father—not the

Medal of Honor winner who was something of a legend within the Teams. Mark loved his father but was also a bit in awe of him. If he could be even half as good as the elder Halstead, Mark thought, he'd be happy, and at the same time, he knew his father was already proud of him. If he got booted out of BUD/S, it would be a disappointment that he hadn't made it into the Teams like his dad, but not a crippling one.

No, it was his mother that he was concerned about, in a back-handed sort of way. His mother, who'd been dead-set against having two SEALs in the family, who'd separated from Dad because she didn't even want to have to worry about one. He'd overheard enough of the late-night discussions, the arguments, the outright shouting matches as he was growing up to know exactly where Wendy Halstead stood.

Yeah, she'd been upset enough that he'd insisted on joining the Navy. Why? There was no draft, with the Navy as an honorable alternative to the Army. Money was tight—it always was in a Navy enlisted family—but there were programs that would let him go to school. Was it some twisted notion of glory? Honor? A silly, adolescent desire to follow in Daddy's footsteps?

But when he'd announced that he'd applied for the SEAL candidate program—as he'd promised ever since he was a kid, in fact—she'd really hit the overhead. *"My God, Mark!"* she'd screamed at him, that last time home on leave. *"Why? Kids die just going through training! And then they die in hellhole countries all over the world, and they don't even tell the families where or how they died!"*

Mom was going through a rough time now. He hated like anything to add to her worries. But . . . well, he'd wanted to be a SEAL for as long as he could remember, ever since he and his best friend, Dave Tangretti, had played SEAL with their G.I. Joes as kids. They'd been how old, then? Six? Younger? At that point, he'd not even known what a SEAL *was,* but his father was one, and at the time, that had been enough.

Later, though, as he got older, he began to understand something of his father's pride at being the very best. Guys who made it through BUD/S had made it through the toughest military training program in the world. Man, that had to count for something.

And there was also that sense of belonging that his dad always talked about—knowing that your swim buddy, your commanding officer, and everyone else in your Team had been through the same training as you.

The same Hell Week experience.

With the split in his family and his feeling that he couldn't take sides, joining one against the other, he felt as if he needed a place where he really belonged.

In fact, he wasn't trying to join the Teams now so much because of his dad as he was because of Dave. David Tangretti, born fourteen months before Mark, had joined the Navy, completed Hospital Corps School, then gone on to the SEAL program and graduated from BUD/S seven months ago. In fact, he'd only just completed his six-month probationary period in December. And now he was a real-deal SEAL, complete with the coveted Budweiser, the gaudy SEAL Team badge worn on his chest.

It was as though Mark were completing a promise sworn and sealed in blood fifteen years ago, when he and David had gone to the beach at La Jolla and pretended to be frogmen, sneaking ashore on an enemy-held island. They would be SEALs together. Brothers in a larger fraternity.

Belonging.

The SEALs were family, family to one another, pulling for one another, always there for one another.

Yeah, he wanted to be a SEAL. Wanted it so bad he could taste it. Wanted it so bad he would complete the runs and the swims and the inhumanly rugged qualifying tests, would endure the sadistic drill instructors, would endure the sugar-cookie treatment and the asinine orders and the telephone-pole bench-presses and all of the nightmare indignity and maltreatment of Hell Week.

Because he *was* going to be a SEAL.

SEAL Training Facility
U.S. Navy Amphibious Training Center
Coronado, California
1515 hours

"Hey, Doc. How's it hangin'?"

HM3 David Tangretti grinned as he entered the proctor's hut, tucking his white hat into the waistband of his blue trousers. "Hanging to the left today, Carl. What's this? While the cat's away? . . ."

Yeoman 2nd Class Carl Evers was leaning far back in his chair with his Korfam shoes propped up on the desk, a mug of steaming coffee in his hand. Normally, the ancient IBM Selectric on the desk was clattering away beneath his fingertips. Today, though, the atmosphere was one of complete relaxation.

Evers laughed. "Hey, Hell Week is Swell Week, so far as the office staff is concerned. They won't be back until the wee hours tonight, if then!"

"Today's oh-one's first day of Hell Week?"

"Sure is. Weyer is running their poor little tadpole asses into the mud right now, and then stomping on them."

"It's good for them," David replied.

It hadn't been that long ago when he'd been out there on the grinder with sixty-some other tadpole recruits . . . or slopping about in the mud pits, or rolling in the surf and the sand of the Pacific, just over the dune line. He'd only just won his Budweiser, and he was still feeling a bit new to the whole SEAL fraternity, but he did know that he was one of those select few who'd actually made it all the way through BUD/S training.

He'd made Carl Evers's acquaintance just before he started his own SEAL training. Assigned to six months ward duty at the San Diego Naval Hospital after his graduation from corps school, he'd been detached from there for special duty at the Amphibious Warfare Center dispensary across the bay at Coronado. Yeoman Evers, assigned to the personnel office at the BUD/S facility, had made the periodic run over to the dispensary to pick up first aid supplies, and the two of them had become friends. He'd not been able to see much of him during BUD/S, of course; tadpoles weren't supposed to see *anybody* during training but their instructors.

"So plant yourself, Doc," Evers said. "Coffee? Help yourself."

"Sure. Thanks." He walked over to the small coffee mess in the corner of the office, plucked a Navy SEALs mug from a hook on the bulkhead, and poured himself a cup.

"So what can I do for you, Doc?" Evers asked as he sat down. "You making house calls?"

"Actually, I've got a buddy in Oh-one. Halstead. I was wondering how he was doing."

"Halstead. Halstead? Oh, yeah. I remember him. Sure, he's okay. Made all his quals. I think Weyer has it in for him, though."

"Yeah?" He took a sip from the mug. "Why?"

"His dad picked up the Medal of Honor in Vietnam. You know that?"

David nodded. His own father was a good friend of Greg Halstead, and the two families had been close for years.

"Well, shit. With his dad with an MOH, Mark Halstead could've gone to West Point, just like that—without a congressman's recommendation, which is the usual thing. Or

Annapolis. Or anything he damn well wanted. But he chose the SEALs."

"And that's a crime?"

"No, but I think Master Chief Weyer wants to make sure young Halstead doesn't get a free ride. You know, coasting in on his daddy's coattails. He's been riding the guy pretty hard."

David nodded. "Okay. Fair enough. But I'll be stopping by once in a while to check on him, okay?"

"Fine by me."

"Hey . . . can you fill me in on something?"

"If I can. Shoot."

"The Bell." He jerked his thumb over his shoulder. "I know they take it with them everywhere during Hell Week, but I don't even see the post it's usually on. Or the frog prints, or the helmet liners. Where'd they move it to, anyway?"

"What . . . that? Oh, they took it down."

"For Hell Week . . ."

"Nope. I mean they took it down. Retired it. They don't use it anymore."

"What?" David was on his feet. "Who took it down?"

"A slimy bunch of pantywaist pencil-necked bean-counter mommy's-boy wussies with admiral stripes, is who," a new voice growled at David's back.

"Chief Weyer!" Evers exploded from his chair, vacating the desk. "Sorry, Chief. Wasn't expecting you back."

David stood as well. Habit died hard. "Hello, Chief. Don't know if you remember me. I'm—"

"HM3 David Tangretti," Weyer said. He was tall, hard, and muscular, wearing shorts and the SEAL black instructor's T-shirt. Unlike the stereotypical Marine DI, he looked as if he'd been living in those clothes for a long time, and there was mud on his shins and tennis shoes. His eyes dropped to the heavy gold Budweiser on his blue uniform jumper. "Got pinned, I see."

"Five weeks ago, Chief."

Weyer advanced, gave David a light punch on the Bud-weiser, and—unexpectedly—grinned. David didn't remember *ever* seeing the guy smile. "Welcome aboard, son." He shook David's hand. "You're Team One now."

"Sure am."

"Good crew."

"Chief!" He couldn't hold back the outrage longer. "They . . . they took away the Bell?"

The smile vanished, and David felt the storm behind Weyer's gray eyes. "Yes, the sons of bitches. Seems the Bell represented unfair and poh-litically incorrect harassment of SEAL trainees. This is the *new* SEALs, the *modern* SEALs. Any tad—any *trainee* who wishes to DOR must first receive *counseling* in several successive interviews with petty officers and officers. He is given a chance to rest, to think, and to change his mind. Without prejudice on the part of his instructors or his classmates."

The rigid way he talked, the darkness in the eyes, spoke volumes about how Weyer actually felt.

"*Jesus,* Chief!"

"Yeah, we asked Him about it, but He couldn't do anything about it. There are . . . people in Washington who out-fucking-rank God."

"What are they doing? Trying to water down BUD/S?"

"In a word, son, yes. Seems some think that SEAL training was too sadistic, too unrelenting, and some of the poor trainees might actually have their *feelings* hurt. Fuck that!"

David blinked, startled. During BUD/S, David had always been amazed at Weyer's astonishing use of invective to belittle, shame, embarrass, humiliate, and above all *motivate* the trainees in his charge, and never once use a swear word. If he ever did swear, well . . .

Shit. He'd just heard Weyer use profanity twice, a sure sign that the apocalypse itself was imminent.

"We'll see how long it lasts," Weyer continued, his voice a growl. "When the Teams heard about that, there was a roar heard from Coronado to Iran. Damn it, the Bell is *tradition!*"

"You have no idea how close I came to ringing that damned thing, Chief."

Weyer's eyes narrowed, and he gave David a dark grin. "Oh, yes I do."

David believed him. Master Chief Weyer and his team of assistant proctors had seemed to know everything. They never seemed to sleep, never got tired, and were always, always, *always* in the tadpoles' weary and often mud-coated faces.

Especially during Hell Week.

"You didn't come down here to gripe about the Bell," Weyer observed.

"Nope. I've got a buddy in Class Oh-one. I wanted to check up on him."

"Who?"

"Halstead."

"He's hanging in there," Weyer said, nodding. Then he gave an evil grin. "'Course, it's only Day One of Hell Week. He's got a long, long way to go."

"The way I see it, Chief, if I could survive you, I'd bet money that he will."

"How much?"

It was David's turn to grin. "Now that would be counterproductive, Chief . . . giving you an incentive to make him quit!"

"Nah. It's my job to make them *all* want to quit. You know that. The ones that stick it despite my best and most loving efforts . . . *those* are SEALs."

"I hear you, Chief."

"So, want to come see?"

"Sure."

"Just let me get a quit-chit." He walked around behind his desk and began fishing through a drawer.

"Somebody folded?"

"*Two* somebodies folded. Couldn't take log PT any more."

"So, what do they do if they don't have a bell to ring?"

Weyer sighed. "They get to talk to Chief Jimenez, maybe get a shower and some sleep and some dry clothes. Have a chance to rethink this whole quitter thing."

"Shit. They can decide to keep going? Rejoin the class?"

"Hell, no. If they decide they want to be rough, tough SEALs after all, they get to roll over to the next class. They get to take Weeks One through Four all over again, and then they get another crack at Hell Week." He grinned. "And you can bet I won't let 'em forget they're quitters! C'mon."

Class 9001 was in the mud pit just beyond the dune line, pulling log PT. David well remembered the hours he'd spent in that filthy, stinking pit, drilling with logs until every muscle in his body was shrieking in protest.

Each boat crew lay in the mud, a creosote-soaked log the size of a telephone pole across their chests. Black-shirted proctors stalked among them, barking out numbers. "An' *one!* An' *two!* An' *one!* An' *two!* . . ." The trainees performed bench-press after bench-press by the numbers, hoisting the log high, then lowering it back to their chests.

David scanned the faces of the recruits, trying to spot Mark. Every face looked identical, however, completely masked by sticky gray mud. He could see eyes opening wide, then squinching shut with exertion, could see teeth bared in clenched rictus with each hoist of a log skyward . . . but he couldn't see Mark.

"Halstead's in Boat Crew Five," Weyer said. He pointed. "They drew Ol' Misery."

One of the logs was considerably larger than the others, and it was reserved for boat crews that had somehow failed to measure up, screwed up, or simply lost a race. Engraved in its side were the words MISERY LOVES COMPANY, which had led to its popular name, "Misery."

"What happened to them?"

"Someone tripped and fell . . . while the crew was engaged in a rubber duck race. Dumped Petty Officer Vosinski on his ass. So they're receiving special motivational encouragement."

"I only see five guys there."

"Yup. Both of the quitters were in Crew Five. Your buddy's still holding on, though. He's second from the left."

David squinted and shielded his eyes against the westering sun, trying to see. Shit. Even having Mark pointed out to him, he couldn't recognize his friend through the mud and the pain.

"So far, Halstead's doing great, I suppose," Weyer said. He almost sounded disappointed. "We'll see how he's doing by Tuesday . . . maybe Wednesday. That's when they start having the hallucinations."

"I remember," David said. "I remember too well."

Mark Halstead, he knew, was always the precise one, the one who needed to know the answers, the one who expected things to make sense. Beginning at midnight on Sunday and lasting through the following Friday, Hell Week was designed, among other things, to cause extreme sleep deprivation among the SEAL recruits. Though they were scheduled for two hours of sleep every night, they rarely got more than an hour or so of *uninterrupted* sleep, and some classes received a grand total of two or three hours sleep for the entire six days. By late on Tuesday, those mud-covered tadpoles down there would be so exhausted they would be seeing things, and none of what they were going through would make any sense at all. He knew well from personal experience how easily dedication and ideals could shrivel up and vanish when a man became tired enough.

He wondered if Mark would be able to hold out.

Chapter 12

6–7 February 1990

BUD/S class 9001
U.S. Navy Amphibious Training Center
Coronado, California
2240 hours

The tide was going out. The damned sadists had timed the exercise so that the BUD/S trainees would be trying to paddle back to shore against the outgoing tide.

Why do I want this? Why do I want this? He couldn't shake the words, the desperate cadence from his mind. He was too tired to think any more.

Mark Halstead squatted in the bottom of the CRRC, gripping a paddle and trying valiantly to match each of his strokes to the strokes of the other tadpoles in the raft. It felt as though he'd been crouching there for hours. The cramping muscles of his thighs burned like fire, while the rest of his body trembled at the ragged edge of uncontrollable quaking, a trembling born of the chilly water and brisk wind. The sky was achingly clear, the stars brilliant. A full moon gleamed high overhead, brilliantly illuminating the Strand in the distance. A glowing haze above the city of San Diego on the far side of Coronado backlit the amphibious base, providing a clear indicator of just how far they had to go . . . and of how little their back-breaking efforts were winning.

Why do I want this?

The exercise had begun simply enough—with the boat crews paddling straight out to sea from the Coronado Strand for an hour, then turning around and paddling back to the beach. For the past thirty minutes, ever since they'd turned the CRRC, it had felt as though they were making scarcely any headway at all.

And now he knew why. The tide had turned, and they were battling the ebb tide as well as exhaustion and cold.

How long had it been since he'd had any sleep? He honestly wasn't sure. Since he and the rest of Class 9001 had been rousted from their racks at just past midnight on Sunday morning, they'd been allowed brief rests, but never more than about twenty minutes or so of actual sleep. There'd been none at all from Sunday through Monday. He thought, *thought* they'd been allowed to sleep a bit sometime late Monday evening, but he honestly wasn't sure.

God. He'd never realized just how absolutely and indispensably precious simple sleep could be.

"You'd do better to swim back."

Huh? He blinked. Who'd spoken? That had sounded like a woman's voice. He could hear nothing now but the grunts and movements of the other men in the raft, the soft surge of the ocean, the hiss of the offshore breeze.

"Why don't you swim back?"

He looked to his left, over the side of the CRRC. A woman was swimming there, five yards off the port side of the raft, black-haired and bare-breasted. Somehow, the scales gleaming in the moonlight across her hips and buttocks, the flick of the fish's tail above the surface as she jackknifed and submerged, didn't surprise him. A mermaid. . . .

"Hey, did you fellas see that?" he asked. No one answered him, and he wondered if they'd all gone deaf. Then he wondered if he'd spoken aloud. He was having trouble getting his mouth to work, to say what he wanted to say, and he was willing to believe that he'd only thought he'd spoken.

A mermaid. Well, he wasn't going to swim ashore, that was for damned sure. His place was in the CRRC, paddling with his boat crew. He *couldn't* leave them behind, with only four men to fight this damned current into the beach. Besides, if he did, Weyer would have them all in the Pit again, pumping away at Misery. He was beginning to hate that log.

He stared at the water again, searching for his new friend. Nothing but moondance on the waves. Besides, he told himself groggily, there *were* no mermaids. At least, not in the SEALs. The Teams only accepted men. Women were not part of the club, even if they did have fish tails instead of legs. . . .

Several long moments passed before Mark realized what was happening. *Hallucinations,* he thought. *There are no mermaids. You're fucking* seeing *things!*

"Come on in, sailor! The water's great!"

He kept his eyes doggedly locked on the back on Jenkins, the man in front of him in the CRRC, and kept paddling.

There are no mermaids. . . .

It was well past midnight by the time the weary boat crew guided their CRRC through a hissing, tumbling surf just in front of the glowing lights of the Coronado Strand Hotel, several miles south of the BUD/S training facility. By day, this stretch of beach was the playground for guests of the hotel—bikini-clad sun worshippers, tourists in flower-print shirts, retired couples soaking up the San Diego sun. Training classes frequently found themselves running through the sand past the hotel's beach entrance, drawing stares and ribald comments from the watching civilians. At two in the morning, however, the beach was deserted, and a good thing, too. It meant that there were no civilians watching when the CRRC overbalanced in the surf and sent Mark and his four teammates flopping into the water.

Water blasted over Mark, sending him sprawling, driving the breath from his body. Picking himself up, he braced himself against the relentless tug of the water as it receded from the beach, then scrambled to grab hold of the CRRC before it could be swept away. Jenkins helped him hold the raft for a few dangerous moments . . . and then Colby, Anderson, and Minkoskowicz joined them, tugging the water-filled craft toward the shore. They reached the wet sand above the surf line and collapsed facedown, too tired to move.

"Where the hell have you miserable creatures *been?*" a voice boomed out of the moon-bright night. It was BM1 Walczewski, one of the class proctors. How in God's name had he known they would be coming ashore *here?*

Then he realized that the binocular-like device hanging from his neck was a set of starlight goggles. Walczewski had been watching them all the way in.

Where were the rest of the trainees? He couldn't see them. Either they'd already made it back . . . or they were so far out they were invisible from this stretch of moonlit beach. Other proctors would be watching them from the shore.

"Looks to me like you tadpoles need a lesson in boat maintenance!" Walczewski yelled. "Your rubber duck is a goddamn freakin' *mess!* Now fall in for sandblasting!"

Mark joined the other four in a chorus of groans. *Sandblasting!*

That was a special torture levied on wayward tadpoles. The five BUD/S recruits sat on the beach just below the high point of the incoming surf, legs spread toward the sea, hands grasping the cuffs of their utility trousers and holding them wide open. In a few minutes, the surging ocean had deposited a thick and gritty layer of cold, wet sand in every crevice, hollow, and fold of skin from the waist down.

"Awright, tadpoles! On your feet! Pick up that CRRC! Okay, now right *face!* Double time . . . *har!*"

It was, Mark thought with grim stoicism, a bit like wearing sandpaper underwear. No . . . worse, because the sand continued to work and rub and coat into the folds of tender skin in a way sandpaper never could. In seconds, all five men were rubbed raw, their crotches and the crevice between their buttocks searing like white fire, each jolting step blasting them with scraping, burning pain.

It was worse still, he knew, for those tadpoles who still wore their Navy-issue boxers. By this time in their BUD/S training, most recruits had learned not to wear the things under their fatigues. Boxers somehow managed to trap even more sand against the skin without affording the wearer any protection at all. Mark had stopped wearing his weeks ago, once he realized that his father *had* known, from personal experience, what he was talking about when discussing the sartorial choices available to the well-dressed SEAL recruit.

The run back to the training compound with the rubber duck hoisted above their heads was a mild one by BUD/S standards . . . only a couple of miles north along the silver strand. By this time, Mark was in a perpetual state of exhaustion, a dreamlike state that felt for all the world as though he'd somehow detached from his body and was carrying on through momentum alone. How much longer did he have to endure? What day was it? Since the beginning of Hell Week the days and nights had blended together into a blurred and unending succession of disjointed images and scattered memories.

And pain. *Lots* of pain. The disconnect from his body wasn't quite sharp enough to anesthetize the agony of muscles driven too far, of sand abrading his crotch, of knees and legs forced to carry him as far as he could possibly go . . . and then to carry him farther still.

And as bad as the pain might be, the mental torture was worse. All he needed to do was say "I quit," talk with the officers and petty officers who would discuss his decision with him and make sure that that was what he wanted most in the world . . . and then he would be out, out of the program, out of the pain, and into a hot shower followed by a soft and comfortable bunk. Knowing that he was that far from blissful and uninterrupted sleep was by far the most devilish torture of all.

Time blurred. Somehow, they'd made it back to the BUD/S compound, joined up with other tired and muddy tadpoles still straggling in from their rubber duck evolution, and jogged back down to the beach.

"So, are you girls tired yet?" Weyer shouted at them as they ran. "You want to stop and rest? Just give me the word and in half an hour you can be sawing logs like a fat and happy civilian. . . ."

Weyer had them all plop down on the sand. A fire was burning brightly on the beach, and Weyer walked among the recruits, hands on hips, talking to them about the joys of quitting. Walczewski held a boombox and at Weyer's signal, switched it on.

From the speakers came soft and gentle music.

Mark wasn't sure what it was . . . something New Age, he thought, with strings and woodwinds intertwining in meaningless but inexpressibly peaceful harmony. Elevator Muzak was more intense. This soporific melody was as gentle as a mother's lullaby and even more effective, especially on sleep-deprived tadpoles.

Mark sat with the others, letting the soft music wash over him, its tones mingling with the hiss and wash of the surf. Damn . . . this had to be a trick, but there was no defense, no way to keep his mind focused, no way to keep himself *here.* Almost before he knew it, Mark was dreaming, deep in REM sleep. His mother was there, arms folded, looking cross. He knew she was disappointed in him, hurt by his joining the Teams. Why did he keep on fighting for something that obviously hurt her so? Why? . . .

She was saying something to him . . . he couldn't quite make out the words. He leaned closer, listening . . .

"Aw-*right,* you slimy tadpoles! Enough damned lolly-gagging! Hit the water! *Move-move-move-move!*" Mark wasn't awake—not really—until he hit the water.

And the torture of being snatched from the dream was worse than a dozen long, hard runs on the sand.

San Diego Zoological Park
Balboa Drive
San Diego, California
1215 hours

"Why?" Wendy asked, the pain and the genuine confusion evident in her voice. "Why does Mark have to be a SEAL?"

Greg shook his head. They were strolling slowly through a favorite haunt of earlier, happier days, the sprawling expanse of the San Diego Zoo. A gibbon hooted, a weird, high-pitched ululation in the distance.

He was taking a long-deferred two-week stretch of leave in the wake of the Panama op, and she'd agreed at long last to see him again, to drive all the way down from San Francisco, where she'd moved, and meet here for another chance to talk through the yawning emotional chasm that sundered them. They both loved the San Diego Zoo, and in happier times had come here every chance they could. There'd been so much he wanted to talk with her about, and yet the conversation always turned back to this. "I can tell you why *I* became a SEAL," he said. "But all I can do is speak for myself. You'll have to ask Mark if you want his reasons. I imagine he's discovering a few of them right now."

"Why now?"

"Hell Week," he told her. "Or 'Motivational Week' as they prefer to call it nowadays. It makes you dig way down inside and find out exactly why you want to be a part of the Teams."

"What . . . is he trying to save the world or something?"

"I don't think so."

She didn't seem to have heard him. "There are so many ways to save the world. Why the damned SEALs?"

"I joined because I knew the Teams were the very best," he told her. "If I could make it into the SEALs, I could make it anywhere."

She gave him a cold, sidelong stare. "You were trying to prove yourself. Some kind of macho thing."

"No," he told her. "I don't think so. Well, maybe I was trying to prove something to myself, a little."

"And maybe you were just suffering from testosterone poisoning." She managed half a smile, then, "You know, I never took you for a knuckle-dragging choot thumper, Greg."

"Hey, not all SEALs are knuckle draggers, Wen. I think you must have us confused with the Marines."

Her mood sobered again. "I don't want Mark to be a SEAL, Greg. You know that."

"Ye-e-es," he said, drawing out the word. "But I don't have anything to do with that decision. He's a big boy now. He can make his own choices."

"Oh, give me a break! He's worshipped you since he was old enough to sit on your lap! You filled him so full of those gung-ho war stories, of course he'd want to follow in his daddy's footsteps!"

"*Gung-ho* is definitely the Marines, hon, not the SEALs."

"Don't patronize me, damn it! Do you have even the slightest idea what it was like for me, all those years? Never knowing when you were coming home? If you were coming home at all?"

Greg closed his eyes and sighed. It was a familiar argument, one played out countless times over the years. Damn it all, Wendy had known she was marrying a SEAL. Once, she'd supported him and his choice of career. But for the past ten years . . . no, more, ever since the covert op into Iran during the hostage crisis there. . . .

"Are we talking about my career now? Or Mark's?"

"Both, I guess. I don't know. I don't know anything, anymore. Damn it, Greg, I hate being this way."

I hate it too, Wen, he thought, but he carefully said nothing. Wendy had been going through some really rough patches lately and was on medication for depression.

He knew some of the story, of course, though Wendy didn't like to talk about it. Her father had died when she was little, and her stepfather had been an alcoholic and abusive, both emotionally and physically. Greg could only imagine what her life had been like when she was growing up, never knowing if, when he came home at all, it was going to be the happy, distant Daddy or the angry, drunken one.

About eight years earlier, Wendy had begun seeing a therapist, working her way through a morass of memories and of emotions. At first, it had been an on-again, off-again pursuit, but during the past eighteen months she'd been digging in hard, working with emotions attached to memories buried so deep she couldn't consciously access them. The way she described it, huge chunks of her life were simply . . . gone, memories blanked out as completely as though they'd never existed. The hell of it was that she could still feel the emotions attached to those vanished memories, emotions that could come bubbling out at the damnedest times or attached to the most inconsequential things in a storm far out of proportion to what had triggered them.

Greg was glad he had real-world enemies to face. You could drop a tango armed with an AK-47 with a tightly grouped triplet of rounds from an H&K, yell "clear," and move on. You could prepare ahead of time for the encounter with endless hours of practice in a team fun house, dodging through mock-ups of rooms and streets, capping pop-up wooden terrorists, holding your fire when the pop-up represented an unarmed civilian or a member of your team.

Wendy, he thought, had the tougher job, battling demons of mind and memory and emotion, and never knowing just what she was going to uncover next.

Unfortunately, understanding even a part of what she was going through didn't help when he was on the receiving end. It was like taking friendly fire—as deadly as the hostile variety, but you couldn't shoot back.

And sometimes, shooting back, in the metaphorical sense, was exactly what he had to do. The fights that had erupted from those sessions had led inexorably to their separation.

He loved her, damn it. He didn't want a divorce. But sometimes seeing her emotional torment was more than he could handle. Greg Halstead—BUD/S trained to work well under pressure, to endure long stints of wretched discomfort without moving or saying a word, to carry out missions under conditions that would quite simply destroy lesser-trained men—was not exactly well trained in dealing with his own emotional responses. Suppress them, yes. Override them, ignore them, or accept them and soldier on, yes. But *deal* with them?

If only it was as simple as accurately planting a three-round burst in a hostile target.

"What made you decide to become a SEAL?" Wendy asked at last.

"What do you mean? Nothing made me. It was a career path decision. A choice."

"Seems to me like a heck of a career choice. It's not like you can get a job as a SEAL once you're out of the service."

They were walking over the crest of the hill above the primate compound. The valley below was thick with trees—a forest of eucalyptus and palm that forcibly reminded Greg of the jungles of Panama . . . and of Vietnam, long ago.

"If you'll recall," Greg replied slowly, "I started out as an electronics technician. You know, 'ET.' A 'twidget.' " He grimaced. "Yeah, I could earn really big bucks with that as a civilian."

She heard the irony in his words. "So what's wrong with that? Do you know how hard it is to get a good electrician to come out to the house?"

"An ET is more than an electrician, hon. But that's not the point. I joined the Teams because, well, they gave me something more. A lot more. I . . . belonged."

"You *belonged?* That's a hell of a reason."

"Look, it's not like I can go back and change my mind!" he said, angry now. "And if I could, I wouldn't. The Teams are my *life,* damn it."

"Take it easy, Greg. I'm just trying to understand."

"Maybe it's not the sort of thing that outsiders can understand."

"Is that what I am? An outsider?"

"You're not a SEAL."

"I'm your wife."

"I know. But you'd still have to be a SEAL to see things the way I do."

"You just told me it was a career choice."

"Yeah. . . ."

"So it's a job. And you are *not* your job. What you do for a goddamn living doesn't determine who you are, okay? It doesn't determine your worth. It doesn't have anything to do with what you contribute to society. It's just what you happen to do to bring home a paycheck."

"The Teams are more than a paycheck, Wendy. I wouldn't be a SEAL if I didn't believe in what I'm doing."

"Hey, I create databases for an insurance company, okay? And I'm damned good at what I do. But that's not what I am!"

"I know that."

"So what's the big deal about being a frogman?"

Wendy was really starting to get under his skin now, with a relentless line of questioning that felt more like an attack than a meaningful communication. Maybe if he interjected some humor. . . .

"Mostly, I get to visit exotic foreign lands, meet interesting people, and kill them." He clapped his hands together, rubbing them vigorously. "I also like the part where I get to blow things up. That's important. I really like blowing things up."

"Come on, Greg! Be serious!"

"I am."

"No you're not! Being a SEAL isn't something you can take with you when you leave the Navy!"

"That's beside the point."

"No, it isn't! What is Mark going to do when he gets out? Blow things up? Kill people?"

"Wendy, there are a hell of a lot of reasons for joining the military that have nothing to do with the paycheck." He hesitated a moment, trying to put words to the thoughts, to the feelings. "Duty. Honor. Love of country. And, with the Teams, it's, well, I guess pride is as good a word as any. Pride at being the best of the very best."

She sighed. "Good old *esprit de corps.*" She reached out and touched his chest, just where he would wear his rack of service ribbons if he'd been in uniform. He was wearing civvies, now, but he understood the gesture. She'd done it often enough in times past when he was in uniform, almost as if, by touching them, she could feel what it was like to wear them. To earn them. She tapped a particular spot on his chest. "It's that damned little blue ribbon again, isn't it?"

The little blue ribbon. His Medal of Honor, won in the closing days of the Vietnam War, up in the DMZ. "What does that have to do with anything?"

"I don't know. Your gung-ho attitude, maybe." She grimaced. "Yes, I know that's a Marine term. Your 'hoo-yah' attitude?"

He smiled. "That's better."

"Anyway, it's part of why Mark worships you so. And a lot of the reason for why he wanted to be in the Teams."

"I don't think the medals have anything to do with it," he said. "If anything, it's the Budweiser." He tapped his own chest, a bit higher up, where he wore the gaudy trident-eagle-cutlass-pistol insignia of the Teams when in uniform. "Up here." He thought a moment, then tapped again, over his heart. "And here. That's what's important. The heart. The spirit. That's what makes a SEAL what he is. It's what gives him the oomph he needs to make it through BUD/S and be accepted as a member of the Teams."

"You're proud of him, aren't you?"

"I could not possibly be prouder."

"What if he doesn't finish the training?"

"He's my son. I'll still be proud." He smiled. "Remember, I served as an assistant instructor at Coronado for six months last year. I *know* what they put those kids through."

"And you went through it yourself, once."

"About a million years ago, yeah."

"And . . . you love it, don't you?"

"The SEALs? Hell, yeah."

"The SEALs, the Navy, all of it. You could have retired by now."

"Maybe," he replied. "But I didn't. They'll have to retire me at gunpoint after thirty."

He'd joined the Navy in the spring of 1967, beginning BUD/S a year later. And, yes, he'd had the chance to retire after twenty. He could have gotten out in 1987 and been drawing half pay, plus retirement bennies. He was forty-two. He could easily start a new career now, especially with the help of retirement pay.

But . . . damn it all. What would he do? Not what could he do, but what would he *want* to do?

In twenty-three years of naval service, all he'd ever wanted to be was a member of the Teams. . . .

"Seven more years and they kick me out, Wen," he added.

"Seven more years of running around in black Spandex and Kevlar playing commando," she said, angry. "Welcome to the nineteen-nineties, sailor," Wendy said. "The Soviets are gone. *Ffhhht!* No more Cold War. And Vietnam is ancient history. Do you understand? No more bad guys! What do they need SEALs for nowadays, anyway?"

"Hey, the Soviets might be gone, but that doesn't make the world a safer place. Quite the contrary, in fact. Used to be, us and the Russians were the two big kids on the block, squared off against each other, and we kept all the smaller kids in line, you know? We couldn't afford to let a small tiff between our allies and their allies expand into something bigger, not when something bigger might mean nuclear Armageddon. Now, it's just us . . . and all the little guys are going for each others' throats like wild dogs."

"So? Is America supposed to be the policeman for the whole world? If they want to fight, let them! We should stay out of their business."

"It's not that simple, Wen, and you know it."

"No! I don't! What the hell business did we have in Panama, anyway?"

He couldn't answer that one, not directly, anyway. He'd been thinking a lot about that very question, ever since his return from Panama. Yes, Noriega was a nut case, and he'd been dangerous . . . at least to his own people. And it was vital to U.S. interests to keep the Panama Canal open to shipping. But that wasn't an answer that would satisfy Wendy. It didn't really satisfy him. *Why* was the canal vital to American interests? Mostly for strategic military reasons that had to do with the U.S. as a global policeman again. And Noriega had been up to his bushy eyebrows in drug trafficking, obviously. But, frankly, the drugs were there because the demand was there. Shut down the cocaine conduit in Panama, and another would open someplace else. Too many *norteamericanos* were willing to pay and pay and pay to keep the drugs flowing.

Greg didn't like looking at the big picture in any case. He was just one man, after all, and the Teams, good as they were, were a tiny, tiny fraction of the totality of U.S. military might. What good *were* they in this new age, anyway?

For Greg, the answer lay more in the faces of those two Panamanians he'd helped rescue just before Just Cause went down. That had not been a situation amenable to a sortie by B-52s. Only a small, elite, highly trained and experienced commando unit could have executed that hostage rescue.

And while Greg couldn't prove it, he had the feeling that this brave, new world without the Soviets was going to offer plenty of opportunities for that type of operation, carried out by those kinds of men.

"The point isn't whether or not we were needed in Panama," he told her after a long and reflective silence. "The point is that Mark has made up his own mind about what he wants to do, and that's the way it should be. I would be just as proud of him if he'd decided to be a Franciscan monk . . . or a grocery store stock clerk. He's still our son, and he deserves our support. Whatever he decides to do."

"I know," she said. She was crying softly now. "I know. I just pray to God he doesn't make it through Hell Week."

9 February 1990

BUD/S class 9001
U.S. Navy Amphibious Training Center
Coronado, California
1230 hours

Exhaustion had blurred time into a meaningless jumble of events and exercises. Mark wasn't even sure what day it was. He thought they must be getting close to the end, but he couldn't really be sure.

Some of the exercises lately had seemed particularly meaningless. That letter-writing evolution this morning, for example. Had it been this morning? He thought so, but wasn't sure. They'd sat the surviving BUD/S tadpoles down at desks, passed out paper and pencils, and told them all to write a page telling exactly why they wanted to be SEALs. So far as the instructors were concerned, the whole thing was pretty academic, since none of this crop of tadpoles was going to make it. But . . . why did they want it so bad that they were willing to put up with this crap?

Mark at first had thought the order a simple one. Why did he want to be a SEAL? Easy! It was obvious! He wanted to be a SEAL because . . . because . . .

He knew he'd scrawled something on that paper, but he couldn't for the life of him remember exactly what. What bothered him most was that, while the desire to be a SEAL was still white hot in his mind, the only thing keeping him going right now, he was having a terrible time picking up on the reasoning behind the desire. He knew it had to do with duty, country, honor. He knew it had to do with being a member of the best of the best. But how to put that into words? He couldn't even find the thoughts.

Eventually, the proctors had collected the papers and they'd been run down to the beach for yet another long, cold swim.

Mark was sitting in the mud, now, completely coated head to foot with thick, black, reeking mud after repeatedly crawling through a stinking pit. Once, these crawls had been through the mudflats of the Tijuana River that, rumor had it, was an open sewer. After several BUD/S trainees had come down with various creeping awfuls, classes had begun using the much healthier slop to be found in San Diego Bay.

It still stank, it still clung to the body, it still left the trainees weak and shivering and miserable. Others were completing the crawl. All Mark could do was sit there in the mud, teeth chattering loudly. He was so cold . . . so cold . . . and so terribly close to giving up.

The thought of giving up had been growing more and more clear for him these past few days and endless nights. Hell, it wouldn't be such a bad thing, would it? What was the fucking *point* of going through this torture?

At the moment, the only thing keeping him from getting up and announcing that he'd quit was that he was just too freaking tired to move, or even speak.

"Now hear this!" blared from a speaker mounted on a pole above the pit. "Now hear this. Class 9001, secure from Hell Week. That is, secure from Hell Week."

It took almost a minute for the meaning behind those words to sink in. Secure from Hell Week? He'd . . . made it?

Other survivors of Hell Week sat around him, as dazed, as blank-faced as he. The proctors were wading in now and helping the recruits to their feet. Somehow, he rose, sham-bling into line, and then the ragged column of twos began the trudging march back to the barracks.

Back to the barracks! Hot showers . . . hot meals . . . and most of all, *most of fucking all,* a full night's uninterrupted sleep! In six days, he'd had a total of perhaps four hours' sleep, and never more than half an hour at a time.

Mark Halstead survived Motivational Week, but the celebration would come later.

Right now, the important thing, the *only* thing, was sleep.

Chapter 13

SEAL Desert Test Range
North of Niland, California
0315 hours

With a grinding hum of machinery, the tail ramp of the C-130 Hercules slowly ground open, admitting a blast of thin, cold air. The platoon of sixteen Navy SEALs had completed checking one another's gear—tightening buckles, examining connections, tugging at weapons and rucks to make sure they were properly secured—and were clustered together now at the top of the Herky-bird's ramp.

BM3 Mark Halstead stood with the others, tasting the dry, chill flow of oxygen through his face mask. The tail door yawned open on a cold, hard darkness, while the C-130's cargo deck was illuminated in a faint, red glow, a light identical to the light used on board submarines before a nighttime surfacing, and for the same reason. When they exited the aircraft in a few seconds, their eyes would be dark-adapted.

Nearby, weirdly lit in red, EM3 Tom Gannet caught his eye through his goggles and gave a jaunty thumbs-up. Gannet was another survivor of Class 9001, brash and loud, a football jock, but fast becoming a good friend. Mark grinned back, then remembered no one could see his face through his oxygen mask. He raised a hand in a casual wave instead.

"Jumpers, stand by," the voice of the Herky-bird's crew chief sounded in Mark's radio headset. "Thirty seconds!"

"Right, guys," added the voice of the platoon's wheel, Lieutenant Ivan Maslowsky. "You heard the man. We go out tight. Stay together. Watch your altimeters. I want every one of you to pop your chute at three thousand feet. *No* heroics. *No* show-offs. I will *not* tolerate that kind of cowboy shit in my platoon. Do you all mark me?"

"Yes, sir!" the platoon shouted back, in chorus.

"Are you with me?"

"Hoo-*yah!*"

"Okay! Platoon ready!"

"Ten seconds," the crew chief's voice warned.

Mark tensed, ready to roll. He felt the dark-clad bodies around him more than he saw them. He could sense their excitement—and, yes, their fear. This was the first group nighttime HALO many of them, including Mark, had experienced.

The training, he thought. *It never stops.*

They'd hammered that particular lesson into his brain throughout BUD/S, right up there with "The only easy day was yesterday." Technically, Mark had completed BUD/S. But he wasn't yet a *real* SEAL. Not quite.

"Green light!" the crew chief yelled. "Go!"

"*Go-go-go-go!*" Lieutenant Maslowsky added, and the SEALs raced together down the sloping ramp, booted feet clanging on ribbed metal, and flung themselves as one into the predawn darkness of the night sky high above the California desert.

The cold wind, thin at 27,000 feet, blasted at Mark's body, plucking at his heavy coveralls and equipment satchels, threatening to tumble him. Arms spread wide, he arched his back and rode the wind, free-falling toward the desert five miles below.

The op was a HALO training exercise—*HALO* for "High-Altitude/Low-Opening," an insertion technique requiring the SEALs to leap from the aircraft at such a high altitude an enemy on the ground couldn't even hear or see the plane, dropping in free-fall to open their chutes at low altitude—three thousand feet or lower. BUD/S might be over and done with, but the training relentlessly continued.

BUD/S training was divided into three phases. Phase One had lasted just nine weeks, with the memorable experience known as Hell Week coming in Week Five. After that, there'd been four more weeks of training in "hydrographic reconnaissance," as good old-fashioned beach surveys were known nowadays. He and the other survivors of Hell Week had been treated with a bit more respect by the instruction staff after Week Five, but the reconnaissance classes had still been supremely challenging physically, with lots of cold swims, muddy crawls, and wallowing in the pounding California surf. Class 9001, originally seventy-five strong, had numbered only forty-one by the end of Week Nine.

Next had come Phase Two, a seven-week stint of intensive training in all aspects of diving—learning about scuba, closed-circuit rebreathers, dive physiology, and all about the myriad things that could go wrong in underwater operations, from simple mistakes to equipment failure to nitrogen narcosis. There'd been less emphasis on the purely physical, much more on the academic skills, though they'd continued making long, long swims every day as they became familiar with the tools of the underwater aspect of their trade. By the end of Week Sixteen, Class 9001 had numbered thirty-three.

Phase Three had been the Demolitions/Recon/Land Warfare portion of the program, four weeks of classroom training in blowing things up, sneaking and peeking, and the tactics of small-unit combat, followed by five more weeks at the SEAL range on San Clemente Island, putting what they'd learned into practice. By this time, the SEAL recruits were a lot more confident of their abilities and were beginning to see the proverbial light at the end of their tunnel. They lost only four more men in this final phase, three of them due to injuries in training. All three had been rotated back to a following class, as soon as broken bones would permit.

Twenty-nine survivors, out of an original class of seventy-five, for an attrition rate of a little over 61 percent—almost two-thirds. That was actually pretty good, Mark thought. Everyone remembered the lesson of the vanished Class 78 and of other classes with attrition rates of 80 percent or more.

How much of that, he wondered, was due to the new way of handling recruit DORs? A kinder, gentler BUD/S, with the chance to talk things over with chiefs, officers, and counselors when you got discouraged. And no goddamned Bell.

Every SEAL in the Navy must be wondering by now if the new training routine was going to weaken the Teams in the long run.

Mark had acquired his father's feelings about BUD/S. Damn it, an elite force was supposed to be highly selective about the people it accepted. SEAL training was all about finding out who could take the punishment and keep on going, and who was going to drop out along the way. Now that he was successfully through Basic Underwater Demolition/SEAL training, Mark could afford the somewhat smug and superior attitude that said, "*I* made it through when getting through meant something. Why make it easier for the newbies?"

BUD/S kept out the riffraff, as the old hands liked to say.

Class 9001—what was left of it—had graduated on Friday 29 June, and from there they'd flown to Fort Benning, Georgia, to complete the Army's three-week airborne qualification course. The instructors there had done their best to keep things interesting for the SEALs, Rangers, and Marines in the class, but after BUD/S, those three weeks had felt like a genuine vacation.

A deadly vacation, if you weren't paying attention to what you were doing.

The roar of the wind filled his helmet; the intense cold clawed at him despite the protective layers of his jumpsuit. Above him, the stars shone impossibly clear and bright. Below, there was only an empty expanse of darkness, the ground far below invisible in the night, betraying its presence only by the absence of stars. He checked his altimeter. Twenty-one thousand, four hundred . . . and falling.

Mark had discovered he loved parachuting—the sheer, heady joy of free-fall, the adrenaline-pounding excitement of the leap into space, the light-headed relief after a successful landing. It was one area where he differed strongly from his dad. *"Parachuting in is a damned stupid way of inserting,"* the elder Halstead had told his son once. *"There are just too damned many ways for something to go wrong, for someone to get hurt or killed. If you're ever planning an op, you'll have to be real desperate to consider jumping in. If you're that desperate, you'd better rethink the whole thing and see if the mission is even worth the risk."*

To Mark's way of thinking, HALO jumps and their close cousins, HAHO—for High-Altitude/High-Opening jumps, allowing the operators to literally fly for miles to their target using a steerable MC-1 chute canopy—simply gave the Teams another string on their bow.

Besides, the SEALs were Sea, *Air* and Land. They had to bring the air component into the acronym somehow.

"The Leap Frogs are one thing," his dad had told him—

a reference to the SEAL parachuting team, that thrilled air-show audiences worldwide with impressive aerial maneuvers and apparently daredevil stunts. *"They're pretty and they're fun to watch. But, like they say, leaving a perfectly good airplane while it's still in flight is not a sane act. It can get you hurt. It can get you killed. Worst of all, it can alert the enemy and that could ruin your whole day. If you have a choice, go in on foot or go in wet."*

Nineteen thousand. Still so high he needed to breathe oxygen from the tank strapped to his belly, just beneath his reserve chute. It was a little eerie, falling through the night like this. He knew that there were fifteen other guys around him, but he couldn't see any of them. They'd dispersed slightly upon exiting the aircraft so that they wouldn't interfere with one another when they started popping canopies, and the vagaries of wind and random motion would have spread them out farther. The op, though, was to give them practice in making this sort of blind jump and—by following book and op plan with religious fervor—coming down more or less in a group.

But, except for the rush of the thin air around him, he fell in complete silence. In fact, it didn't *really* feel like he was falling. With legs and arms outstretched and back arched, it felt more like he was floating on a stiff breeze. Without any visual references, it would be easy to become confused, disoriented . . . or to lose track of where you were and fly straight into the ground at a *very* terminal velocity. Some newbies had done that in training. No one he knew, no one in his class . . . but the instructors had been sure to impress them all with stories, and even with films of a few gruesome finales.

Fifteen thousand. Almost three miles up.

Finally, after his three-week vacation in Georgia, he'd returned to Coronado, wearing the silver wings of a qualified military parachutist, and ready for assignment. He'd drawn

SEAL Team One, Bravo Company, Second Platoon. But that didn't mean he was a real-deal SEAL just yet. He would be on probation for the next six months, always with the knowledge that if things didn't work out, if he didn't meet his quals or toe the mark, if he simply didn't fit in with the team, he would be back in the fleet . . . an ordinary sailor once again.

After six months, he would get his Budweiser, the coveted emblem of a true SEAL. That would be . . . when? January. He was looking forward to that with a keen anticipation as sharp as anything he'd felt toward the conclusion of BUD/S.

Ten thousand.

Still nothing below but black. Their objective was supposed to be marked with chemical light sticks, but those wouldn't be visible from more than a few hundred feet away.

He rode the wind.

All too soon, it seemed, he checked his altimeter and noted that he was dropping through thirty-five hundred feet. He prepared himself, gripping the ripcord and keeping his eyes hard on the luminous dial of his altimeter. Thirty-three hundred . . . thirty-two hundred . . . thirty-one hundred . . . *now!*

He pulled hard on the ripcord and felt the canopy snaking out of the sack. The canopy unfolded . . . and then he felt the savage yank on chest, shoulders, and groin as his harness took the strain. For a dizzying moment, it felt as though he was going *backward,* rising back into the sky, but then the sensation vanished, replaced by the slow drift to earth beneath his chute.

Quickly, Mark went through the postdeployment checklist, tugging on his risers and pulling them apart to make sure they hadn't twisted during deployment. There were a number of possible dangers he needed to be concerned about—twisted risers; a "cigarette roll," where one side of the chute was curled under, robbing him of lift; a "Mae West," more properly known as a semi-inversion, where the canopy had twisted in the middle giving it the comical— and deadly—appearance of a gigantic brassiere; a blown gore or canopy panel; or an inadvertent landing on another SEAL's canopy.

He could barely make out the shape of the parachute canopy overhead—more by the way it blocked out the stars than anything else. What he could see looked okay. And he was still unaware of any other jumpers around him—no canopies to the side or below.

There was a particular chuting stunt performed by the Leap Frogs called "stacking," where one jumper deliberately rode down with his feet on the canopy of a second jumper below him. The maneuver was safe enough— though ten years earlier two SEALs had died when the top man had inadvertently cut loose from his harness and collapsed the canopy of the man below. Such a stunt would never be performed in training, however, and never *never* at night. Accidentally coming down on a buddy's chute was very bad form indeed, and might necessitate one or both jumpers yanking their harness releases and using their reserve chutes.

But he appeared clear. So far, so good. He pulled the lanyard at his side that fired off a chemical light stick attached to his gear. Not the preferred way to sneak up on a real enemy . . . but in training it saved lives. Magically, greenish-hued lights were coming on around him as other jumpers triggered their light sticks as well. Good. They were scattered all around, and with dispersal enough not to collide with one another.

Next he released his third-line gear bag, a rucksack attached to his harness by a long, canvas tether, and let it dangle beneath his feet.

Clinging to the risers, he concentrated on keeping the chute drifting straight and forward as well as down, keeping with the group. When his altimeter read fifty feet, he prepared for landing, extending his hands straight up, grasping a pair of risers with knuckles to the front; head up, eyes on the horizon—or, in this case, on where the horizon would be if he could see it; knees slightly bent, toes slightly pointed, so that he would come down on the balls of his feet; and just enough muscular tension in his legs to make sure that they wouldn't buckle when he hit and put most of the impact on his butt. Ass-first landings were a great way to break your tailbone or, worse, snap your spine.

In the last few seconds, he could finally see the ground, a faint blur in the darkness. It was enough for him to make sure he wasn't coming down on another jumper and to judge his forward momentum. If he was slipping forward too fast, he could still be killed on impact, parachute or no parachute.

He heard his third-line gear hit the ground with a heavy thud, and then a heartbeat later he hit as well, taking the shock in his legs, dropping and rolling as he'd been trained. The touchdown was actually gentle enough that he would have been able to walk it through, staying on his feet, but he was taking no chances, especially in the dark.

In another second, he was on his feet again, hauling in the risers and punching down the canopy, gathering the nylon up into as small a package as possible.

All around him, other SEALs were touching down as well, their positions marked by the jiggling glow of their chemical light sticks. In less than a minute, and in complete silence, all sixteen men had secured their parachutes, checked the area for hostiles, and gathered together for a quick head count.

All present. The men began stripping off their jump gear—reserve chutes and oxygen bottles, masks and jump helmets, and burying them all beneath a tarpaulin covered with sand. Within seconds, the platoon was transformed, from creatures who looked a little like space men in their heavy HALO jump gear, to black-clad raiders in full combat harness, watchcaps, Kevlar vests, and black camo paint smeared on their face. EM1 Hopkins unshipped his GPS, checking their position, while the rest of them readied their weapons. As usual, the SEALs were pretty eclectic in their weaponry tastes. Most popular was the H&K 5MD with integral sound suppressor, but Mark had chosen a folding-stock AK-47. The Russian-built weapon was rugged, light, and forgiving of mud, grit, and sand, features that endeared the weapon to Special Forces units everywhere.

The platoon waited silently while Hopkins completed a four-sight fix, then showed the result to Lieutenant Maslowsky. They needed to know exactly where they were before they made another move.

Hopkins's GPS was one of the latest of the new toys being issued now to special warfare forces, and it promised to be a very useful toy indeed. The size and shape of a brick, weighing less than three pounds, it was properly known as the Rockwell Collins AN/PSN-11 Portable Lightweight GPS Receiver, though the SEALs who'd used it tended to shorten that tongue twister to "plugger." The NAVISTAR Ground Positioning System included a constellation of twenty-four navigational satellites in orbit around the Earth. The handheld Magellan plugger could take a sight on any three satellites and automatically triangulate your position, guaranteed accurate to within one hundred meters. Get a lock on any four satellites, and you reduced your positional uncertainty to a footprint less than thirty-five meters across.

Not only did the little magic box calculate your position on the ground anywhere in the world with astonishing accuracy, it could keep track of routes already traveled, calculate routes to programmed objectives, give altitude and speed, store waypoints and other navigational information, and even key into aircraft targeting systems to help guide incoming missiles and smart bombs. The plugger promised to revolutionize the way battles were planned, organized, and fought.

Maslowsky studied the GPS, nodded, then pointed. Their objective—with its GPS coordinates already provided to the team while they were still en route—was *that* way, toward the southeast. Without a word, the platoon fell into a cross-country dispersal, moving like black and silent ghosts against the night.

The idea for this training op had been to demonstrate that they could come down as a tight group, without scattering themselves all over the California desert and as close to their first objective as possible. As it turned out, they'd missed that objective by less than a kilometer—a pretty decent score when you considered that they'd jumped from five miles up over a target they could not even see.

Mark felt a sharp thrill of excitement at that. *Damn, we're good!* Working together as a team . . . no, as a *Team,* the way they'd been trained . . . there was nothing like it.

As they approached the target, though, they could see the soft glow of light sticks against the darkness. Sometime earlier in the night, another C-135 had come low over the desert, tail ramp down. Parachutes had blossomed, tugging a pair of airdrop cargo pallets free of the transports and bringing them down to a hard but intact landing on the desert floor. The SEALs, taking nothing for granted, approached the two crated objects cautiously, watching for booby traps or enemy forces lying in ambush.

Nothing. So far, so good.

They began unshipping the cargo pallets' contents, a pair of DPVs.

The first time Mark had seen one of these vehicles, during a familiarization lecture in BUD/S Phase Three, he'd almost laughed out loud. The Desert Patrol Vehicle looked like nothing so much as a beefed-up dune buggy, a black OTR with a very bad attitude. Its 200-horsepower Volkswagen engine could send it skittering across the desert at eighty miles per hour or kick it from zero to thirty in four seconds flat. The big tires let it claw through soft sand or bounce high over dunes, rocks, and rugged terrain of all types. It had plenty of ground clearance, a large skid pan, and a rugged roll-bar cage, and outboard wire-mesh racks for carrying supplies or rescued personnel. The gas tank held twenty-one gallons, good for 210 miles of cruising, though that range could be boosted to a thousand miles or better with a hundred-gallon fuel bladder stowed onboard.

There were seats for three—two up front for commander and driver, a third seat elevated in the rear for the gunner. Standard weapons load-out included a .50 caliber M2 heavy machine gun, two light M60 machine guns, a Mark 19 grenade launcher, and a couple of AT-4 antiarmor rocket launchers mounted on the roll bar, plus whatever personal weapons the SEALs chose to bring along.

At the moment, these fast and ugly little machines were the sole property of SEAL Teams One and Three, which worked directly with Chenowyth Racing in El Cajon, California, to have the vehicles manufactured to spec, though the Army Green Berets had a version which they called the FAV, for Fast Attack Vehicle. You could carry three in a C-130 Hercules and either fly them into a friendly airfield or drop them on a cargo pallet. They were ideal for fast reconnaissance, long-range patrols, and especially for CSAR—pronounced "Caesar," an acronym standing for Combat Search and Rescue. In any war where downed friendly pilots needed to be rescued, something like the DPV could be invaluable.

The only real problem SEALs had with them was that the damned things couldn't swim.

It seemed a little strange that Navy SEALs would need such a vehicle, when their traditional element was the water. But ever since Vietnam, SEALs had been operating farther and farther inland. One SEAL, when asked what he was doing at a South Vietnamese village not far from the Cambodian border a hundred miles inland, had just grinned and patted the two canteens he wore on his belt. "As long as we've got our canteens, we're as close to water as we need to be," he'd said. Special Warfare strategists referred to it as the "greening" of the SEALs, tasking them with more and more missions that carried them far from shore.

And the odd little dune buggy certainly reinforced the idea of *Land* in the SEAL acronym of Sea, Air, and Land. If nothing else, they could get a small recon force of SEALs back to the water in one hell of a hurry, even if their mission had taken them a hundred miles inland.

The next part of the training exercise was going to be just plain fun. Six of the SEALs, including both Mark and Tom, would mount up in their dune buggies and set off across the desert toward the south, while the remaining ten SEALs would come along behind on foot. The DPVs would perform a night recon of a simulated enemy position in the foothills of the Chocolate Mountains.

A flare burst high in the night sky, burning a brilliant green as it slowly descended above the weirdly shifting shadows it cast. A tall figure seemed to rise out of nowhere, then yards away, and advance toward the SEAL platoon.

"Halt!" Tom Gannet called out. "Identify yourself!"

"Stand down, gentlemen," the shape called back. "This mission is terminated, Lieutenant Maslowsky."

"Here!" Maslowsky stood, eyeing the figure now silhouetted by the light of the dying flare. "What the hell is this? Who are you? What do you mean, terminated?"

"Lieutenant Commander Lake," the other said, identifying himself. "Group One. Team Three has just received a warning order. We're going on full alert."

"Group One" meant Naval Special Warfare Group One, the next step up the ladder of command for SEAL Team One. It was essentially the Coronado headquarters unit for Teams One, Three, and Five, for SDV Team One, and for the three units of Special Boat Squadron One.

"Yes, sir," Maslowsky said. "What the hell's going down?"

"Things have just hotted up in the Persian Gulf, gentlemen, big-time. Approximately fourteen hours ago, elements of the Iraqi Republican Guard crossed the border into Kuwait. Reports are still sketchy, but it is probable that they've already taken over the entire country. The National Command Authority is concerned that Iraq may not stop with Kuwait. Saddam may be interested in bigger fish."

Which meant Saudi Arabia.

Thanks to CNN and periodic briefings, all of the SEALs had been kept aware of recent developments in the Middle East—of Saddam Hussein's feud with tiny, neighboring Kuwait; of Saddam's rhetoric against Israel, the United States, and any and all Arab countries who continued to hold the cost of oil low at a time when Iraq was drowning in debt; and of intelligence reports that at least two crack Iraqi armored divisions were massing on the border north of Kuwait. There'd been plenty of barracks scuttlebutt about the possibility of a war over there, but most SEALs felt that Saddam was way too savvy a character to risk taking on the United States in a war he could not possibly win.

Maybe the guy was more desperate than savvy.

"Now we know why we've been doing all this desert training," TM Chief Connors said. "Someone knew we might be going to the gulf."

"Oh, and by the way, gentlemen," Lake told the group, "You're all dead."

Mark saw a trio of bright, red pinpoints of light dancing against Maslowsky's Kevlar vest. Looking down, he saw a couple of laser targeting dots on his chest as well. *Shit!* . . .

Silently, other shapes rose from the desert around them. Mark swallowed. Damn it, they'd *checked* the area! Where had these guys come from?

One of the shapes was grinning at Mark, the teeth startlingly white against black-painted skin in the faint light. He was wearing desert camo and a floppy, broad-brimmed hat; somehow, he'd made himself completely invisible against the desert floor. "Bang-bang!" the figure told Mark. "Got ya!"

"*David?*"

"Just like war games in the backyard when we were kids, huh?" HM3 David Tangretti was carrying a CAR-15/M203 with a laser targeting unit clipped to the sight block.

"Not quite. The toy guns are a lot neater. Shit, what are you doing out here?"

"Hunting for you guys, of course." The grin turned predatory. "We heard you coming all the way from the drop zone. Piece of cake!"

At least his friend's presence answered the question about these guys' identity. David was in Team One, Alpha Platoon.

"But we checked the area!"

"Hey, the training never stops, right? Welcome to STT! And the only easy day was *yesterday!*"

STT was SEAL Tactical Training, the program Mark and his classmates would be engaged in for most of the next six months while they won their tridents. It was a period of intensive practice of all the techniques they'd learned in BUD/S and at Fort Benning, putting together what they'd learned into a cohesive and deadly whole.

The two platoons began forming up for a march to an alternate recovery point, some four kilometers to the west, where a couple of trucks were waiting for them on the road. "What do you think, David?" Mark asked his friend as they buried their third-line gear and extra ammo for later pickup. They would be traveling light to the extraction point. "Are they going to use frogmen in the desert?"

"There'll certainly be a place for us in the gulf. All those islands, oil platforms, maybe reconning beaches for an amphib landing. Sure!"

"I was wondering more about using those dune buggies over there. Can't take one of them onto an oil platform."

"Ah. You want to joyride on the dunes, huh?"

"Well . . . sure! You can't show us cool toys like that and not expect us to want to play with them."

"Don't know, buddy. I guess that's up to the Powers That Be. Me, I'm just trusting in Shakespeare."

"Huh? What's Shakespeare have to do with it?"

David grinned. "Cry havoc!" he said. "And let slip the frogs of war!"

Mark groaned and shook his head. "Damn. Poor old Saddam isn't going to know what the hell hit him!"

Chapter 14

Advance SEAL base
Half Moon Bay
Dhahran, Saudi Arabia
1455 hours

Hoisting his seabag onto his shoulder, Master Chief Greg Halstead clanked down the off-loading ramp of the C-141 transport, stepping into a searing, 115-degree furnace.

The heat was staggering, a physical assault on the senses. The afternoon sun blazed in the west, intolerably brilliant in a deep, deep blue sky. The air above the runway shimmered and swam, making it difficult to tell whether the tarmac was real or illusion. A cluster of tents sprawled toward the metallic blue waters of the gulf in the east; elsewhere, there were only the endless dunes and chessboard-flat hardpan.

Other SEALs and naval personnel stepped off the ramp behind him. "Jesus freakin' *Christ!*" one man said. "Let's fry up some eggs, why don't we?"

"Can it, Weed," Lieutenant Russell, the platoon's CO, said. "It's too hot to listen to your bitching."

RM1 Weidenfeld dropped his seabag, resting it against his leg on the tarmac. "Too hot is right, Wheel. Think they got air conditioning in the barracks?"

"Sure, Weed," Greg said, pointing at the tents. "I'm sure the soft, gentle desert breezes blow right through the tent flaps. Cool you right off."

"Or you could take a swim in the Persian Gulf," GM1 Maskell said. "I gather it's a nice, cool, fifty-five degrees."

"I may take you up on that, Mask," Weidenfeld replied.

"Yeah, but watch your mouths, guys," RM2 Vickery said, laughing. "It's the *Arabian* Gulf now, not the Persian Gulf. 'Persian' means 'Iranian,' and the Saudis don't like it if you name their gulf for Iran!"

"Shit," Weidenfeld said. "There's other countries here than Arabia and Iran!"

"Sure," Chief Gunner's Mate Larry Drexler said, "but 'Arabian' doesn't mean just Saudi Arabia. Except for Iran, all of the countries bordering the gulf—Iraq, Kuwait, Saudi Arabia, Bahrain, the Emirates, they're all Arab, see? A Semitic people related to the Jews. Iranians aren't Arabs. They're Persians—Indo-Europeans. Ever since U.S. diplomacy out here tipped away from Iran and into the Arab camp, it's been the *Arabian* Gulf."

"You were here with Earnest Will, weren't you, Drex?" Greg asked.

Drexler nodded. "Yup. Eighty-seven."

"Shit, Master Chief," Maskell said. "He don't talk about it much, but Drex here took down the *Iran Ajr!*"

"All by his lonesome, huh?" Greg asked. The others laughed.

SEALs had been involved in the chaos of the gulf for several years now. Between 1987 and 1989, at the very end of Iraq's ten-year war of attrition with Iran, Navy SEALs had participated in a special operations task force deployed to stop the Iranians from seeding mines throughout the Persian Gulf waterway. The West knew that period as "the Tanker War," when Iran kept trying to close off the sea lanes to oil tanker traffic, in part to starve Iraq into submission. Several tankers leaving Iran's Kharg Island terminal had been hit by missiles, some launched from shoulder-fired launchers on speedboats. A U.S. frigate, the USS *Stark*, had been hit—apparently by mistake—by an Iraqi missile in May of 1987, and thirty-seven American sailors had been killed.

Iraq had immediately apologized, blaming Iran for the escalation of tensions in the region. The United States had responded by reflagging eleven tankers belonging to Kuwait in an effort to discourage further Iranian attacks. They'd also launched Earnest Will.

Operation Earnest Will lasted a total of two and a half years, during which hundreds of SEALs were rotated in and out of the region. Many were deployed aboard U.S. ships. Others, together with Army helicopters and Navy Special Boat Units, operated off of a pair of rented barges, patrolling the tanker lanes for mines and boarding and searching ships suspected of planting them. The best-known action of the deployment was in '87, when an Iranian ship, the *Iran Ajr*, was spotted laying mines. Army helicopters had opened fire on the vessel, which was then boarded by a SEAL VBSS team—a bit of mil-speak alphabet soup standing for "Visit, Board, Search, and Seizure." They'd captured the crew and sent the *Ajr* to the bottom. Drexler had been part of the *Ajr* VBSS unit.

"Let's see where we check in," Lieutenant Russell said.

"Roger that, sir," QM2 Cordy said. "We gotta get outa this fuckin' sun!"

"So stand in the shade, Cord," Drexler said. Most of the twenty SEALs in the group were standing in the shadow cast by the C-141's tail. None of them wanted to venture beyond the scant shelter of that bit of shade, even though it was furnace-hot. It was a lot hotter in the direct sun.

Unfortunately, the Starlifter's crew chief was waving them off from the invitingly cool, dark interior of the aircraft's cargo deck. The pilot was revving the C-141's four big turbofans, which had never entirely stopped after landing. Their source of shade was about to taxi off to the line of military transports visible off the runway to the north.

"Let's move, people," Russell said, hoisting the satchel he used instead of an enlisted man's seabag. As the Hercules's props revved up, dust and grit whirled about the little group of SEALs.

"I think we may have a ride," Greg said, pointing. A small convoy of Humvees was arrowing toward them from the base, sending up a rooster-tail plume of white-yellow dust. As the C-141 slowly taxied away, the SEALs started hiking toward the oncoming vehicles.

The lead hummer pulled up a few feet away, and a Navy chief in olive-drab utilities and a floppy hat—SEALs never called them "boonie hats"—climbed out. "Lieutenant Russell, sir?"

"That's me."

"Chief Morrison, sir." He had a soft, southern accent— Virginia, possibly, Greg thought. "Welcome to the Kingdom of Saudi Arabia, and NAVSPECWAR Task Group Central."

"Thank you. Is the weather always like this?"

"Nah. This here's just a little cold snap. It'll be warmer tomorrow."

Several of the men groaned. "Belay that," Russell said. "Where are we being billeted?"

"We'll take y'all over there right now, so you boys can get showered up and presentable and maybe grab a bite to eat. The Skipper's gonna want to talk to you, welcome you aboard and all that. He'll also want to talk to the guys assigned to Ops Staff right away."

Greg thought he detected a note of urgency in Morrison's voice on that last. "Is there a particular problem, Chief?"

"Problem? Hell, no, Master Chief. It's just that . . . well, see that horizon yonder?" He pointed to the northwest.

"Yeah."

"You go about three hundred kilometers up the coast in that direction. Know what you find?"

"Kuwait," Greg replied. He'd been memorizing maps of the region ever since his orders had come through a week ago.

"That's right. And you also find one hundred thousand of Saddam Hussein's best troops, camped out right on Kuwait's southern border, where they've been sittin' for the past nine days. And right here, now that you boys are here, we've got one hundred and five SEALs and ground support personnel.

"And right now, us hundred and five are the *only* combat force standing between Saddam's Republican Guard and the rest of Saudi Arabia."

"Shit!" Cordy said.

"Yup. Gives ya somethin' to think on, don't it?"

"How long is that going to be the case, Chief?" Russell asked.

"Shit, sir, your guess is as good as mine. Better prob'ly. President Bush can declare Operation Desert Shield and promise that we are absolutely committed to protecting Saudi Arabia and kicking Saddam the hell out of Kuwait, but it's gonna take time, a *lot* of time, to move the whole goddamn U.S. Army over here, M-1 tanks, Cobra gunships, and all. In the meantime, like it or not, we're it. *All* of it."

All of which Greg had heard already in briefings back in Coronado. No one was quite sure of Saddam's intentions, but the threat that he might not stop with tiny Kuwait, that he might keep rolling south to gobble up the Kingdom of the House of Saud, was very real, very credible. There were strategic planners back in Coronado, at Fort Bragg, and in the Pentagon who felt that Saddam's only target was Kuwait, that he would not risk inciting a major war by gobbling up Saudi Arabia as well. But there were plenty more, and Greg was among them, who thought that the man was just unbalanced enough to want to swallow everything from Kuwait to Oman. He had the most powerful, most deadly military force in the region, and Allah knew he had the motivation—hundreds of billions of dollars of debt incurred by ten disastrous years of war with Iran.

And if he *was* going to keep moving south, he'd be smart to jump the Kuwaiti border sooner rather than later, before the full might of the U.S. military machine could block his way.

Iraq's Saddam Hussein might be a psychopathic murderer, a bloody-handed dictator, and a deranged megalomaniac, but one thing he was *not* was stupid.

Greg gave a lot of thought to this as he checked himself into his quarters. Their barracks consisted of a half-dozen large tents with sleeping rolls, their shower a five-hundred-gallon tank on an eight-foot wooden tower, operated by yanking a handle on a chain. Chow was MREs—the "Meals, Ready to Eat" that veterans insisted embodied three lies in one.

Kuwait had been the obvious first target on Saddam's hit list. He had some long-standing disputes with that tiny, desert emirate, and there was a history of animosity there. Lately, Saddam had been publicizing the fact that Kuwait was actually an administrative district of Iraq called the Nineteenth Province. The border between Iraq and Kuwait had long been under dispute, and Iraq complained that two Kuwaiti islands, Warba and Bubiyan, were choking off the only access Iraqi oil tankers had between the port of Basra and the gulf beyond.

The real reasons for the cross-border animosities, though, had more to do with old-fashioned greed and jealousy than with the rarefied language of international disputes. The war between Iraq and Iran, which had ended with a cease-fire in 1988, had wrecked both nations. Determining a victor in that insanely bloody conflict was problematic, at best. Both nations were bankrupt. If there was a victor, it was—by the slimmest of margins—Iraq, solely because Saddam Hussein had emerged with a military stronger than ever, the preeminent military force in the entire region, while Iran's Revolutionary Army had been bled almost to death, a wan shadow of its former power. Perhaps a million people died on both sides, with twice that number crippled. The true human cost of that war—which had seen Iraq using nerve and mustard agents against Iranian human-wave attacks, carried out in some cases by children as young as nine roped together so they couldn't flee—would probably never be known.

Despite financial assistance from all over the world, including the United States, Iraq was on the verge of complete bankruptcy, despite its considerable oil reserves. Its oil industry, which accounted for almost two-thirds of Iraq's gross domestic product, had been crippled by Iranian bombings. Iraq was importing two-thirds of its food. The Iraqis owed the Russians billions for their weapons and technical support; they owed fifty billion on the world markets beyond the Arab states. And they owed close to two hundred billion dollars in loans from other Arab nations—especially Saudi Arabia and Kuwait—and those loans were far overdue, with the interest alone threatening to strangle Iraq's economy.

Desperate for currency, then, Baghdad had begun lashing out at its Arab neighbors to the south. Oil prices were currently at eleven dollars a barrel; Saddam wanted the price boosted to fifty-three dollars a barrel, a move that would send shock waves throughout the unsteady world economy and might even threaten OPEC itself. Kuwait, especially, was overproducing and driving down oil prices, a calculated plan by Kuwait's emir to help end the global recession that had gripped the world during the late eighties. There was a healthy dose of self-interest in that plan, of course; once the world economy was healthy, oil prices could rebound.

In addition, Kuwait, which alone had loaned Iraq one hundred billion dollars for its war effort against Iran, was demanding repayment in full. There were also charges by Iraq—and they might well have been true—that Kuwait was engaged in something called slant drilling, sending in their drills down and out at an angle to siphon off oil reserves that actually lay across the border, beneath Iraqi land. Baghdad claimed that the Kuwaitis had already stolen hundreds of billions of dollars of Iraqi oil and demanded restitution.

So Iraq's big beef at the moment was with Kuwait, a rich but tiny nation that alone was the source of a lot of Saddam's headaches. Greg could accept that he might well be satisfied with absorbing Kuwait, which had enormous oil reserves, easy access to the Arabian Gulf, and, well, if Kuwait suddenly became Iraq's Nineteenth Province, they wouldn't be demanding that hundred-billion-dollar loan repayment. Maybe they didn't need to move on to Saudi Arabia as well.

Greg wondered about that, however. A man with a passionate interest in history, especially military history, he was well aware that appeasement was not a healthy choice when it came to dealing with despots with a powerful military and a taste for conquest. *Could* Saddam stop with Kuwait, or would he need to keep on conquering?

Could Hitler have stopped with Austria and Czechoslovakia?

"What do you think, Drex?" he asked the other SEAL as they sat on lengths of steel tubing, eating their MREs. Greg had learned back in Vietnam that the cardboard-tasting rations could be made palatable with a liberal application of hot sauce, and he was industriously spreading packets of the stuff across his chicken and noodles. "Will Saddam stop with Kuwait?" He respected Chief Drexler's experience in the region. He seemed to understand the people.

"Real hard to tell, Greg," he replied. "I wish to hell I knew. I imagine Washington would like to know that right now, too."

"Well, if he controls Kuwait, his immediate financial problems are taken care of, right?"

"Yeah. Maybe."

"You don't sound convinced."

"Well, everybody thinks it's all about religion, oil, and money over here. It's not. Not really."

"Oh?"

"Those things are important, sure . . . but there's this damned, I don't know. A tribal mentality, I guess. The enemy of my enemy is my friend, and all that. Makes for some really twisted politics. The thing is, the Iraqis are insanely jealous of the Kuwaitis."

"How come?"

He sighed. "The yearly income for the average Iraqi is something less than one thousand dollars. The annual income for the average Kuwaiti is twenty-seven thousand dollars. The Iraqis look south, and they see indulgent, spoiled, and pampered playboys. There's a story going around that rich Kuwaitis on vacation in Egypt would rent horses and take them on mad, all-out runs around the base of the Great Pyramid until the poor animals' hearts literally burst. Then they'd toss a wad of cash at the guys who'd rented out the horses and walk off laughing."

"Shit."

"Yeah. Too much money, too few brains. Or maybe it's just too little maturity. I don't know.

"Anyway, most Iraqis think the Kuwaitis are spoiled rich kids."

"And the Kuwaitis?"

"They see the Iraqis as poor country cousins. You know. Trailer trash. Rude, stupid, ignorant louts. The kind of clod that would forget to wipe his feet when he came in, use his sleeve to blow his nose, and maybe make off with some of the silverware if you invited him home for dinner. Believe me, they both might be Arab countries, but there's no love lost between the two!"

"So, you think he'll be satisfied with humbling Kuwait? Maybe teach the playboys a lesson?"

Drex smiled. "You don't understand. The Saudis are even worse than the Kuwaitis. That much money tends to really twist people's heads around, you know? The only thing really protecting them is the fact that they're the care-takers of the two holiest spots in Islam, Mecca and Medina, and that gives them an awful lot of clout through the Arab world.

"Trouble is, Saddam Hussein and his Ba'athist Party aren't exactly religious fanatics. Oh, they use the guise of Islam, sure, but in fact they're about as secular as they come. I wouldn't be a damned bit surprised if Saddam just decided to take them all out, Kuwait, Saudi Arabia, all of them. It would make him the protector of the Islamic holy places and give him a power base that the rest of the Muslim world couldn't really challenge."

"Could he take them all on?"

"Are you kidding? The Saudis field an army of 73,000 on paper. And from what I've seen here so far, they're pathetic. Maybe seven hundred Main Battle Tanks. The UAE has something like 50,000 men and 131 MBTs, and they're worse than the Saudis. Kuwait has an army of maybe 12,000 . . . or they did until Iraq moved in.

"Against that, Saddam has at least one million, two hundred thousand men in the regular army and another 650,000 reserves. He's got something like 5,500 MBTs—T-55s,

T-62s, and T-72s. Seven thousand APCs. Three thousand towed guns. Greg, the Iraqi army is the fourth goddamn biggest army in the world. A lot of those troops probably aren't that well trained, but Saddam's got two armored divisions, a mechanized division, four motorized divisions, and a special forces unit in the Republican Guard, and they are veterans of the Iranian war and they are *good*. You think Republican Guard, think German SS. Just like the SS, they started out as a political paramilitary force, Saddam's personal bodyguard, and expanded to become the real heart of his army. So, could Saddam mop up everything in the Middle East? Oh, yeah. No problem."

"I don't think I'd realized things were quite that grim."

"Well, they're not. Saddam knows that if he marches south, he's going to face *us* and not just the locals. He's also got to know that we're going to try to make him cough up Kuwait, though, and he might decide to take over as much as he possibly can early on, so he has a lot to bargain with later."

"Yeah. There was a lot of discussion about that back in Coronado before we came over," Greg said. "The son of a bitch is sitting on a pretty good hand, actually. He knows, or, rather, he *thinks* he knows, that the United States is going to be reluctant to get into a war. He may be hoping for a negotiated settlement."

"Hell, for all I know, he still thinks we're bosom buddies."

"I doubt that," Greg said, chuckling.

It was painfully true that the United States had been shamelessly supporting the Iraqi dictator, but then, Greg reflected, the U.S. had a long history of supporting bloody-handed dictators, so long as they were *our* bloody-handed dictators. Ironically, Saddam was as strong as he was now at least partly because of help from the United States. Washington had feared that an Iranian victory would enable the majority Shi'ite population of southern Iraq to over-throw Saddam's secular state and establish an Islamic theocracy along the lines of Iran's revolutionary government. *Any* kind of a union between Iran and Iraq, the largest and most powerful nations in the region, especially under the fanatic guidance of the Shi'ite mullahs, would be a catastrophe. The United States was currently getting only about 7 percent of its oil from the Middle East, but American allies, Japan and the industrial nations of Europe, got up to half of all of their oil supplies through the narrow Strait of Hormuz at the mouth of the Persian Gulf. If the strait was shut down, if an Iranian-Iraqi alliance managed to control not only their own oil reserves but those of their far richer neighbors to the south, the economies of western Europe and Japan could be overthrown . . . and in the newly emerged globalized economy of the 1990s, that would spell economic disaster for the United States as well.

Besides, most policy makers in Washington still had a mindset that recognized the Iranians as the enemy . . . the fanatics who'd overthrown the Shah, a longtime American ally, and who then had held fifty-five Americans hostage for an agonizing 444 days. *The enemy of my enemy is my friend. . . .*

With all of that in mind, the United States had done everything it could to covertly support Iraq in its war against Iran. Saddam Hussein might be a murdering thug—reportedly he'd killed his first man at the age of eleven, and for a time he'd served as a torturer for Iraq's Ba'ath Party leaders in the early sixties—but the U.S. State Department insisted that it was imperative to U.S. interests that he remain in power, a foil against the Islamic fundamentalists of Iran. U.S. support had included funneling intelligence reports on Iranian movements to Baghdad, boosting American oil purchases from Iraq, urging more credit for Iraq through the international banking community, and slipping several billion dollars to Saddam under the table as long-term loans. In addition, he'd received plenty of other help from other nations with similar interests—especially tanks, guns, ammo, aircraft, and other military supplies from the Soviet Union. There were those in the Pentagon who feared that Iraq was fast becoming a Soviet satellite, but that, too, had failed to undermine the support coming in from the U.S. As recently as October of 1989, President Bush had signed a National Security Directive calling for yet more financial and military aid for Iraq.

Lately, though, relations with Saddam had been deteriorating at an alarming rate. In February, he'd demanded that all U.S. warships leave the Arabian Gulf and viciously attacked the United States in a speech to the Arab Cooperation Council. In March of 1990, an Iranian-born journalist with British citizenship was arrested, tortured until he confessed to being an Israeli spy, and hanged, an act that shocked and outraged the civilized world.

There was also the small matter of his genocidal war against the Kurdish population in Iraq's northern region. In March of 1988, Iraqi MiGs had made some twenty runs over the town of Halabjah, scattering warheads containing mustard gas, tabun, sarin, and VX chemical agents on the Kurdish civilian population. In a town of fifty thousand, at least five thousand men, women, and children were killed, and twenty thousand more were horribly burned and disfigured, blinded, or maimed. Other chemical attacks were leveled against other Kurd targets throughout northern Iraq, but the immolation of Halabjah was the worst.

The trouble was, word of these atrocities was slow in leaking out from under the veil of secrecy enfolding Iraq, and what stories did make out were too horrific to be believed, unsubstantiated rumors to be dismissed as fearmongering aimed at the Iraqi-Soviet alliance or as Israeli propaganda. Only by early 1990 was an accurate picture emerging about just what kind of monster the United States was facing in the gulf, a monster at least partly of America's own creation.

Unfortunately, that realization had come a bit late. A series of disastrous diplomatic snafus throughout the spring and summer of 1990 had led Iraq to set the tanks rolling south, and Washington to declaring that it would go to any lengths to safeguard the flow of oil from the Arabian Gulf.

Finished with their meal, Greg and the other SEALs assembled at the tent marked as the HQ for the commander for Naval Special Warfare Task Group Central. That individual, it turned out, was well known to all of the newly arrived West Coast SEALs. Just over a week earlier, Captain Roy R. Scott, the commodore of Naval Special Warfare Group One, had been presented with both a dazzling career opportunity and a daunting challenge—command of NAVSPECWAR Task Group Central. He'd been given seventy-two hours to put together a task force, requisition equipment, and load everything onto three Starlifters and three C-5 Galaxy transports for the flight to Dhahran. Over the next week, more men and materiel had continued to trickle in, with Greg's flight only the latest.

"Welcome, gentlemen," Scott, with a handful of officers and enlisted men on his staff, told the twenty new arrivals as they trooped into the large tent serving as the Task Group's temporary HQ. A folding metal table held a large map of the Saudi coast between Bahrain and Kuwait City. "Welcome aboard!"

"Good to be here, sir," Russell said. "Which way to Iraq?"

Scott and others on his staff chuckled. "That way," Scott said, pointing north. "So right now, we're all making plans to go *that* way," and he pointed east, toward the waters of the Arabian Gulf, "if we have to get out of Dodge."

"I thought the best defense was a good offense, sir," Lieutenant j.g. Henry Lederer said.

"Lieutenant, the mission of the Navy SEALs is not to throw ourselves in the path of several hundred tanks. If Saddam's T-72s roll south, our job is to get the hell out of their way!"

"Seems like a less than glamorous way to prosecute a war, Captain," Russell observed.

"Maybe so. But Master Chief Halstead, there, could give you a lecture on the need to preserve trained men, so they live to fight another day. Right, Master Chief?"

He was grinning, and Greg had the feeling he was trying to make it a joke.

"Well, it's sure not our job to take on enemy armor," he said. "Not without laser designators and close air support!"

"Right. So let's review the tacsit."

Scott began roughing out the events of the past couple of weeks. The SEALs had all been briefed back in Coronado, of course, but this added a bit of spice, to actually *be* here in Saddam's path while Scott discussed the possibilities of an Iraqi attack on Saudi Arabia.

The tactical situation was not encouraging. Over a hundred thousand Iraqi troops—some estimates put the number at *three* hundred thousand men—and over 1,500 tanks, all sitting on the border between Kuwait and Saudi Arabia, evidently waiting for the order to roll south. If they came south, most could be expected to move down along the Gulf Coast, taking the major cities, oil-producing facilities, and oil fields—Ra's al Khafji . . . Ra's al Mishab . . . Munifah . . . Khursaniyah . . . Al Jubayl . . . Al Qatif . . . and finally Dhahran, or Ad Dammam as it was shown on the map. Likely, the Iraqi thrust would go all the way south to the twin cities of Al Mubarraz and Al Hufuf, on the main highway to Qatar, before swinging east to take down the Saudi capital at Riyadh.

And 150 naval personnel, including some sixty SEALs, were all that stood in their way.

"Gentlemen," Scott said after reviewing the tacsit, "our job here today is three-fold. First and foremost, we develop a contingency plan for E & E, should the Iraqis come south. We are *not* expected to stop Iraqi tanks."

"Thank God," Lieutenant Russell said. "Especially when there are a few thousand of them. We wouldn't be much more than a speed bump."

"If that," Scott said. "Second. We begin looking for ways to expand SEAL presence in Saudi Arabia. This assumes that the Iraqis stay put, and that additional SEALs are deployed to this region. Now, the Army high command has been pretty good about our being here so far. They've provided some old recreational facilities here at Half Moon Bay, and as we get squared away, we'll be expanding those to serve as SEAL Southwest Asian Command.

"However, operationally we're way too far south, too far from the likely action." He reached out, tracing a line up the coast to a point just south of the Kuwaiti border. "It is my intention to establish our headquarters here, at Ras al Gar. That's close to Jubayl, which is a pretty large population center for this region, about a hundred twenty kilometers north of here.

"I also intend to establish an advance SEAL base here, at Ra's al Mishab. That's just sixty kilometers south of the Kuwait border. We'll be able to operate all kinds of small boats out of there and be within striking range of the Kuwaiti coast.

"Third . . . and this may be the most important. We are going to brainstorm, gentlemen. We are going to work out, in detail, just exactly what the SEALs are good for out here."

"What do you mean, sir?" Lederer said. "I mean, begging your pardon, but don't we *know* that?"

"We know a lot of things, Lieutenant. We can do beach surveys. We've been trained to blow up enemy shipping, obstruct waterways, sabotage shore installations, board and capture enemy vessels. We can target-designate. We can pull search and rescue for downed pilots. The problem is that others in the special warfare community and, above them, others in the military overall, don't quite know how to use us. Panama was a case in point. Two missions . . . one along classic SEAL lines, and one that used SEALs as infantry. The classic op scored brilliantly. The other, well . . . some good men died. The objective was met, but some good men died. I do *not* want that happening here.

"Our problem is to see just how a unit trained and equipped as we are can be integrated into a much, much larger operation. When Uncle Sam gets his ass in gear, we're going to have the biggest damned buildup of American forces anywhere in the world since World War II. This is a *big* war, people. Bigger than Korea. Bigger than Vietnam. It's the sort of war the U.S. Army has been expecting to fight all along, with the Soviets.

"The Teams were designed to employ small-unit tactics against limited objectives in Vietnam. The question is whether we can continue to operate as a distinct and useful combat element, carry out useful missions, and not find ourselves being employed as cannon fodder, charging Iraqi bunkers. I'm going to want ideas from all of you, I don't care how far-fetched. How can the Teams best be employed in this theater?

"It's a damned important question. I don't need to tell you all that there is a certain amount of, shall we say, interservice rivalry going on right now. Budget battles over shares of military appropriations, and all of that. It's no secret that a lot of high-ranking military planners do *not* like us, do *not* like the concept of special forces. The supreme U.S. commander over here, General Norman Schwarzkopf, doesn't like the idea of specwar one bit, and I gather he has a particular grudge against the SEALs. So far, the powers that be have been pretty good about accommodating us, but

I suspect that's because, right now, we're all there is between Riyadh and Saddam Hussein.

"So how well we answer that question—how can the Teams best be employed here—may determine the future of the SEALs. We didn't shine very brightly in Grenada, remember. And we didn't shine very brightly at Paitilla, either. There are some in the Pentagon who think the SEALs are obsolete, a relic of the Vietnam War.

"I intend to prove them wrong."

"*Hoo-yah!*" was the resounding response from Greg and every man in the tent.

Chapter 15

Southwest Asia Combat Zone
Early morning hours

The sky was on fire.

UN Resolution 678, on 29 November, 1990, had authorized member nations "to use all necessary means" against Iraq unless it withdrew all forces from Kuwait by 15 January 1991. The deadline for Iraq's withdrawal had come and gone without a response from Baghdad.

And now the international coalition Washington's diplomats had forged was using all necessary means. Operation Desert Shield had suddenly and spectacularly become Operation Desert Storm.

The first salvo in the air war against Iraq was a Tomahawk Land-Attack Missile, a BGM-109 TLAM/C, fired minutes into the early morning of January 17.

Launched from a guided-missile cruiser, the USS *San Jacinto* (CG-56) steaming south in the Red Sea some 700 miles southwest of Baghdad, the weapon rose on a dazzling plume of yellow flame from the deck hatch of the ship's Mk. 41 Vertical Launch System. Momentarily, the moonless night, the black-shrouded sea, and the stark gray superstructure of the cruiser were fiercely illuminated, and then the TLAM cleared the ship, discarded its spent booster, and angled over into horizontal flight mode, stubby wings extending, air scoop deploying beneath its tail, onboard radar probing the sky ahead and the sea below.

In flight, the missile appeared pencil-thin, eighteen feet long but only a hair over twenty inches in diameter. Without its booster, it weighed just over a ton and a quarter, and half a ton of that weight consisted of high explosives.

Boosting quickly to high subsonic speeds—nearly 550 miles per hour—the TLAM began following an intricately precise flight path, guided by its onboard computer. It flew low, skimming the sea at an altitude of one hundred feet. In moments, the missile went "feet dry," hurtling across the desolate shoreline of Saudi Arabia's Red Sea coast, climbing rapidly to clear the two-thousand-foot rise of the Madvan Mountains along the coast, then higher still to clear the Al Hijaz range just beyond, passing close to the isolated town of Tabuk.

The TLAM's guidance system could be programmed to follow a precise course, from waypoint to waypoint, using its terrain contour matching capability—called TERCOM—to actually recognize key landmarks and steer by them. The first part of the flight, however, was handled by conventional inertial guidance and by the missile-borne equivalent of GPS, using navigational satellites to stay on course but using the terrain-following capability to maintain a constant altitude of one hundred feet above the ground.

An hour after launch, having traversed the empty, sandy wastes of the northern reaches of Saudi Arabia, the TLAM flew over the low but rugged rise of the Al Widyan near Badanah and crossed the border into Iraq along the southern reaches of the Badiyat Ash Sham, the Syrian desert.

Still skimming the ground at what would be treetop height had there been any trees, the TLAM hurtled beneath the gaze of Iraqi air-defense radar in the region. Even if the missile was tagged by tracking radar, its narrow diameter offered an impossibly tiny radar cross-section.

Besides, by this time, Iraqi Air Defense was becoming concerned about other incoming targets, and the sudden blackout or jamming of large corridors of radar coverage.

The cruise missile carried a conventional warhead, the "C" in TLAM/C, a thousand-pound warhead of high explosives. As it streaked low across the broad meander of the Euphrates River just north of the silent ruins of fabled Babylon, its onboard navigation system switched to terrain contour matching mode. Weaving now through a complex series of programmed waypoints, the missile's onboard intelligence identified its target, locked on, and initiated terminal descent.

An hour and twenty minutes after launch, the first salvo of the war slammed into its target, a highly defended military command-control post on the outskirts of Baghdad, detonating with a precision undreamed of by veterans of earlier wars.

By this time, other cruise missiles and bombs—"force packages" in the oblique terminology of milspeak—were beginning to reach their targets as well. The attack had been meticulously planned, orchestrated minute by minute with a stunning precision and attention to detail. The opening salvo had consisted of a total of fifty-two TLAM missiles fired from nine U.S. warships, including the ancient battleships *Wisconsin* and *Missouri*, only updated within the past year to fight this new kind of war, this long-distance, high-accuracy war that would have astounded their skippers of half a century before, during World War II.

All fifty-two cruise missiles were aimed at targets that were both high-value and highly defended—Iraqi military command-control-communications centers, radar installations, headquarters bunkers, telecommunications buildings, and various Iraqi Defense Ministry facilities. Of those fifty-two Tomahawk launches, only one failed to hit its target within the missile's CEP, its "Circular Error Probable," of thirty feet.

Of course, striking a thirty-foot target from 700 miles away was a little like taking the left wing off of a particular mosquito with a .223 round fired at a range of four hundred yards. Such was the accuracy implicit in this new kind of war. The strike was a dazzling vindication of these high-tech weapons that were now being used in live combat for the very first time.

As the Tomahawks streaked in on the terminal descent phase of their trajectories, a vast air armada was already closing in on Iraq from north and south.

They'd been assembling in air space just beyond the caress of Iraqi radar since 0200 hours, some seven hundred aircraft representing the coalition forces, each with a specific target, a precise timetable.

First across the border, almost in tandem with but high above the incoming TLAMs, were F/A-117 Stealth attack aircraft belonging to the U.S. 37th Tactical Fighter Wing. Death-black, with sharply angular design components and surfaces comprised of exotic composite materials that absorbed or scattered incoming radar, the Stealth fighters were nearly invisible to Iraqi air defenses. Each carried a single bomb within its internal payload bay, a one-ton laser-guided "smart bomb" for pinpoint-precision attacks on key Iraqi assets such as the Baghdad telecommunications building and the Iraqi Air Ministry.

The F-117 would soon become known to the Iraqis as *Shaba*, a word meaning "Ghost." Throughout the duration of the bombing campaign against Iraq, they would fly only 2.6 percent of the total missions flown and yet account for 31 percent of the high-priority fixed targets destroyed.

At about the same time as the Stealth fighters began their bombing runs, eight AH-6 Apache helicopters of the U.S.

101st Airborne Division roared across the far western border between Iraq and Saudi Arabia, skimming scant feet above the sand dunes in pitch darkness, lights off. Pilots and gunners on board the aircraft wore helmets that looked like something out of sheerest science fiction—IHADSS helmets, the letters standing for Integrated Helmet And Display Sighting System. IHADSS allowed a pilot to see in the dark through a night-vision sensor, navigate through an electronic heads-up display projected in front of one eye, cue sensors by merely looking at an icon . . . and even to aim missiles and the Apache's chin turret simply by moving his head.

At 0238 hours, the Apaches dune-hopped to within a few hundred yards of two particular Iraqi radar stations, popping up before the defenders even knew they were there and loosing laser-guided AGM-114A Hellfire missiles, salvos of unguided 2.75-inch Hydra rockets, and a firestorm of 30mm rounds from their M230 Chain Guns.

In seconds, the radar stations were enveloped in flame, smoke, and the thunderous detonations of Hellfires and Hydras striking home. The destruction instantly created a radar-black corridor, a pathway through which coalition aircraft could enter Iraq unseen.

And enter they did. Seven hundred strike aircraft—CF-18 Hornets from Canada, Jaguars from France, Tornado and Jaguar fighter bombers from Great Britain, Tornados from Saudi Arabia, and even A-4 Skyhawks from Kuwait, pilots and aircraft that had escaped the invasion—each directed at a specific target in Iraq or occupied Kuwait. The majority of the aircraft were from the United States and represented all four services—Navy F-14s, A-6Es, A-7Es, and F/A-18s; Air Force F-15s, F/A-117s, and F-111s; Marine F/A-18s; Army A-10s and AH-64s. The sheer power of the bomb load dropped on Iraqi military targets that night was staggering and devastating. A single F-15E Strike Eagle aircraft carried four times the weight in bombs as a World War II B-17.

Besides the seven hundred aircraft actually involved in strikes against Iraqi targets, another three hundred aircraft patrolled the skies above northern Saudi Arabia, Kuwait, and Iraq in support of the strike missions. Fighters flew Combat Air Patrol—CAP—for the attack aircraft to protect them from any sorties by Iraqi fighters. Air Force KC-135, Navy KA-6D and Marine C-130 tankers cruised in leisurely ovals above the Saudi desert and the gulf, topping off the fuel tanks of the strike aircraft just before they turned north. U.S. and Saudi E-3 AWACS—Airborne Warning and Control System aircraft—and Navy E-2C Hawkeyes patrolled the border, the huge, rotating radar disks mounted like flying saucers atop their fuselages probing deep into hostile territory, tracking the hundreds of aircraft in the strike and providing overall air control for the titanic effort being mounted over Iraq. Navy EA-6B Prowlers and Air Force E-8A JSTARS, F-4G Wild Weasels, and EF-111A Ravens carried out electronic warfare missions, jamming enemy radar, identifying Iraqi missile tracking sites and communications networks, and launching HARM high-speed antiradiation missiles that homed in on enemy radar emitters.

Before long, Iraqi defenses began responding . . . but sluggishly, at first, unable to target their opponents. From the skies above Iraq, the major population centers remained brightly lit. A thin layer of broken clouds at 25,000 feet intermittently blocked sight of the ground but could not dim the spectacle of the well-lit cities. Triple-A fire sped into the sky—solid streams of colored tracers from 57mm and 85mm AA guns, and the sharp, popping flashes of 100mm and 135mm shells exploding at twenty to thirty thousand feet. Occasionally, big surface-to-air missiles, the Russian-built SAMs, rose skyward on trails of flame, seeking targets invisible in the night. Below, dazzling flashes strobed and pulsed as bombs struck home, and fires burned brightly against the darkness.

From Kuwait City to Basra to Baghdad to Mosul, fire and death rained from the moonless sky.

Unseen, undetected, there was a ground component to the air strikes. Dozens of laser targeting teams—from Army Special Forces and Rangers, from Marine Recon, and from the Navy SEAL Teams—had already slipped across the border before the air armada had been unleashed. Dropping from helicopters in the desert or slipping ashore along the Kuwaiti coast in CRRCs, these teams positioned themselves with a clear line of sight to certain key Iraqi targets.

There were essentially two ways to steer a laser-guided bomb or missile home. The attacking aircraft—or a companion aircraft—could illuminate the target from the air, which meant the weapons officer aboard the plane had to keep the crosshairs of his laser targeting system centered on the objective. If the aircraft was forced to twist or turn or perform other maneuvers—to avoid antiaircraft fire, for example—the WO could lose his target. Clouds, smoke, windblown sand, all could interfere with the invisible beams of coherent light slicing down out of the sky.

A surer solution was to have a ground team in place, using an AN/PAQ-1 target designator, a hand-carried device like a fat, stubby gun with a massive telescopic sight. It *was* a gun, in a way, a laser weapon of considerable potency. Rather than destroy the target directly, however, the AN/PAQ-1 bounced invisible laser light off the target, "painting" the target, in military terms. Incoming bombs and missiles detected the signature of laser backscatter and homed in on it unerringly. Often, weapons such as Hellfire missiles could be simply fired in the general direction of the target, while the target itself was still out of sight, and the weapon would pick up the laser reflection from the AN/PAQ target designator and home in to destroy the target.

A number of the targets on that first night, then, were painted by SEALs concealed in the darkness a few hundred yards away, holding a pinpoint of laser light steady on command post bunkers and radar installations and communications centers as an American aircraft miles away dropped its force package and veered off into the night. Briefly, the night would be shattered by the weapon's detonation; so accurate was the targeting that many bombs, as audiences of CNN worldwide soon learned firsthand, were literally steered through windows, ventilation shafts, and open hangar doors.

And after the thunder stopped reverberating across the empty desert, the SEALs and other laser designator teams would assess the damage, determine whether or not a second strike would be needed, then slipped silently away into the night.

And across the world during the next few hours, millions of people watched, spellbound, the images from CNN of the devastating campaign called Desert Storm, the first time in history that the opening battle of a war was actually televised. They watched the grainy images from attack aircraft weapons consoles as bombs hurtled through windows or down open ducts with uncanny precision, destroying military targets with a truly surgical finesse, usually without touching civilian structures nearby. These opening hours of Desert Storm, for many watching civilians, was more video game than war. There was no sense of the dirt and dust, the blood, the terror, the pain, or the thundering death from above inflicted on thousands of Iraqis.

And there was no clue that many of those precisely guided warheads were following beams of light aimed by small teams of men on the ground, men including U.S. Navy SEALs.

18 January 1991

Southwest Asia Combat Zone
Early morning hours

White fire lit the desert night, rising slowly, balancing atop its thunderous might a long, slender missile with the Iraqi flag emblazoned on the side. Ground personnel gathered around the MAZ-543 launch vehicle waved caps and helmets, cheered wildly, and fired automatic weapons into the deep night sky. *"Allah akbar!"* someone shouted, and the cry was taken up by a hundred voices. *"Allah akbar! Allah akbar!"*

God is great. . . .

Gaining momentum with every passing moment, the weapon began angling slowly over until it was arrowing into the west.

In his face-off with the United States and the rest of the Arab world, Saddam Hussein had already made two major gambles and lost. He'd expected that the world would condemn the invasion of Kuwait but accept it, eventually, rather than going to war. And he'd expected the Arab world to side with Arab Iraq in this conflict rather than the imperialistic and Zionist United States. He'd lost on both throws of those particular dice.

The *Al-Hussein* missile clawing its way into the night sky above Iraq's western desert represented a third gamble, one with a much higher chance of success than the first two. The United States might have forged an international coalition against Iraq that included such Arab nations as Saudi Arabia, Egypt, Morocco, Qatar, Bahrain, Oman, the UAE, and Syria, but that alliance was a tenuous one indeed, an alliance held together solely by the diplomatic muscle exercised by the United States . . . *and by the key fact that Israel was not in the war.*

None of the Arab nations would remain in the coalition if Israel joined the war against Iraq. To join the Zionist state in an attack against Arab brothers was almost literally unthinkable. And Israel, Saddam knew, was a big bomb with a short fuse. Hit them hard enough, push them far enough, and Israel *would* come into the war.

And that would spell the end of the coalition, at least for the other Arab states.

And so, minutes after 0100 hours on the morning of 18 January, as hellfire and devastation rained down on Iraq and occupied Kuwait, the ponderous *Al-Hussein* missile thundered into the night, bearing upon itself the hope of ultimate Iraqi victory.

The West called them Scud-Bs, a NATO designation from the Cold War era when the Soviets fielded them against the West. Saddam's Scuds had been upgraded from the Soviet design, mostly to give them a longer range, but compared to the incoming TLAMs, the Scuds represented incredibly primitive technology.

A direct descendant of the V-2s unleashed on England by Hitler almost fifty years before, it was purely a terror weapon designed to cow civilian populations. With a high explosive warhead just half as heavy as that of the sleek and elegant TLAMs, with primitive inertial guidance, and with an appalling tendency to break up and tumble in midflight, the Scud was aimed and fired virtually blind. One western observer had described them as having "all of the aerodynamic characteristics of a falling bathtub." Where the TLAM had an accuracy/CEP of less than thirty feet, the CEP of an *Al-Hussein* was about two miles. That was far too large a targeting footprint for the weapon to be any good at all against individual ships or buildings, but it was fine for targeting something as large as a city.

At just past 0200 hours, some twenty-four hours after the first cruise missiles began impacting on their targets, the first *Al-Hussein* missile tumbled into a street in the outskirts of Tel Aviv, Israel, leveling several buildings and gouging a horrific crater in the earth. Throughout that first night of terror, seven more missiles slammed into Israeli territory—another into Tel Aviv, two into Haifa, three harmlessly into unpopulated areas, and one into an area undisclosed by the security-conscious Israelis.

Damage and casualties were light, but terror spread through the Jewish state. No one knew at first if the warheads that had hit so far carried chemical or biological warheads, and it was anyone's guess as to what payload future Scuds might deliver into Israeli population centers. Civilians donned gas masks and withdrew to underground shelters.

And throughout it all, the clamor rose from the Israeli population demanding that their military strike back.

Saddam Hussein was close to scoring an important victory in his war for survival against the allied coalition.

Chapter 16

SEAL Observation Post
Al Khafji, on the Kuwaiti Border
Saudi Arabia
1450 hours

Greg peered through the high-powered binoculars, trying to makc some sense of the ghostlike shapes shimmering in the heat rising from the desert. It was the end of January, the depths of winter, but temperatures along the gulf coast could still rise into the nineties, and the harsh sun was not to be taken casually at midday.

Nothing. The shapes were illusions, a kind of mirage.

Greg was in a makeshift bunker with three other SEALs—Chief Gunner's Mate Larry Drexler, Radioman 2nd Class Mike Vickery, and Torpedoman's Mate 1st Class Fred Gerrold. The first three were all West Coast SEALs, Team One and Team Three; Gerrold was a new arrival to the gulf, detached from the East Coast's Team Four. Together, they'd been assigned to an ad hoc SEAL recon team, code-named Romeo One. The bunker was actually a kind of natural rock shelter, a hollow space beneath a large boulder, with sand and rock piled up across the opening to leave only a narrow observation slit.

Thunder rolled low overhead. Greg lowered his binoculars and glanced up into the hard, metallic blue sky, trying to see past the overhang of the rock. There they were, a two-by-two quartet of Air Force F-15 Strike Eagles, heading north.

Almost two weeks had passed now, since the vast coalition air armada had begun hammering at targets throughout Kuwait and Iraq. Though combined U.S. forces handled the majority of sorties, a very large number were being carried out by the forces of other nations in the carefully and delicately forged international coalition arrayed against Saddam Hussein. British Tornados, for instance, had been carrying out astonishing low-altitude bombing runs with munitions designed to crater Iraqi runways and render them useless. And less than a week before, a Saudi pilot in an F-15 had downed two Iraqi fighters, the first air double-kill of the war.

For two weeks the bombardment had continued day and night, hitting everything from buildings housing Iraqi C^3 centers—Command, Control, Communications—to bunkers to bridges to SAM sites to airfields to individual military vehicles. Planes thundered through the sky above al Khafji almost continually, most headed northwest. The return legs of each sortie tended to be over the gulf or over the desert farther to the west. There'd been no ground actions to speak of at all, save for occasional artillery duels across the border, duels that the Iraqis invariably lost, since as soon as a gun revealed itself, it was pounced on by A-10s, F-111s, or British Tornados.

And Captain Scott had gotten his wish. The SEALs were fast learning how best to support the larger, conventional war.

Ever since their arrival at Ra's al Mishab, the SEALs had been operating up and down the gulf coast, using everything from patrol boats to CRRC rubber ducks. Before the air war had begun, most of those missions had been hydrographic, taking soundings of the bottom off the beaches as far north as Kuwait City, in preparation for a possible Marine landing at some date in the future.

Scott's vision for SEAL operations in the gulf had eventually been distilled into five points.

One, there had to be a high probability of success.

Two, operations should be conducted in a maritime environment, meaning either offshore or very close to the beach.

Three, all operations had to be in support of the commander in chief's published directives and of the central command elements. That, unfortunately, meant no intelligence raids for purely SEAL-related purposes.

Four, each operation had to contribute to the overall war effort, in essence a repeat of Point Three.

Five, all operations would be carried out at squad or platoon level.

That last one, to Greg's way of thinking, was the most important of all. If the Teams needed to carry out a bit of recon or intelligence-gathering not directly related to Schwarzkopf's Grand Scheme, well, they could fudge that, if they had to. But Point Five meant that Scott, at least, had taken the lesson of Paitilla Airfield to heart. In the gulf, SEALs would not be thrown into multiple-platoon forces or used like regular infantry. Point One was good as well. Platoon commanders would have input as to what they considered feasible or not, and the SEALs would not be expected to storm prepared defensive positions or take on other high-risk missions. Oh, sure, there was risk associated with every SEAL mission. That was the name of the game. But there had to be a good possibility of success before an op was okayed. So far as Captain Scott was concerned, success meant having the operators return to base with no casualties.

Even before the air war had begun, then, small teams of SEALs had been slipping across the border or infiltrating from CRRCs along the coast. SEALs—along with similar teams in Army Special Forces and Marine Recon—had set up concealed observation posts within sight of certain high-priority targets such as radar facilities, communications centers, and command bunkers. As Desert Storm began, they'd painted those targets with invisible laser light, guiding home incoming smart bombs and missiles to make the actual kill.

It was a task to which SEALs were well suited, Greg thought. In Vietnam, SEALs had prided themselves on the ability to move undetected through enemy territory all night, find a place of concealment at the objective—a railway tunnel, say, or an important bridge—and simply wait, often in deliberately uncomfortable positions in order to stay alert and awake. When night came again, they would carry out their mission of sabotage or reconnaissance, then slip away, still undetected, to their recovery site.

The press and popular culture—he was thinking of a movie about the Navy SEALs released a few years before—tended to present the Teams as gun-happy Rambos, high-tech gunslingers who took on all comers and left behind little but dead bodies and smoking rubble. Many of the SEALs Greg knew considered themselves to be something more akin to military technicians, highly trained specialists who performed extremely specialized and specific tasks, usually leaving the enemy completely unaware that they'd been there. That was one reason members of the Teams assigned to combat duty referred to themselves as *operators*. It took some of the Hollywood out of what they did.

SEAL Teams worked with a decidedly un-Hollywood ethic: If you have to use your weapons, your mission has *failed*.

The current mission called for no gunplay at all. The four

of them had driven north from the SEAL advance base at
Ra's al Mishab before dawn that morning, using a Humvee
borrowed from the Marines stationed near al Khafji. Over
the past week, satellite reconnaissance and other intelligence sources had reported considerable activity among
Iraqi forces just across the border in Kuwait. Though most
of these had been "F-squared," meaning "filed and forgotten," enough reports were coming through now that CENT-
COM was beginning to take notice.

Romeo One had come north to set up an observation post
overlooking the four-lane highway running up the coast
into Kuwait, an OP from which they could keep a watch on
the border. The Humvee was hidden a hundred meters to
the south of the makeshift OP under a desert-camouflage
tarp, and the reassuring safety of the water lay only a few
hundred meters to the east. The four SEALs fit snugly into
the pocket beneath the boulder, with just enough room for
themselves lying prone, their weapons and gear, and an
LST-5C SATCOM transceiver.

At the moment, Vickery—"Vicky" to his teammates—
was on the radio, talking into the handset. The SATCOM
unit was a marvel of engineering compared to the bulky,
shoulder-carried PRC-74 "pricks" and similar equipment
Greg had used in Nam. It weighed just ten pounds, a third
of a prick-74, and through a satellite channel it could literally communicate with any properly equipped station in the
world. At the moment, Vicky had the unit shoved up against
the rock and sand barrier at one corner of the boulder, so
that its thick antenna could extend outside enough to establish a satellite link.

"Hey, Twidge?" he said.

"Yeah."

"They want to talk to you."

Inwardly, Greg groaned. SATCOM communications
were one of the greatest things that had happened to SEAL

ops in recent years. They were also a curse. You could reach out and talk to anyone you wanted in the world . . . but *they* could also talk to *you.*

He held the handset to his ear. "This is Spock. Go ahead."

As communications handles, Romeo One had adopted the names of characters from the old *Star Trek* series. Greg was "Spock," Drex was "Scotty," Gerrold was "Bones," and Vicky, the team's RTO, was "Uhura." Their Humvee had been given a further Star Trek persona—NCC-1701, *"Enterprise."*

It was an old joke, actually, and one based on a bit of history. There was a story popular back in Vietnam of an Army patrol leader who used the handle "Captain Kirk" and had named his jeep the *Enterprise.* The story claimed that one day, "Captain Kirk" and his platoon walked into an ambush and found themselves surrounded, outnumbered, and in very serious trouble indeed.

"Kirk" had radioed his headquarters with the words, "This is Captain Kirk of the Starship *Enterprise,* NCC-1701, calling Starbase One. We are under attack. Set phasers on kill. . . ."

It would have taken long minutes more, even hours, for the HQ to respond with an airstrike, artillery support, or a relief force, and the NVA knew that. They could easily have completed the job they'd begun and been long gone by the time help arrived. Instead, the incoming hostile fire had ceased before "Kirk" completed his call, the enemy melting away into the jungle in full retreat. It seemed the enemy also knew American pop culture, though it was generally both interesting and amusing to see how they responded to it. Apparently, the NVA thought that the *Enterprise* was an actual starship in the U.S. arsenal, and the threat from phaser fire real.

Whatever others might think today, however, the practice

of using icons of popular culture within the Teams was fairly common. SEAL Team Six, the Teams' antiterrorist unit, referred to themselves as "the Jedi Knights," after figures introduced in the *Star Wars* movies. That nickname apparently had also been picked up just recently by Schwarzkopf's advance planning group in Riyadh, which Greg found ironic in the extreme.

Listening into the handset, he could hear only the rush and crackle of static. SATCOM units could deliver crystal-clear communications, but those communications were ever susceptible to the problems of maintaining a clear channel through the satellite.

"Starbase, Starbase, this is Spock at Romeo One," he said after a moment.

"Romeo One," the voice said after a long moment, ignoring Greg's personal communications handle, "this is Starbase. We're patching you through on a channel to Castle Tower."

Shit. "Castle Tower" was the current code name for the Special Operations Command Center at the Pentagon, a branch, actually, of the Joint Chiefs of Staff operating under the National Command Authority . . . the president, in other words. He'd thought he was going to be talking to Captain Scott or one of his staff back in al Mishab. Instead, he was talking to someone in the Pentagon who might or might not have a clue as to what was actually going on.

Greg's money was on "might not."

"Romeo One, this is Castle Tower. How do you read, over?"

"Castle Tower, Romeo One. I read you. Over."

"Ah, Romeo One, we have updated intel from NPIC." The voice pronounced the acronym "en-pick." It stood for the National Photographic Interpretation Center, a facility at the Navy yard in Washington, D.C., operated by the CIA and tasked with interpreting imagery from the nation's reconnaissance satellites. "Talent-Keyhole, repeat, Talent-Keyhole. Please confirm with security watchword. Over."

The code phrase referred to the security classification of photographic information coming through from one of the KH-11 or newer KH-12 spy satellites in Earth orbit. Anything connected with Keyhole had a security classification so high you couldn't see over the top of it, even on a supposedly secure direct satellite channel.

"Copy, Castle Tower. Security watchword Ruff, I say again, Ruff. Whatcha got? Over."

"Romeo, we have a confirmed target, probably a small patrol moving south on the road across the border. It is in your immediate area, probably within two hundred meters, bearing three-five-niner, your position."

"Roger that, Castle Tower. We do not, repeat, do not have eye contact with the target yet."

"Understood, Romeo. Advance to contact and report. Over."

"Ah, Castle Tower, I do not copy you. Please repeat." Damn it. He'd heard them perfectly. The assholes *couldn't* mean that.

"Romeo, I say again, advance to contact and report. Over."

Briefly, Greg considered turning off the radio and simply insisting later that the thing had gone down. The SEALs needed the SATCOM, though, to stay in touch with their base at al Mishab, and the high command frowned—rather severely so—on *convenient* communications breakdowns. He would have a hell of a lot of explaining to do when they returned to base.

Simpler to have a misunderstanding, if necessary, and save the hardware breakdowns for some really serious interference from the rear. "Copy, Castle Tower," was all he said.

"Keep us informed, Romeo. Castle Tower, out."

"Roger that. Romeo One, out."

Advance to contact. Yeah, right. In a pig's bloodshot left eye. *Keep us informed.*

No wonder so many SEAL platoon leaders developed radio trouble. The curse of having anyone up the chain of command, all the way to the NCA itself, looking over your shoulder sometimes more than offsets the convenience of always being in touch with your immediate headquarters. Even that could be a pain, when some hot-shot junior officer decided to lend the benefit of his expertise and knowledge to the operators actually in the field.

During Operation Eagle Claw, the failed attempt by Army Delta Force to rescue the American hostages in Iran back in 1980, there'd been a certain amount of micromanagement of the op from the NCA. President Carter himself, in a basement office of the White House, had been trying to direct Colonel Charles Beckwith, the Delta commander, in the middle of the operation. At one point, just before the disaster at Desert One, the NCA had been urging that the mission continue. Beckwith had "developed radio difficulties" and ordered the mission aborted. He was, after all, *there,* with too few helicopters to support the mission and a busload of Iranian civilians who'd stumbled across the supposedly remote and unvisited stretch of emptiness known as Desert One. He knew what the true situation was in a way no man sitting in a basement twelve thousand miles away could possibly experience.

Everyone in the teams had had experience with micromanagement from the rear, and most hated it.

"You look mad enough to spit napalm, Twidge," Drexler said.

"Damned armchair-strategist micromanaging wonks," he said. "They tell us an enemy patrol is coming, and then tell us to go out and meet it."

"Well, shitfire," Gerrold said in his easy, Down-East drawl. "Mebee we should just go out and shake hands with them. Might be they're friendly."

"Might be," Greg agreed. "I think I'm going to advance . . ." He crawled a few feet up the berm of sand spilling into the shelter, so he could raise his binoculars again and peer into the sunlight outside. "*This* far."

"That's not to 'contact,' Chief," Vicky said.

"It's enough contact for me. Uh-oh."

"What is it?" Drex asked.

"I just spotted our patrol." The shimmers and ghosts he'd seen before had been real. The heat rising off the desert floor, however, had masked them. Now they were close enough to easily be seen.

A column of about twelve people was moving slowly south on the four-lane al Khafji road, "Route 101" as the Americans had begun calling it, straight toward the SEAL OP. Several were on horseback and . . . was that a camel? No, *two* camels, heavily laden with gear.

The people themselves looked like civilians, though several of the men carried rifles. They wore the traditional burnoose and robes of the Bedouin; the men were without exception bearded. Five of the figures, though, were women, heavily swaddled in traditional robes and veils.

"This could be trouble," Greg said softly.

The Bedouin were still largely an unknown quantity in this war. Relatives of the long-settled Arab population of Saudi Arabia, the true Bedouin were nomads who wandered through the area, usually from water hole to water hole, following the traditions of their people that extended so far back in time no one knew when or where they'd begun. The Bedouin disregarded international boundaries; they were, in fact, openly contemptuous of borders, considering the entire desert to be free for the roaming.

And they felt more loyalty to family ties than to the artificial ties of citizenship. They took no sides in the current war.

However, if these wanderers weren't Iraqi, they were an almost religiously mercenary lot. There was every possibility that they would be happy to sell information to the Iraqis.

Information such as the precise location of a SEAL observation post.

Greg watched as the line of nomads walked closer, leaving the highway and climbing the low rise toward the OP. He wondered how they'd made it through the Iraqi lines. Had the Iraqis simply let them through, assuming them to be harmless neutrals? That didn't seem likely. Maybe they knew someone in the Iraqi army over there.

Or maybe there was something more sinister afoot.

They were too close for the SEALs to use the radio now, close enough that a sneeze would give the hidden men away. Greg inched back a bit deeper into the shadows but continued watching the Bedouin tribesmen moving in the glare of the afternoon sun.

The group had stopped less than twenty meters from the boulder sheltering the SEALs and appeared to be preparing to set up camp. Greg scowled. *Any* noise might give the SEAL position away, or simply a twist of bad luck. In fact . . .

He watched as one of the men, an ancient bolt-action rifle slung over his shoulder, walked closer to the boulder. His eyes were on the ground, and he appeared to be looking for something.

Or studying something.

Footprints. The SEALs had left footprints in the sand before they'd scrambled under the boulder and barricaded the shelter's entrance. There'd been no way—or reason, really—to scuff them out after the fact. The sand was soft enough in any case that footsteps left little in the way of identifiable tracks.

These Bedouin, though, were experts at reading the signs of passage on the desert floor, as expert, perhaps, as Native American trackers had been in the American West. The bearded man appeared to follow the tracks toward the boulder, looked into the darkness beneath, and . . .

"Khatar!" he shouted, eyes widening as he looked straight at Greg. *"Aiee, khatar!"*

He scrambled backward, almost falling in the soft sand, reaching over his shoulder for his rifle. Vicky tensed at Greg's side, aiming his H&K, but Greg laid a hand on his arm. "Don't shoot!"

Damn it, these were civilians. Armed civilians, yes, but they were noncombatants, and the SEALs had express orders about noncombatants and nonmilitary targets, best summed up in the word *"No!"* If that Bedouin armed his rifle, they might have to fire in self-defense, but . . .

But no. The nomad turned and ran, sand kicking up at his sandaled heels, burnoose flapping like great brown wings. The other Bedouin reacted at once to the alarm, moving back into the desert, shouting orders at the women and hauling at the bridles of their bellowing camels. In a few more moments, they were racing into the distance . . . not north, back toward Kuwait and the Iraqi army, but toward the west, deeper into the Saudi desert.

"What do you think, Twidge?" Drexler asked. "Should we pull out?"

"Schwarzkopf would love that," Greg said. He chewed on his upper lip for a moment, considering. On the one hand, those Bedouin could easily give their position away to the Iraqis.

But on the other, the SEALs were still well inside the Saudi border, and the Iraqis wouldn't come across that line unless they were intent on invading anyway. The nomads might well ignore the encounter; Greg might have decided differently if they'd fled back toward the north, but the fact that they were moving west suggested that they were merely intent on avoiding any entanglements with soldiers on either side. They would be in for a surprise when they stumbled into the front lines of the 1st Marines, a few kilometers to the south.

And the SEALs had not yet carried out their mission. They were to remain in place for another night at least, staying under cover by day, reconnoitering toward the border at night, listening and watching for any sign of enemy movement. It was possible that if the Iraqis were preparing for a push down the coast into Saudi Arabia, they would send out advance patrols to scout out the al Khafji road. If so, the SEALs were perfectly positioned to hit the patrol with a classic hop-and-pop and possibly take some prisoners.

No, Greg thought, they were better off staying put. There was a story circulating about Schwarzkopf and the Special Forces, and it rankled. He sure as hell wasn't going to be the one to throw gasoline on that particular fire.

According to the scuttlebutt, the first contingent of Army Green Berets had arrived in Saudi Arabia and met with General Schwarzkopf—a man whose dislike for all elite or special forces was well known. "General, we have good news and we have bad news," the Green Beret commander had told him. "The bad news is . . . we're here. The *good* news is . . . we didn't bring the SEALs!"

Greg had no way of determining whether that story was true or apocryphal. Most likely, he thought, it was the latter, a story circulating among members of Schwarzkopf's headquarters or planning staff, perhaps. Still, myth or not, it highlighted the basic underlying tensions between the regular military forces now flooding into Saudi Arabia and the special forces—SEALs, Green Berets, Rangers, Air Force Special Operations Forces, and others. The SEALs definitely felt as though they were on their best behavior, almost as if they were on unspoken wait-and-see probation.

Well, perhaps this was one time he could make use of the tendencies toward micromanagement displayed by the Pentagon REMFs. While he retained his right to make his own command evaluations, it wouldn't hurt to see what Washington had to say.

"Castle Tower, Castle Tower, this is Romeo One, over."

"Romeo, Castle Tower. Go ahead."

"Castle Tower, contact was a band of Bedouin civilians." He went on to describe the brief contact, adding, "Our position here has been compromised. Repeat, we are compromised. Over."

There was a long and hissing pause. "Ah, Romeo," the Pentagon officer sitting in an electronics-bedecked basement command post seven thousand miles away said at last, "the Arab civilians do not, repeat, do not constitute a threat. Remain in position and continue to report."

"Copy, Castle Tower. Can you track them to see if they might endanger our mission? Over."

"Ah, roger that, Romeo. We will deploy units to detain the civilians. They do not constitute a threat to your mission. Over."

How the hell could they be so certain of that? The KH-11 satellite had a published resolution from orbit of about six inches—the actual figure was something less than that—which didn't allow it to photograph the proverbial license plate number from orbit, but came damned close. Certainly they could have distinguished camels from Iraqi MAZ trucks or BMPs. Why had they been so sure the Bedouin had been hostile earlier?

Castle Tower's confidence in the tactical situation here almost made him want to change his mind about staying. If they thought there was no danger, maybe it was time to get the hell out of Dodge. . . .

He needed more information.

"Castle Tower, what can you tell me about the other side of the line? It might be advisable to change our position. Over."

"Romeo, we are tracking large-scale movements of logistical support traffic northwest of your position. Intel reports suggest an imminent probe-in-force past your position. Remain in place and report on hostile movements. Over."

It sounded like their beady little minds were made up. "I copy, Castle Tower. Romeo over and out." There was nothing to be gained from arguing, not at this point.

"This is Castle Tower, out."

He took another long look out the observation slit toward the northwest, as Allied aircraft continued intermittently to thunder overhead.

"What's the word, Chief?" Vicky asked.

"We're going to stay put until nightfall," Greg decided. It made no sense to move by day in any case. Iraqi observers might see them and call in artillery fire. Better to wait for night, then stay or pull out as the situation dictated.

Sunset would come in another couple of hours.

And those hours passed without any evidence that their position had been given away. The sporadic artillery fire that had made life interesting along the Saudi-Kuwait border for the past couple of weeks could easily have been directed at the area where the SEALs were hiding, but there was nothing. The sun set. The SEALs had their evening meal—MREs, again—and then waited for darkness to fully fall.

It was just before 2000 hours that Drexler suddenly looked up. "Hey! Guys! You hear that?"

Greg lay in the darkness, straining to hear. There was something . . . not a sound so much as a rumbling vibration transmitted through the packed sand beneath them. It was faint but undeniably growing stronger. It was almost like . . .

"Heavy machinery," Gerrold said. "Sounds like some really big tractors."

"Or tanks," Drexler added.

"My money's on the tanks," Greg said, pulling himself up to the open slit with his PVS-7D, a handy and light-weight device that could be worn on a helmet or held like binoculars. In this case, Greg held the eyepiece to his face and peered through it, as the unit's electronics picked up ambient starlight and magnified it several million times. The night-vision scope pierced the darkness, revealing the landscape to the northwest with monochromatic-green clarity.

And there, clearly revealed just as it moved into visual range, was Gerrold's heavy machinery . . . an Iraqi T-62 tank, rumbling down the highway toward al Khafji, with more of the steel beasts strung out on the four-lane road behind. Tanks and armored personnel carriers—it was an all-out assault by mechanized forces.

"Vicky! Get on the horn! Tell them we have company!"

"Aye, aye, Chief!"

The tank fired, the thunder of the shot rolling across the desert seconds after he saw the flash. At the same instant, the round detonated in the air above the rock sheltering the four SEALs with a loud pop and a glare of dazzling light.

Greg turned his head and squeezed his eyes shut to avoid being temporarily blinded. The T-62 had just tossed an illumination round at them and obviously was searching for something . . . presumably *them.*

The tank's main gun fired again, and this time a savage concussion assaulted the SEALs from somewhere to their left, shaking the ground and sending a cascade of sand down on top of them from the rock overhead.

"Shit!" Gerrold called. "They know we're here!"

"Yeah," Greg said. "But not exactly where. They're—"

He was interrupted by a second detonation. This one to the right and behind them.

"They're probing!" Greg continued. "They don't know exactly where we are!" If they had, at this range the Iraqi gunners would have had no problem dropping a 115mm round squarely on top of the boulder.

A third explosion, and this time Greg thought the rock above them shifted a bit with the shock.

"Time for E & E," he told the others. "Grab your gear and go! *Go!*"

Vicky wiggled out of the slit and onto the open desert first, carrying the SATCOM. Gerrold was next, followed by Drexler, then Greg. A sound like an oncoming freight train shrieked through the night, and the detonation smacked all four SEALs like the swing of a titanic fist.

And the T-62 continued its ponderous advance. . . .

Chapter 17

The SEALs picked themselves up and kept moving. That last round had overshot and hit well to the right. The Iraqis were still firing blind, without a clear idea of where the SEALs were at the moment.

Another shot—and this time the boulder they'd been hiding under took a direct hit, the 115mm shell splintering the massive rock and sending fist-sized chunks whizzing through the sky. Shit. Maybe they did know where the SEALs had been hiding . . . but apparently their hurried exit hadn't been observed.

He wondered if the Iraqi commander or gunner on that tank had night-sight optics.

"Move it!" Greg snapped at the others.

"Which way?" Drexler asked. "The water?"

Greg considered that. The gulf lay only a few hundred meters away, across the highway toward the east, and every SEAL, from his first day in BUD/S, was reminded time and time again that the water meant safety. A SEAL squad cut off and outnumbered would probably be safe if it could reach the water. There weren't many who would follow them into their own element.

But he didn't want to exercise that option. Those tanks could roll down the highway a lot faster than the SEALs could swim and would reach the coastal village of Khafji long before they could. They might be able to use the SAT-COM to get help—maybe—but rescue would be long hours away. In the meantime, God alone knew how the Iraqi attack would be unfolding.

The other three were watching him closely in the dim light, waiting for his order.

"Uh-uh," he told the others, shaking his head. "Make for the hummer. We need to let the Marines in Khafji know what's coming down the highway."

Slipping from shadow to shadow, keeping low and moving two-by-two, the SEALs zigzagged through the sand toward the hidden Humvee. *Please God, the Bedouin didn't find it,* he thought. Damn. He hadn't considered that possibility earlier. But then, the nomads had been pretty damned eager to get out of the area. They wouldn't have had time to search for the SEALs' hidden transportation.

Again the Iraqi tank fired its main gun, and again that chugging-train howl thundered low overhead, ending in a deafening explosion. Shrapnel whined through the air or buried itself with pattering thuds in the sand.

The Humvee was right where they'd left it, carefully nestled under a desert-camo tarp held in place by rocks and piled-up sand. It took only a moment to pull off the tarp and discard it, hop into the vehicle, and gun the motor to life.

Only one T-62 had separated from the main column, which was continuing to move down the coast highway, along with a column of armored troop carriers—Soviet-built BTR-60s. The lone tank, apparently detailed to deal with the SEALs, crashed through the rubble where the boulder had been moments before, slewing left, then accelerating. As Gerrold drove the Humvee, Greg turned and watched the tank's progress through the PVS-7D. He could see the rooster tail of sand flung high behind the tank by its spinning tracks, saw the turret tracking to bring the main gun with its big, midbarrel fume extractor to bear.

"He's got us spotted!" Greg yelled. "Hard right!"

Gerrold spun the wheel and skewed the Humvee to the right. The T-62's main gun spoke again, and the detonating shell sent a pillar of sand geysering into the night up ahead and to the left. Bullets snapped and shrieked overhead. The tank was firing its coaxial machine gun, trying to bring it to bear on the small and armorless target.

Greg was running through everything he knew about the T-62 from various indoctrination sessions. Designed to replace the aging T-55 almost thirty years before, it had never lived up to its promise. The 115mm gun was good—the first smoothbore tank gun adopted by the Soviets—with good penetration and fair accuracy out to 1,200 meters, but with abominably poor accuracy at greater ranges. They would be carrying forty rounds in the turret—a number already reduced by five. Or was it six? The explosions had left Greg a bit dazed, and he was having trouble thinking straight.

Road speed was fifty kilometers per hour, slower in the sand. The beast was not very maneuverable. When it first had been introduced, it hadn't even been up to par with the U.S. M60 . . . and it was markedly inferior to the M60A3.

The Soviets had exported a few T-62s once the more modern T-72s had come on-line, most of them to various Arab states. The Iraqis were known to have about a thousand of them in their arsenal, most concentrated within their elite Republican Guard divisions.

Gerroid wrenched the hummer left just as another long burst of machine-gun fire stitched through the sand alongside. Inferior the T-62 might be, but it was still a hell of a match for a Humvee.

"You wanna make it to the highway?" Gerrold yelled over the roar of a straining engine.

"No," Greg said. "That column of BTRs and tanks must be ahead of us by now. We can't let them cut us off. We'll try to move west, then south."

"What's down there?" Drexler wanted to know.

"A Saudi national guard unit," Greg replied, "and I think there's a unit from Qatar. And some Marines, of course." The U.S. Marines were part of Task Force Shepherd—three Marine companies and a headquarters unit positioned just outside the town of Khafji. The SEALs had talked with them that morning and borrowed the Humvee from them.

"Shit," Drexler said. "Saudi National Guard? Let's stick with the Marines."

"Roger that," Vicky said. "I'm not sure I'd trust the Saudis to park my car."

Greg said nothing. Vicky's view of Saudi combat abilities was pretty common throughout the U.S. CENTCOM forces, from what he'd seen so far, but it was hard to tell how much of that was based on reality and how much on American provincialism. Certainly, the Saudis had shown a pretty spirited determination to defend their borders against an incursion by their bullying neighbor to the north, and they were well equipped and in many cases trained by U.S. Special Forces or in special programs back in the States.

The Saudis Greg had met also possessed an alarming tendency to assume that they were superior to anything Saddam could throw at them and seemed to feel that, though the Americans were there to help them, outside assistance wasn't really necessary.

In combat, that kind of hubris could get you killed very, very quickly.

"Hey! We can fight back," Vicky said. He patted the inside roof of the hummer, indicating the TOW antitank missile launcher mounted topside. "Let's take the bastard out!"

"Negative," Greg said. "We stop, we're dead!"

They would have to stop the hummer to draw a bead on their pursuer and hold the aim steady for the wire-guided missile to find its mark. While the SEALs had been trained in the use of TOWs, it was not exactly a weapon with which they were experienced.

Damn it, SEALs were not supposed to engage enemy armor in a stand-up fight!

"We'll use it for a last resort," he told the others, "if we have to." If the hummer were disabled, the TOW might be their only defense against that oncoming steel monster.

Their single advantage now was maneuverability. The hummer wasn't much faster than the T-62 in sand and rough terrain, but it could zigzag and twist, making it tough for the enemy gunner to hit them. At the moment, the Iraqis were trying to spray them with machine-gun fire, hoping to hit them almost at random. Gerrold was working the hummer more and more to the right. There was a depression in the desert there which they'd noted during their survey of the ground early that morning, a wadi or dry gully that might give them a few precious moments out of their pursuers' sight.

Another explosion thundered to their right, the shock tipping the hummer precariously onto its two right-side wheels. Then the rugged little machine's broad wheel base proved its superiority over the tip-prone Jeep, and the Humvee slammed back onto all fours. An instant later, they bounded into the air and plunged into the wadi, slamming into the floor of the ravine hard enough to jolt them all from tailbones to crowns.

Gerrold tugged on the stick, gunning the wheels. They bounced, then dug in, sluing sideways as Gerrold hauled the wheel over. Bouncing and bumping through the night, the Humvee jolted down the wadi to the southwest, the tank now out of direct line of sight.

"You think they'll chase us, Chief?" Drexler asked.

"Don't know," Greg said. He was studying the crest of the slope alongside the wadi behind them through his night scope. "I guess it depends on whether they lose us here or . . . damn."

The T-62 was in view again, nosing up over the edge of the wadi, balancing precariously for a moment, then plunging nose-down, clawing at the sand, then nosing up again on the far slope.

"Okay," Greg said. "He's climbing the south slope. We can use the time to put some distance between us and him!"

"Roger that!"

The wadi gave out a few hundred meters later, the walls opening and dropping away, debouching onto flat, hard-surface desert. Gerrold opened up the throttle, giving the tortured vehicle all it would take. Gradually, he brought them back around to the left, angling more south than west, heading for friendly lines.

An explosion thundered in the distance, followed by another . . . and then by a rapid-fire barrage, one explosion following another in rapid succession. This time, though, the fire wasn't aimed at them. It sounded like a major battle was breaking out somewhere to the east. Heavy guns boomed and rumbled, shells burst, and the eastern sky was intermittently lit by strobing pulses of yellow light.

There was no further sign of pursuit. "I think we lost him," Greg said. "Keep heading south. We have to find us some Marines!"

The first thing they found, though, was less than reassuring—a line of trenches and earthworks dug into the sand that were completely unmanned. As they slowed to pass through a gap in the berm, Greg saw something more alarming than empty fighting positions: M-16 rifles and desert-camo helmets, tossed in a chaotic jumble on the ground.

"Somebody left in a hell of a hurry," Vicky said.

"Not Marines," Drexler said, pointing to a green flag fluttering above a deserted tent. "Saudi."

"Keep driving." Greg felt his fury growing. There was no sign of an Iraqi attack here. Hadn't the bastards held their position at *all?*

Half a mile farther to the south, a man in desert combat gear clambered out of a trench and stepped in front of them, one hand raised, the other gripping his M-16. Behind him, other troops were just visible in the dim light alongside a couple of light armored personnel carriers, aiming their weapons at the Humvee as it slowed. TOW missile emplacements were dug into the sand.

"Halt! Identify yourself!"

Greg stood up in the overhead hatch, his head and shoulders above the roof. "U.S. Navy, Task Force Romeo One," he called back.

"Let's have the password!"

"Geranium," Greg replied—an unlikely enough word to hear in the Saudi desert.

"Petunia," the challenger said, giving the countersign and relaxing only slightly. "Come on in."

"Marines?"

"Affirmative. Staff Sergeant Walsh."

"Master Chief Halstead." He climbed down out of the Humvee. He could hear the rumble and boom of heavy artillery fire in the distance. The sky to the east looked as if it were ablaze. "What's the situation?"

"Your guess is as good as mine, Master Chief. All we

know right now is that the Iraqis are hitting Khafji with a major force."

"Staff Sergeant?" another voice called. "Who is it?"

"The U.S. fuckin' Navy, sir," Walsh replied.

Another Marine materialized out of the gloom, a young man with lieutenant's bars on his collar.

"Sir!" Halstead said, coming to attention. "Master Chief Halstead, reporting!"

"At ease," the lieutenant said. "I'm Lieutenant Kresgin. What do you have for us?"

Greg relaxed. "T-62s and BTR-60s, sir," he said. "At least a battalion of them, heading south on the coast road." Quickly, he gave the Marines a run-down of what they'd seen and where.

Kresgin nodded. "Your armored column hit Khafji about ten minutes ago. That's six miles inside the Saudi border. Looks like Saddam wants to come out and play."

"He can't be meaning to punch a hole through the allied line," Walsh said. "I'd bet a month's pay he's trying to lure us into a counterattack. If he gets us to chase him north, chase him onto *his* turf . . ."

"That may be," Kresgin said, "but he's done a good job of hole-punching so far."

"Sir?" Greg said. "What do you mean?"

"I mean we're here as a reconnaissance in force. This part of the line is being held, was *supposed* to be being held, by Saudi troops." Kresgin sounded bitter. "You'll notice that our Saudi friends are in kind of short supply around here right now."

"We passed their fighting position a few hundred yards back that way."

"Fighting position!" Walsh said. "Shit. They didn't even *see* the Iraqis, and they fucking ran! The shooting started and they were gone! So much for the fucking coalition!"

"Shit," Greg said with some feeling. "Can you stop them?"

"With three companies and a headquarters platoon? Negative. But we can sure as hell slow them up a bit. At least we can keep them occupied until CENTCOM can bring up reinforcements and some air strikes."

"Sir, I need to contact my base," Greg said, suddenly feeling the exhaustion hitting him. It sounded like three companies of Marines were all that stood now between the Iraqi armored thrust and the rest of Saudi Arabia. It promised to be a long, long night.

"We've got a radio here, Chief," Kresgin told him, "but it won't be set to the right channels."

"We don't have much call to talk to the Navy out here," Walsh added.

"S'okay. We have our own SATCOM gear. Just let us park, okay?"

"Right over there, pal. We'll let you know if the Iraqis come over the hill."

"Thanks."

"Thank *you* for your report," Kresgin said. "It will help."

"Aye, aye, sir." He came to attention again but didn't render a salute. Old, old training had taken over. A salute could identify an officer to enemy snipers.

"Carry on."

"Aye, aye, sir."

He turned to go. Walsh stopped him. "Hey, Navy . . . a question?"

"Sure."

"What the hell is the U.S. Navy doing out in the desert? I don't see any water!"

Greg shrugged, then patted one of his canteens. "We've got all the water we need, Staff Sergeant, right here."

"Shit," Walsh said, shaking his head. "You must be fucking crazy!"

"Nope," Greg replied. "We're SEALs."

"Like I said, Master Chief. Fucking crazy!"

31 January 1991

SEAL Headquarters
Ra's al Mishab
Saudi Arabia
1620 hours

By the final day of January, the Battle of Khafji was all over.

Greg and the other SEALs sat out the engagement at their base at al Mishab, on the coast twenty miles or so south of Khafji. They received updates and briefings, but they soon found that the best and most up-to-date information could be had by watching CNN on a television set in the Quonset hut they used as mess and recreation facility.

Staff Sergeant Walsh had been right. Saddam Hussein's thrust south from Kuwait had been designed to draw Allied forces back north into the tangle of berms, oil-filled trenches, minefields, and Republican Guard divisions massed on the border. The attack had had a second goal as well. With the U.S. Army's heavy divisions shifted some hundreds of miles west, the coalition forces along the coast above al Khafji had consisted almost entirely of Arab units—Saudi, Qatari, Syrian, and Egyptian. By engaging Arabs, Saddam hoped to test the coherence of the coalition arrayed against him and perhaps convince the Arab members to break away.

The Iraqi attack had been planned as a multipronged thrust by three full divisions. Their 5th Mechanized Division would push straight down the coast, engaging Saudi units and rolling through al Khafji. Their 3rd Armored Division would race south through the desert west of the 5th, then hook to the east to seize Ra's al Mishab. Even farther to the west, the Iraqi 1st Mechanized Division would protect the main attack's right flank. At the same time, Iraqi commandos would land from small boats along the coast well behind Saudi lines, disrupting communications, breaking supply lines, and spreading panic.

At worst, the Iraqi High Command reasoned, they would control some Saudi territory, which might convince the Saudis to rethink their alliance with the West. At best, the Allies would find themselves bogged down in a major land battle which—based on experiences in the Iran-Iraq War— could drag on for months and inflict tens of thousands of casualties on the enemy.

The Americans, after all, had no stomach for the sort of casualties that *this* kind of war would create.

The plan was well thought out, as far as it went, and the execution, at least initially, hadn't been bad. The problem had been, first, the U.S. Marines, and, second, the overwhelming effectiveness of U.S. air power.

Romeo One had had the dubious honor of becoming the first U.S. troops to fight the Iraqis on the ground, face to face. Moments later, the Marines of Task Force Shepherd had begun engaging Iraqi tanks with the only weapon at their disposal—their TOW missile launchers—at around 2000 hours on 29 January. Within half an hour, two F-15s, two F-16s, a pair of Specter gunships, and four A-10 tank-killers were overhead, providing close air-ground support.

Before long, more Allied aircraft were vectoring in to the battle area . . . then more, and still more. Initially, the majority of air assets had been deployed on Scud-busting missions, searching for the elusive long-range missile launchers that were dropping several missiles a night into population centers in both Israel and Saudi Arabia, but within hours the full might of Allied air power had been redeployed against the Iraqi ground assault.

The Iraqi 1st Mechanized Division was pounded from the air until they broke off their attack and retreated in confusion hours after crossing the border. The 3rd Mechanized Division stumbled blindly south, smack into lead elements of the U.S. Marines' 2nd Light Infantry Battalion.

Only on the coast did the Iraqi plan succeed as advertised, when at just past midnight on the morning of 30 January the 5th Mechanized Division rolled into Khafji.

Khafji lay so close to the Kuwaiti border it provided an easy target for Iraqi artillery, so the town's 15,000 inhabitants had been evacuated during the opening days of the war. A major desalinization plant drank water from the gulf at Khafji, but that was the only facility of strategic importance in the entire area, and Saudi Arabia's fresh water supplies were more than adequately met by other plants farther down the coast. All that was left in the town as the Iraqi tanks rumbled in were deserted buildings, a couple of journalists hiding in an empty seaside hotel, and two six-man squads of U.S. Marines from Task Force Shepherd.

CENTCOM's plan called for containment of the Iraqi force, cutting them off north of the town, and starving them out. The supreme Saudi commander, General Prince Khalid bin Sultan, his pride stung, demanded an immediate counterattack even if it meant house-to-house fighting and threatened to pull his air assets out from CENTCOM control if he didn't get his way.

The counterattack proved to be a delicate balance of U.S. tactical needs with bin Sultan's political muscle. Arab forces—Saudis and Qataris—struck north into Khafji with U.S. Marine support. The twelve Marines inside the occupied town remained hidden on rooftops, reporting on Iraqi movements in the streets below and identifying potential targets for air and artillery strikes.

Allied air power, meanwhile, was given the task of pulling off a first, something never done before in the history of warfare—breaking the back of an armored offensive by sheer airpower alone.

Air strikes rained down on Iraqi positions from Khafji to Kuwait City, a devastating torrent of death and destruction by tank-killing A-10 Warthogs, Specter gunships, Harrier Jump Jets, Tornados, F-15s, F-18s, F-111s . . . everything up to and including the wholesale devastation inflicted by flights of carpet-bombing B-52s. CENTCOM air planners divided the land into so-called kill boxes, each measuring thirty by thirty kilometers. Every eight minutes by day, every fifteen minutes by night, Allied aircraft entered their assigned kill box and blasted anything that moved, anything not naturally a part of the already torn and tortured landscape.

Within hours, the Iraqi 1st and 5th Mechanized Divisions ceased to exist as coherent military units, while the 3rd Armored Division tumbled back into Kuwait, leaving dozens upon dozens of tanks burning in the desert. Iraqi units above the border kept trying to punch reinforcements through to the south, but every attempt was smashed. By noon on 30 January, remnants of the 5th Mechanized were effectively trapped inside Khafji, though they did manage to repulse one Saudi attack just after sundown. The Saudis regrouped and attacked again, with support from the Marines, and by midday on the thirty-first, Khafji was again in Allied hands.

The victory was not without cost, however. A Specter gunship, call sign Spirit 03, was downed by an Iraqi shoulder-launched missile, killing all fourteen men aboard.

Two soldiers in a transport battalion were captured when they made a wrong turn in their Humvee west of Khafji. One of them was a woman, the first American servicewoman to be captured by the enemy since the fall of the Philippines to the Japanese.

And eleven U.S. Marines were killed when two APCs were destroyed on the night of the twenty-eighth—victims of so-called friendly fire.

Greg learned after the fighting that Lieutenant Kresgin and Staff Sergeant Walsh were among the dead.

He'd just received that news on the final day of January. He was on the dockside at Ra's al Mishab with several other SEALs and a contingent of Special Boat Squadron people, checking out one of the new Fountain-class high-speed patrol boats recently delivered to the gulf. He had made a phone call to the headquarters of the Marine's 2nd Light Infantry Battalion, hoping to speak with Staff Sergeant Walsh. Instead, he got a return call from a personnel officer attached to the HQ.

He'd scarcely known them, had spoken to them only for a few minutes that night as the sky to the east pulsed and flashed with the fury of U.S. air strikes. But the thought of those few Marines holding the line against the oncoming Iraqis while the Arab coalition forces fled had been troubling him.

He'd run into this feeling twenty years before, in Vietnam, when South Vietnamese ARVN troops—"Arvin Marvin," as they were derisively known—had repeatedly fled an enemy onslaught, leaving U.S. troops to face the storm alone. That wasn't universally the case, of course. He'd known plenty of brave Vietnamese troops, especially within their counterpart unit to the Navy SEALs. Still, what the hell were they doing fighting and dying for people who couldn't or wouldn't defend themselves?

He felt that now, even more strongly, as he thought about the Saudi troops who'd fled the Iraqi armored columns thrusting toward Khafji.

That was turning into a diplomatic debate that would not soon be settled. The Saudis claimed now that Iraqi tanks had approached their position with their turrets traversed to the rear, a sign that they were surrendering. When they got close, however, the turrets had spun around, and the Saudis had been caught in a withering fire, forcing them to withdraw. Later, the Saudis had insisted that CENTCOM had ordered their retreat, a statement that CENTCOM flatly denied. All that could be known for certain at this point was that the already shaky coalition of Arab states with the Western forces in Saudi Arabia was now that much shakier. There was open talk of the Saudis pulling out of the war entirely, and few Americans now trusted their Arab allies.

Saddam Hussein, Greg thought bitterly, might be licking his wounds after Khafji, but he must at the same time be delighted at the cracks appearing in the supposedly solid front poised against him.

Damn it, he thought. *What are we doing here? Trading lives for oil? Or just proving to the world that we're the toughest damned bastards on the block? . . .*

"Dad?"

The word brought Greg up sharply out of his brown study. He'd been sitting on the fantail of the Fountain patrol boat, helping to set a .50-caliber machine gun into its mount, when a couple of men stepped onto the dock. He'd not paid any attention to their approach, but . . .

"Mark! My God, what are *you* doing here?"

"Surprise, Dad," Mark said, grinning broadly. "We thought you old farts might need a hand!"

"Good to see you, Master Chief," David Tangretti added. "I hope you guys left some Iraqis for us."

"This is . . . this is great!" He stood up, then clambered out of the patrol boat and onto the dock. His eyes dropped to Mark's chest. His son was in whites, and he was wearing a shiny new Budweiser prominently above his left chest pocket. "What's this?"

"Won my trident," Mark said, grinning happily. "They pinned it on just before we left Coronado!"

"Geeze, another raw newbie," David said, shaking his head in mock dismay. "What they're sending us these days . . ."

"Congratulations, son." Playfully, Greg threw a punch—a reasonably gentle one—slamming the badge against Mark's rock-hard chest. "Welcome aboard!"

"Ow! Thanks!"

"So! When did you guys get here?"

"We flew into Dhahran yesterday," Mark told him. "Third Platoon, SEAL Team One. I gather they're putting us on a Scud-hunting detail."

"Scud hunting?"

"Yup," Tangretti told him. "CENTCOM pulled all their air assets in to hit Khafji. Took 'em off their Scud-hunting duties, and that's playing hell with the Israeli situation. *We're* the answer!"

Greg nodded. The Scuds had been falling nearly every night on population centers in Israel and in Saudi Arabia. Before the Khafji attack, coalition air assets had largely been directed toward Scud-busting missions in the knowledge that if Israel came into the war, the Arab alliance would almost certainly dissolve, neutral countries like Jordan might openly ally with Iraq, and erstwhile allies might even switch sides entirely.

With the Iraqi attack, though, the Scud hunters had been redeployed to attack enemy units around Khafji, and that left the enemy free to escalate its terror assault against Israeli and Saudi cities.

Evidently, CENTCOM was considering using SEALs to fill in the gap.

"The Battle of Khafji's already over," Greg told them. "The flyboys will be pounding Scud launchers again any day, now. Looks like you're too late."

"The hell with *that* noise," Mark said. "The Teams can do things that a whole squadron of F-15s couldn't dream of!"

"Our only fear was that the war was going to be over before we got here," David added.

"You don't have to worry about *that,*" Greg told them. "This fight isn't over by a long shot."

"Yeah?" Mark said. "From the sound of it, Saddam is on the ropes just from the air campaign. According to CNN, there's not much left of the guy!"

Greg sighed. "You know, I have great respect for CNN," he said. "Some of our best intel has been coming from their coverage lately. But I don't care how many live-from-Baghdad broadcasts they do . . . they can't possibly have an accurate understanding of what Saddam still has waiting for us."

"They're saying that Khafji is the first time ever air power alone has stopped an armored attack," David pointed out.

"So I've heard," Greg said. "But the reality is that we could throw smart bombs at Saddam's troops from now till doomsday, and it still wouldn't pry the son of a bitch out of Kuwait. That's a job for ground troops, son. Lots and lots of ground troops. When the ground war starts, it's going to be big, and it's going to be very, very noisy."

Mark laughed. "You're saying we haven't missed it, then, right? I mean, after the Battle of Khafji, it looks like everything else is going to be anticlimax!"

"Yeah," David added. "There are reports that the Iraqi Army is already falling apart."

What is it about the younger generation, Greg wondered, *that's always so damned impatient to go off to war? You'd*

*think we'd learn after a while that it's not something to
chase.*

And for the first time, he thought he truly understood
Wendy's sense of abandonment, as he and her son both
went off to war.

"Khafji was just a skirmish," Greg said, shaking his
head. "When the ground war starts for real, trust me. You'll
know."

Chapter 18

Port Facilities
Al Jubayl
Saudi Arabia
0207 hours

Minutes before, the *Al-Hussein* missile had launched from the so-called Scud Basket north of Al Qurnah, where the Tigris meets the Euphrates. Aimed simply at the general vicinity of the port of Al Jubayl 350 miles to the southeast, its simple-minded ballistic navigation did not allow for anything like a precise aim point.

Sooner or later, however, one of the quarter-ton warheads was bound to hit something vital—at least so reasoned the command staff of Iraq's strategic missile forces. At worst, the steady rain of warheads over military and civilian targets would worry the military forces arrayed against the homeland and cause morale, already shaky among the Arab members of the coalition, to plummet.

Surprisingly, this particular *Al-Hussein,* the sixty-sixth to be launched so far in this war of rockets, arrived over its target area more or less intact, with only a few chunks of the aft fuselage trailing the main body of the missile.

Below, extending like a broad concrete platform almost a

mile out into the waters of the Arabian Gulf, the main pier of the Al Jubayl port facility provided a most tempting target—one of the largest commercial piers in the world.

A number of ships were tied up at that pier. There was the Polish hospital ship *Wodnik* and two American aviation support ships, the *Curtis* and the *Wright*, all moored along the south side. On the north side were two supply vessels, the *Cleveland* and the *Santa Adela*.

A mountain of supplies, many of them highly explosive or flammable, occupied space on that pier. One U.S. general described the military sea-lift to the gulf as equivalent to "moving the entire population of Alaska, along with their personal belongings, to the other side of the world on short notice." During Desert Storm so far, some 20 percent of all troops and supplies coming into Saudi Arabia had arrived at the Al Jubayl commercial pier. Several thousand U.S. Marines were also on the pier, quartered in the long line of warehouses along the south side of the structure.

The prize, though, was the LHA-1 *Tarawa,* a Marine amphibious assault ship tied at the very end of the dock. The *Tarawa* had arrived at Al Jubayl just thirteen hours earlier to offload a six-plane marine AV-8B detachment. On board were 2,793 sailors, Marines, soldiers, and civilians.

A mountain of supplies was stored in the open at the end of the pier, directly alongside the *Tarawa*, including aviation fuel, 155mm high-explosive rounds, white phosphorus, cluster bombs, and 500-pound bombs. More supplies, many of them highly explosive, were stored in nearby warehouses.

At 0207 hours, a lookout on board the *Tarawa* reported a bright flash in the sky and a loud boom. Seconds later, the missile plummeted into the waters of the gulf only 150 meters south of the pier, and 125 meters off the starboard bow of the *Wodnik*. Fragments scattering out of the sky struck the *Wodnik*, the *Curtis*, and the *Wright*, though, fortunately, no major damage was done, and no casualties incurred.

The strike was a frighteningly close call, a near miss that could have had catastrophic consequences. The missile's warhead failed to explode. It had missed the *Tarawa* by something just less than 1,000 meters and missed the supply dump alongside the LHA by perhaps 700 meters.

Had either the *Tarawa* or the munitions dump been hit, the secondary explosions would have obliterated every ship at the pier, ignited all of the explosive ordnance, and claimed thousands of lives.

The timing of the launch, so soon after the *Tarawa*'s arrival, strongly suggested that the attack had been deliberately aimed at the ship and the supply dumps. Though probability statistics later downplayed the danger—a one-in-2,000 chance of a direct hit on the *Tarawa,* and a one-in-200 chance of striking the stored munitions—the near miss sent repercussions throughout CENTCOM. Saddam's Scuds were proving to be much more than an annoyance. Even one hit resulting in a serious loss of life might break the coalition, might even erode popular support for the Gulf War among the millions of American CNN viewers back home.

The next time, the coalition forces still pouring in through Saudi Arabia's gulf ports might not be so lucky.

SEAL Headquarters
Ra's al Mishab
Saudi Arabia
1430 hours

"Gentlemen," Captain Scott told the assembled platoon, "it's time we started earning our keep."

The SEALs gathered around the table in the Quonset hut briefing area chuckled at that. The two hundred or so SEALs in the gulf had been kept pretty busy over the past month, and no one could say they hadn't contributed a lot to the Allied cause already. Had it been enough to convince CENTCOM's senior officers that special forces had their place in modern warfare? That question remained unanswered . . . but Mark was willing to bet that the Teams, at least, had more than earned their place in the American order of battle.

He, however, had been champing at the bit since he'd arrived three weeks before. "Getting acclimated," they called it. Shit, he'd had all the desert heat and sand acclimation he wanted. He wanted an *op*.

"As you've all heard by now," Scott went on, "CENTCOM wants us to participate in the Scud-busting campaign. Most of the Team assets that have been in-country since January or earlier are already spoken for—carrying out hydrographic studies of Kuwaiti beaches, training Kuwaiti commandos, and supporting U.S. and Allied naval operations in the gulf. You boys haven't been assigned yet, so you draw the short straw."

"Hoo-*yah*!" MM1 Jack McKenzie cried. "It's about damned time!" The others chuckled.

"Hoo-yah," Scott replied, with considerably less enthusiasm. "We're violating one of our prime commandments by doing this, but CENTCOM is getting downright frantic about those Scuds."

Mark had been briefed on those commandments during his first week in Saudi Arabia; Scott was referring to his decision that the SEALs would only be employed in a maritime environment. *Not a problem,* he told himself, and he smiled. His dad had told him the story about the SEAL and the canteens in Vietnam, and about his own exchange with the Marine staff sergeant outside of Khafji. *We'll have our canteens with us.* . . .

Scott turned to rap a pointer on a large blow-up of a satellite photograph set on an easel at his back. "The Scud-B," he said. "Or the *Al-Hussein,* as the Iraqis call it. Thirty-seven feet long, a bit less than three feet wide. It weighs seven tons and has a speed of about Mach one to one point five. The original Scud-Bs designed by the Soviets had warheads packing one ton of high explosives, but the *Al-Hussein*'s warhead has been stepped down to five hundred pounds in order to give it a greater fuel capacity and a longer range. Range for the *Al-Hussein*—pretty close to four hundred miles.

"When the air war began," he continued, "Iraq had an estimated four hundred *Al-Hussein* missiles. About half of those were in fixed launch sites. The rest were fitted to be fired from mobile launchers, like the MAZ-543. So far, Saddam has fired sixty-six missiles, half at Israel, the rest at targets in Saudi Arabia. General Horner, the supreme CENTCOM air commander, has been going after Scud sites aggressively. We believe that air strikes to date have accounted for perhaps half of the fixed launch sites and several mobile launchers . . . estimates range from twelve to eighteen. That leaves Saddam with something like two hundred missiles remaining in his arsenal, and that, gentlemen, is *not* good."

The SEALs at the table murmured among themselves at that. Scott pushed ahead. "It's no secret that the ground phase of this war is coming up soon, perhaps *very* soon. CENTCOM deems it imperative that the remaining Scuds be found and destroyed. They are too inaccurate to pose a major *consistent* threat to ground units, but every once in a while, the Iraqis could get lucky. And the real question on everyone's mind is when they're going to start putting chemical or bacteriological warheads on top of those things."

Mark thoughtfully fingered the weight of the pouch slung over his shoulder and resting at his hip. They'd all been issued gas masks before their deployment to the gulf, and spent hours of training learning to work with the things on. Everyone knew Saddam had chemical and biological weapons. They knew he'd used gas before—against the Iranians and against Iraqi Kurds—and they knew he'd vowed to use them against both Israel and the Americans if he was attacked. There'd been several scares already, when chemical agents had been detected in the aftermath of a Scud strike, but so far those had all proven to be false alarms.

CENTCOM planners must be having kittens right now, kittens with big, fuzzy tails, over the possibility of a chemical strike against U.S. troop concentrations in Saudi Arabia.

A hand went up at the table. "Mueller," Scott said.

BM Chief Steve Mueller took down his hand. "Sir," he said, "begging your pardon, but what about the Patriot batteries? CNN keeps trumpeting about how our Patriots keep knocking the Scuds right out of the sky."

The Patriot was a tactical air defense system, a one-ton missile flying at Mach 3, radar-guided to incoming aircraft or, in this case, incoming Scuds. A number of batteries had been rushed to Saudi Arabia as soon as the standoff with Saddam had begun last August. Several batteries were rushed to Israel immediately after the first attacks to reassure the Israelis and persuade them to keep their promise that they would not strike back, would not join in the war against Iraq. The boxlike Patriot launchers, with their attendant radar trailers, electrical generator trucks, and engagement control station vehicles, were familiar and welcome sights wherever coalition forces were gathered. There'd been some pretty spectacular footage on the news lately of night engagements between Patriots and Scuds, of fireworks lighting up the night sky.

Scott frowned and shook his head. "I'm afraid, Mueller, that you can't believe everything you hear on CNN, okay? Hate to break it to you, but there's no tooth fairy, either." The men at the table laughed, and Scott went on. "Gentlemen . . . and I must emphasize that this is classified information . . . it's beginning to look as though the Patriot isn't the cure-all CENTCOM thought it was. They're putting the best face on the thing to the news agencies, of course, but too many Scud warheads are getting through. What we think is happening is that the Patriots are locking onto the biggest target in front of them. Unfortunately, those damned Scuds tend to break up during flight. The Patriots are destroying the missile's main fuel tanks, and ignoring the warheads. It's almost like the Scuds come with their own ready-made decoys. We just don't have any way to identify and target a 250-pound warhead tumbling to earth amid several tons of flying scrap.

"You've all heard about the Scud strike in Dhahran."

Mark nodded his agreement along with the others. In a way, the potential deadliness of this science-fiction warfare had been driven home just a few nights before, when a Scud had struck the barracks occupied by the newly arrived 14th Quartermaster Company, an Army Reserve unit based in Greensburg, Pennsylvania. Twenty-eight soldiers, men and women, had died and eighty were wounded—the highest number of casualties in a single Scud attack yet.

"That Scud," Scott said, "apparently was intercepted by a Patriot salvo. That seems to be a case where the Patriots did more harm than good, by dropping part of the Scud onto that barracks.

"Here's another story for you," he went on. "And this, I'll remind you, is classified secret. This is one we *don't* want to air on CNN, okay? Early this morning, an Iraqi Scud was fired at the port facilities at Al Jubayl. It landed in the gulf at oh-two-oh-seven hours, local time. It just missed a Polish hospital ship and came within a kilometer or so of an LHA, the *Tarawa*, and a major munitions dump. Intelligence has reason to believe the strike was aimed at the *Tarawa* herself, rather than at the general area. They were hoping to get lucky. They almost did.

"Gentlemen, that one could have been bad, *very* bad. Had that missile fallen just a thousand yards to the north of its actual impact point, the resulting explosion would have taken out the *Tarawa,* several other ships, and possibly claimed thousands of lives.

"And for your information, Mueller, there was a Patriot battery at the port, but it was down for a swap-out of a part of its main computer and didn't come back on-line until five minutes after the attack. Given what happened at the barracks in Dhahran, that may have been what saved the *Tarawa.*

"Needless to say, details of that incident are being kept very, very quiet. SEAL and EOD personnel are already at Al Jubayl, attempting to recover the missile, but CENT-COM has put out a report that it hit ten miles from the port, well outside of the Patriot battery's coverage area."

Mark thought of the Team members and Explosive Ordnance Disposal personnel diving to find that missile, with its 250-pound unexploded warhead. That was *not* a job he would care to tackle himself.

"We don't want Saddam's people to know just how close they came that night to scoring a major victory in the Scud war," Scott went on. "And we don't want the fact of that near miss to frighten either our allies or the folks back home.

"What we want . . . what we *need,* is to destroy the remaining Scuds!"

But that, Mark thought, would be a lot easier said than done. Iraq was a very large haystack in which to hide a handful of very small needles. . . .

Scott tapped the satellite image again. "This photo shows a typical *Al-Hussein* mobile launch site. These cylinders here and here are missiles still in their shipping tubes. This is a fuel truck. And this, here, is the MAZ-543 launch trailer, with a missile in place. The tactical problem we face is the fact that these mobile launchers are so damned mobile. They can arrive at a firing site and have the missile fueled and ready to launch within a few hours. After launch, they can pack up and be gone in minutes.

"Scuds launch out of two main areas—the desert in the extreme west of Iraq, where the launches against Israel have been fired from—and the so-called Scud Basket in southeastern Iraq, from the Al Hajarah Desert in the west, to the Tigris Valley in the northeast, and south to Iraq's border with Saudi Arabia and Kuwait. Finding a hundred or so mobile launchers in all that space in time to stop even one launch is damned near impossible. Even if we manage to spot one before launch, as we did with this satellite imagery here, the bird has flown long before we can vector strike aircraft into the area. The MAZ can be reloading for another shot fifty kilometers away by the time our planes can respond.

"For that reason, gentlemen, we are going to attempt to initiate a new program, a new way of doing things. CENT-COM is deploying several dozen hunter-killer teams into Iraq. We're going to actively track the Scud launchers before they can reach their launch sites.

"And this is how we're going to do it."

Mark listened intently and with something approaching awe. The odds for any one HK team still weren't good, but a large number of such teams, operating on the ground inside Iraq's Scud Basket, just might be able to come up with a few lucky hits.

They would be deploying by helo in six-man teams, with two predropped DPVs for transport. While it was impossible to pinpoint with any accuracy where the mobile Scud launchers might turn up next—after all, if Intelligence could turn up *that* bit of information, the job could be left to the Air Force—satellite reconnaissance had located several general areas where MAZ-543 launchers were frequently spotted. Roads were few and far between in the mostly trackless wastes of the southern Iraqi desert, but the mobile launchers *did* use roads where possible. MAZ tractors and launch trailers could navigate offroad, but slowly and always with the possibility of becoming mired in sand or of losing an axle on rough ground. Road travel was faster.

It was also more predictable. The Scud HK teams would set up observation posts overlooking certain key roads in the southern Scud Basket and notify CENTCOM Air Command by SATCOM whenever a likely target moved past. They would also perform broad sweeps of key target areas, searching for MAZ-543 tracks in the sand and looking for hidden or camouflaged supply dumps and truck parks.

The HK teams would go in heavily armed, with supplies for five days and carrying laser target designators in case they found themselves in a position to guide smart munitions in for the kill. Their most deadly assets, though, would be their eyes and their minds. Keyhole satellites might be able to photograph license plates from orbit, but it took a brain and what SEALs liked to call their Mark 1 MOD 0 eyeballs to distinguish decoys from reality—or, and Mark chuckled at the thought, a camel caravan from an Iraqi Army patrol.

"There's one major catch, gentlemen," Scott said as he wrapped up the briefing. "We all know that the ground war is going to commence any day now. The Iraqis know that too, and they're going to be on the alert. CENTCOM is particularly anxious that we not tip our hand. If any of you clowns run into trouble—shooting trouble—the Iraqis might think that the ground offensive has begun and react by moving in troops and tanks.

"While we are not privy to General Schwarzkopf's battle plans at this date, I can tell you that the idea will be to keep the Iraqi Army pinned down in one place, not letting them chase all over the desert.

"So take extreme care, gentlemen. Do not let yourselves be seen. Do not get drawn into a firefight. I have General Schwarzkopf's solemn promise that he will personally skin alive any special forces operative who risks giving away the game to the enemy. Am I understood?"

"Yes, sir!" the men chorused.

"Consider this your warning order. We will begin loading up at 1800 hours tomorrow. You are dismissed."

"Hoo-yah!"

Mark was on his feet with the others, fist punching the air, shouting the SEAL battle cry. This was it. He was going into combat—his first time.

He was glad his mom didn't know.

19 February 1991

The Arabian Gulf
Off Kuwait City
Kuwait
0015 hours

"Luck, guys. Bring back Saddam's mustache as a souvenir."

Greg acknowledged Gerrold's good wishes with a jaunty

touch of forefinger to brow, before rolling over the side of the CRRC and into the black waters of the gulf. The water was cold—fifty-five degrees—but Greg was wearing a black wetsuit that insulated him well enough from the chill. Drexler splashed into the water right behind him, and together the two SEALs began swimming toward the shore.

In a way, this was a return to the days of World War II, when combat swimmers of the early UDT swam unarmed onto the beaches of Japanese-held islands in order to perform hydrographic reconnaissance, clear beach obstacles, and determine whether the beach shelf could support armored vehicles.

Those men—"naked warriors," they'd been called by men who'd chronicled their exploits—had carried out their mission wearing nothing but swim trunks, flippers and mask, an underwater chalkboard for making notes . . . and occasionally a coating of blue paint to help ward off the cold. Tonight, their SEAL descendants were reconnoitering an enemy-held beach without much more.

The wetsuit warded off the cold. He wore flippers but no swim mask. There was too great a chance that a stray reflection off the plastic faceplate would give them away. Rather than donning a Draeger rebreather, SCUBA gear, or other underwater breathing apparatus, he carried a "bail bottle," a small tank containing three minutes worth of air. If he was spotted, the tank would let him stay submerged just long enough to get out of range.

Instead of a chalkboard, he carried a battle board, a plastic board with a built-in compass that allowed him to record depth readings, bearings, and other hydrographic data. His knife, a Sykes-Fairbairn commando blade that he carried strapped to his leg in preference to the standard-issue Mark I SEAL knife, rounded out his gear. He carried no other weapons. This was definitely one of those situations where, if shots were fired, the mission was a failure.

Greg swam on the surface with an easy sidestroke, his head above water, navigating by the light from Kuwait City. Parts of the city were blacked out, but other areas, surprisingly, were brightly lit. There was light enough to easily see Kuwait City's signature water towers, huge spheres pierced by vertical, needle-tipped towers in architectural mimicry of Islamic minarets.

The stretch of beach immediately ahead was broad and flat, a smooth black shelf running from the splash of the surf to a row of waterfront buildings. Farther north along the coast was the ritzy part of town, opulent hotels, gleaming white beachfront resorts, and the mansions of Kuwait City's wealthy elite. Here, though, the buildings were shabbier, darker, and less inviting, reminding him a bit of the Mataznillo District in Panama City, a bizarre mingling of the very rich with the very poor. A low, rumbling seawall divided the buildings from the beach. Steps led up to alleys or short, dead-end streets between some of the buildings.

Though the buildings along this part of the waterfront were blacked out, there was plenty of light. In the distance, numerous oil fires, brilliant orange beacons, flared against the night. Though it was a clear night according to the Met boys and girls, the sky was shrouded in a moody, turgid veil of poisonous blackness, a pall of smoke lit from below by the burning oil wells. The stink of oil hung in the air.

A surge of water broke over Greg's head from behind. He squeezed his eyes shut and kept swimming. The water stank worse than the air, and a viscous, somewhat slimy scum blanketed the surface. It stank even worse than the Pit back in the dunes above San Diego Harbor, but Greg ignored the assault on his senses and gave a small inward thanks for the training that had inured him to mere discomfort.

At least this oil slick was relatively minor, unlike the black sea engulfing the beaches farther south.

The oil here was fallout from the burning oil wells, a toxic rain of raw petrochemical soot drifting across the gulf as far east as Iran and far down the coast into Saudi Arabia. It covered everything—buildings, sand, water, skin—and burned the mouth, nose, and lungs. A month earlier, on 22 January, in what the newscasters were calling acts of ecoterrorism, Saddam's troops had begun detonating explosives in oil wells across Kuwait. And on this day, 19 February, they'd stepped up the destruction, igniting oil wells wholesale throughout the country—over two hundred so far. The massive oil field blazes were perhaps the *second* most destructive assault by the Iraqis on Kuwait and Saudi Arabia. Two days later, they'd opened wide the valves on the refinery at Mina al Hamadi, just north of the Saudi-Kuwaiti border, dumping 250 million gallons of crude into the waters of the Arabian Gulf—the largest oil spill in history. Saddam's target, evidently, had been the desalinization plant at al Khafji, but Allied aircraft, in a dazzling display of pinpoint-precision bombing on 27 January, had destroyed one key pumping station in an oil terminal complex with a 2,000-pound laser-guided bomb and closed off the spill.

But now a pall of carcinogenic black smoke hung over Kuwait and northern Saudi Arabia, and the oil slick clung to the sands of the gulf beaches, miring thousands of sea birds and threatening to kill off the wildly diverse and delicately balanced ecosystem of the gulf. Saddam's use of the offshore oil slick as an offensive weapon had backfired. In terms of Iraq's public relations campaign to turn world opinion against the coalition, Saddam had done far more damage to himself than to his enemies.

However, the damage to the shoreline was still incalculable, as was the damage to Kuwait's oil-based economy.

Many CENTCOM planners felt that Saddam knew the Allies were going to oust him from Kuwait sooner or later and that he was taking this opportunity to settle old scores by wrecking the Kuwaiti oil industry.

Reports coming out of Kuwait suggested that some, at least, of Saddam's troops were engaging in the wholesale rape of the tiny country, stripping it of national treasures, cash, and luxury goods, wrecking factories and oil facilities, and brutalizing its people.

He's going to have to pay for all of this, Greg thought, his head breaking through another oily wave. *The bastard's got to know we're going to hold him accountable for it.*

Which didn't help the Kuwaitis right now. All Greg and his fellow SEALs could do was to continue to run hydrographic missions up and down the coast as planned, gathering information for the upcoming invasion of occupied Kuwait. That the invasion was coming the SEALs had no doubt. For months now, U.S. Marines had been practicing landings up and down the Saudi coast, and some thirty-one amphibious assault ships carrying 17,000 Marines of the 4th and 5th Marine Expeditionary Units cruised back and forth a few miles offshore, ready for the word to go.

In preparation for the coming Marine offensive, SEALs deployed to the KTO, the Kuwaiti Theater of Operations, had been carrying out an aggressive program of support. On 19 January, SEALs on board the guided missile frigate *Nicholas* had stormed the Durrah oil platforms fifty miles out into the gulf off the Kuwaiti coast. Iraqi forces had been using the platforms as lookout posts and as convenient bases from which to take pot shots at Allied aircraft passing overhead. Moving in under a bombardment of Hellfire missiles launched by a pair of Army AH-58 Kiowa helicopters, the SEALs had boarded the platforms, killed five Iraqis, and captured twenty-three, the first combat POWs taken in the war. On 24 January, SEALs from the destroyer *Leftwich* had heloed in to the island of Qurah, fourteen miles off the coast, after other helicopters had come under fire from the site. Three Iraqis were killed in that fight, and fifty-one were captured. After the skirmish, the SEALs ran a Kuwaiti flag up a flagpole above the beach, making Qurah the first bit of Kuwaiti territory officially liberated from Iraqi occupation.

More recently, SEALs had been moving up and down the Kuwaiti coast, probing Iraqi defenses, using machine-gun fire against enemy patrol boats and calling in air strikes on juicy targets ashore. And, of course, there was the endless work of finding and disarming Iraqi mines, work done by both the SEALs and the elite Explosive Ordnance Disposal teams, the EOD.

Greg and his platoon hadn't been in on any of those actions, most of which were carried out by SEAL detachments on board ships patrolling the gulf waters off Kuwait. They and dozens of other SEALs continued to carry out the far less glamorous but vitally important job, as routine as a nine-to-five career in accounting, of sampling, measuring, and exploring the beaches of Kuwait in anticipation of the Marine landings sure to come.

Another oily surge carried Greg forward, and this time his knees and forearms dragged across the sandy bottom.

Oil coated the skin of his face and hands as effectively as camo paint. He belly-crawled a few feet farther up the beach shelf. Drexler came ashore, a black shadow agleam with oil, a few feet to his left. They made eye contact, then began carefully moving forward.

Pylons, barbed wire, steel girders, chunks of concrete, and other obstacles made this stretch of coastline look like the beaches of Normandy on the night before D-day. It was low tide right now, and most of the obstacles rose from the sand just above the waterline. A fire burned brightly farther down the beach, a hundred yards away.

Carefully, Greg and Drex moved up the shelf of the beach, using the obstacles for concealment, recording what they saw on their boards with each pause in movement.

The buildings beyond the seawall showed signs of recent construction activity. Holes were knocked in some of the walls, giving them the look of firing ports in a fortress. Some doorways had been half filled with sandbags or concrete blocks; someone had gone to a lot of trouble to fortify those structures, turning them into bunkers. Greg was willing to bet a year's pay that there were machine guns, mortars, shoulder-fired rocket launchers, and plenty of small arms stashed away behind those building walls, ready for the moment when the Marines stormed ashore. The alleys between the houses had been fortified as well, blocked off with sandbags, concrete, and piles of debris, all topped by coils of barbed wire and tank obstacles.

This particular stretch of beach, at least, was a death trap, as heavily defended, evidently, as Omaha Beach in WWII. Intelligence reports suggested that at least five Iraqi divisions currently occupied the Kuwaiti coast, backed by plenty of artillery, and with mechanized divisions in reserve. Current estimates put Marine casualties at 10 percent when they stormed these beaches.

Not good. Not good at all.

A shrill scream, a woman's scream, cut through the night. It was coming from the left, toward the south . . . possibly from the fire on the beach. Greg held up a hand to block out the light of the fire, trying to see.

By the flickering glow, he could make out three figures, apparently struggling together. It looked like three Iraqi soldiers were grappling with a woman, half dragging, half carrying her down the beach. Greg felt a sick certainty in the pit of his stomach about what was happening over there.

Drexler looked back over his shoulder at Greg. His hand

moved in the silent sign language SEALs used in situations where silence was vital. *Let's go!*

Greg's fingers closed in the sign meaning *no*. He added a second sign. *Freeze!*

The woman screamed again, and Greg caught the sound of tearing cloth. Damn it all! If the two SEALs tried to help her, they could easily be spotted, and the mission would be compromised.

And yet how the hell would he live with himself if the two of them just turned away and swam off into the night?

Chapter 19

South of Kuwait City
Kuwait
0104 hours

One of the soldiers stepped away from the fracas up the beach, turned, and lurched unsteadily toward the surf. His path took him among the beach obstacles, weaving almost directly toward the two SEALs where they lay hidden in the shadows beside a concrete pylon. The man was drunk, barely able to stay on his feet. They could hear him humming tunelessly under his breath.

Behind him, close by the fire, the woman screamed again, and one of the soldiers holding her slapped her, hard. The screaming stopped, replaced by a low, sobbing moan.

Dear God in heaven, Greg thought. *This can't be happening! . . .*

The lone Iraqi soldier was less than ten feet away now, leaning with one hand against a steel girder and fumbling with the waistband of his pants with the other. He called something back over his shoulder in Arabic, and his companion gave a harsh, nasty laugh.

The soldier began urinating in the sand.

Greg's mind was racing. Their orders tonight were explicit: under *no* circumstances whatsoever were they to reveal their presence to the enemy. Hell, Schwarzkopf himself had promised to skin alive any special forces personnel who endangered his strategy through cowboy antics, as he called them.

And yet there just might be a way.

Quietly, he reached down and drew the jet-black Sykes-Fairbairn from its sheath. Drexler saw the movement, and his eyes widened. Greg nodded. They were going to do this, but they would have to move fast, move silent, and move deadly.

The Iraqi's night vision would be shot, thanks to that fire on the beach, and his reaction time would be way down, thanks to the alcohol he'd obviously been consuming. If Greg could take him down silently, they might have a chance at the remaining two soldiers, if they moved fast.

Moving belly-flat on the sand, circling wide to keep the concrete pylon between himself and his target, Greg closed the last few feet, reaching the Iraqi just as the man fumbled again with his trousers, buttoning them up.

The Sykes-Fairbairn, designed by a British commando in World War II, was a slender, almost delicate blade, designed for one thing and one thing only—a swift and silent kill. Rising just as the Iraqi started to turn away, Greg brought his left hand up over the Iraqi's mouth from behind and dragged the head back; the blade plunged home at the same instant, driving up beneath the angle of the man's jaw, slicing open his throat and penetrating the base of the skull. The Iraqi's arms and legs jerked spasmodically once, then went limp. Something like a soft, gurgling sigh escaped the bloody mouth. Greg eased the dead weight to the sand.

Drexler was at his side. Greg pointed, and his swim buddy nodded. Two more soldiers, one apiece. It sounded as though they were occupied at the moment and oblivious to anything else.

Drexler faded into the shadows, but Greg stood upright and began walking toward the fire, lurching unsteadily in imitation of the drunken Iraqi. *At least,* he thought, *we know there aren't any mines on this part of the beach.* Silently, he thanked the dead Iraqi for pointing that fact out. That would be an important piece of intel when they got back.

One of the remaining Iraqis was holding the woman's hands. The other lay full-length on top of her, tugging at the remnants of her clothing. Surprisingly, she appeared to be in western dress rather than the traditional all-covering shroud worn by most Arabic women in this part of the world. Many Kuwaitis, Greg remembered, especially in the wealthy classes, were quite western in their thought and culture. Maybe it had been her dress that had singled her out for this attack.

Three AK-47 rifles rested in a tripod nearby, butts in the sand, barrels clipped together. The fire—a blaze inside a fifty-five gallon drum resting upright in the sand—cast a surreal and shifting glow over the scene, adding a night-marish touch. The soldier holding the woman's hands looked up as Greg approached, grinned broadly, and said something in a guttural burst of Arabic. Probably the only thing he could see of Greg was an upright shape, black against the smoke-shrouded night.

Greg grunted in reply, then stepped into the circle of light, grabbed the hair of the Iraqi on top of the woman, and sliced through trachea and carotid together in a single slash. The other Iraqi let go of the woman's hands, voiced a shocked gobble of sound, and jumped back—straight into Drexler's waiting arms. Drex thrust his SEAL knife up under the angle of the man's jaw, cracked bone, and severed the spinal cord.

Greg turned to the woman, who was sitting up, dark eyes wide with shock and fear. She was young, probably in her midteens, and the vision of these two frogmen looming up out of nowhere, dressed all in black and with blackened hands and faces, must have been almost as terrifying as the ordeal she'd just been through.

"Take it easy, Miss," Greg said, keeping his voice soft and gesturing with his free hand. "It's okay. . . ."

The woman scooped up the crumpled rags of her dress, holding them against her body as she scrambled to her feet and began running back up the beach.

"Wait!" Drexler called quietly, but the woman didn't stop. Greg touched Drex's arm. There was nothing else they could do for her, especially if she didn't want to stop and talk with the two black-garbed swimmers.

Greg and Drexler dragged the two bodies down to the waterline; Drex stayed with them then, while Greg fetched the third body. The sand showed little in the way of drag marks; in a few more minutes, the tide would be in far enough to obliterate any marks they did leave, wiping them away so completely even a Bedouin couldn't track them.

They left the rifles. Greg's guess was that the three Iraqi soldiers were a sentry detail on this part of the beach. At some point they would be missed, but not for several hours yet if the SEALs' luck held. Greg and Drexler donned their flippers, then hauled their burdens into the water. There were concrete pylons out there, positioned to tear the bellies out of incoming Marine landing craft. One of those would serve nicely as a snag that would keep the bodies permanently out of sight.

Allied Intelligence had been full of reports lately on the poor morale of most Iraqi soldiers. A number had managed to desert already, and there were stories circulating about deserters being caught and shot behind Iraqi lines.

These three would be listed as AWOL, with the assumption that they'd deserted.

The only loose end was the girl. If she was stopped by

other Iraqi soldiers as she ran half-naked through the streets . . . would she tell them what she'd seen?

Unlikely, Greg thought. She certainly had no love for the Iraqis, and she was already so deeply in shock any story she told would be fragmented and hysterical.

No, Greg was pretty sure they'd gotten away with these "cowboy antics."

Well out from the shore, they found a concrete block dropped on the bottom, its top just barely beneath the surface at low tide. There were hundreds of the things out here, waiting for the onslaught of American landing craft. Diving deep in the ink-black water, Greg's fingers found the iron hooks that had served as attachment points for the shipboard cranes that had set them in place. They made convenient attachment points for the belts on the three bodies.

His biggest question as he secured one of the bodies down near the sandy bottom was whether or not he and Drexler were going to report this little incident when they got back to Ra's al Mishab.

After all, the incident in question had never happened, and the two SEALs had never been there on that Kuwaiti beach.

22 February 1991

Near As Salman
South-Central Iraq
0210 hours

"Five minutes!"

Mark watched Lieutenant Francis Hunter nod and give the helicopter's crew chief a thumbs-up. He sat on the narrow bench in the Blackhawk's cargo bay, watching black desert streak past. The ground, barely visible by moon and starlight but rendered bright by the light intensifier goggles he wore, blurred past beneath the helo's belly, rough, rocky, and unforgiving.

At least it's not a HALO insertion this time, he thought. Back in California, during the intensive post-BUD/S training, he'd thought SEALs who didn't care for high-altitude parachute jumps were wrestling a bit with the wimp factor. Now, though, out here in the real world, on a real op, looking at that unforgiving terrain, he knew that the operative problem was not a wimp factor but the infamous pucker factor.

Just how tightly puckered could a man's asshole become with the stress of the last few moments before showtime?

Except for the fact that he and five other SEALs were hurtling across the desert at dune-hopping altitude in a Blackhawk helicopter instead of leaping from a C-130 at 25,000 feet and that the DPVs hadn't been dropped yet, this could almost be an exact replay of that last mission in the desert above Niland.

He hoped the C-130 with their transport was on time and on-target. If they weren't, it would be a damned long hike back to Ra's al Mishab.

David Tangretti, sitting to his right, slapped his shoulder and grinned, his teeth startlingly white against his black face paint. "We're a long way from the ocean!" he shouted, pitching his voice above the roar of the Blackhawk's rotor.

"Hey, SEALs go anywhere!" Mark shouted back. "Sea, air, and land!"

"Button it up!" the lieutenant shouted. "Two-minute warning!"

They *were* a long way from the water, though—almost three hundred miles from Ra's al Mishab, and a good hundred miles inside the Iraqi border. He wondered if Schwarzkopf knew.

Well, of course he did, in general, if not in specific. But the leader of the Allied coalition, though brilliant, was also mercurial. And the pace of the war had been stepping up for the past few days, until things were moving so quickly that no one could really keep up.

During this past week there'd been a number of cross-border raids, penetrations into Iraqi territory in order to capture prisoners, gather intel on Iraqi positions and equipment, and take out key defensive positions. Just yesterday, elements of the 101st Airborne—the "Screaming Eagles"—had launched a cross-border raid just west of this place, scouting Iraqi positions and taking down a command bunker complex known as "Objective Toad." By the time that little skirmish had resolved, the bunkers had been blasted to bits, and the paratroopers found themselves in unexpected possession of over four hundred prisoners, troops from the Iraqi 45th Infantry Division. The 101st boys hadn't intended to take more than a few prisoners for interrogation purposes, but as the bunkers had begun blowing up, the Iraqi soldiers had begun emerging from trenches and shelters everywhere, hands high or waving bits of white cloth. According to all reports, most had been delighted to be captured; food and water, evidently, were in short supply out here, and morale within the Iraqi Army was piss-poor. They'd had to call in seventeen additional helicopters in a massive airlift effort to transport the prisoners back to Saudi Arabia, an operation carried out with brilliant success.

But the word was that Schwarzkopf had hit the ceiling when he'd heard. Something big, something *very* big, was in the works, and CENTCOM's entire command staff was terrified that such incursions would tip off Saddam, give him warning about Allied intentions.

From the look of things, though, Schwarzkopf had little to worry about. The Iraqi command-control-communications infrastructure, after a month of savage bombing, was a shambles, and captured Iraqis so far showed no sign of anything beyond hunger, relief, and dazed fatigue.

And the incursions were being carried out all along the 300-mile front, from the far western border between Iraq and Saudi Arabia all the way to Kuwait and the sea. U.S. Marines were infiltrating Iraqi positions along the Kuwait border; SEALs were patrolling up and down the coast, blazing away with heavy machine guns and mortars at targets along the shore; the 24th Infantry had raided an antiaircraft position; and the 6th Cavalry had had a dust-up with Iraqi troops farther east, taking out twenty trucks, several triple-A batteries, two aircraft hangars, and lighting up the morning sky by detonating an artillery munitions dump. Even the French had gotten in on the action. Their 6th Light Armored Division had pushed forty miles into Iraq, in pursuit of some fast-moving—meaning fleeing—targets. By now, Saddam must know the massed might of the coalition was coming, as indeed he'd known all along, but he couldn't have a clue as to *where.*

Still, it was a little unnerving to know that, with so much going on along the desert lines of battle, the Iraqis must be thoroughly alerted by now. Demoralized or not, they still had a hell of a powerful force. Captain Scott had given the SEALs a run-down of intelligence estimates just a couple of days ago. The air campaign had been enormously successful, but it was simply impossible to nail everything the enemy possessed from the air. According to Intelligence, the Allies had accounted so far for 1,700 tanks—with 2,700 more still operational. They'd destroyed 1,500 artillery units, but there were 1,700 still in the field. Nine hundred fifty APCs had been taken out, but over two thousand remained.

There were no estimates as to the number of Iraqi dead and wounded so far, and those certainly numbered in the

tens of thousands, but their army was still very much intact—including six divisions of the vaunted Republican
Guard, positioned just outside of Kuwait. CENTCOM Intelligence had concluded that, after massive aerial pound-
ings by everything from A-10 Warthogs up to B-52 Arc
Light carpet bombings, no unit in the Iraqi army, including
the Republican Guard, could now mount an offensive, but
that defensive operations were another story entirely.

Forget about that, Mark told himself. *Focus on the
Scuds. They're your target, nothing else. . . .*

The Blackhawk jolted suddenly, a savage thump from
below and behind that kicked Mark in the small of the back
and set several of the SEALs to shouting bitter obscenities.
"What the fuck was that?" Tangretti demanded.

"Take it easy, people," Lieutenant Hunter replied. "Our
tail wheel just clipped a sand dune, is all."

The Blackhawk remained in the air—barely. Through
the open side door now, Mark could see the lights of a small
town in the distance—brilliant green through the LI goggles attached to his helmet. Sand dunes gave way to a road
and the sudden flash of a power-line pole. Shit! The Blackhawk pilot had just taken them *under* a set of power lines!
The guy must be as crazy as a SEAL.

Then they were too busy for fear. The Blackhawk flared
out, nose high, settling toward the desert in a swirling blast
of rotor-stirred sand. "Go! Go! Go!" Hunter was shouting,
and Mark leaped out of the door, hit the sand, and tumbled,
rising to his feet an instant later as other SEALs dropped to
the ground around him.

He dragged a full magazine from an ammo pouch and
snapped it home in his H&K's receiver. They'd been carrying their weapons unloaded, a safety precaution on board
the heavily loaded chopper, but now they were deep inside
enemy territory and ready for a fight. The six SEALs spread
out from the landing zone, crouching low in the sand as the

Blackhawk's rotors revved to full and the ungainly, insect-like machine roared into the sky once more. Sand burned and bit at exposed skin. Mark's night goggles kept the sand out of his eyes, though, and he rode out the sandblasting as the Blackhawk roared through a tight half-circle and clattered off toward the south.

And then the six SEALs were alone, alone in a dark, wide, and empty desert a hundred lonely miles behind enemy lines.

The silence, after an hour aboard the Blackhawk with its rotor noise hammering in his ears, was almost unsettling.

In silence, then, the SEALs began carrying out the list of details on their op plan. They gathered up their gear, including food and water for five days, ammunition, and both an LST-5C SATCOM and a bulkier AN/PRC-113 UHF/VHF transceiver. Their RTO, RM1 Bill Kennedy, broke out the SATCOM, opened a channel to a satellite, and began calling softly into its handset. MM Chief Yancey took a fix with a Magellan GPS unit, feeding data to Kennedy. Lieutenant Hunter stayed by Kennedy, while the rest of the team—HM2 Tangretti, BM1 Ernie Bowdon, and Mark—provided perimeter security, spacing themselves out in a triangle around the others.

One thing was clear right off. They'd come down close to the As Salman Road, as planned, but they were damned close to that village Mark had glimpsed from the air. From the top of a low ridge west of the LZ, he could see the village lights less than two hundred yards away—easy rifle range. He wondered if they'd heard the helicopter . . . and if any Iraqi troops were stationed there.

As Salman was a smallish desert town at the end of a major road leading south from As Samawah, a major city on the Euphrates River just 110 miles farther to the north. Intelligence believed that Iraqi mobile launchers used that highway in their ongoing shell game with Allied Scudbusters, speeding back and forth between the Euphrates Valley to the north and a series of dry wadis, dune seas, and open, rocky plains to the south. The planned LZ was twenty miles north of As Salman and supposedly well clear of any other population centers.

But if that was so, what the hell was *that*?

The village west of the ridge was little more than a straggling jumble of mud-brick buildings. Through low-light binoculars he could just make out a well at what passed for the town center, a stable, and what might be a mechanic's garage. Lights were on in several of the buildings. Had they heard the Blackhawk and sounded an alarm? Or were they by now used to the constant roar of aircraft low overhead, enough so that as long as bombs didn't fall, the roar could be safely ignored?

Lieutenant Hunter joined him behind the crest of the ridge overlooking the village. "Anything?"

"Negative, sir . . . except for that village. Damn it, we're a little close, aren't we?"

"Yeah, that we are. The Blackhawk put us exactly where we're supposed to be. Trouble is, the maps we have for this area are out of date and weren't that accurate to begin with. Either that, or that 'ville got up and walked six miles northwest."

"Sir . . . the Herky Bird with our DPVs'll be inbound by now. Shouldn't we move to a different drop zone?"

He sensed the lieutenant's shake of his head. "Negative on that, Halstead. We can't afford the time or the risk of missing that drop . . . and we sure as hell can't afford to go chasing around the desert looking for a secondary DZ. Any sign of an alert down there?"

"Except for those lights, no, sir. But it's zero-dark thirty. If I had to guess, I'd say we woke someone up."

"Here's what I want you to do, Halstead. I'm taking the others to set up the DZ ground signals well behind this ridge. I want you to keep a sharp eye on that 'ville. If you see anything so much as twitch down there, you sing out on the Motorola. Got it?"

"Aye, aye, sir. You'll hear me sing."

"Good man."

Lieutenant Hunter faded back into the shadows and was silently gone.

Mark soon felt the isolation, the nerve-wracking loneliness, of his watch post. The night was death-quiet, save for the dry whisper of the wind across the crest of the ridge, and it was dark. The moon, a waxing crescent, had set some hours before, and when he lifted his night goggles, the sky was a cold and infinitely deep sea of night gloriously strewn with ice-brilliant stars. The scene might have been in the high desert of California, one of the training ranges used by SEALs for weapons familiarization, say, but the unearthly clarity of those stars reinforced the sense of alienness, of sheer distance from the places and people he knew.

He brought the night goggles back down, and starlight turned almost day-bright, albeit in monotone shades of green against black.

Checking back over his shoulder, he found he couldn't see or hear the other SEALs, even with the LI goggles. He was tempted to use his Motorola—the small, short-ranged radio with an earplug and a lip mike each man wore strapped to his Kevlar vest for intersquad communications, for a radio check—but knew better. The rule was radio silence, unless he needed to give the others warning. He settled down, belly against cold sand, to wait. At least he wasn't sleepy, despite the hour. Adrenaline had been pumping through his system all day now, to the point where he felt as though he would never sleep again.

Movement. He wasn't sure, at first, but he thought he'd seen something move in the shadows close by that garage in the town. He lifted his LI goggles and brought his LI binoculars to his eyes, trying to penetrate the darkness.

Yes! There! Two men, obviously soldiers, with slung automatic rifles, standing outside the garage. A sudden, sharp flare of light moved toward one of the men's strangely glowing face—a match lighting a cigarette. As he watched, a third soldier joined them. They appeared to be talking, but every so often their faces would turn toward Mark, almost as if they could see him. That, of course, was impossible . . . but it did suggest to a suspicious or paranoid mind that they'd heard the Blackhawk and might even be discussing the need for a small night recon.

But as minutes passed, the soldiers did nothing but smoke and talk. Apparently they weren't about to go traipsing around the night-shrouded desert unless they absolutely had to. One of the men tossed down the butt of a cigarette, waved at the others, and walked out of sight behind the building.

A droning, deep-throated hum swelled in volume, coming from the south. Mark turned, searching the sky with his starlight optics. Yes . . . there it was, a ghostly pale green against the cold, black sky, looking almost like a photographic negative, a C-130 Hercules coming in across the desert at extremely low altitude.

Not as low, perhaps, as the dune-hopping Blackhawk earlier, but the big military transport was flying at something just less than a hundred feet, excruciatingly low for night flying over unfamiliar territory. The pilot and copilot would be wearing night goggles similar to those worn by the SEALs, of course, but it was still not a maneuver that Mark would have cared to try.

Mark returned his attention to the two Iraqi soldiers. Had they heard? The C-130 was almost certainly blocked from their sight by the ridge, even if they could see the blacked-out aircraft at all in the dark . . . but could they hear it?

Checking back over his shoulder a second time, he saw

the glow of chemical light sticks on the desert floor, two rows of three, the signal from the other SEALs. An instant later, a parachute blossomed from the C-130's open tail door, dragging a large and solidly packaged object down the ramp. No sooner was the first object clear of the aircraft than a second parachute appeared, dropping a second package.

The parachutes were not for landing the objects, but strictly to drag them clear of the aircraft. One after the other, they slammed into the desert, skidding on solidly built sled runners until they came to rest on the ground roughly between the two lines of chemical light sticks. The Hercules was already grabbing altitude, banking as it climbed, turning toward the east to begin the homeward leg of its flight.

Again, Mark checked the activity in the village. Yeah, they'd heard all right. One of the soldiers was sprinting for another building, and more and more lights were coming on.

He keyed his radio. "Lieutenant? Halstead. We have activity in the village."

"Roger that. Talk to me."

"Looks like they heard the delivery. Lights coming on. Soldiers moving around. It looks like they might be . . ." New motion caught his eye. "Wait a sec . . . shit."

"Whatcha got?"

"I see two trucks coming out of one of the larger buildings, the one that looks like a garage. Flatbeds, pickups. There are soldiers in them . . . looks like six in the back of one . . . maybe eight in the back of the other. PKMs on pintel mounts on both vehicles over the cabs. And they're definitely coming this way."

"How far?"

"They're still in the town. Maybe two hundred meters from my position."

"Okay, Halstead. Listen up. You are authorized to use

deadly force as soon as they are within effective range. You got that? Wait until they're in effective range, then open fire. See if you can drive them to cover."

"Roger that." He snicked back the bolt on his H&K and released it, chambering a round.

"We'll have the DPVs unshipped in a minute, then we'll come pick you up. Hold your position, see if you can pin them down, okay? We only need a few minutes grace."

"Aye, aye, sir."

"Excellent. Good hunting!"

Good hunting . . . right.

The 9mm Parabellum ball ammunition in Mark's weapon could travel a good thousand yards, but the H&K MP5SD3's relatively short barrel meant that even an expert shooter would have trouble making that bullet hit anything at much more than 130 to 150 yards—the H&K's *effective* range. The problem was that 150 yards was damned close to knife-fighting range when it came to modern combat. Those Iraqis down there carried AK-47s, assault rifles with an effective range of something like 300 yards.

However, the SEAL course in squad-level infantry tactics had taught Mark quite a bit. Back in California, he'd practiced a lot of crawling around in the boonies on San Clemente and in the desert above the Salton Sea, stalking U.S. Marines and other SEALs—and being stalked in turn. He'd learned a key axiom of modern warfare. One man *could* stop a platoon if he had to, at least temporarily. If he had the advantages of surprise and position, and if he had a certain amount of cold, raw nerve.

And of course his father had told him about the clusterfuck in Panama, where a handful of Noriega's PDF bullyboys had killed four SEALs, wounded eight more, and nearly deep-sixed the Paitilla op.

Mark's thumb stroked the weapon's fire select lever, checking that it was set to single-shot. Each SEAL was carrying just ten thirty-round magazines for his weapon, three hundred rounds of ammunition total . . . not very much at all for an extended stay deep behind enemy lines. The idea, after all, had been to get in and out without having to stop and play tag with Saddam's employees.

The lead truck was well clear of the village buildings now, pale green-on-green in Mark's LI optics. Both vehicles had their headlights on, which indicated that they weren't really expecting trouble out here . . . but which also made visibility through the sensitive light-intensifier goggles less than ideal. He aimed for a spot just above the green-white glare of the vehicle's left headlight, taking an educated guess at how far the round would drop in 150 yards, and allowing for the fact that the round would strike slightly above the bull's-eye when fired from a higher elevation to a lower one.

He braced his H&K on a flat rock at the crest of the ridge and then waited . . . waited . . . took in a breath, let part of it out . . . waited a moment longer . . .

Chapter 20

22 February 1991

Near As Salman
South-Central Iraq
0216 hours

Mark stroked the trigger, and the weapon gave a soft chuff of sound through its integral suppressor. The noise of the receiver snapping back and forward was louder than the shot itself. The spent brass cartridge flipped into the darkness behind and to his right.

But the truck kept coming; no change so far as he could make out. Mark took another look through his binoculars, then settled down into a second shot . . . bracing the weapon . . . aiming . . . holding . . . *squeeze*.

Still no change in the vehicle's progress. Well, the H&K wasn't exactly designed as a sniper's weapon. Try again. The lead truck wasn't much more than a hundred yards off, now . . . the length of a football field. It was beginning to climb, too, coming up the gentle slope leading the ridge crest where Mark was hidden. Both trucks were bouncing heavily now over uneven ground, sending billowing plumes of dust swirling in their wakes.

He fired again . . . and this time, the lead truck swerved sharply to the left, jounced over a body-sized boulder, and jolted to a stop. Iraqi soldiers spilled from the truck bed and dove for cover among the rocks. One stayed in the back of the truck, clinging to the grip of the mounted PKM, blazing a long and chattering stream of full-auto gunfire into the night.

Yeah . . . *that* had grabbed their attention, all right!

The machine-gun fire was wild, with yellow tracers spraying through the night high above the ridge and well off to Mark's right, but he wasn't going to take chances. He ducked down behind the top of the ridge and began crawling left, moving twenty yards before cautiously peeking over the top once more.

The second truck had pulled to a stop next to the first, and both machine guns were in action now. The PKM fired 7.62x54mm rounds, putting it in the same class as the American M60. The weapon's design was such that there was little recoil and little muzzle-climb, making it an extremely easy full-auto machine gun to fire. The question was how well trained those Iraqi soldiers down there were.

As he watched the Iraqis deploy, he decided that, whatever unit they were from, they weren't up to Republican Guard standards. They all were firing up the ridge, but there didn't appear to be any fire discipline or order. Some, he could see, were simply holding their AKs up above the boulder they were hiding behind and firing blind, emptying their magazines into sky or sand. Twice Mark heard the snap of stray rounds passing over his head. He stayed pressed flat against the ground, bracing his H&K with his left arm, flicking the selector switch to burst fire and taking careful aim.

The soldiers manning the two machine guns were the most dangerous of the enemy troops, as well as the most exposed. He squeezed the trigger, the weapon's soft, triple thump barely audible above the crack and chatter of the

Iraqi gunfire. The H&K's built-in sound suppressor slowed the nine-millimeter rounds to subsonic velocity, eliminating the loud crack of bullets breaking the sound barrier. Using the three-round burst setting, he could lay down a heavy volume of fire, yet stay on-target. Full-auto fire, as the Iraqis were learning now, tended to drag the weapon's muzzle high and waste the bullets.

The machine gunner slumped heavily to the side, dragging the PKM's muzzle around and almost vertical, before tumbling over the side of the truck. Mark shifted targets, taking aim on the second gunner . . . but that man was already leaping out of the truck, his weapon abandoned.

"Halstead," sounded in his earphone. "This is Hunter. What's your situation?"

"I've got at least sixteen Iraqi soldiers at the west base of the ridge," he replied, crawling back to the right with the ridge crest as cover. He found another spot to stop and cautiously peek over the top. "I've taken down one, maybe two. And . . ." He raised his binoculars to check the town again. "Looks like we've kicked over the hornet's nest, sir. I see more troops in the village. They know we're here, all right."

"Keep 'em cautious, Halstead. We're still unshipping the DPVs." There was a heartbeat's pause. "Some assembly required."

"Roger that, Lieutenant. Just like Christmas morning."

The DPVs would have been solidly packed and padded on the sled-pallets they'd ridden on board the Hercules, a system designed to let them fall a hundred feet at a couple of hundred miles per hour, hit, slide, and come to rest intact. Mark had seen light tanks delivered that way . . . but tanks seemed a bit more robust, a bit more of a solid, single unit, than the SEAL DPVs. His teammates would be busily mounting the machine guns, stowing fuel and ammunition, attaching the carry racks and roll bars, and taking care of anything else that would have been packaged separately in order to let it survive the rough handling.

"Hang on," Hunter told him. "We need ten minutes. Do you require assistance?"

He thought about that. It would be reassuring to have a swim buddy up here watching his back. On the other hand, the more hands they had for uncrating the dune buggies . . .

"Negative, sir. It's going to take at least that long for these bozos to sort themselves out."

"Copy. Hunter out."

Four Iraqis had begun working their way up the ridge, crouched low and stopping every few feet to have a look around. They looked nervous—and with damned good reason, Mark thought. Their companions at their backs were still firing wildly, raising the very real possibility that they would accidentally score an own-goal.

He aimed at the adventurous troops and fired another couple of three-round bursts. One of the soldiers slumped and lay still. Another rolled over on his back, cradling his knee against his chest and rocking back and forth. His two comrades left him there, diving for cover behind the nearest scattering of large rocks.

Another couple of trucks were leaving the village now, but they were moving south, not east. That made sense. The soldiers caught by Mark's sniping would have radioed for help; the reinforcements would try to cut around the SEALs' flank, to hit them from the side or the rear.

Mark passed this bit of tactical news on to Hunter, then concentrated on the Iraqis immediately in front of him. They didn't seem predisposed to show themselves any longer, not with two more of their number down. They weren't even firing now but appeared content to wait until reinforcements arrived to bail them out. Mark began a systematic campaign of firing, then pulling back and moving, firing, then pulling back and moving. The MP5SD3 didn't have much if any of a muzzle flash, but he wasn't going to take the chance of someone getting lucky and spotting his flash signature. From one position well to the north he managed to get a clear line of sight on an Iraqi crawling up the slope and put him down with a well-aimed burst.

He caught movement out of the side of his goggles and rolled onto his back. It was David, scrabbling up the east slope of the ridge. "How's it going, hotshot?"

"Just fine. The party's getting boring, though."

"Your limo awaits you, sir. If you'll come this way?"

"Hoo-yah!"

Together, they jump-and-side-stepped down the soft sand of the east slope. Both Desert Patrol Vehicles were waiting at the bottom. "Hop on!" Hunter called. "Time to get the hell out of Dodge!"

Mark and David scrambled onto the nearest DPV, David sliding into the seat beside Yancey, who was driving, Mark taking the high seat behind the sixty-gun.

"Let's roll!" David called. With a jolt, the two light DPVs leaped forward, their big tires spraying sand as they slued around and headed north.

A rattle of machine-gun fire sounded above the roar of the DPVs' engines. The other two pickup trucks had completed their flanking maneuver and were bouncing down the east slope of the ridge perhaps a hundred yards behind the SEAL vehicles. Their headlights bobbed and jolted with the rough terrain; those pickups weren't designed for open desert and must be giving their passengers a damned rough ride.

Machine guns blazed in the night, their muzzle flashes snapping above the bouncing headlights. Mark doubted that the gunners could see a thing in the dark; they were firing wildly, randomly, an attempt to use pure firepower to flush the SEALs from hiding and cut them down.

Were *they* ever in for a shock!

The Desert Patrol Vehicle might be little more than a glorified dune buggy, but the powerful Volkswagen engine gave it speed and power, and the operational weapons load-out echoed the SEAL philosophy of delivering overwhelming firepower where and when it was needed.

In four seconds, they hit thirty miles per hour and kept accelerating. Yancey hit the right-side cutting brake and they pivoted sharply, turning on the proverbial dime, and raced headlong onto the desert flat.

"Hoo-yah!" Mark screamed into the wind. Back in the seventies, when he and David were growing up in San Diego, a favorite rerun series on TV had been a silly little war drama called *The Rat Patrol*. The series had been entertaining enough, especially to a couple of nine-year-olds enamored of all things military, though its main premise appeared to be how three Americans and a Brit had won the desert war in North Africa single-handedly in a couple of jeeps fitted out with M-2 machine guns. Somehow, the show's signature image—of two jeeps momentarily taking flight as they crested the sand dunes, of the blazing devastation wrought on German trucks and tanks by those machine guns as the jeeps literally ran circles around them—had stuck with Mark through the years.

And now he was living that image . . . but with firepower and maneuverability way beyond what *The Rat Patrol*'s creators could ever have imagined.

Mark clutched the double handgrips of the big Ma Deuce, the .50-caliber machine gun mounted on the roll bar above the driver and navigator seats, leaning to the side to pivot the weapon around. He ratcheted back the charging lever, took aim at the closest headlights, and thumbed the butterfly trigger. The muzzle flash stabbed into the night, momentarily obliterating the IL-green image of the oncoming pickup. Mark had a blurred, split-instant's impression of windshield and windows shattering, of soldiers leaping, of the truck nosing into a ditch and flipping onto its side.

Flashes stitched across the path of the second truck, accompanied by a sharp, rattle-cracking thunder. Lieutenant Hunter, seated in the navigator's position in the other DPV, had just opened up with his Mk. 19, a full-auto grenade launcher that could pump out 40mm grenades at the rate of five per second. The effect—one SEAL had once referred to it as "saturation bombing"—was like calling in an air strike. The pickup went airborne as explosions lifted it from the ground . . . and then the gas tank exploded while it was still in the air.

An orange ball of roiling flame crawled into the sky, illuminating the desert and the Iraqi soldiers pressing themselves down against the ground.

"Hey, David!" Mark yelled, shrill above the roar of the engine. "Just like *The Rat Patrol!*"

The DPV went airborne off a dune, sailed through the air for a long second, then hit with a thump and a bounce of protesting hydraulics.

"Shit-*fire!*" David yelled back. "Those guys would never be able to keep up with us!"

In minutes, they were miles away, racing up the As Salman highway to avoid leaving tracks, then ducking off-road to travel through the dunes.

Mark wondered how aggressively the Iraqis would look for them.

So far, the op wasn't off to a real promising start.

SEAL Headquarters
Ra's al Mishab
Saudi Arabia
1500 hours

"All right, gentlemen," the Army colonel told the roomful of listening SEALs. With a dramatic flourish, he whipped a sheet off the easel at the front of the room, revealing a large map showing Kuwait, southern Iraq, and northern Saudi Arabia. "Now we can tell you what you've all been guessing at for the past month. The invasion for the liberation of Kuwait is about to begin. G-day is set for just before dawn on Sunday, 24 February."

Two more days! Greg felt the electric shock of that revelation crackle through the room, heard the murmur of low-voiced conversation among the listening SEALs.

Greg leaned forward, looking at the neatly arrayed rectangles marking military units—blue for American and Allied, red for Iraqi. The surprise was in the placement. Most of the heavy-hitter U.S. forces, units that a month ago had been lined up across Saudi Arabia closer to the Arabian Gulf behind a screen of U.S. Marines and Saudi units, had been shifted far, far to the east, throwing the overwhelming majority of the Allied thrust onto the left flank.

Blue arrows punched north across the Iraqi border, then swung sharply to the right; Schwarzkopf's master plan appeared to bypass Kuwait almost entirely, flanking the Iraqi army in the open desert, then smashing in on it, not from the south, but from the west and the northwest.

Farthest west were three French units—the 6th Light Armored and the French foreign legion's 2nd Parachute Infantry and 1st Cavalry—anchoring the U.S. flank and guarding against Iraqi counterattacks from the north and west. The American 101st Airborne and the 82nd Airborne formed the muscle of the end sweep, leapfrogging hundreds of miles north, then east into Iraq, all the way to the Euphrates River.

Moving east toward the gulf, blue rectangles marked the 24th Mechanized Infantry Division and the 3rd Armored Cavalry, the 1st Infantry Division and the 1st Cavalry, the pan-Arab forces and the U.S. 1st and 2nd Marines. According to the map, the Marines and armored units below the

Kuwaiti border would punch through the enemy's defenses and move north to Kuwait City, pinning the Iraqis in place, but the major fighting, it appeared, would be inside Iraq and in the west of Kuwait.

Prominently absent, however, was the long-expected invasion from the sea.

"General Schwarzkopf has been calling this our 'Hail Mary play,' an end-run around the main body of the Iraqi Army. The idea is to keep Saddam looking one way, toward the south, and sucker-punch him from his right."

Colonel Randolph Sanders, the briefing officer, had been introduced to the SEALs as a member of the CENTCOM planning staff. He was a small and rabbity-looking man whose glasses and Clark-Gable mustache seemed out of place with his baggy camo utilities.

"Our strategy to date has been to misdirect the Iraqis as to where the actual blow is going to fall," he continued, using his pointer on the map. "Obviously, the longer we can keep the enemy in the dark about the true nature of our move, the better." The pointer tapped the map at the southwest corner of Kuwait. "The 1st Cav has made several probing attacks in the past few days here, at the Wadi al Batin, which is a natural highway straight into the heart of Kuwait and which the Iraqis have fortified to an almost absurd level. That misdirection will continue. We intend to use continued pressure in this region to keep Saddam's attention focused there.

"In the south, the 1st and 2nd Marine Divisions are lined up opposite the main Iraqi defenses along the Kuwaiti border. Saddam's people have built up an enormous berm and created something right out of World War I, complete with trenches, bunkers, ditches, barbed wire, minefields . . . and a new twist. They've dug miles of trenches and filled them with petroleum. When the party starts, we expect them to light those oil trenches in order to block our attack.

"The Marines are set to go despite this rather formidable barrier. The most elaborate and carefully constructed line of fortifications in the world is only as good as the soldiers backing it up, and our intelligence over the past few weeks has painted a pretty consistent, a pretty grim picture of what's going on over there. By all reports, the Iraqi army is absolutely falling apart. Their Republican Guard is still a potent fighting force, we think, but their guard units are being held in reserve, north of Kuwait City. The Marine and Arab coalition forces are probably facing raw recruits and unwilling conscripts, half-starved and by this time completely dazed by the bombing.

"In any case, the Marines will actually start moving forward ahead of G-day. Their engineering battalions will begin moving tomorrow, dynamiting sections of the berm, clearing corridors through the minefields, and taking down Iraqi strong points while Marine task forces will punch through several key points in the enemy line. The Marines are moving early just to keep Saddam's people looking right where we want them to look, toward the south.

"CENTCOM wants to add one more flourish to the deception. For weeks, now, the Iraqis have been aware of our Marine units offshore, here in the gulf, and knowing the Marine penchant for amphibious landings, they've been expecting an invasion from the sea, somewhere here, close to Kuwait City. Naval forces have been instrumental in this part of the deception, everything from your SEAL small boat units up to bombardment by the battleships *Missouri* and *Wisconsin.*

"Your SEAL CO has presented an operational plan in support of our diversionary activities, and it has been approved by CENTCOM.

"Captain Scott will fill you in on your part of the operation." He hesitated, then added, "I know things haven't always been the smoothest between the various special forces units and Central Command. I would like to say for the record, though, that General Schwarzkopf is enormously impressed by SEAL Team operations carried out so far in this conflict. He told me to tell you people, from him, personally, that he knows he can count on each and every one of you to do what has to be done to see this thing through. Thank you. Captain Scott?"

The SEALs in the room applauded as Sanders left the podium, a way, perhaps, of saying "No hard feelings." Sanders's platitudes notwithstanding and despite the wry jokes floating around CENTCOM and occasionally reaching all the way down to the men in the field, relations between the special warfare community and the regular military had been remarkably cordial. Both sides had work to do. Both sides did it, and for the most part left the other group alone.

Greg had decided, after all, to report the dust-up on the beach at Kuwait City. There was important intelligence there . . . the lack of a minefield and the fact that the Iraqi troops manning those defenses were ill disciplined, more interested in loot and rape than anything else. Lieutenant Dietz, whose platoon Greg had been assigned to weeks before, had given him a fairly mild chewing out, scarcely even blistering the paint on the wall behind him. He'd been told that there might be an official and very negative reaction from CENTCOM. Reportedly, Schwarzkopf had been on a fuming rampage over false starts that might give away the game for weeks now. There was every possibility that Greg would be singled out for disciplinary action.

But the only response from on high was a thunderous silence. Perhaps, with the pickup of the pace over the past week, Greg and Drex's little incursion into Kuwait was being seen as just another element in the grand strategy of deception. Anything that made Saddam look south and east—and away from the west—was good.

Commodore Scott walked up to the podium. "Thank you, Colonel. And may we say that it's been a pleasure working with the regular army as well.

"Gentlemen," he said. "A select few of you are going to convince the Iraqis that seventeen thousand Marines are coming ashore right here in Kuwait City, right in their laps. Do you think you can handle that?"

The thunderous chorus of "Hoo-yah!" was answer enough.

"Up until now, our primary focus has been on hydrographic reconnaissance of the beaches up and down the Kuwaiti coast." Scott turned his head, scanning his audience, until he spotted Greg, and grinned. "Some of you men have been carrying out that reconnaissance with, shall we say, excessive enthusiasm? I've had reports of several SEALs who've managed to carry out their own, personal and temporary invasions of Kuwait.

"For most of you, though, it's been a damned long and tedious job. No glory. No excitement. Unless you want to call hypothermia exciting."

The listening SEALs chuckled at that.

The public perception of Navy SEALs—thanks to several movies and popular books—remained one of larger-than-life action-heroes, of macho Ramboesque warriors carrying out daredevil missions in blazing displays of large-caliber pyrotechnics.

But in actuality, since the very beginning of the U.S. buildup in the Gulf, the Navy SEAL presence in Southwest Asia had been one of quiet and rigorous professionalism. The firefights and skirmishes—the take-down of the Durrah oil platforms, the capture of Qurah, the brief encounter at al Khafji—had all been unusual variants in the weave of a much larger pattern. By far the most common type of SEAL mission to date had been offshore reconnaissance.

SEALs had been slipping into the waters off Kuwait almost every night since January, watching Iraqi coastal traffic, studying the beaches, making detailed notes and photographs of Iraqi defensive preparations. The most common op involved three-man teams dropping into the water from CRRCs or small patrol craft and swimming up close to the beach—not actually going ashore, but lying in the shallow surf, using night-vision optics to pierce the darkness.

When the Teams' direct predecessors, the Navy's UDT, had performed almost identical missions around Japanese-held islands in World War II, they'd been forced to go in by day just so they could see what they were doing. LI technologies gave the SEALs a tremendous advantage here. The frogmen of WWII had frequently been spotted and fired at. So far as the SEALs in the Gulf knew, the Iraqi high command remained blissfully unaware of this surveillance off of the Kuwaiti beaches.

And any individual Iraqi soldiers who'd happened to discover otherwise had simply, and quietly, vanished.

Those small teams of SEALs had floated in the surf for hours at a time, studying the beach, studying the defensive fortifications, watching for signs of Iraqi movements or prepared positions. Their number-one priority had been to find and report on any beaches suitable for a Marine amphibious landing.

That search had been singularly frustrating. Nearly the entire length of the Kuwaiti coast, from Bubiyan Island south to Mina bad Allah, was built up to one degree or another. Buildings—everything from oil refineries and tanker loading facilities to warehouses to palatial mansions to sprawling slums—were scattered along the coast in thick profusion. Only the region around Kuwait City itself was truly urban, but Marines coming ashore anywhere along that eighty-mile stretch of coastline would find themselves fighting in an urban environment—the dirtiest, nastiest, and most deadly type of combat. The Iraqis could be expected to turn every house into a fortress; to defend every street with hidden machine guns, mortars, rocket launchers, and mines; to force the Marines into a brutish house-to-house combat guaranteed to inflict as many casualties on the attackers as possible.

The Marines might easily find themselves pulling a reprise of the landing at Tarawa in WWII, where over eleven hundred men of the 2nd Marine Division had died in seventy-six hellish hours—due largely to poor intelligence about reefs, beaches, and tides—in front of a labyrinth of carefully prepared and heavily fortified Japanese defensive positions. Bloody Tarawa had drawn a clear picture of the need for careful reconnaissance of the beaches slated for invasion. Tarawa, in one sense, had been the birthplace of the Navy UDTs, the combat swimmers who'd made those daylight explorations of Pacific islands, from Saipan to Iwo to Okinawa.

The SEAL recon teams had finally found one beach on the Kuwaiti coast that might fit the bill. It was a mile and a half of dunes and flat sandy shelf south of Kuwait City, between the towns of As Salamiyah and Al Fuhayhil. There were some buildings behind the beach—in Kuwait, *everyone* with a choice preferred living closer to the cool waters of the gulf, rather than in the blazing interior—but they were widely scattered, and the beach zone was backed by broad, open fields ideal for maneuver by Marine armored vehicles.

Designated "Blue Beach," the area had been selected as

the most promising possible LZ for Marine amphib operations.

Of course, every SEAL, and every Marine, knew that Saddam's strategic planners were as aware of that beach as were the Allies.

"For the past week," Scott was saying, "we have been giving that beach extra attention, as if we were softening it up for an invasion. Naval air strikes have been pounding anything and everything that looks like a defensive position, and both the *Wisconsin* and the *Missouri* have been dropping sixteen-inch shells on the place. I think we can safely say we've got the Iraqis' attention firmly locked on to Blue Beach by now.

"On the night of 23 February that bombardment will cease. Two Fountain-class patrol boats will depart from Ra's al Mishab and proceed north to the objective. Six men from Lieutenant Dietz's platoon will swim in to Blue Beach, where they will rig explosives to the beach obstacles, set with timers for staggered detonations. Offshore, other SEAL units will place flotation buoys, making it look like cleared lanes marked for incoming landing craft. Once the SEALs ashore have completed their mission and been recovered, we're going to make so much noise offshore that Saddam is going to think the whole damned U.S. Navy is coming after him.

"Gentlemen, some of us in this room are still stinging from some of the criticism the Teams received after Grenada and Paitilla Airfield, unjust criticism thrown at us when we failed to carry out missions that were not within the purview of our training and experience. There are people in the Pentagon and elsewhere who remember our failures, who remember the SEALs calling for help at Grenada or walking into a crossfire in Panama, who say we're obsolete.

"This is where we heal that old wound, once and for all!"

Greg rose to his feet and cheered with the others. Yeah, forget Paitilla! This would be a genuine SEAL op, the real deal right from the Team handbook.

The SEALs would strike from the sea.

And when they struck, the effect would be far out of proportion to the actual numbers involved.

Chapter 21

Although their official call sign was Copperhead One-Niner, they'd picked up on Mark and David's childhood memories of the TV show and begun calling themselves the Rat Patrol. Now, though, they were no longer bouncing across the desert and going airborne off the dunes. Their DPVs were carefully dug in and camouflaged fifty yards to the east, while they sat above the highway and watched for Scud launchers.

They'd hidden the vehicles and dug the OP for themselves during yesterday's predawn hours after their escape from the Iraqi troops at the DZ, scraping it out of hard, sandy dirt and covering it over with a tarpaulin stretched tight from stakes holding it just above the ground, then covering over the whole thing with earth. With their makeshift roof raised above the hole, they had a narrow observation slit giving them a 360-degree view of the surrounding terrain. They had an excellent position overlooking the As Salman highway; their hilltop gave them an unobstructed view for ten miles in both directions, north and south. Behind them, to the east, the ground rose in a series of bald-topped hills and rocky outcroppings.

The land here was not truly desert but more like the dry scrub country of southern California below the high desert. A lot like home, Mark decided. Hardy grasses and brush cloaked the flats between the outcrops; farther north, the land turned greener—or, at least, less sere—and more fertile as it began to descend in a series of rolling slopes toward the fabled valley of the Euphrates.

So far, though, their long and patient wait had turned up little. They'd reported some ground traffic to CENT-COM—a couple of two-and-a-half-ton trucks going north, a tanker truck probably hauling water going south, a number of civilian vehicles. No Scuds. No armor or other heavy stuff. With the ongoing pounding by the coalition air forces, ground traffic throughout Iraq was getting pretty nervous about moving in the open, especially during daylight.

They'd passed an entire day, the following night, and most of the next day, now, lying in the observation post they'd come to call "the hole," moving little, speaking in whispers or not at all. They split the hours watch-and-watch, four on, four off, with three men observing the surrounding terrain at any given time.

"Hey, Lieutenant?" Yancey called softly from the east side of the hole. "I got movement here."

Mark had been sleeping but lightly, and Yancey's voice brought him fully awake. He rolled over and crawled up next to Yancey and Hunter.

What he saw chilled him.

"Shit," Hunter whispered almost under his breath. "Shit, shit, *shit*. . . ."

An Iraqi was approaching the OP . . . not a soldier, but a girl, a child no more than nine or ten years old. She wore a ragged robe and sandals. Her dirty, stringy black hair hung

in greasy ringlets over an equally dirty face. She was leading several shaggy, brown- and black-wooled goats, picking her way among the boulders, moving directly toward
the SEALs' hiding place.

"Damn it, Wheel!" Bowdon whispered. "What'll we
do?"

"Sit tight," Hunter replied. "maybe she won't see us."

Bowdon fingered his H&K. "We'll have to cap her.
She'll blow the mission."

"Fuck *that!*" Mark said, his whisper carrying the intense
rejection of the idea. "She's just a kid!"

"Yeah," Tangretti added. "We don't make war on civilians, Bow."

Mark had heard the story from his father about the
Beduoin at al Khafji, and he'd wondered what he would do
in similar circumstances. Back in the good old days of clas-
sical armies parading across the battlefield, civilians
weren't targeted unless they were unlucky enough to be
caught in a besieged city. World War II had introduced the
concept of open cities and strategic bombing. Korea and
Vietnam had presented new problems in distinguishing
civilians from military personnel. Modern warfare presented a kind of ethical minefield to those who cared, for
those who clung to the notion that only soldiers should be
targeted.

"She's coming this way!" Kennedy whispered.

The girl's eyes grew suddenly large and round. *"Ilhaq!"*
she shrieked. *"Ilhaq!"*

"That's fucking torn it!" Bowdon snapped. Scrambling
out from under the tarp, he dashed forward, chasing down
the girl and scattering the flock of goats, snatching her off
the ground by one arm and clamping his hand over her
mouth. "Got her!"

"Okay, what are you going to do with her, Bow?" Mark
said, emerging from beneath the tarp. He was furiously an-

gry, angry at the OP's discovery, angry at the fortunes of war, but especially angry at Bowdon and the cavalier way he'd suggested killing the kid.

"We can't let her go!" Bowdon said.

"The hell we can't. We can't keep her here! And we're not going to kill her!"

"Let her go, Bowdon," Hunter said. "Halstead's right. We don't make war on civilians."

"Especially *kids*," Mark added.

"Kids can still pull triggers," Bowdon snapped, but he let the girl go. Screaming then, she raced down the hill and vanished among the boulders and outcroppings.

"*You're* on report, mister," Hunter told Bowdon. "Okay, let's pack up our gear. It's time we moved on."

"Maybe she's Shi'a," Kennedy suggested. "Maybe she wouldn't give the Iraqis the time of day."

"We can't take the chance," Hunter said. "Halstead. Tangretti. Mount the watch. The rest of you start packing the gear and piling it outside."

So Mark and Tangretti took perimeter watch while the others cleaned out the OP, stowing radios, ammunition, food, and water. All together, each man had to carry better than 130 pounds in his backpack. That, in Mark's heartfelt estimation, was a hell of a good reason for bringing along the DPVs.

As he watched the road below the hilltop outpost, he thought about what had just happened.

Yeah, expediency, the necessity of saving other lives, even common sense, all might demand that a civilian life be sacrificed to save a vital mission. But to a large extent, the Gulf War so far had maintained at least an illusion of aiming solely at military targets. CNN continued to trumpet the spectacular success of smart bombs that could be guided down the ventilator shaft of an Iraqi command bunker and leave the houses on either side untouched.

CENTCOM was justly proud of precision attacks on Iraq's military and government infrastructure with an absolute minimum of what they so blandly called *collateral damage.* Saddam Hussein might casually toss Scud missiles at civilian population centers, but the Allies struck only military targets, struck them hard, and struck them with surgical precision.

Of course, the reality wasn't quite so clean and neat. Ten days earlier, a pair of GBU-27 laser-guided bombs dropped from two F-117 Stealth fighters had taken out a bunker nine miles west of downtown Baghdad. Al Amerieh was supposed to be a military command-control bunker, and there were indications that it did possibly serve that purpose during the daylight hours.

But at 0430 hours on the morning of 13 February, it was being used as a civilian air shelter, and perhaps as many as 500 civilians were incinerated. There'd been plenty of other missed shots as well, bombs that had failed to guide as advertised, targets that were misidentified, intelligence failures, and of course the controversial strike in January at Abu Gharib—identified by Allied strategists as a plant producing chemical and biological weapons but claimed by the Iraqis to be a baby formula factory.

How did you conduct a clean war without civilian casualties, when your opponent parked key military C^3 bunkers in suburban neighborhoods and used foreign detainees as human shields?

SEALs, by virtue of the fact that they engaged in small-unit tactics, rarely had to worry about something as drastic as accidentally blowing up a bunker filled with 500 people, but they did have to be careful they identified their targets accurately. And in the course of a covert operation behind enemy lines, it was possible, even *probable* that they would encounter enemy civilians. Their high level of training, their professionalism, their results-oriented state of mind while on a mission, all served as defenses against random violence. A SEAL team would never be in a position to carry out a My Lai.

But you could never write a blanket rule for any aspect of warfare. There were always exceptions, and all Mark could really hope for was that he would not be involved in one of them.

He wondered about Bowdon. The guy was from Fort Lauderdale, big, tough, powerfully muscled, a quarterback for Miami State until a low GPA had ended his college career and he'd joined the Navy instead. As a SEAL, Bowdon seemed to have found his niche in life, cool, calm, competence with only an occasional flash of temper or macho braggadocio.

How could the guy even consider killing a child?

"Uh-oh," David said. "Somebody's coming."

Mark moved over to a position next to his friend, using his binoculars. North of the hilltop OP, a column of BTRs and BMPs, armored personnel carriers, was making its way south along the highway. They were still miles off, almost lost in the shimmer of heat off the pavement, but it looked like a pretty sizable convoy. There were larger vehicles as well, though they were still too distant to make out clearly.

"Hey, Lieutenant?"

"Yeah."

"Have a look. You might want to call this one in."

Hunter peered through the binoculars for a moment. "Shit," he said at last. "That might be what we're here to find. Kennedy?"

"Sir!"

"Crank up the SATCOM. We've got a target."

"Aye, aye, sir."

"Yancey. Halstead."

"Yessir."

"Get back to where we parked the dune buggies. Get them up here pronto. We may need to make a fast getaway."

"Aye, aye, sir. Uh . . . the ground's pretty rough, sir," Mark said. "We couldn't get them any closer before without going around to the open side of the hill. And moving around in daylight . . ."

"Get 'em as close as you can. Right now, we need to put as much distance between us and here as we can. *After* we report that convoy. Now move!"

Gripping his H&K, Mark followed Chief Yancey out of the OP and down the hill toward the hidden DPVs. The sun was westering, and there was a slight chill in the air. If they could avoid detection until nightfall . . .

Yancey held up his hand, a sharp signal to halt. Both men went to ground. There were voices up ahead.

Iraqi soldiers, dozens of them. They must have come up the hill from the blind side, toward the east, to have gotten this close without being seen. Mark didn't see the girl. He wondered if she'd found the soldiers or if they were here coincidentally.

It hardly mattered. If the two SEALs tried crossing the last ten yards to their DPVs, they would certainly be seen.

Yancey hesitated, sighting along the barrel of his M-16/M-203 combo as if trying to make up his mind. Then he signaled for Mark to move back. *Good,* Mark thought. *There's too goddamn many of them!*

Carefully, leapfrogging back the way they'd come, the two SEALs returned to the OP. "Big trouble, Lieutenant," Yancey said. "We got bad guys, platoon strength at least, and they're close enough to the DPVs we can't get to 'em. They're moving cautious. I think they know we're here . . . or at least suspect it."

"That brat ratted us out," Bowdon said.

"Stow it, Bowdon," Hunter replied. "C'mon, guys. Pick it up! We're out of here!"

They left the tarp still stretched above the hole. If the Iraqis found it, it wouldn't tell them much. Moving by twos, the SEALs slipped into the boulder field, moving back toward the DPVs.

The irony of the situation wasn't lost on Mark. The Rat Patrol possessed incredible firepower. Each DPV mounted a .50-caliber machine gun, a Mk. 19 auto-grenade launcher, and a couple of AT-4 antitank weapons . . . but that impressive armament wouldn't have helped them at the OP, would, in fact, have slowed them down.

Now that they needed firepower, they couldn't reach it. Murphy's Law was a constant companion in combat.

The Iraqis had found the DPVs. They had the camo tarps off and were poking around inside them. One was using an old-fashioned walkie-talkie to call the report in. One soldier picked up one of the AT-4 tubes slung on the side of one of the DPVs. An officer barked at him and he put it back. Maybe they were afraid of booby traps, or possibly they were just under orders to capture Allied equipment intact.

Hunter tapped Mark and David on their shoulders, then swiftly signed at them. *You two . . . stay here. Watch the DPVs. We'll draw them off. You get the vehicles. Lay down covering fire.*

Mark nodded his understanding, and Tangretti gave a thumbs-up. They waited there among the boulders, watching the Iraqi troops gathering twenty yards away, as minute dragged after minute.

Damn it, where were they? Just as he was beginning to wonder if the other four SEALs had run into trouble, an explosion detonated on the far side of the DPVs, the savage, sharp concussion of a 40mm grenade from either Hunter's or Yancey's M-203.

A second grenade blast closely followed the first, as Iraqi soldiers tumbled to the ground, shouted at one another, and began scattering among the rocks. Gunfire erupted across the crest of the hill, the sharp rattle of M-16s crossing with the flatter *crack-crack-crack* of AK-47s. Two Iraqis went down. Mark couldn't see the attacking SEALs, but they must have put the bad guys into a crossfire.

And then, as suddenly as it had begun, the Iraqis were fleeing, some of them dropping their weapons and helmets in their eagerness to get off the top of the hill. David slapped Mark's arm and started forward; Mark followed, crouched low, eyes on the rocks to left and right, watching for any bad-guy shooters who might have stayed behind.

They reached the DPVs. Mark scrambled into the driver's seat of one, while David took the other. He gunned the VW motor to life, ratcheted back on the gearshift, and sent the little vehicle bounding forward out of its hide. David was close behind.

"Good work!" sounded in his Motorola earphone. *"Okay, people! Mount up!"*

AK gunfire crackled nearby, and Mark heard the snap of bullets overhead. Iraqi morale was obviously damned low, but they could still fight. *Don't underestimate them,* he told himself.

Hunter and the other SEALs scrambled out from among the boulder outcroppings. Bowdon and Yancey clambered onto Mark's machine, while Hunter and Kennedy took the other. Both DPVs were moving almost before the SEALs were all on board.

With Hunter in the machine David was driving, Mark became tail-end Charlie, following the other DPV as they maneuvered clear of the outcroppings . . .

. . . and straight into trouble. Three BTR-60s and a BMP-1 were making their way up the east side of the hill. As the DPVs came into their line of sight, they opened fire.

The BTRs mounted machine guns, including a 14.5mm heavy MG in a thin-skinned turret. The BMP mounted a turret as well, this one housing a 73mm smoothbore cannon and the launching rail for an AT-3 Sagger antitank missile.

The BMP's cannon spurted flame, and the round slammed into the rocks just below the lead DPV. Mark saw David hauling around on the wheel and slamming home the right-side cutting brakes, pivoting the nimble vehicle into a full one-eighty and racing back up the slope.

Mark did the same. Heavy machine-gun fire crackled and hammered in the late-afternoon air, the sounds echoing off the rocks. The BMP fired its cannon again. . . .

Mark was looking back over his shoulder when the round hit, slamming into the hillside just to the right of the DPV carrying Hunter, Bowdon, and Tangretti. It was a clean miss . . . but close enough that the dune buggy lifted high on its left-side wheels.

For an agonizing moment, the DPV balanced on two wheels as Tangretti battled to right the vehicle, but momentum and the rough terrain conspired together. The machine wobbled, then lurched heavily, rolling completely over onto its back.

"Mark!" Yancey yelled. "The lieutenant! . . ."

"I see them!" He'd already put the DPV into another tight one-eighty, whipping around and racing back down the path between two high boulder outcrops. Bowdon, in the gunner's position, opened up with the heavy machine gun, blazing away at the oncoming armor.

The three SEALs were clambering out from under the overturned DPV, shaken, but apparently unhurt. Kennedy still had his radios, while Tangretti clutched one of the AT-4 tubes. Mark pulled up alongside, and Kennedy and Hunter both scrambled on board, climbing up onto the wire racks slung to either side of the vehicle. While only designed to carry three, those racks allowed at least two casualties to be carried outboard, and the vehicle was sturdy enough to manage a third extra passenger as well.

David Tangretti dropped to one knee, the AT-4 balanced over his right shoulder, taking aim at the BMP rumbling up the slope behind them. He squeezed the trigger and the blunt tube barked, flame erupting from both ends as the antitank rocket streaked downhill on a hissing white contrail.

It struck the BMP squarely on the slope of its glacis between the two tracks and exploded. Though a BMP was well armored against shrapnel and small-arms fire, even up front its hull armor was only about 20mm thick. The explosion blasted orange flame from the rear doors and up from the turret, transforming the Russian-built armored personnel carrier into blazing wreckage.

David dropped the spent tube and clambered onto the rear of the remaining DPV. Lieutenant Hunter armed a grenade and tossed it under the overturned DPV just as Mark gunned clear. The detonation seconds later ignited the wreck's gas tank with a roar and a fast-climbing ball of orange flame. The Iraqis wouldn't salvage weapons—or GPS mapping data—from *that* patrol vehicle.

Oily black smoke stained the evening sky from two wrecks now. Mark guided the heavily loaded vehicle down the hill once more, picking his way past house-sized boulders and impossibly rugged terrain.

The Iraqi BTRs followed, but cautiously, at a distance.

"Make for those hills to the south!" Hunter shouted into Mark's ear. "Maybe we can lose them there!"

Racing south, parallel to the As Salman Highway but hidden from it by a low ridge, the DPV skittered ahead of its pursuers, twisting away into the deepening shadows of late afternoon. As they began climbing the next hill, he had to downshift hard and slow sharply; the VW engine was laboring under the extra weight of three additional passengers.

Over the crest of the hill and into a tangle of rugged ground along a saddle between that hill and the next. At last, Mark braked to a stop in the deep shade beneath a twenty-foot-high rock outcropping. "Engine's overheating, guys!" he said. "This is as far as we go . . . unless we want to get stuck out in the open when the engine seizes!"

"Right," Hunter said. "Everybody out. Defensive perimeter."

Mark and David took the crest of the ridge overlooking the highway. That stretch of barren road was crowded now with a convoy coming from the north—troop carriers and trucks, mostly.

And right now, it looked like every damned one of them was heading for the top of the Rat Patrol's new position.

"Set up the SATCOM!" Hunter told Kennedy. "We need air support, fast!"

"Bad news, Skipper," Kennedy replied. He held up the SATCOM, showing the ragged hole in the side of the unit's casing. "SATCOM's finished!"

Tangretti groaned. "Just pure, damned, bad luck. Shit!" A piece of shrapnel from that 73mm round must have hit the radio, just *exactly* the wrong piece of equipment to lose right now.

"If it can go wrong," Mark said, "it will. Murphy strikes again."

"Don't forget Murphy's Second Law," Yancey said.

"What's that one say?"

"That Murphy was an optimist."

"Kennedy!" Hunter said. "Can you patch through with your prick?"

"I can try, Skipper, but you know we won't talk to any-body unless they're on top of us . . . and have the right fre-quencies."

"Do it. It's all we've got."

The team's back-up radio was the AN/PRC-113, a "Prick

113." A UHF/VHF transceiver, it weighed fourteen pounds and could be carried on a man's back. But where the LST-5C SATCOM could talk to anyone in the world via satellite, the AN/PRC could only talk to receivers within range—a figure that fluctuated wildly depending on terrain and weather. They were far out of range from the SEAL base, but they might be able to raise Allied aircraft close by. The real problem was finding someone listening on the right frequency. There were thousands of available channels and encryption algorithms that shifted among many frequencies. Some of the problems during Grenada had been caused by radio operators being given the wrong frequencies or the wrong communications codes.

"This is Copperhead One-Niner calling," Kennedy said, speaking into the PRC's handset. "Copperhead One-Niner. Does anybody copy? Over."

Tangretti looked up into the rapidly darkening sky. "So where *is* everyone?" he demanded. "Where are all those hotshot pilots?" Allied aircraft had been thick overhead for the past two days, but the sky was empty now.

"Yeah, never a cop when you need one," Mark replied.

The Iraqis below the hill continued to rumble slowly past, heading south toward As Salman. If they were worried about Allied air, they didn't show it. Several APCs had swung out of the column to the side of the road, and appeared to be setting up camp. Yancey, atop the hill just north of their new position, reported that there didn't seem to be any pursuit.

Maybe they were still searching the first hill, marked now by the twin plumes of black smoke, perhaps two miles away.

"You think they know where we are?" David asked Mark.

"Damned if I know," Mark replied. He held up his binoculars, studying the troops gathered alongside their BTR-60s at the base of the ridge, perhaps a hundred yards away. "Maybe we got away clean."

"I doubt that," David said. "They know we got away, and they have to know we're still in the area. My guess is that they're more interested in getting that convoy out of here before we call in an air strike. That has to be what they're worried most about right now."

"Maybe. And maybe they know exactly where we are, and they're just taking their own sweet time."

"Yeah? Why would they do that?"

"It's a no-brainer, Dave. They know there's not many of us, and they know we can't travel far with only one patrol vehicle. They chased us up here into these rocks, and they have us pretty well pinned down."

"Why would they need to launch a headlong charge when they know they have us completely surrounded? . . ."

SEAL Base
Ra's al Mishab
Saudi Arabia
2015 hours

Greg pressed the phone hard against his right ear, using his free hand to plug his left. The line was terrible, and he could hardly hear her.

"I said," Wendy's voice whispered at him through the hiss of static, "how's Mark?"

"How's Mark? Yeah, he was fine last time I saw him," Greg shouted. "We're both doing fine!"

He was standing in the Quonset hut rec center at Ra's al Mishab, talking to his wife halfway around the world. It had taken him a long time to arrange this call; theoretically, they were *allowed* several phone calls a week, but there were few phones available, and a lot of guys—and gals—who wanted to talk to the folks back home. The time-zone difference made evenings the most popular time to call, too; 2000 hours in the gulf was 0800, eight in the morning, in San Diego, when the people on both ends of the line were awake. He'd traded a bottle of Dewar's scotch—and *that* had been given to him by a machinist's mate chief off the *Wisconsin* in exchange for some critical engine parts and an outboard motor from the SEAL dock-yard—for the chance to bump up his place in the queue by a couple of days.

He'd wanted, he'd *needed* to talk to Wendy before to-night.

Before he went out on the SEAL Team diversionary op up the coast.

"Listen," he said. "I just wanted to tell you . . . I love you!"

There was a hissing pause of static. "What did you say?" Her voice was so tiny, so very, very far away.

"I said, 'I love you!' "

"I . . . I love you, too."

Greg looked back over his shoulder. The line waiting to use this phone was long, and most of the service men and women standing there appeared to be listening with consid-erable interest. Well, they had nothing better to do at the moment.

He ignored them. "I just wanted to tell you, hon. I don't want us to be apart any longer. Do you hear me? I don't want this separation! Whatever you want to do, that's fine . . . and if you need a divorce, well, I won't stop you. I want you to be happy.

"But I want us to be together again. A couple. Like we used to be."

He listened into the static for an answer. "Wendy? Did you hear me?"

"Y-yes." This time, her voice was a bit clearer. "Yes, I hear you."

"If you want me to leave the Teams, I'm . . . I'm willing. At least I'm willing to talk about it."

"You'd leave the SEALs? Settle down and become an avocado farmer?"

"I hate avocados. Make it oranges."

"Listen to me, Greg. I've been doing a lot of work. The therapy, you know?"

"Yes."

"And I've been thinking a lot since our talk in the zoo, back last year. Remember?"

"I remember."

"I don't own you. I don't own Mark. And neither of you own me. Okay?"

"Right."

"So I can't tell you, *either* of you, what to do. That would be . . . very wrong. Like I was trying to live your lives."

"Wendy—"

"Please don't interrupt, Greg! I had a father who died, and then I married a guy who's courting death every minute. I had a stepfather who was never there when I needed him, and then I married a guy who . . . well, he's never around when I need him. It's like a pattern, you know? My life coming around full circle. It's something I keep bumping up against, keep having to struggle with."

Damn. He'd never seen it that way before.

"But the point is, Greg . . . it's my issue. Not yours. I think I'm starting to see that."

"So . . . what does that mean? What do you want to do?"

"I want to get back together again, too, Greg. Just as soon as you come back from the gulf. The only thing I insist on is that we're *honest* with each other. We've got to stop the lies, stop the covering up. If you're going out on a mission somewhere, I want to know. Not the secret stuff, but I want to know whatever you can tell me."

This time, it was Greg's turn to be speechless.

"Greg? Are you still there?"

"Yeah, Wen. I'm here. That's . . . that's just wonderful. I wish I could kiss you right now."

"Just bring our son back with you, okay?"

In truth, he didn't know where Mark was right now. He hadn't quite lied earlier, when she'd asked him how he was, but he'd skated around the truth. He knew Mark was on an op somewhere over the border in the Iraqi desert, knew he was hunting Scuds.

But Mark could be dead right now, for all he knew. That was the way it was with war. There were no certainties, no promises you could make knowing you would keep them.

"I will do my best, Wendy," he said.

And he meant it.

"Twidge! Hey, Twidge!"

It was Drexler. He waved, then waved the other SEAL away.

"It's time, bro!" Drexler shouted. "Wrap it up!"

He checked his watch. Time to go.

"Listen, Wendy. I have to go. They're calling me."

"An op?"

He hesitated. He was tempted to tell her no, to save her the worry.

But that would violate this new pact they had, this new way of communicating. He couldn't be too specific without violating security regulations, but . . .

"Another one of those late-night calls, hon. But I'll do my best to come back. With Mark!"

"I understand. I . . . I love you, Greg."

"And I love you."

He passed the phone on to the next in line and followed Drexler back toward the waterfront.

He and Wendy were going to make another go of it.

Greg was determined that *this* time it would work, even if he had to fight his way across Iraq and through Saddam's entire army to do it.

They would do it together.

Chapter 22

"Why the hell haven't they attacked?" Mark asked. He lay on the ground beside a massive boulder, using night-vision binoculars to study the vehicles gathered a hundred yards away at the base of the hilltop. The Iraqis had set up an encampment down there. The west slope of the hill wasn't very steep—twenty degrees, at most. Those APCs could easily make it all the way to the top.

The other SEALs were with Mark, discussing the enemy's apparently casual attitude. "Shit," Bowdon said. "They're still just sitting down there."

"They're being cautious," Hunter replied. "Playing it smart. I don't think they know for sure we're up here."

Mark grinned. "They can't know we're right here above them, or they wouldn't be so relaxed right now." He patted the top of the Mk. 19. "We could take 'em all out right now, one burst."

"And have half the Iraqi army on top of us in five minutes," Hunter replied. Other Iraqi encampments were scattered about the landscape in all directions. They appeared to be taking up defensive positions but were ignoring the hills and ridges.

"What they do know," David said, "is that we have a nasty bite. We took out those trucks yesterday and a bump this afternoon. Figure . . . what? Maybe forty, maybe fifty Indians KIA and wounded. And they know we have anti-tank weapons, too, and full-auto grenade launchers." Indian was the SEAL code word for Iraqis, from the phonetic alphabet of signal flags and radio calls. Tango for terrorist, India for Iraqi . . . and the obvious if nonpolitically-correct extension of India to Indian.

"Yeah," Hunter said. "If I was their CO, I'd be playing it *real* cautious right now!"

"So they're waiting for reinforcements, sir?" Bowdon asked.

"Could be. Or maybe they're just mustering up the courage to come up here and nab us."

"Doesn't make sense, sir," Mark said. "They don't know our SATCOM's out. They don't know we can't raise home base. What are they doing, *waiting* for us to call in an air strike?"

"Could be they're just playing games with us," Kennedy suggested. "I mean, they know if we were going to call in an air strike, we would've done it hours ago, right? So either they don't know we're here, or, like you say, they're playing it cagey. If *I* were their CO, I'd be planning on sending out small teams tonight, try to infiltrate our perimeter, get an idea of how we're deployed."

"Seems to me," Yancey said, "that the likeliest scenario is that they don't know we're here. It's stupid to just park that many APCs around in the open like that, if they know we're here and that we might call in a strike."

"Could be," Hunter agreed. "Could very well be. They don't know the capabilities of our DPVs. They might have just assumed we took off for the border and are long gone."

"Out of sight, out of mind," Yancey agreed.

"So," Mark said, "all we can do is wait 'em out, huh?"

"That's the plan," Hunter agreed, nodding in the darkness. "It ain't much, but that's the plan for now, anyway. Okay, this is what I want. Only one man asleep at any time. The rest, be on your toes. Watch for infiltrators. Yancey . . . you rack out first. We'll call you at oh-one-hundred."

"Aye, aye, sir."

The other SEALs moved off, Yancey to get some sleep, Hunter, Bowdon, and David to watch south and east quarters of the perimeter, Kennedy to return to his radio. Mark went back to studying the Iraqi encampment through his IL scope. The Iraqis—if they knew the SEALs were up there—appeared completely unconcerned. About twenty were gathered in small groups alongside three BTRs. Two more BTRs and a BMP were positioned on the other side of the hill, to the east, along with another twenty men. All appeared to be eating rations and just . . . waiting.

The SEALs had shifted their position once again a few hours ago, moving from the ridge-back saddle between the two rocky hills to a better, more defensible position straddling the crest of the taller, southern hill. Their combat tactics training had emphasized the need to choose your ground for a fight and to choose it carefully. If you were forced into a defensive posture and couldn't flee, your use of the terrain might make the difference between survival and death. There was a shallow depression up here, bordered by several large boulders, forming naturally an excellent, ready-made fighting position for six men. If they stayed low, they could use the depression to move unseen to any part of the perimeter, sifting to meet an attack from any quarter.

They'd moved the DPV to a new hiding place, putting it in the depression only a few feet behind and below Mark's position. Yancey, their "gearhead" on this patrol, had been tinkering with the dune buggy's engine, cleaning it and putting it back into first-rate condition, despite the omnipresent sand and dust. They'd not removed the machine gun from its mount; they might need to exit in a hurry once again and were not eager to leave their Ma Deuce behind. They'd positioned the DPV hull-down but with the MG high enough to give themselves a clear field of fire down the hill, and they'd removed both of the AT-4s, the M60 machine gun, and the Mk. 19 and its 40mm ammo, setting them up around the perimeter of their position where they could be swiftly moved to any part of the circle.

They'd also set out almost all of their supply of Claymore mines, stretching tripwires across obvious pathways between the rocks and aiming the convex, "this-side-toward-enemy" faces downhill in interlocking crossfire patterns. The idea was to make things very noisy if anyone tried sneaking up the hill in the middle of the night.

And, of course, their RTO, RM1 Kennedy, continued his low-voiced vigil on the PRC-113, crouching next to the DPV. "This is Copperhead One-Niner, Copperhead One-Niner. Does anybody copy? Over. . . ."

The loneliness was rising up again, threatening to overwhelm him. Carefully, Mark edged to his right, moving toward the northwest portion of the circle. David was just a few feet away, lying flat alongside one of the big boulders, watching the south.

"Hey, David? *Sst!*" His whisper carried easily. David joined him after a moment, crawling over with his CAR-15 cradled in his arms. "Yeah?"

"I don't know if we're going to get out of this one. What do you think?"

He felt David's shrug. "A SEAL always feels safest if he

has some water to retreat to," he said. "We're a long way from the water."

"Yeah."

"I figure we're stuck until one of two things happens. Either the bad guys go away, or they come and get us. If it's the latter, we make 'em pay, y'know?"

"It'd be better if we could sneak out."

"Sure. But then what? If we take the dune buggy, they'll hear us, and we won't get far with six on board. We leave it here and crawl out, we'd probably get past those clowns down there easy enough . . . but then we're on foot a hundred miles behind Iraqi lines. What do we do? Walk out?"

"If we have to," Mark said.

"Sure. If we have to. But the lieutenant won't want to try that until there's no alternative." He paused. "To tell the truth, I've been thinking this is a lot like Camerone."

"Like what?"

"You know anything about the French foreign legion?"

"Not much. I saw *Beau Geste* once."

"They've got one of the toughest training programs in the world. Not as tough as BUD/S, maybe, and not as technical, but damned good. They're good soldiers, a true elite. Did you know only their officers are French?"

"No, I didn't."

"That's why they're the *foreign* legion. All of the enlisted men are from other countries. I think today most of them are supposed to be from Eastern Europe. If they survive five years in the legion, they get to become French citizens."

"I heard the foreign legion is in the gulf right now, with the French contingent."

"Yup. Part of it, anyway. So anyhow, Camerone was a battle in their early history, back in 1863. The French were trying to prop up their own guy as emperor of Mexico, and the Mexicans weren't having any of it. A small detachment of legionnaires, sixty-four men under a Captain Danjou, found themselves surrounded by two thousand Mexican rebels at the Camerone Hacienda, near a town called Puebla."

"Geez! What happened?"

"They fought to the last five men, killed, I don't know, hundreds of Mexicans . . . then staged a bayonet charge."

"All KIA?"

"Not quite. There were a few survivors—something like seventeen wounded. And when the last three legionnaires on their feet were asked to surrender, they said they would *if* they could keep their weapons. The Mexican commander is supposed to have replied that he could refuse nothing to such brave men as these."

"So there were survivors. Not like the Alamo, then."

David shrugged. "Actually, Mexican accounts of the battle say there were a few survivors at the Alamo. Only there, the Mexican commander ordered the survivors bayoneted."

"So . . . what's the point? That we fight to the last man? That we should surrender to the Iraqis?"

"SEALs never surrender," David said, quoting a line heard by every recruit every day in BUD/S. "No, I think all I'm saying is that the point of *ésprit de corps* is that a small, highly trained, highly dedicated group of professional warriors is going to have an overwhelming advantage over conscripts and armed rabble every time, if only because they believe in what they're doing and because they believe in each other."

Mark nodded. "SEALs never surrender. They also *never* leave behind one of their own. Swim buddies."

"Absolutely. You know, Captain Danjou had a wooden hand, a souvenir from an earlier campaign in the Crimea. Somebody found it after the battle and returned it to the French. The legion has it now. They trot it out every year on the anniversary of Camerone. It's part of the legion's *esprit*.

That was what we learned in BUD/S, right? If you have the spirit, you can do anything."

"I don't know. The Teams can do damned near anything, but six men taking on a whole battalion? Looks to me like a suicide charge is just about our only option."

"Nah. You know how someone can have the head for something, like numbers, or the heart to do something tough?"

"Sure."

"Well, Lieutenant Hunter doesn't have the *hand* for it."

"Shit, David! That's awful!"

"And frankly, I don't think the Iraqis down there are as good as those Mexican peasants. Not as dedicated, know what I mean?"

"I agree. What we've seen so far haven't been exactly top-of-the-line troops. But still, six men . . ."

"Numbers have nothing to do with it, Mark. You know, if we get into a shooting match with them, we're going to hurt them, and I mean hurt them *bad*. We know it, and *they* know it. That's why they're not pushing harder to find us, you know? And that's something we can use to our advantage. Maybe it's our *only* advantage . . . but it's a damned big one."

The two SEALs lay there side by side a moment longer in silence. Then Mark said, "Back to work. Hang tight, brother."

"You, too."

Mark crawled off toward the south as David moved back to his position in the west. The night was still, profoundly quiet.

Mark checked the Iraqis at the road encampment again, then settled into watch mode, alone with dark thoughts. SEALs weren't supposed to be suicide troops, weren't supposed to face these kinds of odds. It was like his dad had told him after Panama . . . using highly trained elite forces like combat infantry. Not quite the same, perhaps. Scud-hunting was a proper task for the Teams.

But they shouldn't have let themselves get into this damned hole, backs against the wall and all the numbers against them.

He thought about Camerone and about the Alamo and about other last-ditch, fight-to-the-last-man actions he'd heard or read about.

There was, though, the well-known tale from the early days of the Texas Rangers. A town was having trouble with an unruly armed mob of vigilantes, and they asked for a company of Texas Rangers to come help. One Ranger arrived. When asked why more men weren't sent to deal with the trouble, the Ranger reportedly replied, "One mob, one Ranger." The guy had dispersed the mob, too, without firing a shot.

One mob, one Ranger.

One Iraqi battalion, one SEAL squad. Yeah, it made a strange kind of mathematical sense. . . .

Something was moving on the As Salman Highway, coming from the north, ill defined in the green glow of Mark's night optics. He used the LI binoculars to try to bring the object into better resolution. What he saw sent a cold chill down his spine, and he silently breathed out a single word. *"Yes!"*

There were a number of vehicles in line; Mark guessed twenty, though he was having trouble sorting them all out. In front was a ZSU-23-4, a "Zoo" in popular military parlance—four 23mm antiaircraft guns mounted in a broad open turret atop a tank chassis. It was followed by a van with a large radar dish on top, and that was followed by a miscellany of vehicles that looked like flat-bed trailers hauling long, heavy payloads shrouded by camo tarps.

And the prize came rumbling along at the rear of the pack, flanked by three more ZSUs—a squat box of a tractor cab hauling a flatbed trailer with what looked like a shrouded white sewer pipe on top.

"Lieutenant!" Mark called, his voice a harsh stage whisper pitched to carry to the east side of the hilltop position. "Hey, *Lieutenant!*"

Hunter joined him a moment later. "What?"

"Have a look," Mark said, handing him the binoculars. "I think we just struck pay dirt!"

Hunter took the night-vision binoculars and peered toward the northern horizon for a long moment. The new convoy was still a good eight miles off, and moving slowly, its velocity restricted to the road speed of the tracked ZSUs—perhaps thirty miles an hour.

"Bingo," Hunter said, lowering the binoculars. "We got us a Scud. Now if we could just do something about it!"

"If they come down this road," Mark said, "it'll be in easy range of this baby." He patted the breech mechanism of the Mk. 19 in front of him. "Not as good as a laser-guided bomb, but I'll bet we could do some serious damage."

"Roger that." Hunter lifted the binoculars and watched a moment more. "This proves the Iraqis think we're out of the area, though. They wouldn't risk bringing that monster this way if they thought there was even a chance that we were here."

"They just got careless?" It seemed literally too good to be true.

"They think they chased us out this afternoon. Didn't know we'd gone to ground. Those people," and he nodded at the Iraqis at the base of the hill, "were probably told to check out these hills and report back. They took the easy way out, checked out the area all around the hill, and reported back 'all clear.'"

"So we lucked out."

"Halstead, the number-one rule of warfare is that victory goes to the side that makes the fewest mistakes. We've made our share, yeah . . . but those guys down there are *not* having a good day!"

A thunderous blast echoed across the hilltop, from the north. "*Shit!* Not *now!*"

"One of the Claymores!" Mark said. "I think our luck just ran out, too!"

**Off Objective Blue Beach
Kuwait
2238 hours**

Greg Halstead rolled off the Zodiac and into the quiet waters of the gulf. The water was a biting fifty-three degrees, a far cry from the ninety-degree-plus waters of last August, so warm they'd threatened SEAL swimmers with heat exhaustion. As before, he wore a full wetsuit, with swim fins over the rubber booties on his feet, but no mask, no air tank or rebreather gear. A lightweight helmet strapped over his head helped prevent hypothermia as he radiated body heat through his scalp. His face was painted black, partly for camouflage, but partly, too, because the waterproof paint helped keep his face warm.

As before, he carried a three-minute "bail bottle" that would let him swim underwater far enough to escape gunfire if he was spotted. He'd traded his Sykes-Fairbairn, reluctantly, for a standard-issue K-Bar knife; the heavier blade was better suited to cutting barbed wire if he managed to get tangled in the stuff in the surf. And as he swam, he pushed along in front of him a Hagensen Pack of C-4 explosives. A small flotation bag attached to the satchel kept the twenty-pound haversack afloat. This time out he was armed, with a waterproofed H&K MP5 braced across the top of the Hagensen Pack.

As he swam, he couldn't help thinking about his last op

in Vietnam—Christ! Was it nineteen years ago, now? That had been the mission where he'd picked up his "little blue button," the Medal of Honor. He and one other SEAL and three South Vietnamese LLDN commandos had been put ashore to carry out a recon. The problem was, the junk that had dropped them off had put them down way off-target, inside the DMZ and almost inside of North Vietnam itself. After almost walking into North Vietnam, they'd recognized their mistake and tried to extract—an operation that brought them under heavy fire. His MOH had come from the nightmare moment when he'd gone back to pick up the op's CO—*another* SEAL who would receive the Medal of Honor for another op six months earlier.

Nineteen years had made such a tremendous difference in the technology that SEALs now took for granted. The team had made the forty-mile trip north from Ra's al Mishab in a couple of Fountain-class patrol boats, then moved in to within five hundred yards of the shore on board a couple of Zodiacs, a military version of the commercial rubber boat, a decided step up from the clumsy CRRCs. Every step of the way, they knew their exact position, thanks to the black-box magic of their GPS satellite receivers.

There were only six men in the water, a tiny invasion force. Nine more waited in the pair of Zodiacs offshore, while still more SEALs and brown-water naval personnel waited a mile out in the patrol boats.

A little ways offshore, he went vertical in the water, his feet brushing the sandy bottom at a depth of perhaps six feet. He floated there for a long time, his H&K resting on the floating Hagensen Pack, studying the objective.

Objective Blue Beach was as advertised, a long stretch of beach almost empty of buildings, though the shelf above the waterline was thickly infested with steel pylons and other obstacles. Somewhere behind the beach, Greg knew, Iraqi troops were waiting in trenches and fighting holes, preparing to face the long-awaited onslaught by the United States Marines.

Tonight, the SEALs would give them just what they were looking for.

Near As Salman
South-Central Iraq
2240 hours

"Fuck!" Mark and Hunter swore in unison as the Claymore blast echoed off the hilltop. Murphy again. If something could go wrong, it would. The bad guys sure as hell knew the SEALs were up here now, and it was a sure bet that they wouldn't let that MAZ transport and the Scud it was carrying anywhere near them.

At the bottom of the hill a number of Iraqis leaped to their feet, staring up into the rugged heights above them. "Take the Mk. 19," Hunter told him.

"Yessir." Mark lowered his binoculars, adjusted his LI goggles, and moved behind the bulk of the auto grenade launcher off the DPV. Machine-gun fire rattled in the night, coming from the north slope. Bowdon, awakened by the Claymore blast, crawled up to their position, clutching his H&K. "Jesus! What's happening?"

"Don't know," Hunter replied. "One of our tripwires just went."

"I got movement, north perimeter!" David called over their squad Motorolas. "Looks like a patrol, a big one, coming up the slope!"

"Well," Mark told Bowdon, "if they didn't know we were here before, they sure do now!"

The rattle of small-arms fire chattered from the north side of the hill, the flat crack of AK-47s all but drowning out the lighter rattle of David's CAR-15, firing short, precise bursts.

Another Claymore mine went off, farther around the hilltop toward the east.

The Iraqis at the bottom of the west slope of the hill had grabbed their weapons at the first blast and, after a moment's confused hesitation, had started moving forward. "Take 'em down!" Hunter growled, dragging back the cocking lever on his M-16/M-203 combo. Mark took the double handgrip of the Mk. 19, checked to make sure the feed mechanism was locked down, then squeezed the trigger.

With a stuttering stream of thumping concussions, the auto grenade launcher spat its 40mm rounds in a curving arc down the hillside. A line of explosions walked across the slope just behind the advancing infantry, savage, shattering blasts that ripped men apart or sent them flopping to the earth like rag dolls. One of the BTRs parked next to the highway took a pair of direct hits and exploded with a thunderous double *whump,* orange flame lighting up the terrain.

"I've got Indians on the north perimeter!" David's voice called over the squad frequency. "Too many of them! They're coming through!"

The ground there was rocky enough that it would be almost impossible for one man to hold off a large number of attackers.

"Bowdon!" Hunter snapped. "North side!"

"Aye, aye, Skipper!"

He was halfway across to David's position when two Iraqi soldiers rushed past a nearby boulder on the northwestern quarter of the perimeter, stumbling into the hilltop depression, as startled at their sudden arrival, apparently, as the SEALs. Bowdon raised his H&K and cut them down before they had a chance to recover. Another Claymore blast echoed among the boulders, and Mark could hear screaming now, the screams of wounded men.

"Where's Dave?" Mark shouted. Those two infiltrators

had come right past his position. "Tangretti!" he called over his squad radio. "Tangretti! Come in!"

"I'm okay!" David replied. "But we've got ten . . . maybe fifteen Indians, north perimeter!"

"Yancey!" Hunter called into his Motorola. "North side!"

"Aye, aye, sir!"

Abandoning the south and west slopes to support the north perimeter was dangerous but a reasonable risk. It sounded as though a patrol-in-force had finally been sent to check the two hills and the ridge between them, while the Iraqis on the west side were just following the sound of gunfire. This was nothing like a coordinated attack.

Mark continued to fire the grenade launcher, loosing short, precisely controlled bursts as the surviving BTRs wheeled clear of the hilltop and moved out of range. The blasts caught several more Iraqi soldiers in the open and scythed them down with devastating sprays of shrapnel.

Mark was all too aware that there'd been Iraqi encampments on the plain to the east as well. If they decided to come check out the shooting . . .

The Iraqi attack ended almost as soon as it had begun, the troops—those still on their feet, at any rate—spilling back down the slope in a disorganized rout. Silence settled once more across the hilltop, a silence broken only by the moans of the wounded and the far-off crackle and roar of the burning APC.

"Squad!" Hunter called over his Motorola. "Sound off! Anyone hit? Tangretti!"

"Just a scratch, Lieutenant. I'm okay."

"Bowdon!"

"Okay!"

"Yancey!"

"A-OK!"

"Halstead!"

"I'm okay," Mark replied. Hunter was lying next to him beside the Mk. 19, but protocol and discipline *would* be observed.

"Kennedy!"

"Okay."

"Bowdon, south perimeter!" Hunter ordered. "Yancey, west side! Stay sharp!"

"Aye, aye, sir."

"Right, Lieutenant!"

"Lieutenant!" sounded sharply from his earphone. "Lieutenant! Come quick!"

Mark winced. *What now?*

After successfully fighting off so many Iraqis without any casualties in return, it seemed inevitable that the unwanted Murphy would take the opportunity to strike at the SEALs again. . . .

Chapter 23

23 February 1991

Off Objective Blue Beach
Kuwait
2255 hours

After a long, silent look at the beach in front of them, the six SEAL swimmers had spaced themselves out in a line parallel to the shore, fifty yards between one man and the next, the six of them covering almost an eighth of a mile. The beach ahead, viewed through waterproof night optics, remained empty, though it was a certainty that Iraqi troops occupied the trenches and bunkers known to straddle the slightly higher ground beyond the beach dunes. There were no sentries on the beach itself, however. No vehicles. No sound. No sign of life . . . which in itself seemed a bit strange. At the briefing session, they'd been informed that the Navy had been pounding this stretch of beach for some time now. If this was indeed the first time in days that there'd been no bombardment, the beach defenders *should* be wondering why and taking extra steps to be on high alert.

Well, if the local defenders weren't curious, it was a sure bet that their commanders, farther inland and better dug-in, were wide awake and watching. The Iraqi military had showed signs of incompetence, yeah, but their leaders weren't *stupid*.

That was a cardinal rule of warfare, as old or older than the doctrines of Sun-tzu. Never, *ever* underestimate the enemy.

Greg started forward again, pushing his weapon and the Hagensen Pack in front of him.

The chilly waters of the gulf were almost absolutely calm . . . and that was a real godsend. On some of the night missions north along the coast out of Ra's al Mishab, the water had been so rough that the SEALs riding their small, high-speed boats through the waves had returned bruised head to toe from the violence of their ride, and a rough surf on the beach tonight would have made coordinating the placement of explosives a tricky proposition.

But, as it was, the gulf tonight was almost mirror-smooth, with only a low and quiet splash of rolling surf at the water's edge. There was no moon. Even if there'd been one, the black pall from burning oil wells inland acted as a blanketing overcast. The only light at all came from the faint red glow on the undersides of the cloud ceiling, reflections from flaming wellheads.

Greg reached a point where the water was about two feet deep, just a few yards out from the shore. He pulled two pins from the timers attached to the Hagensen Pack, then drew his knife, slashed the air bladder on the flotation collar, and let the pack sink.

The twenty-pound pack of C-4 explosives would easily remain in place in this gentle surf. There was no need to fasten it down or bury the thing. With this charge in place and the timers quietly counting down, he turned and side-stroked away from the beach, slipping further and further into the black and comforting emptiness of the sea.

Half an hour later, he rendezvoused with the Zodiacs, homing first on a sonar beacon operated by one of the

SEALs on board, then by a SEAL waving a chemical light stick. The other swimmers were homing on the sound and light as well, and in minutes, all six were back in their craft and the helmsmen were gently opening up the throttles on the almost-silent electric engines, motoring deeper into the night.

At their backs, the beach remained silent and empty, with six packs of high explosives at the waters' edge, their timers silently counting off the seconds. . . .

**Near As Salman
South-Central Iraq
2322 hours**

"Lieutenant, this is Kennedy! I've got someone! I've got a live channel!"

The radio operator's excitement lit up the other five SEALs like an electric charge. Hunter slithered back from the lip of the depression, joining Kennedy at the PRC-113 behind the dune buggy, at the center of the circle.

Mark turned his attention back to the rolling terrain to the west, but his heart was racing now. If the squad's RTO had actually managed to patch through to someone, even a spotter plane . . .

There was a lot of activity now to the north and to the west. The convoy built around the MAZ transporter and its deadly cargo appeared to have halted in confusion, with some vehicles pulling off to the side of the road and others remaining on the highway. BMPs, BTRs, and BDRMs had left the column and were racing toward the string of ridge and hills where the SEALs lay hidden, armored personnel carriers each carrying six to eight troops. The encampment at the western base of the hill was deserted now, with nothing marking it save the burning wreckage of the BTR.

"Lieutenant?" he called into his Motorola. "This is Halstead. We're about to have company. A *lot* of it."

There was no answer, and he turned in place, looking past the SEAL DPV. Hunter was crouched at the bottom of the depression next to Kennedy, holding the PRC-113 handset to his ear. Clearly they were talking to someone.

Abruptly, Hunter replaced the handset and opened his squad channel. "Heads up, everyone! Our call was picked up by an AWACS over the Saudi border! They're vectoring in some fast movers! ETA . . . twenty minutes!"

"Hoo-*yah*!" Yancey's voice called over the Motorola link. "Let's hear it for the Tinkers!"

AWACS—Airborne Warning And Control System—was the E3A Sentry, the Air Force long-range radar surveillance aircraft with a huge, disk-shaped radome rotating above its aft fuselage. The advanced computer system on board provided an uncluttered view of airborne targets across an enormous area—a two-hundred-mile range for low-flying targets and even farther for targets at higher altitudes. Primarily used to spot enemy air threats and to vector in friendly aircraft for the kill, AWACS possessed an advanced communications suite, including UHF, VHF, and HF radios as well as a Tactical Data Link, or TADIL, which gave them direct contact with both air and ground units. U.S. Air Force AWACS were assigned to the 552nd Airborne Warning and Control Wing, operating out of Tinker Air Force Base in Oklahoma, hence Yancey's excitement about the "Tinkers."

The AWACS was probably orbiting over the Saudi-Iraqi border somewhere to the south, helping to coordinate the vast armada of coalition aircraft operating over Iraq, and had by chance picked up Kennedy's UHF radio call for help. They would be in direct contact with dozens of U.S. and Allied aircraft operating throughout the area and be able to vector in some close ground support. "Fast movers" in SEAL slang meant strike aircraft—F-15s, F-18s, F-111s, even the ungainly A-10 Warthog tank-killers. The SEALs would have all the help they needed in just twenty minutes.

At least, that was the idea. Mark took another look at the oncoming Iraqi forces. Right now, it looked like the whole damned Iraqi army was heading straight for the SEAL position. Did they *have* twenty minutes? . . .

"Lieutenant?" Mark called. "Someone's taken an interest in our work up here. We're going to have visitors inside of fifteen minutes . . . maybe ten."

"I see them," Hunter replied, standing up next to the DPV. "Okay, fighting positions, everyone. We'll just have to hold out until help arrives."

"Can we use the DPV to get out of Dodge?" Bowdon asked.

"Negative. It won't carry all six of us fast enough. They'd be on us in no time."

"Yeah," David said. "We're better off staying put. We wouldn't want to be caught by friendly fire out in the open, either."

"Do the Tinks have a solid fix on our position?" Mark asked.

"I think so," Hunter replied. "I was having . . . a little trouble communicating."

"Bad atmospherics?" David asked.

"That's not the problem," Hunter told them. "Those aren't Tinks up there. They're part of Peace Shield."

"Oh, *shit!*" Yancey said. "That's just fucking great!"

"What's the matter?" Mark asked. "What's Peace Shield?"

"It was a special program tasked with transferring AWACS technology to the Saudis," Yancey replied. "That's not an Air Force Sentry up there. It's Saudi AWACS, with a goddamn Saudi crew!"

Mark digested this disturbing bit of news. He'd heard all the rumors and stories back at Ra's al Mishab, of course . . . about how the Saudi ground troops had fled at the first sign of trouble at al Khafji, about the cracks appearing in the alliance between the U.S. high command and the Arab coalition as the commander of the Saudi ground forces publicly blamed the U.S. for the loss of Khafji, about complaints on all sides that the Saudis were somehow less than competent in this war or, worse, less than entirely supportive in their own defense.

Mark hadn't put a lot of credence in those rumors. After all, the first double kill in the skies above Iraq had been credited to a Saudi pilot flying a Saudi Air Force F-15, and from what he'd observed so far, they seemed to be pulling their share of things.

But it did make him think about things again, realizing that his life, and the survival of the tiny SEAL Copperhead team, now depended on their Arab allies. . . .

An explosion thumped hard against the west side of the hill, throwing a huge spray of sand and debris skyward. The SEALs dropped flat, clutching the earth, as a second blast thundered among the boulders to the north.

"Mortars!" Tangretti snapped.

"More likely seventy-three mike-mike fire from those bumps," Yancey said. "They're gonna try to blast us off this fuckin' hill!"

Specter AC-130 Gunship
Callsign Spirit 07
North of As Salman
2343 hours

"Say again, Saudi AWACS Yankee-Three-Seven." Air Force Major Roger Pierce strained to hear through the speaker's thick accent. It had sounded like the Saudi had said the guys on the ground were . . . SEALs? "Your transmission garbled. Over."

"I say again," the voice on the other end of the UHF channel said in clipped, almost British-sounding tones. "Copperhead One-Niner requests immediate assistance. They say they are six Navy SEALs on a hilltop, map coordinates . . ."

The Saudi speaker began rattling off alphanumerics again, and Pierce shook his head. Navy SEALs?

"I copy that, Saudi AWACS Yankee-Three-Seven. We're almost at those coordinates now. What is the situation on the ground, over?"

"Copperhead One-Niner reports they are taking heavy fire from numerous armored vehicles. Their position is surrounded and their situation desperate. Over."

"I think I see ground fire up there, Captain," his copilot said, pointing. "See those flashes?"

"That I do." He picked up a mike, keying the intercom for the aircraft's Battle Management Center. "Okay, back there. Get ready to rock. We have a job to do."

"What'd they say, Major?" Captain Wilkins, his copilot, asked.

"That we're being deployed to rescue a bunch of Navy SEALs."

"*SEALs?*" Wilkins said. "What the fuck are Navy SEALs doing way out here?"

"I think," Pierce replied, shaking his head, "they're lost. Okay, here we go!"

**Near As Salman
South-Central Iraq
2344 hours**

Explosions continued to rain down on the SEALs, though fortunately, the fire so far had been scattered and inaccurate enough that none of the rounds had come closer than thirty or forty yards or so. The enemy had spread out to virtually surround the hilly area east of the highway, and troops were advancing both on foot and on board APCs and trucks. Mark estimated that they were looking at a full battalion.

He shoved the Mk. 19 around, aiming at the oncoming light armor. The weapon was awkward and clumsy when not mounted on the DPV, and difficult to point, but the sheer volume of firepower it could lay down more than made up for the trouble it took to aim the thing. He pressed the trigger and sent bursts of high explosive flashing and cracking among the lead Iraqi vehicles. The lead vehicles began to slow up, which meant the APCs in the middle of the pack began bunching up—a lovely traffic jam creating what military tacticians liked to call "a target-rich environment."

Nearby, David was using the M60, its harsh chatter echoing among the surrounding boulders. Yancey clambered into the DPV and swung the M2 into action, its hammering thunder thudding just above Mark's head.

And then the last of the 40mm grenade belts for the Mk. 19 ran to an end and the weapon locked open. Mark rolled out from behind it and unslung his H&K. Fires dotted the plain and highway west and north, now, but the Iraqi forces kept coming, crowding closer to the base of the hill—unwilling, it seemed, to make that final vault up the slope in the teeth of the devastating fire from the SEAL position, but closing slowly nonetheless. Bowdon reported more Iraqis climbing the hill from the east. At Hunter's orders, Mark abandoned his position on the west side of the perimeter and joined Bowdon on the east. Troops were spilling from a stalled BDRM halfway up the hill, and he began loosing bursts of nine-millimeter fire into the crowd.

His left arm was sore, and when he glanced down at it, he saw a black stain spreading across his utilities. Hell, he'd been hit, probably by a piece of shrapnel, and hadn't even known it. He ignored it and kept firing.

And then the darkness to the east fled before what for all the world looked like some sort of science-fictional death ray, a dazzling beam of light stabbing at a forty-five-degree angle out of the night sky. The sound . . . the pure, raw, ground-shuddering *sound* of that onslaught was more felt than heard, a palpable blast of shuddering air slapping skin and clothing that only gradually resolved as a grating shriek clawing at the senses.

The source of that death ray was moving, circling from the east of the perimeter toward the north. Tracer fire, streaks of brilliant yellow, fast-drifting stars, streamed from the unseen shooter; explosions sent thunderclaps of sound echoing across the plain.

Mark looked up at that dazzling light show illuminating the Iraqi night, his jaw dropping open, the stress and fear of the firefight lost now, in a rising tide of sheer awe.

For the Iraqis below the hilltop, the night must have seemed like Armageddon.

The death ray cut off, then lit up again at a different angle, sweeping right to left across the plain at the base of the hill.

"It's a Specter!" Yancey called over the Motorola channel, but the noise, a deep, hammering *thrum* mingled with the high-pitched scream and the thundering detonations of high explosives all but drowned out his voice. Secondary explosions savaged the ground as Iraqi vehicles began to cook off. . . .

A Specter gunship. Mark had never seen one in action, though his training had certainly described them.

David was yelling at the sky. "Pour it on, guys! Pour it the fuck on!"

The AC-130 was a derivation of the ubiquitous C-130 Hercules turboprop transports, modified as a close-ground-support airborne gun platform. With a crew of fourteen, a single Specter gunship could dominate the battlefield. Its fire control officer, riding in the Battle Manage-

ment Center in the fuselage, could view the battlefield
through an all-light-level television monitor, as well as in-
frared, radar, and a laser illuminator assembly, and direct
the aircraft's fire from a single console, delivering devas-
tatingly precise ground support. The Specter's sensor suite
nakedly revealed the target by night or day, smoke or dust
or solid overcast.

The death-ray effect was caused by the tracers for the
gunship's GAU 12/U Gatling cannon. That awesome
weapon fired 25mm rounds at the incredible rate of 1,800
rounds per minute—thirty rounds *each second*—delivering
tracers from an altitude of up to 12,000 feet so quickly that
they created the illusion of a solid beam of explosive light,
the sound of individual shots blurring together in human
perception to a buzzsaw howl.

The Gatling wasn't the only weapon in the AC-130's arsenal, either. Mounted along its port side were a 40mm Bo-
fors gun and a 105mm howitzer—that last a field artillery
gun modified for use inside the aircraft.

Approaching the target in a left-hand bank, the AC-130
could circle an area for hours, leaving in its path nothing
save twisted wreckage and death.

It took Mark some minutes to realize that the SEALs had
just been saved.

Specter AC-130 Gunship
Callsign Spirit 07
North of As Salman
2352 hours

Major Pierce held the AC-130 in its steady, left-hand
turn, left side tipped down at the optimum angle of forty-
five degrees, giving the gunners aft the best possible shot at

their targets. From an altitude of five thousand feet, the roar of explosions was muted to a distant rumble almost over-ridden by the buzzsaw howl of the Gatling cannon. An Air Force officer for fifteen years, this was his first time in combat.

And it was, for him, damned personal.

The Air Force's fleet of AC-130s operated out of the 4th Special Operations Squadron of the 16th Special Operations Wing. It was a small, tight unit, one with close bonds between the different aircraft crews.

On 31 January, toward the end of the Battle of Khafji, a Specter gunship, call sign Spirit 03, piloted by Major Paul Weaver, had been called in by embattled Marines on the ground to target an Iraqi Frog missile launcher—one suspected of mounting chemical warheads. It was nearly dawn, and Spirit 03 had been RTB—returning to base—but Major Weaver had diverted the plane to help the Marines.

They wiped out the Frog launcher with no problem. In the growing light of the dawn, however, the low-flying AC-130 made a perfect target for a lone Iraqi soldier with a shoulder-fired SAM. Spirit 03 plunged into the waters of the gulf; there were no survivors among her crew of fourteen. It would be the single greatest air loss of the war.

In retaliation, the Air Force had dropped a daisy cutter on Iraqi positions in Kuwait a few days later. The daisy cutter—properly the BLU-82—was a 15,000-pound bomb dropped by parachute from the tail ramp of a specially equipped C-130. Developed in the Vietnam War, originally to clear jungle, the device was billed as the most powerful conventional bomb ever developed. Thermal effects vaporized everything within a hundred yards or more; the blast created an overpressure of 1,000 pounds per square inch with a Mach-1 concussion wave that killed everything across an area of 120 acres. The mushroom cloud rising above ground zero looked exactly like the aftereffect of a small nuclear weapon.

So devastating was the blast that an SAS recon team on the ground several miles away had reported that the Yanks had just nuked Kuwait.

Major Pierce had welcomed the news of the daisy cutter's vengeance with quiet satisfaction, but it was not, somehow, enough. Major Weaver had been a close friend; Pierce's sister was married to Spirit 03's fire control officer.

Tonight, he thought, would mark his *personal* payback to the Iraqis for the death of his friends.

He picked up his radio mike, switching to the channel passed on to him by the Saudi AWACS. "Copperhead One-niner, Copperhead One-niner, this is Spirit Oh-seven. Do you copy? Over."

"Spirit Oh-seven, this is Copperhead. Go ahead."

"Hello, Navy. You boys just kick back, relax, and enjoy the show. We're going to burn some raghead butt!"

"Ah, roger that, Oh-seven. We have coordinates for you on a probable Scud north of our position. Over."

Pierce glanced toward the north but couldn't see anything. "Don't worry, Copperhead. We have some fast-movers inbound. They'll take out the Scud. We're just here to bail your asses out. Over."

"Copy that, Oh-seven. Do you require target identification? Over."

"Negative, Copperhead. What you can do for us is keep your heads down. This is gonna get noisy."

Below the Specter's left-hand side, flame and pulsing splashes of explosions painted an eerily surreal landscape of light.

Yeah, he thought. *Oh-three . . . this is for you!*

24 February 1991

Off Blue Beach
Kuwaiti Coast
0059 hours

"Any time now," Lieutenant Dietz said.

Greg glanced at his diving watch, checking the time. The explosives were set to go off at different times, rather than all at once, but the first one was due to go almost any—

The thunderous detonation of twenty pounds of C-4 cleaved the night. The explosion itself was invisible from two miles offshore in the middle of a moonless, overcast night, but the blast must have put every Iraqi soldier within a mile of Blue Beach on high alert. The two SEAL patrol boats continued riding silently on the gentle swell of the gulf, waiting. Almost two minutes later, the second charge went off, the deep-throated boom as direct and as personal as a punch in the face.

"Hey, Saddam!" one of the SEALs called. "Lookie here!"

Lookie here was right. Greg was willing to bet that before the remaining four charges had gone off, Saddam and his generals would be looking at Blue Beach and the Kuwaiti gulf coast very hard indeed.

Lights were coming on along the darkened coast. Searchlights snapped on both to the north and the south, the beams clearly visible in the smoke-laden night air as they swept across the water.

"Time to boogie," Dietz said. He made a revving motion with his hand, signaling the patrol boat's coxswain. "Let's do it!"

The patrol boat's engine kicked in, churning up water astern. The coxswain rammed the engine into gear, and the craft leaped forward, bow rising on a plane. The other Fountain-class cigarette boat followed.

Racing in close to shore, angling toward the north and the opening to the bay in front of Kuwait City, the two SEAL PCs roared at high speed, unconcerned now with silence or stealth. At a range of less than a mile, buildings and oil storage tanks were visible on the shore, along with the glare of dozens of spotlights illuminating all of Kuwait's beaches. One young SEAL, Gunner's Mate 2nd Class Gary Duvall, grasped the hand grips on the big M2 .50-caliber machine gun on the Fountain's aft deck, swung the weapon around on its mount, and thumbed the trigger. Full-auto gunfire echoed across the water, the muzzle flash stabbing and flickering like a bright orange tongue of flame.

The third Hagensen Pack went off, and this time they were close enough to shore and the shore was brightly illuminated enough that the SEALs saw the explosion, astern and to port, a thundering pillar of white water erupting into the black and smoky sky, then collapsing in a cascade of spray and sea foam.

The cigarette boat leaned into a hard turn, swinging about 180 degrees toward the south and bouncing across the water in jolting leaps and thumps. Duvall walked the M2 around and continued his bombardment of the shore, sending long, sweeping streams of tracers arcing across the water and plunging into the beach.

Searchlights continued to sweep the water, and by their light, Greg could see two lanes marked out in the water ahead by small buoys, the work of another couple of SEAL patrol boats that night. When the Iraqis saw those, he thought, they would have to assume they were seeing lane markers for incoming landing craft.

Another explosion from the surf line. Iraqi troops ashore were beginning to open fire now, though not at any particular target. Green, yellow, and red tracers crawled across the sky as antiaircraft defenses behind the beach opened up on nonexistent targets, and small-arms fire swept the empty beach and water.

The SEAL patrol boats continued their wild zigzag through the waters just offshore, hammering at the beach defenses with machine-gun fire. One of the beach searchlights flared suddenly and went out, and the SEALs on board the PC cheered as wildly as if they'd just scored a major victory. From farther offshore, various small patrol and amphibious craft mounting rocket launchers began firing barrages at the beach—swarms of yellow flares hurtling into the sky, brilliant for just a moment before burning out. Explosions rang from the open field behind the beach dune line as the rockets fell. Flashes of light strobed and flickered as the bombardment struck home.

Greg found himself cheering with the other SEALs, as their one-platoon invasion of Kuwait continued.

Chapter 24

**North of As Salman
South-Central Iraq
0125 hours**

The SEALs rose from their hide atop the hill and took a long and somber look at the devastation below and around them. F-15s, A-10s, and most especially the circling angel of death designated Spirit 07 had left a scene of stark destruction akin to the desolation in the aftermath of a nuclear blast. Vehicle after Iraqi vehicle had been struck by bomb or shell, often repeatedly, and transformed into flaming, twisted wreckage. Mark's imagination was especially captured by an Iraqi BMP that had made it all the way to the western slope of the hill before being flipped over onto its back, its tracks stripped from its road wheels, its thinly armored belly ripped open and gutted. Flames had completed the destruction, leaving an empty and burned-out shell.

Despite their tracks, BMPs were not tanks by any stretch of the imagination, and their thinly armored hulls offered little protection to their passengers on the battlefield save from chance bits of shrapnel. That personnel carrier had been picked up and tossed aside like a toy by an impatient giant child. The soldiers on board could not have had a chance.

There were places along the As Salman Highway where the military vehicles had crowded up together in their eagerness to flee, creating an immense and terribly lethal traffic jam that the bombs had transformed into a kind of jumbled, jagged carpet of wreckage, the skeletal remnants of one armored personnel carrier merging indistinguishably with the twisted and flame-blackened ruin of another. Fires continued to burn everywhere.

And as Mark and the other SEALs scanned the destruction through their IL optics, nowhere, nowhere did they see any sign of a living soul. Every Iraqi soldier on that plain had fled on foot—or died in the thunderous blasts and all-consuming flames. If there'd been wounded left anywhere on or near that wreckage-littered highway, they'd either been helped away by their comrades or been left to die in the hellfire that had swept across the plain.

To the north, a towering pillar of flame marked the smashed and tortured chassis of the MAZ-543 transport, along with whatever was left of its cargo. A pair of F-15Es had arrived perhaps ten minutes after the circling Specter, seeking out the MAZ transporter, the fuel tanker, the radar van, and the C^3 vehicle and hammering them all with AGM-65 Maverick missiles. The new F-15E had been upgraded to carry a weapons load of up to twelve tons, and the pyrotechnic display erupting from the northern horizon was nothing short of spectacular.

At last, munitions expended and targets eliminated, both the F-15s and the Specter had banked off toward the south.

The Saudi AWACS was already out of range.

Had the F-15s taken out a Scud? From here, damage assessment was impossible. There was no way to tell what the transporter had been carrying—a length of shrouded sewer pipe or an *Al-Hussein* missile. No doubt, though, it would be tallied up on the Air Force scorecard as a probable Scud kill.

For a long, long time, no one said a word.

"Jesus H. Christ," Yancey said after a while.

"C'mon," Hunter told them. "Let's put some distance between us and here."

"Yeah," David said. "I don't know about you guys, but I don't want to have to explain this mess to the Iraqis."

"Roger that," Kennedy said.

They loaded up their weapons, ammo, and gear on the DPV, remounted the sixty-gun and the Mk. 19, and climbed aboard. Slowly, tortuously, with David at the wheel, they began picking their way down the slope, past boulders, shell holes, and the twisted bodies of dead Iraqi soldiers.

For nearly three hours, they drove south, sticking to the highway at first but then veering off into the desert when they spotted Iraqi vehicles coming north to meet them. The Iraqis didn't appear to be looking for them. In fact, they showed every sign of trying to flee, racing north, trailing rooster-tail plumes of dust in their wakes.

The sky was just barely beginning to show light in the east when their DPV broke down once and for all, the rugged little VW engine unable to continue pulling the load its SEAL masters demanded of it. They rolled it into a defile behind a low hill, loaded as much gear, food, water, and ammo into their rucksacks as they could carry, then used a satchel charge to reduce the DPV to another blazing tangle of wreckage.

From there, they walked.

Each man was carrying ninety pounds or more on his back, and by the time the sun finally dragged itself into the eastern sky, all six SEALs were feeling the strain, an aching, gnawing exhaustion as familiar to them all as their shared experience of BUD/S.

"The only easy day was yesterday," Mark told the others, breaking a long silence.

No one laughed.

SEAL HQ
Ra's al Mishab
Saudi Arabia
0825 hours

Greg and the other SEALs had returned to base long before first light, tying up their cigarette boats at the Ra's al Mishab waterfront and heading for their barracks for a shower and a change into something other than a cold wet suit. After that, they were too pumped to sleep, so they'd rendezvoused at the mess hall for breakfast.

Lieutenant Dietz's comment on their return still tickled Greg. *"Yeah, everything went fine. It was pretty boring, actually."*

In an operation like this one, Greg thought, boring was good. It meant everything had gone according to plan, with no surprises, and no intervention by the evil Mr. Murphy. In fact, all of the SEALs on the diversionary force felt that it had been a pretty routine op, easier than most training missions. They were more excited by the news back at their base: just before dawn, at about the same time that they'd been coming back to port at Ra's al Mishab, General Schwarzkopf had launched his long-awaited assault.

The invasion of Iraq was well and truly under way.

Lieutenant Dietz walked up to their mess hall table, a lopsided grin on his face. "At ease, at ease," he said, as the SEALs started to rise. He produced a carefully folded sheet of paper. "I just thought you'd want to hear this. It just came down from Commodore Scott." He cleared his throat. " 'Tom: Please pass to your men an "extremely well done" on last night's mission. CENTCOM has passed to us that elements of two Iraqi divisions reacted and moved, based on your operation. That reaction was exactly the objective we had hoped for. Keep up the great work. Commodore sends.' "

"Two divisions!" Drexler exclaimed. "Now *that's* something!"

"It's damned impressive, I'd say," Greg added.

"From the sound of things," Dietz told them, "CENT-COM is pounding the Iraqis flat, and the Airborne guys are sweeping way, way around behind the Iraqi flank. If we made Saddam pull two divisions back from the front to protect a useless strip of beach, we've probably saved a bunch of coalition lives. Good work, men!"

"Thank you, sir."

How far would the coalition go? To the Euphrates? All the way to Baghdad? The first order of business would be to trap the Iraqi army—especially its still-deadly Republican Guard—in a pocket in Kuwait and southeastern Iraq and dismantle it, pound it until there was nothing left to pound. After that, Greg thought, the obvious move would be to take down Baghdad and see to it that the bloody-handed madman who ran that country ceased ever to be a threat to the populations of other nations or of his own.

He felt good, exultant, even. And . . . chances were, the SEALs' part in the war was over. SEALs would not be taking on the Republican Guard or securing vast areas of desert. It was hard to imagine what they could do now, beyond mop-up and continued surveillance along the coast. Maybe CENTCOM would send them in to tackle Bubiyan, the big island close by the gulf opening of the Shatt al Arab, which carried to the gulf the mingled waters of the Tigris and Euphrates.

Maybe. He doubted it. The war now would be settled in the desert, by tanks and mechanized infantry divisions, by Apache gunships and Airborne troops, by F-15s and AC-130 Specters. The SEALs were now pretty much irrelevant.

Soon, the Teams would be going home.

He could see Wendy again. Talk with her. Hold her. Make love to her.

Start over with her.

Yeah, this was a good op to end his career on. After this, it would be up to the younger generation.

And again, as he had so many times during the past several days, he wondered where Mark was, what he was doing. He must be somewhere out in the desert still, hunting Scuds.

Keep your head down, son, he found himself thinking. *We're almost home free. Keep your head down. . . .*

After all, he'd promised Wendy that they *both* would come home. . . .

South of As Salman
South-Central Iraq
1120 hours

For hours, now, the terrain had been becoming more and more inhospitable, each step taking the six SEALs deeper into the desert wasteland of dunes, sand, and blazing sun. It wasn't actually that hot—in the eighties—but the air was so dry it sucked the moisture from their bodies. Their water, almost gone, was closely rationed. How much farther?

They'd just decided to try to find some shelter among some large boulders to the east when Tangretti called to the others. "Hey! You guys hear that?"

They stopped for a moment to listen. Mark could hear nothing at first except the sigh of windblown sand off the dunes. Then he felt it, a slight shiver in the air, a pulsing sensation that rapidly grew louder . . . and louder, and still louder.

"Helicopters!" Yancey called.

The Iraqis were known to have a few hundred helicopters in their arsenal, Russian-made Mi-24s, French Alouettes and Gazelles, and West-German-made BO-105s, mostly, but those wouldn't be flying by day, not while Allied aircraft prowled the Iraqi skies unchallenged. These were almost certainly American helicopters, and a hell of a lot of them, if the volume of that oncoming thunder was any indication.

They appeared above the sand dunes to the west, a line of angular, dark-olive machines with oddly buglike visages of Plexiglas and hard angles.

"It's Apaches!" Bowden yelled. "It's our Apaches!"

As they watched from a dune top, one of the aircraft suddenly peeled out of the formation and swung to face them, arrowing toward them across the desert at dune-kissing altitude.

"Down!" Hunter yelled, suddenly, and the SEALs dropped behind the crest of the dune as the M230A1 chain gun slung beneath the attack helo's chin opened up with a stuttering burst of 30mm cannon fire.

The rounds chewed into the top of the dune in cracking explosions and a shower of loose sand. The SEALs pressed themselves flat as the AH-64 Apache roared low overhead, banked, and came around for another pass, this time from the northeast.

One of the maxims of modern warfare—humorously stated but dead-serious in content—was that friendly fire isn't. There'd already been a number of friendly fire incidents in this war so far—those Marines killed outside of al Khafji, Mark remembered, among them. For a moment, it looked like the SEALs of Copperhead One-niner might be added to the list.

Mark stood up, facing the oncoming aircraft, bracing himself . . . then raising his hands high. *SEALs never surrender . . .*

. . . but maybe that didn't count when your attacker was on your side.

The Apache slowed in its approach, slowed more, then

hovered, drifting very slowly toward the SEALs until it was only twenty yards away. Its rotor wash slammed into Mark, clawing at his clothing, whipping clouds of stinging sand against eyes and exposed skin, but he held himself absolutely still, hands in the air. Damn it, couldn't that guy see his camo utilities, his combat harness . . . or the floppy-brimmed hat that the rotor wash had just sent skittering across the sand? Iraqis didn't dress like *this*.

Hunter and the other SEALs were standing now as well, following Mark's example. The Apache faced them like an enormous insect, hovering motionless as its chin-mounted chain gun tracked them, following the movements of the gunner's head.

And then, abruptly, the Apache lifted higher above the desert floor, drifted backward a step, and turned away. Mark caught sight of the pilot and gunner both in profile, waving from the Apache's armored cockpit.

"Now *that* would've been a kick in the pants," Yancey said, "coming all this way and getting gunned down by our own side!"

"That sort of thing could ruin your whole day," David said, his teeth showing white against the grit-smeared skin of his face.

Kennedy broke out the PRC-113 and began trying to raise someone. This time, an answer came almost at once. By chance, the SEALs were almost at the center of the north-sweeping axis of flight for the Eight-Deuce, the 82nd Airborne Division which, this time up, was fighting as a ground-bound mechanized infantry force. The Apaches were Air Cavalry elements flying in advance of the 82nd, which was tasked with seizing the As Salman Highway and an Iraqi airbase at As Salman itself.

Walking west now, toward the highway, they encountered a bizarre procession coming toward them from the north . . . a group of surrendered Iraqi soldiers, stumbling through the sand with their hands high . . . being herded along by, of all things, an Apache helicopter hovering just behind them.

The SEALs trained their own weapons on the Iraqis, who seemed uncommonly happy to encounter six Americans out here in the desert. The Apache pilot grinned at them from his cockpit, gave a jaunty thumbs-up, and flew off to the north again, leaving the bemused SEALs with twenty-three dirty, unshaven, half-starved, and very *relieved* Iraqi POWs.

"We friends!" one Iraqi said, grinning broadly with badly decayed teeth. "We friends! All friends!" Mark wondered if this crowd had been part of the battalion hit by the Specter last night. It was possible; several of them were wounded, and most had that faraway glaze to their eyes that suggested they'd seen too much.

Friends or not, the SEALs kept their weapons on their new charges and marched them south along the highway.

Half an hour later, they encountered the first northbound APCs of the 82nd, and their Scud-busting mission was over.

3 March 1991

Kuwait City
Kuwait
1525 hours

Greg stood on a Kuwaiti City street just outside the walls of the American embassy, watching the crowd go insane. The news had just come through. General Schwarzkopf had met with Iraqi commanders at Safwan, in southern Iraq, to receive the Iraqi surrender, formally ending the Gulf War.

In fact, a cease-fire had been in effect since 0800 on 28 February, on orders direct from the commander in chief, George Bush. Schwarzkopf's meeting with General Sultan

Hashim Ahmed had merely formalized things as they already stood. Already, people were calling it the 100-hour war.

Why? Greg wondered. *Why the hell stop now? . . .*

It was a question on the minds of most fighting men in Southwest Asia. In four thunderous, triumphant days, CENTCOM's forces had smashed through stunned Iraqi defenses, destroying hundreds of vehicles, killing tens of thousands of Iraqi soldiers, and capturing many tens of thousands more. On a stretch of six-lane highway leading north from Kuwait City toward the Iraqi border at al Mutwa Ridge, fleeing Iraqis became entangled in a monumental traffic jam of armored personnel carriers, tanks, eighteen-wheelers, military and civilian transports, taxi cabs, limousines, and automobiles of every description. At 0130 on the morning of 26 February, U.S. Marine pilots flying Harrier jump-jets and F-18 Hornets with Marine Air Group 11 began pounding the mass evacuation with relentless precision, turning the highway into what reporters were soon calling the "Highway of Death."

It was strange, Greg thought. The video images of the carnage along the Highway of Death had swiftly become the defining symbol of the Gulf War—not the liberation of Kuwait City with its jubilant citizens dancing in the streets, not the stunning combat victories and heroic battles at the Euphrates, at the Kuwait City Airport, of 73 Easting, of Phase Line Norfolk, of Medina Ridge. The vaunted Iraqi Army had crumbled away in hours; four days after the ground assault had begun, the fourth largest army in the world had become the twenty-second largest . . . and had for all practical purposes ceased to exist as a fighting force. It was a triumph of American arms without parallel in history, and yet what the folks back home saw and remembered were the burning oil wells and the charred and reeking carnage along the Highway of Death.

President Bush, many thought, had ordered the cease-fire precisely because of those scenes of carnage on the nightly news; public support for the war, for Bush himself, was visibly dwindling, with the United States now perceived as a roughneck bully trampling the little kid after he was down.

"Dad! Hey, Dad!"

He turned at the familiar voice. A Special Forces DPV was driving up the street a few yards away, and Mark Halstead was clambering out of the navigator's seat.

"Mark!"

The two SEALs embraced, slapping backs and shoulders. "Hey, I was wondering where you were. They told me at the airport you were guarding the embassy!"

Greg smiled. "I'm going to have to transfer to the Marines, I guess. Embassy honor guard, y'know?"

"Shit, Dad. You know the SEALs always hit the beach first, before the Marines even get there!"

That had certainly been true this time, though Greg knew some Marines who would take exception to that heretical notion.

Gunfire rattled nearby—joyous Kuwaitis celebrating by loosing whole magazines full-auto into the sky. Greg winced. He'd heard stories of several people killed by spent rounds falling into crowds during such "celebrations," but those stories hadn't stopped the shooting.

"Let's move over here, son," he said. There was partial shelter nearby, a concrete overhang above the sidewalk that would shield them from falling bullets. *More friendly fire,* he thought.

Mark waved at the DPV driver, and the dune buggy growled and sped off. SEALs and Army Special Forces had found the tough little vehicles wonderfully useful for patrolling the streets of Kuwait City since the liberation. They had to push through a throng of Kuwaiti men, most armed, all wildly happy. One of them grabbed Greg in a bear hug, shouted "Allah bless USA," and kissed him full on his lips before he could push away.

"Jesus!" Greg said, wiping his mouth. "Where are we, San Francisco?"

"Well, it beats those chants of 'Death to America' we were always hearing in the eighties," Mark said, grinning. "It makes getting through the crowd interesting, though, I can tell you."

"I know. The occupation was damned hard on the Kuwaitis. They're pretty happy to see us. Most of them, anyway."

Greg was still having trouble believing the sheer destruction wrought on occupied Kuwait by the vengeful Iraqis. Most of the buildings in the downtown portion of town had been burned or shelled. The port facilities had been torn apart and burned. The animals in the Kuwaiti City Zoo, for God's sake, had been shot, some for food, many for sport. Every home had been stripped of valuables. Most of the vehicles on the Highway of Death, it had turned out, had been loaded with booty stolen from Kuwait—everything from Persian rugs to clothing to jewelry to date trees.

And other, far darker stories were emerging. Iraqi torture chambers had been erected throughout the cities, and some of the torturers had collected Polaroids of their victims. Greg had seen some of those photos, and they still turned the battle-hardened SEAL veteran's stomach. *My God*, he thought, *how can people do things like that to other people?* Hundreds, perhaps thousands had been tortured to death, and an estimated six thousand Kuwaiti citizens had been murdered or taken to Iraq as hostages.

Saddam's regime didn't have the size, the time, or the sheer scope of operations of Nazi Germany, but the dehumanizing cruelty, the tortures, the mass murders were just as vicious, just as brutal, and just as hard for civilized humans to believe.

"Most of them?" Mark asked. "Who's not happy to see us? Besides the Iraqis, I mean."

"The fundies, of course," Greg said. "Islamic fundamentalists."

Mark made a derisive snort. "Them."

"Them," Greg agreed.

"A few disgruntled clerics."

"Safar al Hawali and Salman al Awdah are something more than disgruntled clerics," Greg said. "Their Movement for Islamic Resurgence is gaining a lot of support."

He'd been keeping up to date on the intelligence reports streaming in to the SEAL HQ at Ra's al Mishab. Most Saudis hated—or at least disdained—the Iraqis, and the Kuwaitis, of course, saw them as monsters. But certain Islamic fundamentalist *ulema*—religious scholars—were loudly criticizing the House of Saud for inviting U.S. soldiers onto holy soil. Americans weren't in the gulf, they claimed, to protect Saudi Arabia or liberate Kuwait, nor even to secure the region's oil reserves for themselves. Americans, the fanatic *ulema* claimed, had come solely to degrade and conquer Islam. They'd issued a *fatwa*—a holy proclamation—to that effect, and CIA reports noted that some thousands of disaffected Saudi, Omani, Yemeni, Palestinian, and other Islamic volunteers were gathering in military training camps in Afghanistan, Yemen, and the Sudan.

There was going to be real trouble, Greg thought.

"What I want to know," Mark said, staring out at the unruly mob of celebrants, "is why they stopped us after a hundred hours. Man, the road to Baghdad was wide open! We could've rolled right in, knocked on old Saddam's door, and escorted him to a special cell in Florida right next to Noriega's."

"I think the administration was . . . *disturbed* by the CNN coverage of the Highway of Death. Pretty graphic stuff. Public support for the war was dropping. Can't have another Vietnam, you know, with antiwar protests and demonstrations and all of that."

"Shit. The hell with Vietnam. We had the sons of bitches *beat!*"

"Yup. Kind of a lopsided win. Even if we did score some own goals." Coalition casualties had been astonishingly light—not at all the tens of thousands predicted by Saddam when he promised that this would be the "Mother of all Battles." According to the latest reports, 367 Americans had been killed in Desert Shield and in Desert Storm. A sobering footnote, however: 165 of those troops had been killed by friendly fire.

Casualties of war. . . .

"That's not what I meant," Mark said. "We had them cornered. We let them go with most of the Republican Guard still intact!"

"True." There were a couple of full divisions of the Guard in northern Iraq that were virtually untouched, and large numbers of Guard troops in the south had been allowed to retreat to safety in the hours before the cease-fire had taken effect.

"And what's with the order to leave the Iraqi helicopters alone?" Mark continued. "We set up no-fly zones where we promise to shoot down any Iraqi aircraft that pokes its nose above a runway . . . but their helicopters get a free pass. Why?"

"Publicly, to let the Baghdad government maintain order at home and to help provide humanitarian assistance. Parts of Iraq are pretty rugged, and helicopters are the only way to get food and supplies in."

"Humanitarian assistance. Oh, yeah, like 57-mike-mike rockets."

"The scuttlebutt I heard," Greg said, "is that the U.S. military is courting the favor of the guy in charge of Iraq's helicopter force. They hope he'll lead a military coup against Saddam."

"Good luck," Mark said. "Hell, why leave Saddam in power at all? That's a little like winning World War II and letting Hitler keep his job as Führer, isn't it?"

Greg sighed. "Look at it this way. If we'd taken Baghdad, we'd have had to occupy Iraq, set up a new government, station occupation troops in-country, all of that. How long do you think the locals—especially those disgruntled clerics you mentioned—would put up with that state of affairs? Our Arab allies might pull out of the coalition, and we'd find ourselves with a really nasty guerrilla war on our hands. Welcome to the brave new world, Mark. A new way of doing things. No more colonialism. Besides, we did what the UN resolutions called for us to do. We liberated Kuwait. They didn't say anything about conquering Iraq."

"Huh. What I heard," Mark said, "is that the Pentagon thinks Saddam is going to be offed by his own people. Either a military coup, or the Shi'ites in the south, or the Kurds in the north. They all have reason to put a gun to his head."

"Maybe. But Saddam, he's not going to be that easy to shoot. He's a survivor, that one." Greg thought for a moment. "And you know, come to think of it, that may be exactly why we left the bastard in power. I think there are folks back in the Pentagon and the State Department who are scared shitless that the Shi'ites are going to take over Iraq, just like they took over Iran twelve years ago. An Islamic fundamentalist world power, covering Iraq *and* Iran, controlling that much of the world's oil reserves? Hell, they'd keep the devil himself in power if that was the only option."

"Never thought of that one," Mark said. "We have kind of a rep for propping up megalomaniac tinhorn dictators, don't we?"

Greg thought about Noriega. "Yup. As long as they're *our* megalomaniac tinhorn dictators."

"So what do *you* think, Dad? Did we do the right thing by stopping when we did?"

"I think," Greg said slowly, "we should have gone in and kicked Saddam's sorry ass clear to Siberia."

"Well, maybe we will some day. Or maybe we won't have to."

Greg shrugged. "It's always the same. The end of one war plants the seeds of the next one. It's going to come back to haunt us."

"Maybe," Mark said. "But the Teams'll be ready. After all, the only easy day . . ."

They completed the line in chorus. ". . . was yesterday."

And the jubilant celebration in the streets of Kuwait City continued.

1991–2000

The desert sands and oil-stained coastline of the gulf seemed at first and literal glance less than fertile, but seeds had indeed been planted. A new war, a new way of *waging* war, was in the offing.

At Safwan, a member of General Schwarzkopf's honor detachment stood at attention alongside his Bradley armored fighting vehicle. The AFV's nickname was *Bad Company*. The soldier, who would win the Bronze Star, was Sergeant Timothy McVeigh. The world would hear that name again, seven years hence. McVeigh's hatred and mistrust of the U.S. government had its roots in the sands of the gulf.

Another name that would soon be heard again belonged to the son of one of the wealthiest families in Saudi Arabia. During the surrender talks, Osama bin Laden was in

Dhahran, still seething over Riyadh's rejection of his plan to defeat the Iraqis without the help of infidel Americans on sacred Saudi ground.

In the days following the surrender talks, rebels in both the north and the south of Iraq rose against the Baghdad government, attacking Republican Guard troops in Basra, Najaf, and Karbala. The Iraqi military struck back, with tanks and the fleet of helicopter gunships that, by the terms of the surrender treaty, would be allowed to continue flying even within the no-fly zones. Gunships strafed Karbala; Iraqi troops followed, herding hundreds of captured civilians into soccer stadiums and killing them wholesale. Survivors fled in a panicked stream south toward Najaf. Iraqi helicopters flew low overhead, drenching the mob with kerosene. The gunships that followed opened fire with incendiary bullets. . . .

American aircraft were circling nearby at the time and, under orders not to interfere in Iraqi affairs, did nothing to stop the fiery carnage.

And in the north, the Kurds fought T-72 tanks and helicopter gunships with small arms and rocks. Forbidden to use poison gas as they had in the past, Saddam's forces used instead white phosphorus, incinerating thousands and choking thousands more in the poisonous fumes. Survivors fled, some toward the Turkish border, where the Turks— who'd been trying to exterminate their Kurdish population since the 1920s—opened fire. Most fled east toward Iran . . . struggling through snow-choked mountain passes 8,000 feet above sea level to cross the rugged Zagros Mountains. One estimate put the number of refugees fleeing across the mountains at 800,000 . . . with a thousand a day dying from cold and starvation. The survivors were packed into refugee camps, where thousands more died of starvation and disease.

But Washington's official policy was "hands-off in Iraqi

internal affairs." Like the South Vietnamese of twenty-six years before, the Kurds and Shi'ites both knew that they'd been encouraged to act . . . then abandoned by the American government.

Within the next few years, a new player on the scene began to make its presence felt.

In 1993, a truck bomb exploded beneath the World Trade Center in New York City, killing six and injuring a thousand people. The mastermind was Ramzi Yousef, a Kuwaiti revolutionary financed by Iraqi intelligence . . . and by a shadowy group organized in Saudi Arabia shortly before the Gulf War called *al-Qaida*, Arabic for "the Base."

Later the same year, Somali militiamen trained by al-Qaida shot down an American helicopter, killed eighteen U.S. Army Rangers, and dragged their mutilated bodies through the streets.

In November of 1995, a car bomb exploded in Riyadh, Saudi Arabia, killing seven, five of them Americans. Seven months later, a truck packed with two and a half tons of TNT exploded in Dhahran, killing nineteen American servicemen. Bin Laden's al-Qaida was implicated in both attacks. A *fatwa* issued by bin Laden in September of 1996 called for jihad against all Americans, in retaliation for their "occupation" of Saudi Arabia.

In 1998, truck bombs detonated in front of the U.S. embassies in Kenya and Tanzania. Hundreds died, most of them Kenyan civilians on the crowded streets of Nairobi. Again, bin Laden was implicated, through the al-Qaida–funded and organized World Islamic Front.

In 2000, a U.S. guided-missile destroyer, the USS *Cole,* was attacked by suicide bombers while docked in the port of Aden, in Yemen. The blast tore a forty-foot hole in the ship's side and nearly sank her; seventeen U.S. sailors died, and thirty-nine were wounded. American intelligence had reason to believe that, once again, bin Laden and al-Qaida were behind the attack.

It was as Greg had said, that afternoon in the chaotic streets of Kuwait City. *It's going to come back to haunt us.*

There could be no doubt, now, that Osama bin Laden and al-Qaida had declared all-out war against America.

In 1992, Master Chief Greg Halstead retired from the Navy after twenty-five years of service. Some of his fellow SEALS, were horrified; another five years and he could have retired on full pay and benefits.

But Greg had had enough. In one sense, he shared McVeigh's mistrust of a government directed by political expediency, though not, of course, to the murderously paranoid extent of *Bad Company*'s gunner. His attitudes toward war, and about the Teams and their mission, had been forged in the cauldron of Vietnam. Sure, the politics of that conflict had been impossibly murky, but it had still been possible for individuals to exercise their moral sense, to do what they perceived as *right*. There, you didn't have the Pentagon breathing over your shoulder by satellite, telling you what to do. . . .

Besides, the Teams and their high-tech wizardry belonged now, and rightfully, to the younger generation.

In any case, he had a campaign of his own to face back on the home front. Greg and Wendy, together again, moved back to the area where he'd grown up, in the town of Jenner, on the Russian River in northern California. He began writing, and within four years was making a respectable name for himself writing military fiction—and the collected nonfiction memoirs of his fellow Navy SEALS.

One constant, though, one undeniable law imposed by training and character and dedication, remained, despite politics, despite poor intelligence, despite all the sycophantic and self-serving idiocy that Washington could muster. There was no such thing as an *ex*-SEAL.

The SEALs were *family,* a part of him born of duty, blood and honor, and Greg Halstead always would be one of them, a member of the Teams.

Epilogue

September 11, 2001

**Manhattan,
New York, New York
0845 hours, EST**

The hijacked airliner slammed into the first of the World Trade Center towers above the southern tip of Manhattan at 0845 on a beautiful, blue-skied morning of late summer. The second tower was struck by another airliner minutes later, while a third aircraft plunged into the Pentagon, and a fourth, Flight 93 hijacked over Pennsylvania, was deliberately crashed by its passengers to prevent another suicide attack, one aimed at the nation's capital.

Nearly three thousand died in the collapse of the twin towers of the World Trade Center, since the 1970s an icon of capitalism and the West.

A few blocks from the World Trade Center, on Chambers Street, 650 children at Public School 234 were evacuated to safety moments before the towers' thunderous collapse. A quarter of a mile above their heads, some hundreds of people, trapped by the flames on the floors beneath them, chose to leap to their deaths rather than burn. Many were already aflame as they plummeted to the street.

One child of five stopped and pointed skyward. "Teacher look! The birds are on fire!"

The new war, born in the fires of the Gulf, had come home to America in a roar of thunderous carnage.

In Jenner, California, Greg and Wendy watched, together with millions of other horrified Americans as CNN played out the drama time after time after horrific time—of airliners plunging into glass facades, of billowing flames and burning tower tops, of first one tower, then the other, majestically settling vertically into clouds of dust, raining destruction onto the crowded streets of lower Manhattan.

After a long time, Wendy pulled closer to Greg, inside the half-circle of his arm. "This will mean another war, won't it?" she asked.

"It's been war, hon. All along. Most Americans just haven't realized that fact." He paused. "I guess this will wake them up, though. My God. . . ."

"Mark. He'll be in it." It wasn't a question, but a statement of simple fact.

"I imagine so. I don't think this war will lend itself much to high-tech gadgets, you know?"

In the Gulf War, the SEALs had fought to establish a place for themselves alongside the larger, more conventional service arms of the American war effort. They'd won a distinguished, an honored place there, too, doing things that the other services simply could not manage.

At the same time, the Gulf had been a high-tech war, one fought with Stealth fighters and the down-the-ventilator-shaft accuracy of laser-guided bombs, with Magellan GPS receivers and cruise missiles, with M1A1 Abrams tanks and Specter gunships. Saddam's army had been outmatched from the beginning, by technology as well as by the skill and training of the American fighting man and woman.

Again—not for the first time by far—voices were being raised in the Pentagon's halls that the SEALs were an anachronism, that modern warfare had no room for the small-unit tactics of a handful of sailors, no matter how highly trained or dedicated they might be.

Each war carried within its ending the seeds of the next war to come. But this new war would be unlike any fought before, with the technological might of the United States military squaring off with hate-consumed fanatics with medieval worldviews, a new breed of *kamikaze* who gladly gave their lives for a chance at killing Americans.

And Greg had a feeling that in that war the SEALs would be coming into their own.